IRISH ANGEL SERIES

HEART
—of—
STONE

A Novel

Book One

JILL MARIE LANDIS

New York Times Bestselling Author

ZONDERVAN®

ZONDERVAN.com/
AUTHORTRACKER
follow your favorite authors

D0005184

ZONDERVAN

Heart of Stone
Copyright © 2010 by Jill Marie Landis

This title is also available as a Zondervan ebook.
Visit www.zondervan.com/ebooks.

This title is also available in a Zondervan audio edition.
Visit www.zondervan.fm.

Requests for information should be addressed to:

Zondervan, *Grand Rapids, Michigan* 49530

Library of Congress Cataloging-in-Publication Data

Landis, Jill Marie.
    Heart of stone : a novel / Jill Marie Landis.
        p.   cm.—(Irish angel series; bk. 1)
        ISBN 978-0-310-29369-9 (softcover)
        1. Single women—Fiction. 2. Irish—United States—Fiction. I. Title.
    PS3562.A4769H425 2010
    813'.6—dc22   2009026814

Cover design: Curt Diepenhorst
Cover illustration: Aleta Rafton
Interior design: Michelle Espinoza

Printed in the United States of America

10 11 12 13 14 15 • 20 19 18 17 16 15 14 13 12 11 10 9 8 7 6 5 4 3 2

To new beginnings —
forging friendships
strengthening ties
fulfilling dreams
finding peace.
Thank you for reading this book.

He that is without sin among you, let him first cast a stone at her.
John 8:7

ONE

Eleven-year-old Lovie Lane would never be certain what actually woke her the night she learned her life was to become a living hell.

She might have been unintentionally kicked by one of her three younger sisters, all crowded on the pallet on the floor beside her. Or it might have been the gnawing hunger in her belly. She could have been awakened by the sounds of her aunt and uncle's voices raised in anger. Or a shout outside the shack where they lived. The Irish Channel—a New Orleans neighborhood home to penniless Irish laborers newly immigrated to Louisiana—was not known for peace, quiet, or abundance.

Whatever the reason, Lovie sat up. She pushed her matted hair out of her eyes and gazed at the tangle of limbs and threadbare nightclothes illuminated by the lamplight spilling in from the front room. Her sisters slept soundly, like angels, innocent of the tumult around them. Across the room her two male cousins, both older than she, also slept on.

The nasal whine of her Aunt Maddie's voice easily carried through the thin curtain that hung in the doorway to the sleeping area. "We can't keep 'em. Not with our own to feed."

Lovie gingerly slipped out of bed, taking care not to waken her sisters. She crept up next to the curtain, moved it aside just enough to peer out without being seen. Her uncle shuffled to the table and pulled out a chair. He weaved back and forth before he finally sat, and her aunt shot him a dark scowl as she bustled about the stove to prepare him a cup of tea.

Uncle Timothy tried to shush her, but Maddie wouldn't be silenced. "You've been drinkin' again. I can smell it on ya."

"I been out tryin' to solve our *little* problems, is what I've been doin'."

"Whiskey ain't goin' to help. We wouldn't have our 'little' problems if it weren't for your brother and his wife both up and dying on us."

"Thank the angels they're all girls. The Ursulines will take the two little ones." His heavy sigh reached Lovie from across the room.

"And the other two?"

Lovie stifled a gasp, knowing she, and Megan, almost nine years old, were "the other two."

"Found a place for them, too, I have," he bragged.

When Ma lay on her death bed, Lovie had promised she'd watch over her sisters. Now they were going to be parceled out, given away like unwanted kittens. Separated for life.

Maddie set the tea down and shuffled back to the stove. She was rail thin, all elbows and wrists, angles and edges—no softness about her at all. She was nothing like the gentle, soft-spoken mother Lovie had known, the mother she missed so desperately.

"Is it a good place?" Maddie wanted to know.

"What do you care? Besides, they'll live in a big, fine house."

"Oh, really? And how's that?" Maddie turned away and mumbled, "Maybe I should go me'self."

"Don't tempt me." Uncle Tim burst into ribald laughter mingled with a phlegmy cough. When he stopped choking and slapping his knees, he settled back in his chair again.

"They'll have three square meals a day, their own beds, and fine clothes."

When her aunt glanced in the direction of the door, Lovie drew away from the crack in the drape. Aunt Maddie lowered her voice to a gravelly whisper. Lovie was too lost in her own speculation to concentrate on what her aunt might be saying.

Never having known what it was to not fight for pallet space, Lovie found the prospect of sleeping alone a frightening proposition at best. And fine clothes? It was hard to even imagine what exactly that meant, but it was tempting. What little girl didn't want pretty clothes?

A chair creaked in the other room. Lovie peeked out and saw Uncle Tim fighting to stay awake. His head slumped onto his chest and his mouth opened on a snore. Aunt Maddie shook his shoulder with a rough jerk.

"Did you save any coin? We'll need milk tomorrow."

"Once I deliver the two girls in the mornin', we'll have plenty to spare. You get them washed up first thing. Have 'em lookin' as presentable as you can. I don't want to have to be bringin' 'em back."

"And the little ones?"

"Soon as I deliver the older girls, I'll come back for the other two."

Having grown up in the brisk chill of Ireland, Lovie was convinced she'd never grow used to the sultry Louisiana air. Tonight, though, she shivered despite the heat as she tiptoed back to the pallet and knelt down.

She stared at "the baa-bies," as her Ma always called the two youngest girls. They were *her* babies now. Tears wet her cheeks and she pictured the coming morn. She and Megan were to be groomed and taken to a new family.

Were they even Irish? Would anything be familiar?

She wondered if she could somehow sneak all of her sisters out of the house, and thought about waking them. Within another breath she realized the idea was completely impossible. If it were just her and Megan, they might stand a chance of escape, but with a four- and six-year-old along? Impossible.

Besides, she barely knew the Irish Channel neighborhood and it only covered a few blocks near the docks. Ma had told her New Orleans was a huge, sprawling city, big as Dublin, with many, many streets and neighborhoods. Many dangers, too, if the stories her parents told were to be believed.

As Lovie lay staring into the darkness, she blindly reached for Megan's hand. Though her sister slept, Lovie took comfort in slipping her fingers around Megan's own warm ones. Eventually she fell asleep with her tears drying on her cheeks.

Before the light of dawn the next morning, true to her word, Aunt Maddie woke Lovie and Megan and filled a tub in the kitchen with lukewarm water.

She proceeded to have each girl stand in the tub as she sluiced them with soapy water and scrubbed their faces until they shone. She put their dresses back on them, then struggled to make some semblance of their tangled hair.

"Lovie, your hair is a rat's nest."

"Sorry, Aunt."

Somehow Ma had always managed to tame her matted curls. Ma said she took after her English cousins, what with her dimples and hair the color of wheat straw. Megan, with her straight, dark-brown hair and dusting of freckles all over, looked Irish through and through. Lovie longed for straight hair and freckles, but had to settle for blonde ringlets and bright-blue eyes.

"Want me to get the babies, Aunt?" Megan asked. "They need bathed in the worst way, you know." She'd been chatting happily all morning, and the cheerier she grew, the heavier became Lovie's heart.

She has no idea—

"I won't be needin' to bath them. But you'll be wantin' to go and tell them good-bye, I suppose, so you best get to it."

"Good-bye?" Excitement dawned in Megan's brown eyes. "Are we going somewhere? Just Lovie and me? Where, Aunt?"

"I don't rightly know, but your Uncle Tim 'as a surprise for you and Lovie. You'll be movin' to a fine new place where they need two lovely lasses like you."

Megan's perfectly shaped brows drew together. A scar parted her right brow, a reminder of a fall she'd taken aboard the ship on the voyage to America. "But what of the others?" She glanced toward the other room where her sisters and cousins slept on in their innocence.

"They won't be goin' with you. They'll be off to their own place, they will."

"But ..." Megan looked to Lovie for answers. "But Ma said we'd always be together. Didn't she now, Lovie?"

"She did, Sis, but Ma ain't here no more."

Looking down into her sister's trusting eyes, Lovie's heart crumpled like a paper fan. No use in lying or trying to tell her it wasn't so. A million and one questions crowded Lovie's mind, but her uncle was short-tempered and impatient of a morning. He wasn't civil until he'd had his first ration of whiskey for the day. There was no sense in asking him where they were going or if they'd ever see their sisters again.

The thought that she might never lay eyes on Katie and Sarah again was unthinkable. Before their mother died, Lovie had promised not only to be brave and to do as she was told, but above all to watch over the little ones. She was the oldest, the head of the family. She was the one charged with keeping them together.

"Be good, Lovie. Do your best. Work hard. Keep the others safe."

Theirs had been a difficult life. There was famine in Ireland and Da had had no choice but to come to America to meet up with Uncle Tim and seek his fortune. Uncle Tim was a slacker; Da had always said so. But they were brothers, after all. So Da packed up Ma and Lovie and all the girls and, bringing only what they could carry, they'd sailed across the Atlantic in search of a better life.

What they'd found was as bad as the potato famine they'd left behind.

Like the hundreds of other Irish immigrants who'd come before them, they'd settled not far from where they disembarked at the docks of New Orleans and moved into the two-room shack with Uncle Tim, Aunt Maddie, and the boys. Da had found work digging the canals that surrounded the city. The immigrants were hired not only because they worked for pennies, but because they were expendable. The task was so dangerous, disease and accidents so common, that slave owners refused to risk their precious investments. The Irish dug the canals. The slaves did not. At least that's what Da told them, and he never lied.

They hadn't been there but six months before Da caught the yellow fever and died. It wasn't long before Ma fell ill too. Her heart and spirit broken, she followed Da. Her parents had survived what many immigrants called the "coffin voyage" to America only to perish in a filthy, crowded shack near the damp, Louisiana dockside.

Aunt Maddie gave the older girls but a moment to hug the two little ones. The tears and bawling quickly became infectious, and their aunt shooed Megan and Lovie out of the bedroom and held on to the babies to keep them from running after while Uncle Tim quickly shoved the older girls out of the house. Lovie paused to look back. She could hear her sisters screaming for her through the door.

"Come on." Uncle Tim grabbed her by the arm and pulled her along after him. With her free hand she quickly wiped her face and then reached back and grabbed Megan, who was struggling to keep pace as their uncle dragged them through the streets of Irish Channel.

Soon they left the docks behind. The houses around them grew larger. Iron grille work lined the second-floor galleries that hung out over the sidewalks. Moss draped the trees like moldy gray-green beards.

Megan had faltered and was nearly pulling Lovie's arm out of

its socket. She tried to slow down. Uncle Tim stopped long enough
to tower over them. "Hurry up or I'll give ye the back of m' hand!"

"Keep up," Lovie whispered to Megan. "You can do it."

Her own heart pounded to match her footsteps. Her fear of her
uncle was as great as her fear of the unknown.

The city took on a different feel and flair away from Irish
Channel. Well-dressed ladies in fancy gowns and gloves strolled
beside gentlemen with top hats and polished canes. They barely
gave Uncle Tim and the girls a glance as they passed by on foot or
on the high-sprung seats of their glossy phaetons. Away from the
docks, the very air was heavy with opulence.

And yet ... Lovie sensed an underlying sadness that laced the
air, an all-pervasive heaviness that, like the Spanish moss in the
trees, hung in a pall over the city built on the backs of slaves and
the poor.

As they hurried along, panting, Megan dared to ask, "Where
do the Ursulines live, Uncle?" She was rewarded with a dark glower
but wasn't dissuaded. "Will the babies be far from our new home?"

"A world away," he mumbled.

"Are they ... are the Ursulines ... a nice family?"

"The Ursulines are nuns who run an orphanage."

Orphanage? Lovie recoiled. Aunt Maddie and Uncle Tim had
sworn to their mother that none of them would ever be sent to an
orphanage.

Lovie's heart began to pound when she realized what was happening. There would be no loving family for the little ones. No pretty
clothes or beds of their own. They'd be parceled out—separated
from one another like puppies from the same litter—if by chance
anyone chose to adopt them at all.

How would she ever find them again if they were separated?
How could she pull them all back together?

She turned to stare at her sister, taking in Megan's wide, terrified brown eyes, her thin limbs and straight brown hair. The image
of her da had already begun to fade from her mind's eye, and she

imagined the same would soon happen with her ma. What if she and Megan were separated and she forgot what her sister looked like? What if she couldn't recognize the babies?

Her hand tightened on Megan's as their uncle rounded a corner. She was tempted to run, just as she had been last night. As if he could read her mind, her uncle glanced over his shoulder and growled, "Don't be dawdlin'."

He picked up his pace, made a sharp turn off a main thoroughfare, and ducked down a narrow passageway. Shaded by the sides of tall buildings and lined with cobblestones, the lane was cool and damp. Now and again they were treated to the sight of lovely walled gardens crowded with ferns and colorful flowers she couldn't name and palms with long fronds whispering in the breeze. Trickling fountains lent the soothing sound of falling water.

She didn't know exactly what to hope for now that the raw truth had hit her. They were to be living here, in this grand, terrifying new place. Would their new family have a walled garden?

Uncle Tim suddenly stopped before a door of thick planks set in a stucco wall the color of rust. He stared down at the two of them for so long that Lovie didn't know if he was going to hit them or if he might have changed his mind.

She hoped he was about to say, "I've made a mistake. Let's go home."

Instead he barked, "Brush your sister's hair back off her face, Lovie."

Lovie spit on her palm and smoothed back Megan's brown hair. She cupped her sister's chin in her hands and smiled down into her eyes. "It's going to be grand," she whispered. "You'll see. It's going to be grand."

"You promise?" Megan whispered.

Lovie closed her eyes. A shiver slid down her spine. She wanted to scream, "I don't know! I don't know anything. I'm only a little girl myself!"

Instead she whispered, "I promise."

Uncle Tim raised the wrought-iron loop that served as a knocker and let it fall. It made a hollow thud. A moment later, the door was opened by a tall Negress wearing a bright-orange turban and a stiff white apron over a calico gown. The woman took one look at Uncle Tim and then glanced down at Lovie and Megan. A fleeting shadow of concern moved behind her eyes. It passed so swiftly Lovie wasn't certain whether she actually saw it or not. She tried to tell herself she was wrong. Tried to tell herself the look meant nothing.

The woman said something in a soft, lovely language Lovie did not understand and stepped back. Another woman took her place in the open doorway. This one had red hair the color of glowing embers on a grate and skin as white as rose petals. She wore a long, shimmering ivory robe embroidered with huge bouquets of flowers. It was so loosely tied she held the top closed with her hand.

The woman didn't ask what Uncle Tim wanted. She merely looked down her nose at him the way he'd always done Lovie and the rest of the Lanes.

"He wants these two," her uncle said. "We made a deal yesterday."

Lovie couldn't take her eyes off of the woman. Her face and features were perfect. She was slender, yet not in the hard-angled way of Aunt Maddie. With her bright-red hair flowing past her shoulders, wrapped as she was in the long silky robe, she reminded Lovie of a delicate wax candle topped by a shimmering flame. She was stunning.

Lovie stopped staring at the woman's hair and robe long enough to look into her eyes. She couldn't always trust the things people said, but she'd learned to search for the truth in their eyes. But this woman's eyes lacked any expression whatsoever. No curiosity, no warmth. No joy, no sorrow. There was none of the bitterness she'd seen in Aunt Maddie's eyes, none of the eternal hope and bottomless love her mother's eyes possessed.

It was as if someone had snuffed out all the feeling in her.

Maybe this is why they need some children here, Lovie thought.

A glimmer of hope sparked inside her. Ma had always called them her angels, her joy. Perhaps she and Megan were here to bring joy to this woman who looked at them with such blankness behind her eyes.

Ignoring Lovie and Megan, the woman said to Uncle Tim, "Wait here, *s'il vous plaît*. I will get him." Unlike her cold eyes, her voice was warm. It reminded Lovie of the sultry New Orleans air.

The woman walked away, barely holding her robe closed. Lovie peered past her into the room beyond. It was a huge kitchen, larger than Uncle Tim's two rooms put together. Bigger even than their thatched-roofed cottage back in Ireland. There were two other women inside, both seated at a table. Both wore the grandest gowns Lovie had ever seen. The fabric was bright and shiny—one crimson red, the other the color of a ripe plum. Rows and rows of ruffles cascaded from their waists to the floor.

Steaming cups of liquid sat on the table in front of the women. One yawned and rested her head upon her forearm as the other woman slowly turned to face the door. She noticed Megan first before her gaze finally drifted to Lovie.

When their eyes met, the woman across the room turned away—but not before Lovie saw the flash of anger in the woman's eyes. A flash of anger quickly replaced by a wash of shame.

She waved them in but Lovie didn't move. Despite Uncle Tim's threatening presence, despite the women staring at them from across the room, Lovie wrapped her arm protectively around Megan's shoulders and pulled her close. She'd made Ma a promise and she intended to keep it.

She whispered, "No matter what, Megan, I'll watch out for you. No matter what."

Her uncle pushed them over the threshold.

It wasn't more than a few hours later that Lovie saw her sister for the last time. Megan lay draped over the shoulder of a tall, long-limbed man who carried her screaming down a lengthy, narrow hallway.

TWO

GLORY, TEXAS, 1874

Laura Foster awoke in the middle of the night in a cold sweat and bolted upright. It took a moment for her to realize she'd been dreaming, that she wasn't eleven years old anymore. That she wasn't in a brothel in New Orleans.

Her gaze swept the shadowed interior of her room. Momentarily confused, she waited until the foggy remnants of sleep lifted, until she remembered where she was and who she was now.

She threw back the fine Egyptian-cotton sheets and climbed out of the bed that was among her most prized possessions. She'd paid a small fortune for the piece crafted by the famed cabinet-maker, Belter. The side rails were fashioned out of bent rosewood laminate. The headboard was ornamented with a detailed, carved basket of fruit flanked by a pair of cherubs.

If only the bed could ensure sweet dreams, it would be worth the hard-earned gold she'd paid for it.

Barefooted, she padded across the room to her dressing table. A chenille runner covered its marble top, a cushioned base for her feminine paraphernalia—perfume bottles, a silver-backed hairbrush, hairpins stored in collection of alabaster boxes.

She caught a glimpse of her muted image in the mirror above

the table—her long, heavy hair hanging in untamed curls about her shoulders. In the dark, her full white nightgown gave the impression that she was naught but a spirit hovering in the shadows. She turned away, walked to the second-story bay window with its view down Main Street.

Indian summer had arrived. It swept across the Texas plains with a blazing show of heat before fall set in. Her window was open, but the lace sheers beneath the heavier velvet drapes hung limp and still. There wasn't a breath of air to stir them.

Outside all was quiet, the street deserted. Wooden structures lined both sides of the two-block thoroughfare. None of them were as well built or fancy as Foster's Boardinghouse. Her home graced one end of Main Street. With its wide veranda and rococo trim and detail, it had taken over a year to build—something unheard of in these parts where people raised a barn in an afternoon and generations shared small split-log homes.

Everything in the house had been her own personal choice, from the detail in the plaster medallions in the ceiling to the hand-carved chair rail in the dining room. She'd chosen every drawer pull, every doorknob, every lamp, drapery, piece of linen, each and every finely woven carpet. Expensive wall coverings lined the walls of almost every room. Ornate furnishings made of hardwoods were waxed and polished to a high shine. The finest items money could buy had come together to impress visitors and leave no doubt that the widow Foster was a lady of fine quality.

Her grand home was just as she'd planned it: a place fine enough to disguise the woman she'd been, the life she'd led.

In a sense she had designed her very own gilded cage. It was a lovely place of refuge. And yet never far from her mind was the truth—that this life she had so carefully planned and seen to fruition could unravel in an instant, for it was a life built upon a lie.

Laura was proud of what she'd accomplished here, but it had come at a price. She had suffered untold indignities doing the only thing she knew how in order to amass her fortune and establish her independence. And although she no longer lived the life she had and no one could force her to do anything against her will, not a day went by that she didn't wonder if the truth would come out.

That Laura Foster was nothing more than a former whore.

When the clock in the parlor below struck four, Laura ran a hand over her eyes and sighed. Well acquainted with bouts of insomnia, she knew there was no going back to sleep. There was nothing to do but wait for dawn, when Rodrigo, the handyman, and his wife, Anna, arrived and started to prepare breakfast for her guests. Thanks to Rodrigo and Anna and their son, Richard, Foster's was known as much for the hearty and delicious meals she planned as it was for the fine table she set.

She walked back to her bed and lit the lamp on the bedside table, then picked up the novel she'd been reading. *The Count of Monte Cristo* by Alexandre Dumas reminded her of herself. Determined to succeed in escaping the life fate had handed her, she'd educated herself, first by begging one of the other whores, a woman named Jolie, to teach her to read. The process had been painstaking at best, for there was little time to "waste" on something as frivolous as reading. Yet she'd persevered. She'd never forgotten Jolie's advice: *"Study hard, little one. For if you can read, you can slip into the pages of a book and escape into your mind."*

Her efforts to better herself hadn't gone unnoticed. She was chided by the other women in the brothel where she was forced to grow up overnight. She was accused of being aloof and arrogant because she walled off her heart and her soul in order to survive. Through it all, she had cultivated her mind—for it was the only place she could escape to.

No one could touch her there. No man could put his hands on her mind.

She didn't care what any of the other women thought of her. She was too focused on fighting for survival and winning her independence in the outside world. And she'd succeeded. But at great cost. She had everything she could want. Yet every pretty and expensive thing she owned was like her—lovely on the outside, incapable of feeling on the inside.

She'd loved once. She loved her Da and Ma, her sisters. But now . . .

Now it was easier to feel nothing.

Laura had been up for six hours before breakfast was over and the dining room was finally cleared. Two visiting families had departed to return to their hometowns and it was time to prepare for the next.

She was lucky to have a steady stream of guests. Hers was the only boardinghouse in a town quickly spreading in all directions—thanks to its founder's descendants and their offer to sell homesteaders two tracts of land for the price of one. With more settlers came more business, and the threat of renegade Comanche attacks diminished. The stage lines were doubling their schedules, and with luck a railroad spur might one day cut through Glory.

The scents of cinnamon and bacon still lingered in the kitchen as Laura went over the dinner menu with Rodrigo while Anna worked upstairs changing linens. Though she normally trusted Rodrigo to do the daily marketing—he'd taught her how long various cuts of meat should hang in order to reach their peak tenderness, which fruits and vegetables were just ripe enough, how to bargain for a fair price—today she wanted to escape before the walls closed in on her.

In her room, she tried to tame her curly hair into a chignon before choosing a ruffled gray bonnet and a beaded reticule. She made sure the silver derringer she never went without was safely within the purse, then slipped the silk cords over her wrist and collected her parasol from the hall tree near the front door. Armed with her list and a basket for carrying her purchases, she was soon on her way.

The Texas sun was already brutal. She used the parasol to protect her complexion as she headed to the mercantile. As she strolled along, her footsteps sure and confident, she gazed at the familiar landmarks, the neat rows of false-fronted stores on either side of the street, the boardwalk that kept passersby out of the dusty road.

Glory was a fine town, far enough from New Orleans that she felt somewhat safe from recognition, yet small enough to have room to grow her business.

Laura smiled and made it a point to stop and chat with all the merchants she'd come to know: Patrick O'Toole, the butcher, always saved the finest cuts of meat for her. Big Mick Robinson, the smith, made certain her horse was properly shod and her carriage wheels well greased. Harrison Barker, who along with his mother owned the mercantile, was always willing to please.

They all knew her as Mrs. Laura Foster. The respectable, wealthy widow Foster.

She hoped to keep it that way.

She'd nearly reached the mercantile when a cowboy caught her eye as he sauntered across the street and started down the sidewalk toward her. When he tipped his hat, she gave him a quick, cool nod and then angled her parasol so that her face was hidden from his view. She picked up her pace a bit — not noticeably, just enough to put distance between them.

Tempted to glance over her shoulder, she forced herself to keep her eyes on the walk ahead of her and tried to convince herself she was being foolish. What were the chances that even one of the countless men she'd known in New Orleans would show up here? Let alone recognize her now? The odds were a million to one.

When she finally reached the mercantile, she experienced a wave of relief. She folded her parasol and paused on the threshold for a moment as her eyes adjusted to the light inside. Across the room, Harrison was busy helping a woman select canning jars. A cowpuncher in a filthy shirt with tattered cuffs, well-worn denim pants, and sweat-stained ten-gallon hat waited for service. He had piled a small stack of goods — a pound bag of dry beans, a few tins of sardines, and a half dozen potatoes — on the counter.

A child stood alongside him, a little girl in a ragged homespun jumper that sagged off her thin shoulders. Beneath it she wore a soiled white blouse. She was standing in front of an open candy jar full of lemon drops. The child's hand was curled into a fist, no doubt closed around a piece of candy she'd sneaked from the jar.

Laura understood the scene in one glance. The sight reminded her all too much of herself at that same age. It was an image that conjured up memories of Megan too. She turned away, but not before she felt a desperate squeeze in her chest where her heart had once been.

She tried to concentrate on the list of things she needed and was about to move on when she heard the crack of flesh against flesh.

"Drop those sweets 'fore I tan your hide!"

The harshly uttered threat stopped her in her tracks.

She whirled and caught the man towering over the child, his hand still raised. A lone lemon drop lay on the floor beside the little girl's dirty bare feet. She stood silent, but her dark eyes were wide as saucers. Beneath her small fingers, pressed against her cheek, a large, red handprint told the tale.

Without thought, Laura hurried over to the counter and barged in to the small space between the man and the child.

"If you lay another hand on her you'll regret it until the day you die," she said.

The man looked as stunned as his daughter, but he recovered in a heartbeat.

"She's mine and I'll not have her stealing."

The child peeked out from behind Laura's skirt. "I wasn't stealing, Pa. I was gonna ask the man if I could have one." Her tremulous voice broke on the words as she fought back tears.

"We're not thieves *or* beggars. Now get over here." He pointed to a spot on the floor beside him. The little girl slipped around Laura to stand beside her pa. She dropped her hand but the palm print on her face flared red and angry.

The man ignored the child as he tried to stare Laura down. She stared right back, determined to let him know he'd met his match.

"Do you have brothers and sisters at home?" Laura turned her attention to the little girl.

The child glanced up at her father before she nodded yes.

"I'm sending you home with a half pound of lemon drops. Share them, will you?"

"I don't take charity," the man growled.

"It's not for you. It's for your children." Laura knew there was probably very little light in his children's lives. If the girl was any indication, the joy had been beaten out of them a long time ago.

"How I raise my young'uns is my own business."

"You don't have any business hitting a child, mister."

She watched his jaw bunch, knew instinctively that his hand had tightened into a fist.

Just you try, mister.

As she met his hard stare, she felt someone move to stand beside her. Then she heard a voice she recognized. A voice filled with confidence.

"Think twice before you do something you'll regret."

Laura turned and found herself staring into the eyes of Reverend Brand McCormick, the minister of Glory's only church. He was standing as close as he could get. A united front, they stood shoulder to shoulder facing down the cowhand.

"I suggest you graciously accept this lady's kind offer to purchase a bit of candy for your children and in the future you hold your temper," the reverend said.

Used to listening to this man deliver his Sunday sermons, she had no idea that beneath McCormick's confident, smiling exterior lay such courage and strength. Relief swept through her when she realized she was no longer alone. She had reacted to the homesteader's assault on the child without thinking.

She had no desire to even contemplate what might have happened if the good reverend hadn't stepped in.

The man stared back and forth between the two of them, opened his mouth, thought better of what it was he might have said, and closed it.

Harrison hurried across the room and quickly began tallying up the homesteader's small order of goods. He bagged up a half pound of sweets and set them atop the order. Laura reached for the sack and held it out to the child. The little girl looked up at her father for permission to accept, and he gave a slight nod of his head in acknowledgment. She reached out and Laura placed the sack in her hand.

"Thank you, lady," the little girl whispered.

"You're welcome."

There was so much more Laura wanted to say, so much more she wished she could do for the child, but she already feared she'd done too much. She could only hope the man wouldn't take his shame and embarrassment out on the girl after they had left the store.

Laura refused to walk away until the man and child left. When they were finally out of sight, she released a sigh of relief and turned to Brand McCormick.

"Thank you, Reverend." She was well aware that he was staring speculatively. "I really had no idea what I was going to do next."

Short of shooting the man.

His smile lit up his face. "After what I just saw, there's not a doubt in my mind that you could have handled things."

She bit her bottom lip and glanced toward the door before she looked at the preacher again.

"I just hope I didn't make things worse for that child."

"I doubt things could get much worse for her."

Laura sighed and said softly, "Oh, yes, they could."

When the preacher looked at her questioningly, she shook her head, dismissing her comment.

"Do you know that man?" she asked. "Have you ever seen him before?"

"They don't attend church. I've never seen him around."

Harrison spoke up from behind the counter. "Probably new to the area. So many folks settling around here, taking advantage of the land sale. It's not like the old days when we knew all our neighbors."

"Things change, Harrison," Brand told him. "I imagine new folks moving in is good for business."

"That's true, but we'd be better off if there was a way to let only upstanding folks in. Scum like that have no place in our town."

Laura weathered the comment by putting a placid "widow Foster" smile on her face.

She turned to Brand. "What brings you here this morning, Reverend?"

He smiled back. "I could say that I was here to fill an order for my sister, but since I'm not a liar, I have to admit I saw you and stepped inside to say hello—and suddenly you were flying to that child's defense. Impressive, I must say."

"Impulsive and probably very stupid, but I couldn't stand by and watch that man mistreat that child." Embarrassed by his perusal, she tried to change the subject. "How have you been, Reverend?"

"I've been busy sanding and refinishing church pews."

His answer surprised her. Although she knew from observing him every Sunday that he was physically fit, she hadn't taken him for a man who labored much. On closer inspection she noticed the way his shoulders filled out his suit coat and the fact that his hands were not the hands of a man who shied away from hard work.

"And you?" He seemed determined to keep chatting.

"Busy as well, but I sorely needed an outing. I came in to see if Harrison has anything that might tempt me to spend some extra money this morning."

Harrison was still behind the counter. With a smile, he reached up and smoothed down the part in his well-oiled hair. "I was expecting Rodrigo, as usual," he said.

She offered him her list and basket.

"I've a new display of lace and buttons I'd like to show you," Harrison told her.

She didn't sew, but Laura excused herself anyway, thinking Brand might be too polite to take his leave. But as Harrison drew her over to view his new items, she noticed Brand appeared perfectly content to lean against the counter and linger.

Brand was drawn to the graceful sway of Laura's skirt as she moved across the store.

He'd crossed the threshold just as the rancher had slapped his daughter and was on his way to challenge the bully when Laura suddenly stepped in. His fear for her was as great as his admiration for her courage. To hear her admit she had acted without thought for her own safety only underscored her selflessness.

As he continued to admire her demure loveliness from his vantage point, he compared the sophisticated, polished woman she appeared to be with the brave, albeit somewhat foolhardy, champion of an ill-treated child. There was obviously far more to Laura Foster than met the eye.

Brand selected a few items that he knew his sister, Charity, needed — a scoop of beans and a few eggs. He carried them over to the counter, aware of Laura as she moved around the store, stalling as he waited for her to finish shopping.

"How are the children, Reverend?" Harrison had left Laura to her shopping and was behind the counter again, writing out a receipt.

Brand knew full well that he spared the rod too often since his wife, Jane's, passing. Charity did her best with Sam and Janie, but she wasn't the strongest of disciplinarians — a reaction, no doubt, to their own strict upbringing. He'd tried to reconcile his own memories of their father, but time had not done anything to help.

"Reverend?" Harrison drew him out of his dark thoughts.

"Oh, I'm sorry. I was just thinking—"

"How are the children?" Harrison asked again.

"Scamps. Incorrigible. Healthy as ever." Brand paid for the beans and eggs and noticed Laura's basket waiting for her on the counter. He watched as Harrison went to the small mail cubicles along the wall. He pulled a letter out of Laura's box and placed it in the basket.

Brand lingered, chatting with Harrison until Laura finally joined them. He waited while she paid for her items and picked up her basket.

"I'm walking you home," he told her.

"Pardon me?" She seemed astonished.

"I'm walking you home." It wasn't a request.

"I can take care of myself, I assure you."

She might be lovely — ethereally so — yet in that moment the strength of will and determination in her eyes assured him she believed she could indeed take care of herself if need be.

"So it seems," he admitted, "but after what just happened, I'd feel better seeing you to your door."

"Really, Reverend," Laura lowered her voice. "I'm perfectly fine."

She laid her hand on his sleeve for the briefest moment, as if trying to communicate through a gentle touch that all was well. The innocent touch did more than calm him. He became even more determined to escort her home — not only to offer protection, but to enjoy her company awhile longer.

"Mrs. Foster, I insist."

For a moment he thought she would continue to refuse. Then she glanced out the front window and frowned. An instant later, she gave him a slight smile and shrugged.

"Then you may walk me home, if you insist."

"I do."

As they left the store together, Reverend McCormick offered his arm.

Slipping her hand into the crook of Brand's arm was a perfectly innocent gesture—or so she thought until she felt his warmth through the fabric of his coat sleeve and caught her breath at her unexpected reaction. She hadn't thought to be moved by the slight connection. She never, ever sought out intimacy. Too many emotions, too much sensitivity had been stripped from her as a child.

She walked beside Brand and stared straight ahead, hoping to hide her embarrassment behind the lace-trimmed edge of her bonnet. But it was impossible to forget who she was and that she was strolling down Main Street on a preacher's arm.

Who would have thought?

Truth be told, Brand McCormick was *handsome* personified. Tall, with thick light hair and green eyes, he exuded quiet confidence and charm. Surprising, since she'd always imagined a preacher to be much more reserved. But from what she'd seen of him, he always appeared cheerful, eternally optimistic, and compassionate.

She glanced over at him, found him studying her intently, and felt the color rise in her cheeks. Her embarrassment surprised her. She'd been forced to give up all manner of shyness early in life.

As her cheeks blazed, she again reminded herself he was a preacher. Not only that, but he was a father. A widower. A *real* widower with not one but two children. He was a pillar of the community, in many ways the closest thing Glory had to a mayor.

Just as she was wondering how to fill the awkward silence, they passed the front window of the *Glory Gazette* building. She glanced inside and saw Hank Larson sitting behind his desk. Thankfully, he looked up, waved, and signaled for them to wait.

"There's Hank," she told Brand. They paused and she slipped her hand off his arm.

Hank hurried out. His shirt sleeves were rolled up to his elbows, his bowtie askew. His brown hair looked as if he'd been raking his fingers through it, but there was a huge smile on his face.

"It's great to see you both. I'm avoiding work," Hank said in greeting.

Laura had never seen the usually thoughtful writer, publisher, and acting sheriff look as happy as he did now.

Brand must have been thinking the same thing. "Obviously marriage agrees with you, Hank."

Laura studied Hank and found it curious that a forty-year-old man could actually be embarrassed by his friend's comment.

"I'm a happy man," he said. "Now if I can just find someone to take over as sheriff . . ."

Laura couldn't blame him for wanting to hand the job over to someone else. After foiling a bank robbery — he claimed his actions were completely accidental — Hank had been proclaimed the town hero and railroaded into the job of sheriff until a replacement could be found. As acting sheriff, he'd almost lost his life in a shoot-out.

"When can we expect a new edition of the *Gazette*?" She wanted to put a smile back on his face.

"Hopefully before the week is up," Hank said. "By the way, Laura, I'll never be able to thank you enough for hosting our wedding and reception supper." He'd thanked her every time he'd run into her this past month.

Brand laughed and nodded. "If she hadn't stepped in, the wedding would have taken place right there in the middle of your surprise party."

Hank nodded. " 'Hold it right there, all of you!' " he mimicked Laura and she grimaced.

Hank had nearly lost the *Gazette* when he ran out of funds and was laid up after the shoot-out. The town had gotten together to help him out and Laura had hosted a surprise party in her backyard. During the party, Hank proposed to Amelia Hawthorne, who was not only the town healer but Laura's only close friend. Amelia had accepted and Brand had been ready to marry them on the spot.

Laura remembered thinking *What have I done?* the minute she spoke up and stopped them. She was adamant when she said,

"Hank Larson, this is your surprise party—*not* Miss Hawthorne's wedding day. She deserves a celebration worthy of her and I for one intend to see that she gets it."

Laura cringed even now as she recalled the way she'd taken charge, but she hadn't been about to let the menfolk rob Amelia of a lovely wedding day. She'd put on a very small but elegant event a week later in her drawing room and had even had Amelia's gown made for her out of one of her own. To Laura, it was the least anyone could do for the man who had not only established Glory's first newspaper, but had helped rid the territory of a gang of thieves.

Knowing that she would never have a wedding of her own made Laura's part in the planning a bittersweet affair but she took joy in the moment. When Amelia asked her to stand up for her, she'd humbly accepted, though she wasn't fool enough to believe for a moment that Amelia would have befriended her had she known about Laura's past.

She had no regrets. The wedding had been perfect. She only wished the newlyweds would stop singing her praises.

"Amelia is planning a dinner of her own soon," Hank said. "You'll both be our first guests."

"I'll look forward to it," Brand said.

"So will I," Laura assured Hank.

Laura felt Brand's gaze on her and turned his way. Staring into his eyes, she saw no lust there, merely respect. And tenderness.

Laura looked away first. "I'd best be getting back. Rodrigo needs these groceries." She held out her hand for the basket. "I can manage by myself from here, Reverend, thank you."

"You're not going to let a pretty lady walk home all alone, are you?" Hank nudged Brand on the shoulder.

Laura wanted to muzzle the newspaperman.

"Of course not." Brand kept a hold of the basket and offered his arm again. Unwilling to refuse in front of Hank, Laura hesitated and then accepted. The sooner she gave in, the sooner she'd be home. She took a deep breath and lightly rested her fingertips on the crook of Brand's elbow again.

By the time they reached the boardinghouse, they'd fallen into a comfortable silence that wasn't broken until Brand said, "I had an ulterior motive for walking you home, you know."

"Don't tell me *you* harbor any secrets, Reverend."

"I admit it. I'm guilty."

He stepped closer. There was less than a foot between them now.

She wished he would step back, but he didn't move. His nearness affected her in ways she couldn't fathom. She stepped closer to the door. She might have been wary, but his eyes were not only smiling, but brimming with honesty. They weren't full of blarney like her uncle Tim's. Nor was there any lust or perversion there. They were open, honest, and filled with what she could only describe as hope. She was surprisingly moved.

"May I call on you tomorrow?" the preacher asked.

"Call tomorrow?"

"To stop by and chat," he clarified. "I was thinking of something in the nature of a social call."

Shock reverberated through her. Had she given him any reason to think she'd welcome him as a gentleman caller? Perhaps she'd stared at him a bit too long—smiled a bit too openly. She *had* taken his arm.

She set the basket down beside the front door. There was a reason for the sign on the wall behind her. *Women and Families Only.* She wanted no single men under her roof. She needed to keep her reputation impeccable. Her standing in Glory, her business success, depended upon maintaining her spotless character. She hadn't let herself know a man, socially or otherwise, in nearly five years. When she'd first moved to town, she'd turned down so many marriage proposals Amelia had told her the word was out: there was no need to try to woo the widow Foster.

The answer to Brand's question was simple: his intent might

be innocent, but she was not. He was a preacher. She was a whore. If he knew that attending Sunday services was simply a part of her new persona and had nothing to do with faith, he wouldn't be asking at all.

Besides, Brand McCormick might smile down at her with the guileless eyes of an honest man and a preacher, but he was, after all, still a man. To allow him to come calling would surely open a Pandora's box of trouble.

"I'm afraid that's out of the question. I'll be rather busy tomorrow." She glanced behind her, reached for the brass doorknob.

"The next day, then?" he suggested.

"I'm afraid I'll be busy all week. I've a new round of guests arriving by week's end."

"Ah," he said.

She wondered if there was some special punishment reserved for sinners who fibbed to a minister. Even if it was for his own sake.

"Reverend, I've tried to be nice, but I am really not interested in gentleman callers." There were enough black marks on her soul already. What difference did one more little lie make?

She realized her rebuff had not dimmed the determined light in his eyes. Not one bit. Brand McCormick raised his hat and tipped it in her direction. And smiled that smile.

"I understand. Some other time, perhaps," he said.

"I don't think so."

He turned around and stepped out into the sunshine, into the Indian summer heat and dryness that was Texas.

She reached for her basket and watched as he walked down the steps and out into the street. Then she let go a pent-up, heartfelt sigh.

"Not at all, Preacher," she whispered.

Not tomorrow. Not next week.

Not ever.

Once inside, Laura carried the basket directly into the kitchen and set it on the wide work table in the middle of the room. She slipped out the letter Harrison had put in, bid Rodrigo good morning, and hurried upstairs to her room. Once there, she sat on the tufted chair in front of her dressing table, picked up a thick hat pin, and used it to open the envelope.

Her fingers trembled as she carefully unfolded the page.

Dear Mrs. Foster,

I'm sorry to inform you that I haven't any positive news to send along regarding the whereabouts of Megan Lane.

Laura tried not to acknowledge the pain of her disappointment as she lowered the letter to her lap. She knew the rest of the page would detail how Mr. Abbott had spent the last of the retainer she'd sent him and how much more he would require to continue his search for her sister — for whom she had not one clue to help them with their search.

If she hadn't met Tom Abbott during the war, if she didn't know him to be a fine upstanding employee of the famed Pinkerton Detective Agency, "The Eye that Never Sleeps," then she wouldn't even consider sending him another advance. But she did know Tom to be completely discreet and one of the best private investigators Pinkerton had ever hired. He'd honed his skills during the war as a spy for the Union.

If anyone could find Megan after all these years, it was Tom.

If he failed ...

If he failed she would have him start searching for Katie and Sarah.

She refused to let herself dwell on failure. She'd planned too long, paid too high a price to fail. She wasn't about to give up hope.

Not yet. Not until every means had been exhausted. She would find her sisters.

She had to.

THREE

Foster's Boardinghouse was full of life over the week's end. There was much conversation and laughter at the dinner table with two families in residence, but no matter how full her days were, loneliness was Laura's only companion when she locked the door and tucked herself in at night. The hours of darkness seemed to stretch on forever. Restless hours filled with glimpses of what should have been her childhood—or the years between then and now. Her sisters, a loving home, the innocence of a first love, not to mention all she had suffered ... Memories fueled the regret and shame that she hadn't been able to protect Megan and the others, to bind her sisters together.

By day, she combated sleeplessness with hard work. She turned on her charm for boarders, making certain their stays under her roof—whether merely overnight or for an extended time—were memorable. She planned the details of every menu herself, inspected every cut of meat, every piece of fruit, every dish served. She oversaw the laundering of the linens, the polishing of the furniture. She taught Anna how to sprinkle lavender water on the pillows and turn perfect sheet corners.

She set a demanding pace for the Hernandezes only because she demanded perfection of herself.

Throwing herself into her work usually exhausted her by early evening, but invariably, she'd awaken long before dawn. Eventually she'd give up tossing and turning, light the lamp, and read.

On Monday morning there were five guest rooms to clean, five sets of laundry to wash and hang, starch and press. She told Anna she would polish the silverware and dust the drawing room herself. She donned a full-length apron over a sprigged muslin gown, scooped her springy curls into a loose chignon, then made a head scarf out of a clean linen towel and tied it around her hair.

She found polishing the silver soothing. Her hands worked as her mind wandered back to a time when her mother was still alive and her family was whole.

The only piece of jewelry her mother owned was a small circle of brass that represented eternity. It surrounded an Irish shamrock. Her mother wore it tied to a slim leather thong around her neck, and Laura couldn't ever recall seeing her without it. She'd promised that one day it would be Laura's.

When her mother died, Laura's uncle pocketed and sold the modest piece and used the money to buy himself whiskey. His due, he said, for taking in his brother's brood.

When Laura commissioned her fine sterling, she had the design on the medallion re-created on the hollow-handled knives and other pieces of the set. She never looked at the emblem without thinking of her mother.

Once the silver was polished and ready for the noon meal, Laura moved on to the drawing room where the windows were opulently dressed with drapes only seen in the finest hotels and drawing rooms of the very wealthy. She loved the feel of the rose velvet she'd chosen for the side panels and the three swags of the valence. She kept them pulled back with thick gilt cord to reveal the icy Swiss lace panels beneath. Her first task of the day was to shake them to remove any dust that might have come in through an open window.

Then, with rag in hand, she worked her way around the room, stopping now and then to admire her collection of bric-a-brac, the

French Morbier grandfather clock, the assortment of Dresden and Staffordshire figurines. Every tabletop, every surface in the room held vases, urns, and lamps. Compotes filled with hard candies stood beside casually stacked, leather-bound books and candles in silver. A high-back Eastlake parlor organ she'd purchased in Biloxi and learned to play—not well but passably—stood against one wall.

Tucked alongside all her lovely collections she'd scattered silver-framed daguerreotypes and photographs of people she'd never met, faces of nameless men's and women's likenesses that she'd acquired after the war claimed so many lives and fortunes all over the South. The photographs were her "people" now. A family on display lest anyone think she was not who she claimed to be. Like herself, she'd made up an identity for each and every one of them. They were part and parcel of the many signs of gentility she had acquired as she planned her home, a refuge for her sisters.

She not only kept her things on display as a show of respectability—she'd noticed early on that a display of wealth enhanced status no matter what a person's background—but she knew how to use them. Her possessions made it easier for her to accept her own lie.

As she adjusted the floral pillow that she'd painstakingly embroidered in needlepoint—she had hated every excruciating moment—there came a sudden knock at the door. She set down the dust rag, wiped her hands on her apron, and went to answer it. Her new guests were not due to arrive until late afternoon.

Through the lace panels hanging across the window on the front door, she easily recognized Brand McCormick.

Laura sighed and opened the door, prepared to send him on his way—until she noticed the children, a boy and a girl, standing on either side of him. He was holding firm to their hands.

Laura glanced up at the preacher, then returned her attention to the children. The boy, who appeared to be about nine—a shorter, mirror image of Brand—stared back. His brow was furrowed, his bottom lip thrust out in a pout. The girl was a bit younger and dressed in a smocked gingham dress. Her hair sported a crooked part and had been fashioned into two uneven braids.

"Hello, Reverend," Laura said. "To what do I owe the honor?"

She sincerely hoped she'd been clear when he'd asked to come calling. But what man brought his children on a social call? Surely this was something else. She took a deep breath, prepared to be firm.

He proudly introduced Janie and Sam.

"Nice to meet you both," Laura said.

"Why do you have that rag on your head?" the girl asked, her critical stare unwavering.

Laura's hand flew to her head. She pulled off the scarf and started an avalanche of hairpins and curls.

"I was dusting," she said.

Janie shrugged. "Now your hair just looks messy."

"Janie," Brand warned, "mind your manners. Sam, why don't you take your sister and explore the yard?"

Laura had heard from Amelia that the McCormick children were a handful. *Incorrigible* had actually been her friend's description. Before Laura could protest that she'd prefer they didn't wander on their own, Janie piped up.

"We wanna stay here. *Don't* we, Sam?" Janie shot Sam a look that Laura easily read.

"Yeah. We wanna stay here." The boy pulled his hand out of Brand's and crossed his arms.

A buckboard rolled down Main. Laura wondered if she should ask the McCormicks in but then thought better of it. She couldn't imagine these two loose in her drawing room.

"We came to meet you and ask you something important," Sam said.

Janie was silent but watchful as she chewed on the end of a braid.

"Something important?" Laura glanced up at Brand and found him smiling.

"Will you come with us to the church social on Saturday night?" he asked.

"Us?"

"The three of us. My sister, Charity, is leading the choir in their first performance wearing their new robes. Sam and Janie are singing in the children's choir. It's a very special event."

"Church social?" Staring into his eyes had rendered Laura speechless until she pulled her thoughts together. "You want me to come to a church social?"

"Yes. As our guest. I don't know anyone I'd rather spend the evening with."

She tried to picture herself at a staid choir performance, making small talk with the good women of Glory, smiling politely at the men, watching children cavort and do whatever children did at a social. She tried to imagine pretending to be something she wasn't, someone she would never be, for an entire evening.

And on a preacher's arm, no less.

The reality was sobering. Even politeness couldn't keep the smile on her face.

"I'm sorry, Reverend. I don't go to church socials."

Brand appeared undaunted.

"Yes, you do," Janie spoke up. "You were at the masquerade party. You were dressed up like an angel. With big fluffy wings. I saw you."

Laura groaned inwardly. It was true. A few months ago she had on a whim attended a masquerade party at the church hall, an event held to raise money for the very choir robes to be previewed at the upcoming performance.

She'd dressed as an angel on a lark. She thought there'd be no harm in going in disguise. She'd donned a gold silk mask and a long, white robe with flowing sleeves bound by one of her gilt-tasseled drapery cords. She'd made ostrich feather wings out of a feather arrangement she kept in an urn near the fireplace.

From the moment she'd stepped into the hall she'd been uncomfortable.

When three liquored-up cowhands began to stare, she realized she had made a terrible mistake. She gave them an icy glare and their attention turned to Amelia. When Hank Larson came to his sweetheart's rescue, a fistfight broke out. Then Laura slipped out a side door and hurried home.

"I don't make it a habit." She found herself wondering why she had to defend herself to a child. "I'm sorry. I simply can't go."

She remembered Brand at the masquerade. He'd greeted every guest at the door while wearing a Roman gladiator's helmet and a flowing red cape.

"You gotta come," Sam urged. "We brought you a present."

"Present?" She drew back. She hated to think Brand had spent his hard-earned cash on a gift. His clothes were not worn, but they were not of the latest cut. His boots were polished but a bit scuffed around the heels. Preachers relied on the wealth of their congregation and for the most part, rich donors were few and far between in and around Glory.

He reached into his pocket, pulled out a small glass jar with a metal lid. When he offered it to her, she let him drop it into her palm.

"Open it," Sam urged.

Laura obliged. A combination of oil of roses and a hint of almond swirled up from the open jar.

"It's salve for your hands," Janie explained. "Miss Amelia makes it."

"It's lovely." Laura looked at Brand. "Thank you."

"It's from all of us," he said.

She thanked Sam and Janie. Now that the gift had been delivered, the children seemed to have lost interest in her. Sam started to climb on the veranda railing, quickly straddling the top. Janie spied Peaches, Laura's long-haired calico, stretched out on the porch swing. She left her father's side and tiptoed toward the sleeping cat.

Brand drew Laura's attention again. "I'd love to have you hear them sing."

"This really isn't fair, you know," she said softly. "Using your children to get me to join you."

He shrugged, smiled down at her. "A man has to do what a man has to do."

Against her will, Laura found herself smiling. "When is the performance again?"

"Saturday night. So, will you be our guest?" He didn't appear to be leaving without an answer.

"So. How about it?" Sam asked.

"Will you, please?" Janie begged.

Laura sighed. Refusing Brand was one thing. Sam and Janie were quite another.

"Very well. Since you all insist."

She politely listened as he detailed the event and what she could expect. She could always send her regrets later. For now, she couldn't turn him down. Not while he was wearing such a hopeful sparkle in his eyes.

She forced herself to look away. Her mind wandered as he spoke of his sister's plans for the choir. A few moments later, she noticed both children had disappeared. So had Peaches.

"Where are your children?" Laura asked.

Startled, Brand looked around. "They're around somewhere. I don't think that they would stray too—"

A high, bloodcurdling scream rent the air. Brand bolted down the veranda stairs and headed around back. Laura gathered her skirt in her hands and followed. The high-pitched screams esca-lated as she rounded the corner of the house. The sound pierced Laura's shell of reserve, reminding her all too much of the night Megan had disappeared. She had never gotten *those* screams out of her mind.

Brand disappeared through the open doors in the carriage house. Laura followed him inside the dim interior. Her shiny black buggy was parked off to one side of the open room. Sam sat back on the front seat, casually stretched out, watching his sister helplessly dangle by her fingertips from the edge of the open loft high overhead. She was easily twenty feet above the ground.

"Hang on, Janie. Hang on." Brand skidded to a stop directly beneath his little girl.

"Don't move, Brand. Stay beneath her." Laura struggled to lift the ladder that was usually propped up against the loft. Once it was righted, she leaned it against the edge of the loft beside Janie. Arms out, ready to catch Janie if she let go, Brand never took his eyes off his daughter.

"Papa!" the girl shouted. "Help me!"

Laura tied a knot in the hem of her skirt to keep from stepping on it and started up the ladder.

"Your Papa will catch you if you fall. I'm coming up to get you, Janie. Just hang on a little longer." She tried to sound calm and confident despite her racing heart.

"No! Papa, help!"

When she reached the top of the ladder, Laura was close enough to touch Janie, but feared if she leaned out to grab the child, the ladder would shift and they'd both go tumbling down.

"I'm right here beside you, Janie. I'm going to put my hand on your waist. If you move your foot to your right, maybe you can put your toe on the ladder." Laura didn't allow one ounce of her own dread to creep into her tone.

"That's your left foot, sweetie," Brand said. "The other foot."

Laura saw Janie slowly extend her leg. She gently guided the child's foot to the ladder rung above her. She breathed a sigh of relief when Janie's toe was secure.

"That's it," Brand encouraged. "That's it, honey. Now the other foot."

Laura slipped her hand around Janie's waist and held on. "I've got you. Slide your other foot onto the ladder."

"I can't. I'll *die*!" Janie, hanging sideways, started to sob.

At least, Laura thought, *she's not screaming anymore.*

Laura tried to cajole her. "Yes, you can. You can scoot your hands along the floor until you get close and then grab the ladder. I've got you."

"I can't. I won't! Papa, *do* something!"

"Listen to Laura, honey."

"I don't want to listen to her. I don't want her, I want you—"

Laura glanced down at Brand. His face had lost all color. She had broken up bar brawls and tossed ill-mannered patrons out of her establishment on their ears. She'd never backed down from an argument or a fight, never feared for her own safety—not when she had nothing to lose. She could certainly handle a seven-year-old.

Laura lowered her voice and spoke with complete calm. "Once Janie is on the ladder, you grab hold of it, please, Brand. Janie, I'm going to hang on to you while you let go of the loft and reach for the ladder." She tightened her grip on Janie's waist.

"Now, Janie, move your hands. Reach for the ladder," she urged.

"But—"

"Do it!" Laura demanded. "Right now."

Janie inched her right hand and then her left over to a rung above her. Laura knew the minute Brand took firm hold of the ladder.

"I'm going to start climbing down and you are going to follow after me," she told Janie. "Ready?"

The girl's braids bobbed as she nodded.

"Now, come on." Laura started down the ladder. Janie sniffled and whimpered but slowly followed. Laura forgot that Brand was directly beneath her, his hands steady on the rails. When she reached the lowest rung, she realized she had stepped within the circle of his arms.

All the courage she'd mustered to help Janie failed her. She whispered, "You can let go and step back, Reverend."

He let go of the ladder and gave her room to dismount. She

made a great show of brushing off her apron and shaking out her skirt and petticoats while she collected herself. She refused to meet his gaze for as long as she could.

When she finally looked up she realized she needn't have been embarrassed by her reaction to his nearness. His attention was focused on Janie. He was hunkered down on one knee, hugging Janie close before he began to dry the child's tears with his kerchief.

Laura's thoughts drifted back to that long-distant time when she'd been the one to dry her sister's tears, to wash their faces, to sing them to sleep. She quickly smothered the memory the way one snuffs a dangerous flame. She couldn't bear the searing pain.

Instead, she concentrated on the man and child before her. She stood tall and reminded herself who she was, where she was.

"How in the world did you end up there like that?" Brand asked Janie.

"Sam and I climbed up. He climbed down first and when it was my turn he knocked the ladder down and ditched me." The child spoke between sorrowful hiccups.

Laura turned toward the buggy. Sam was no longer there.

"What are you going to do to him, Papa?" Janie slipped her hand into his.

"I'm going to give him a stern talking to, of course."

"I think you should beat him within an inch of his life —"

"Jane McCormick. We've talked about forgiveness."

Janie looked doubtful. "But he did a really *bad* thing. Are we supposed to forgive really *bad* things, Papa? What if I fell and kilt myself? Would you forgive him then?"

Laura watched Brand collect himself. A telling muscle flexed in his jaw. She reckoned he would probably like to shake Sam senseless, but after a moment or two, he slowly nodded.

"I would forgive him, Janie. It's what God wants us to do."

"Are we supposed to forgive really bad *things?"*

It was easy for him to say he would forgive his son, Laura

thought. Janie was unharmed. But what if she'd been badly hurt or, heaven forbid, killed? Would Brand's faith truly stand the test?

Still clutching his handkerchief, Janie continued to snuffle as she leaned against Brand's leg.

"Shall we go back to the veranda and have some lemonade?" Laura suggested.

"What about Sam?" Janie obviously wanted to see justice doled out quickly.

"I'll look for him as soon as we get you settled," Brand assured her.

Laura hoped the boy hadn't snuck into the house. She could just imagine the havoc he could wreak inside.

"Why don't you look for him now?" she suggested to Brand before she turned to the child. "You can sit on my porch swing. Would you like that?"

Janie rubbed her toe in the dirt. "Maybe." Then she turned to her father. "But I think you better find him right away. He said something about skinning Mrs. Foster's cat."

Brand found Sam hiding near the back porch steps and led him back to where Laura and Janie waited on the veranda. He whispered a quick prayer of thanksgiving when he saw Peaches curled up asleep on the veranda swing.

He confined Sam to the far porch corner and made him sit on a stool with his nose pressed against the wall. How long would it take to forget the sight of Janie hanging above the carriage house floor, he wondered. His heart hadn't settled down yet.

"You need to think about what you did to Janie."

"How long?"

"Until I say you're done."

As Brand walked away, he was aware that some would say Sam needed a strong hand against his backside. Brand was tempted to spank him, but whenever his children erred and he wanted to punish them, he was reminded of his own father's overbearing nature and unbending discipline and couldn't bring himself to be firm as he should be.

He found himself wondering what Laura would do if Sam were her child.

Her quick action and courage had amazed and surprised him. A weak-willed woman might have taken one look at Janie dangling high above the ground and fainted dead away. He'd been frozen with fear and all he could think of was catching Janie if she fell. Laura had taken charge.

"How can I ever thank you, Laura?"

She was seated beside Janie on the swing, focused on what the girl was saying as she stroked Laura's cat. Peaches had survived Sam's idle threat and was curled up in Janie's lap.

Laura turned. "Pardon?"

"I was thanking you. You were wonderful in the carriage house. All I could do was wait to catch her when she fell."

"It was quite a shocking sight."

"But you didn't hesitate to act."

"You might say I've had a lot of experience with emergencies."

He noticed how a flush of color always fanned across her cheeks when she was embarrassed.

"I guess you've seen about everything running a boarding-house," he mused. He was still amazed by her courage. Not only had she stood up for the child in the mercantile, but when Hank Larson had been wounded in a shoot-out nearly six months ago, Laura had stepped in without being asked to help Amelia nurse Hank. "Amelia still credits you with helping her save Hank's life," he said, thinking aloud.

"I was just there as another pair of hands and to act as chaperone." Blushing, Laura dropped her gaze to her folded hands. "My being a widow and all," she added softly, "I was able to save Amelia the embarrassment of having to bathe Hank when he was feverish—" She abruptly cut herself off, as if she'd said too much.

From the far end of the veranda, Sam interrupted.

"Am I gonna have to sit here forever? I'm so thirsty, Papa. I might just keel over right here and die."

"You may apologize to Mrs. Foster."

Sam leapt off the stool and crossed the veranda. When he reached the swing, he stared at the floor and mumbled, "Sorry."

"Mean it, please, son."

"I'm sorry, Mrs. Foster, for leaving Janie hangin' in your barn."

"And ..." Brand prodded.

Sam swallowed. "And for saying I was going to skin your cat."

Brand watched Laura reach for Sam's chin, tilt his face up, and made him look her in the eye.

"Would you really skin my cat? Or any cat, for that matter?"

Sam mumbled something.

"I'm sorry. I didn't hear you," Laura said. Her voice was soft, melodic, yet laced with steel.

"No. I wouldn't hurt your cat. Or any cat."

"Yes, he would," Janie piped up.

Laura gently took hold of Sam's hand, effectively keeping the boy close. Brand watched with admiration and amazement.

"I'm talking to your brother right now, Janie. If he says he's not going to hurt Peaches, then I'll take him as a man of his word." Laura turned to Sam again. "Are you a man of your word?"

Brand watched as his son stood a bit taller and squared his shoulders.

"Yes, ma'am. I'm a man of my word."

"Then that's all that needs to be said," Laura told him. "I forgive you. I think you need to ask your sister to forgive you too. She's the one you left in such a precarious position. You need to make her a promise as well."

Laura let go of Sam's hand. The boy scooted over to stand in front of Janie.

"Sorry," he told her. Then he glanced at Laura and added, "Sorry, I left you hanging like that. I won't do it again."

Janie stared at him for a moment, then said, "Wanna pet Peaches?"

When Sam said yes, she proceeded to scoot over and let him sit beside her.

Brand let go a sigh of relief. "We'll take that lemonade now," he said. "If it's not too much trouble."

Laura asked Brand to have a seat while she went inside and told Anna to bring them some lemonade. When she came back, she found Brand seated in the middle of the swing, next to Janie and Sam. If she joined them all, she'd be forced to wedge herself in beside him. Instead, she leaned against the veranda railing. She left her apron on, a reminder that they had interrupted her at her task.

Still, her relief that Janie was safe was so great, she realized she wasn't in any hurry to have them leave. At least until they'd finished their lemonade.

As if he had read her thoughts Brand said, "We won't take up much more of your time. I haven't forgotten that you refused my request to call on you, but what kind of a man would I be if I gave up without a fight?"

His open smile was far too tempting.

"Sensible?" She continued to find herself inexplicably drawn to him.

"And why is that?" His voice was low and warm.

She glanced at the children. They were whispering over the cat.

"Because if you're looking for a romantic relationship, Reverend, I'm not interested."

"Your penchant for turning down marriage proposals is legendary, Mrs. Foster."

"Is it?"

"Very much so."

Good, she thought. *Then you won't be shocked or disappointed when I do not attend the choir performance.*

"I realized this morning I don't know much about you, Mrs. Foster."

"That's because I'm a private person, Reverend McCormick."

He didn't question her. Instead he said, "I suppose my life is pretty much an open book."

"I suppose it has to be, doesn't it?" She tipped her head, studied him carefully. The faithful had a right to know all about this man who was charged with their salvation. They would also want his associations to be of the highest standards and morals.

"That's right." He appeared thoughtful.

"So, tell me about yourself," she said. An expert on men, she hadn't met one yet who didn't care to talk about himself more than anything else.

Brand set the swing rocking to a gentle rhythm. "I was born and raised in Illinois. When the war broke out, I enlisted in the Union Army."

"Were you a chaplain?"

He shook his head no and paused a moment before he went on. "I had a spiritual awakening on the battlefield. After the war, I went back home, met and married Jane, my late wife, and became a minister. I was blessed. Our lives were everything we'd dreamed of when the children came. Then, when Janie was a year old, Jane fell ill and died very suddenly. God presented me with the challenge of living through my grief and raising my children. With the help of my sister, I decided to come to Texas and start over, like so many folks did after the war."

Standing on the veranda of the grand home built from the shame of her past, Laura could barely speak above a whisper. "Texas is a fine place for that."

She'd chosen Texas for its size, hoping she was as well hidden here as a needle in a haystack.

Anna appeared with a tray of glasses and a pitcher of lemonade and set them on a wicker side table near the swing. Laura poured the lemonade, gave some to Janie and Sam. As she handed Brand a glass, their fingers met. The touch was entirely innocent, but an unexpected wave of longing hit her. She never sought a man's touch, never welcomed one. But this — this gentle brush of his fingertips was something altogether different.

She glanced up and found Brand staring into her eyes. Had he felt it too?

She tried to look away but couldn't. Silence stretched between them, silence full of tension that the children beside him were oblivious to. As much as Laura wanted the startling moment to end, a part of her wished it could last forever.

Brand found himself in no hurry to leave as they sipped lemonade and chatted awhile longer, and then he told the children they could start walking home, but to wait for him at the corner. He wanted to bid Laura good-bye alone.

Before today, he'd never entertained any opinions about whether or not Laura Foster would make a good mother for his children. He hadn't thought any further than inviting her to the choir performance on Saturday night. Now he had no doubt that not only was she caring, forgiving, and strong, but loving and gentle.

The direction of his thoughts surprised him. It had been forever since he dared to think about marriage again. Laura would be an easy woman to love.

Laura busied herself with the refreshment tray as Brand watched the children dash across the front yard and head toward the corner. When he turned to her, she appeared to be waiting expectantly for him to take his leave.

"I've kept you from your duties long enough. I'm sorry about what happened—"

"Don't think about it. Children can be unpredictable." Such deep sadness filled her eyes that it took him aback.

He spoke before he thought. "It's unfortunate you and Mr. Foster never had any children. You're very good with them."

She stared silently back. Almost as if she couldn't comprehend a word he'd just said. It quickly dawned on him that his comment had wounded her. Laura might have wanted children desperately.

"I'm so sorry," he said quickly. "That's none of my business."

"I—"

"Really, forgive me."

"There's nothing to forgive, Reverend." She looked away for an instant, as if collecting herself. "Thank you for the hand cream. It's lovely."

It was a clear hint that he should be on his way.

"I'll look forward to Saturday night." He reminded her that he would see her again soon. "The choir performance starts at seven. Would it be all right to come get you at six-thirty?"

She hesitated a moment. "I'll meet you there. In case I'm detained by my guests," she added.

"It's no problem, really. Charity and the children have to be there early."

"I'd prefer meeting you there." Her tone brooked no argument.

Her independent streak presented a challenge, but he wasn't about to risk giving up on her.

The beguiling Mrs. Foster had just met her match.

FOUR

Two days later, Brand finally had time to hunt down Hank Larson. He spent a harrowing morning with the church board, during a meeting in which a heated discussion arose over whether or not it was proper to charge folks for a cup of coffee after church. Members nearly came to blows until he stepped in to remind them they could surely find a peaceful solution to the problem.

Afterward, he hightailed it over to the *Glory Gazette* office, only to learn from Richard Hernandez, Laura's employee and Hank's apprentice, that Hank had ridden a mile outside of town to do some target practice. Brand found the gun-toting journalist shooting cans off a fallen cottonwood log.

"What brings you out here, Reverend?" Hank holstered his Colt. "No trouble, I hope."

Thinking of the board meeting, Brand said, "Nothing a little prayer won't help." He tied his horse's reins to what was left of a four-foot cottonwood stump.

"Actually," he added, "I came looking for advice."

"You're usually the one dispensing advice, Preacher."

"Not this time. This time it involves an affair of the heart. Since you are newly married, I think you're just the man to help."

"This doesn't have anything to do with the beautiful Mrs. Foster, does it?"

Dozens of rusted, bullet-ridden cans lined the ground around the fallen log. Brand planted a boot on it. He shoved his low-crowned hat off his forehead.

"How did you guess?"

Hank laughed. "Oh, could have been the look in your eye when you were strutting down Main with Mrs. Foster on your arm a few mornings ago. Or the fact that you called on Amelia and you let Sam and Janie choose one of her salves for Laura."

"All true, I won't deny it. When did you know for certain you were ready to marry again?"

"The day I realized I couldn't live in the same town with Amelia without having her by my side. But I did have to propose quite a few times before she finally said yes, remember?"

"So many times that you'd about given up hope."

Hank stared at him for a moment.

"Mind my asking how long ago you lost your wife?" Hank asked.

For the longest time, Brand had experienced a sinking feeling when anyone mentioned Jane as his "lost" wife or his "late" wife. But now, although the pain was still there, it was muted, not as swift or razor sharp.

"Almost seven years ago," Brand said.

"You'll love her always, but she's in heaven and you're still here. It's natural to worry about being disloyal. Believe me, I know." Hank had been a widower himself before he married Amelia. "If there are qualities in Laura that you admire—"

"Laura's unlike any woman I've ever known. She's wealthy, refined. Independent."

"Not to mention stunning," Hank added.

Brand smiled. "I've noticed. Believe me."

Hank began to line up more cans.

"A few months back you assured me that Amelia wasn't one to judge a man by the size of his bankroll. If a wealthy man is what Mrs. Foster requires, then she's not the woman for you," he said.

"I've got two children and Charity to support," Brand reminded him.

"Love finds a way, Brand."

"I've asked Laura to the choir performance on Saturday night." Brand shook his head, hoping he'd done the right thing.

Hank looked at him for a long, telling moment. "A good start, I guess."

"Not very romantic." Brand shrugged. He wasn't used to feeling helpless.

"Did she accept?"

Brand nodded. "I think Janie and Sam had a lot to do with her agreeing to go."

Hank patted Brand on the shoulder. "Congratulations. It's a start.

"You just keep the faith, Reverend, and take it one step at a time. Meanwhile, I'll ask Amelia if she's got any ideas. Women are a whole lot better at these things than we are."

The week flew by all too quickly for Laura.

She awoke each day determined to send Reverend McCormick a note to let him know she wouldn't be able to attend the recital. Each time, she balked. It was one thing to live a lie. Quite another to keep lying to a preacher.

Saturday morning she sat alone in her drawing room trying to practice an organ piece. In a valiant attempt to cultivate gentility before she moved to Texas, she'd taken lessons from an ancient gentleman in New Orleans. Monsieur Beaurevaus was patient and talented. He kept his hands to himself and taught her a few basic songs. She could use more lessons, but decided she didn't have the temperament to succeed.

When the doorbell rang, shrill and insistent, she went immediately to the entry hall. Kansas state representative Bryce Botsworth and his family were on their way to San Antonio. The Botsworths and their two daughters were scheduled to stay only one night.

Laura opened the door to greet them, focusing on Mrs. Botsworth first. The woman was short, just an inch or two over five feet. Her hair was bright red, her skin white as a dove's wing. Her eyes were bright green.

Her daughters, reed thin and a bit taller than their mother, favored her coloring. Both girls appeared to be under twenty.

"Welcome," Laura said, smiling at the woman and then the young ladies. "I'm sure you're ready for some tea or other refreshment. Do come right—"

She paused the minute she finally turned to Mr. Botsworth. He was of medium height, portly, with short, thick hands. Dressed in a somber black suit with a silk cravat and diamond stick pin, he whipped off his hat, exposing a bald pate.

When Laura looked into the man's eyes, she couldn't help but notice his speculative stare. Her speech faltered. Her blood ran cold. It took all of her will not to turn and leave them standing there on the threshold.

"Do come in. Please. I'll just … I'll … Please, step right into the parlor. Let me go find Richard. He'll take your luggage up … upstairs."

"Thank you so much," Mrs. Botsworth said, leading the way into the drawing room. "Come, girls." She moved into the drawing room. "Oh, my. This is quite lovely. Very unexpected for a small town like this. Just look, Bryce."

Bryce *was* looking, Laura noticed, but not at the drawing room. He was staring at her. Then, without a word, Mr. Botsworth turned and followed in his family's wake. He didn't break stride, nor did he look at Laura again. Had she imagined his interest? She couldn't be at all certain.

Laura took a deep breath and hoped no one noticed that her hands trembled slightly as she smoothed the front of her gown. "Make yourself comfortable," she said.

She hurried down the hall to the kitchen, forced herself not to run. Once there, she shoved open the swinging door and, without thinking, collapsed against the wall. She pressed her hands to her heart, afraid it was about to beat its way out of her chest.

"*Señora?*"

Rodrigo was at the sink, peeling potatoes. He glanced over his shoulder and, the minute he saw her, set down the paring knife and dried his hands. Concern marred his dark features.

Laura waved him off when he rushed to her side.

"Please, keep working. I'm fine. It's ... it's just the heat."

"*Agua?*" He offered. "Water?"

"Yes. Yes. Some water. And put on the teapot." She gave the bellpull near the door a yank. Soon Anna would come running.

Laura tried to rein in her emotions. She took a deep breath, reminded herself that there were guests to be settled, refreshments to be served.

She tried to convince herself Bryce Botsworth had never, *ever* laid eyes on her. She didn't recognize him at all — but hundreds of men had passed through her life, hundreds had taken pleasure in her arms while she willed herself to feel nothing.

Something in Botsworth's stare sent chills down her spine.

Help me.

The plea for help came from somewhere deep inside. Certainly not a prayer; she never prayed. If there was a God in heaven, He would have never let two innocent children enter that house on Rue de Lafayette.

She took another deep breath. Inhaled the scent of beef and onions roasting in the big stove across the room. Studied the carefully placed crocks and pitchers on the dry sink, the china collection in the cupboards, the starched, lace-trimmed curtains hanging across the wide bank of windows along the back wall.

This was her world. The world she'd created out of the blood, sweat, and tears of her past. This was the home where she would reunite what was left of her family. She had to stay strong, to cling to her dream, or surely perish. She was not about to let Bryce Botsworth or any other man bring her down.

Rodrigo brought her a glass of water. Not trusting herself to hold it, she sat heavily at the table. He set the glass down and hovered. She tried to smile, to reassure him.

"It's all right. You can finish up." She nodded toward the bowl of potato peels.

She lifted the glass, amazed the water didn't slosh. Her hands were a bit steadier. She took a long drink, willed the water to stay down.

Anna walked in and took in the scene. Like Laura, she was still in her thirties. The mother of only one child, sixteen-year-old Richard, Anna didn't appear much older than her son. She was slim with light-brown skin, smooth and flawless. She wore her dark hair in a braid coiled into a knot at her nape.

Her dark eyes flashed toward her husband and there was no missing the look of concern that passed between them.

Laura forced herself to smile. The Hernandez family was as dependent upon her as she was them. She tried to alleviate their fear.

"I'm fine now." She rose, raised a hand to her hair, and found it perfectly in place, as usual. Her appearance was perfect. Her shame was hidden. "Just a bit warm. The Botsworth family has arrived. I'd like you to serve tea and lemonade, Anna. In the drawing room. Rodrigo, their bags are on the veranda. If Richard is here, have him put the luggage in the green and blue rooms. If not, please take them up yourself."

"He is here, señora. I will call him." Rodrigo went out the back door, headed for the small log structure where the family lived near the edge of Laura's property.

There, she thought. *Routine. Normalcy.*

Surely she was mistaken about Representative Botsworth. She had stirred up her own emotional tornado.

As soon as she sent her regrets to Brand McCormick—which she was determined to do before the tall standing clock in the hall chimed again—she could relax.

"Anna," she began, remembering to sound calm and collected,

"I'll have a letter for Richard to deliver in the next few minutes. Please have him wait here after he takes the luggage upstairs."

The Botsworths went out to look at a homestead — their older daughter was engaged and they thought to invest in some land for a wedding gift to the newlyweds. Laura kept to herself upstairs until they went out, then met with Anna and Rodrigo to go over the dinner details. Soon enough, the Botsworth girls returned and took turns at the parlor organ. Both of them played far and away better than Laura. When she heard the older girl tell her parents that she didn't care how much land they bought here, there was no way she would live in Texas, Laura breathed a sigh of relief.

Calm now, convinced she'd been mistaken about Bryce Botsworth, Laura presided at the head of the dinner table as always. She displayed all the finesse she could muster. She had read that the perfect hostess was mistress of the art of small talk. The flow of conversation was in her hands and she kept a list of several suitable topics in mind. Certain topics, of course — politics, religion, and money — were never to be discussed.

She welcomed the Botsworths and her other guests and made certain the serving platters and bowls kept moving around the table. When their plates were filled with steaming pot roast, potatoes, carrots, and flaky biscuits oozing with fresh creamy butter, she even went so far as to ask Mr. Botsworth, since he was the most prestigious among them, to give the blessing. Laura found most of her guests expected the ritual.

He complied without hesitation. Everyone bowed their heads in prayer. Laura snuck a glance at the man seated at the end of the table. Eyes closed, his strong voice resonated as he asked God to bless the food before them and to keep them all safe — no matter where their journeys might take them.

Eventually she became involved in a discussion of books with his well-read daughters, Vivian and Imogene. Mrs. Botsworth — who insisted Laura call her by her given name, Amber — was pleasant, though she tended to go on incessantly once she had everyone's attention. Tonight, Laura didn't mind in the least.

The doorbell rang when they were in the middle of the main course. Since she wasn't expecting any new boarders that evening, Laura remained seated, knowing that Anna, on duty in the kitchen, would answer the bell.

"I've heard that ice water is very unhealthy," Amber Botsworth was just saying as Anna slipped into the room and whispered to Laura that Reverend McCormick was at the door asking to speak to her.

Laura excused herself. She brushed a wayward curl out of her eye before she opened the wide pocket doors separating the dining room from the entry hall. Silently she drew the doors closed behind her.

"Laura," Brand nodded. He was smiling, looking very handsome in a new black suit. His preacher's collar might as well have been a danger sign.

What next? she wondered.

"Oh, Reverend, I'm so sorry. Didn't you get my note?"

He drew his hand out of his coat pocket and flipped her letter up between his first two fingers. "I did." He looked her over from head to toe. "It seems you have recovered from your headache."

Laura blushed. "I . . . it actually faded away a few minutes ago, and I felt obligated to join my guests for dinner. There's a Kansas state representative here tonight. I thought it too late to let you know—"

"Not at all. I was ready early, so I thought I'd stop by and see how you were feeling."

Laughter filtered through the closed dining room doors.

"My guests . . ."

Brand's gaze had not left her since she'd opened the door. Though she tried to look away, she was arrested by his calm, steady perusal. She was lying and knew he knew it.

"I'm sorry to interrupt during your meal. I can wait in the drawing room," he offered.

"Wait?"

"For you to join me."

"But ... I'm not going."

"Because you *had* a headache?"

"As I said, I don't have one now." Laura felt as if she were floundering alone in a sinking rowboat—one she'd drilled a hole in herself.

Brand lowered his voice and stepped closer. "Janie's been primping all day. She had Charity roll her hair in rags so it would curl like yours."

"Reverend—"

"It's an important night for my family, Laura. Charity has been planning this event for weeks. It would mean a lot to me if you were there."

Her presence would mean a lot to him?

She couldn't remember her presence meaning anything to anyone unless it was bought and paid for.

She pictured his children. Scamps they might be, but she remembered how easily children could be disappointed by the smallest thing.

"I'm not properly dressed ..."

Laura was sorry when his gaze swept her gown. When he met her eyes again, they displayed an admiration she couldn't deny. She warned herself to be very, very careful where this man was concerned. He was not someone she wanted to see hurt in any way. He or his children.

"You'll already outshine everyone there," he told her.

She tried to imagine herself primly seated in the church hall beside him.

"Really, Brand. I just don't think—"

Just then, Bryce Botsworth's laughter rang out above the others in the dining room. Loud and boisterous, it resonated through the closed doors.

The distinctive laugh, really more of a bark, sent a cold chill through Laura. She knew without a doubt she'd heard it before. The sound brought back the memory of her first employer whispering in her ear just before she was introduced to Bryce Botsworth . . .

"It would behoove you to make sure the gentleman is well pleased tonight, Lovie. He's a politician from Kansas."

He'd been younger then. Thinner. With a full head of hair.

And she'd been younger than his oldest daughter was now.

She should have put money on her million-to-one odds of running into one of her former patrons.

Brand suddenly took her hand. "I'm so sorry, Laura. You're white as a sheet. I'm sorry I pressed you. I'll come back another time—"

"No." She tightened her grip on his fingers. "Please. Don't go."

The last thing she wanted was to walk back into the dining room and face Botsworth again. If Brand could see it, Botsworth would surely notice her distress. Perhaps the man hadn't yet recognized her. The last thing she wanted was to be around to jolt his memory. She quickly collected herself and tried to smile.

"Please, wait in the drawing room while I run upstairs and get a wrap. I'll go with you."

"Are you sure? You don't look—"

"Yes. I'm sure." *And desperate.* "I'd love to go."

Before he let go of her hands, he promised, "Trust me, Laura, I'll bring you home the minute you say the word."

FIVE

The doors to the hall were wide open as Brand drove his buggy up to the church grounds. Light spilled out from inside.

He set the brake and climbed down, walked around to Laura's side. She took a deep breath and gathered her skirt. But before she could clasp his hand, Brand reached up and slipped his hands around her waist. His eyes never left her face as he lifted her to the ground. Laura tried to cover her surprise as, once more, his nearness breached the wall she had built to protect herself from her emotions. As once more, her reaction astonished her.

Thankfully, he stepped back as soon as her feet were firmly planted, but not before the shock of his touch wore off. She avoided his gaze, taking longer than necessary to straighten her shawl, to adjust the satin bow beneath her chin, to wait for her racing heart to slow down.

There were folks lining up at the door to the church. He was their minister and needed to be there. She took a deep breath.

"You look lovely," he said softly.

"Thank you." She didn't feel lovely. She'd rushed upstairs, grabbed her reticule and a hat — the plainest she owned, though it sported a saucy, iridescent peacock feather — a butter-colored shawl with long fringe, and white kid gloves. She'd been so desperate to leave the house that she hadn't even glanced in the mirror.

He offered her his elbow. In a move that was becoming too familiar, she slipped her hand into the crook of his arm. As they neared those gathered at the front door to the hall, she noticed Brand had been right. Compared to the other women she was overdressed. She raised her chin a notch. It was no sin to own pretty things.

Though how she'd come by them was another story.

Brand was greeted all around as he made his way up the steps. He paused now and again to introduce her. Hearing his easy banter, watching his eyes darken with concern whenever someone asked for his advice, not only deepened her respect for him, but emphasized just how wide was the gulf between them.

She thought to leave him to his work and walk into the hall alone. But when she started to draw her hand out of the warm crook of his elbow, he smoothly laid his free hand over hers. The touch was enough to keep her beside him as he continued to introduce her and greet his congregation. They remained there, side by side, until every last person had entered.

"After you," he said finally, gesturing toward the open doors.

She nodded and stepped over the threshold.

Together they walked toward the front pew near the stage. The hall was full of the young, old, and in-between, some families taking up entire rows. She was certain her walking in on Brand's arm had caused a bit of a stir. She could feel folks watching them with interest. Embarrassed, she tried to focus on the stage where the choir would perform.

She left the seat on the aisle for Brand and settled into the one beside it. Head down, lost in thought, she tried to forget that Bryce Botsworth was in her dining room, and that she'd just used Brand to escape.

You shouldn't be here, she told herself. *He deserves better than you.*

A hushed whisper and a few giggles came from backstage and she was reminded that she wasn't here just for Brand, but for his children. She was here so as not to disappoint them.

He startled her when he leaned close and whispered, "Duty calls. I'll be right back."

He mounted two low steps to the stage and walked to the lectern. There, he greeted the assembly. He spoke of the need for choir robes and the fact that not only had everyone donated, but a generous benefactor had made up the needed difference after the masquerade fundraiser. Then he asked them all to bow their heads in prayer.

Laura remained silent, staring at her gloved hands. She clutched them tightly in her lap and tried to keep her mind blank. She couldn't stop chiding herself for panicking and coming with him tonight. What right had she to sit among these good people? What right had she to lead Brand on?

She rubbed the thumbs of her gloves against each other and remained silent as the sound of prayer swelled. If God existed, if He cared at all, He would have saved her. Or at the very least, He would have saved Megan.

But she had been forced to save herself, to survive alone and hope that her sisters were not lost to her.

"Laura?"

While she'd been mired in thought, head down, the prayer had ended and Brand had slipped into the seat beside her. Everyone was waiting expectantly for the performance to begin.

Charity McCormick appeared on stage and walked up to the lectern. Tall and thin with blonde hair, Charity appeared far more nervous than Laura felt. Brand's sister was obviously forcing a smile as she thanked everyone for their help in raising funds for the choir robes.

"Since they are anxious to begin, not to mention wiggle worms, the children will perform first." She waved her hand toward the side entrance, and twelve boys and girls of all ages filed onto the stage. They were followed by Amelia Larson, who'd apparently been assigned the task of keeping them in line.

When Amelia turned to take a seat, she spied Laura and smiled.

Even seeing her friend didn't help to calm Laura's nerves. She scanned the children's faces and located Janie and Sam. Janie was, indeed, wearing her hair in bobbing ringlets. She smiled at Laura and wiggled her fingers in greeting. Laura flushed with embarrassment but managed to hold her smile. Sam was too busy tugging on the braids of the little girl in front of him to pay any attention to Laura or Brand.

A few chuckles came from the audience, a few hushed whispers as everyone settled down. Charity took her place, lifted her hand, and the children began to sing "Rock of Ages." The song started on a shaky note but leveled out. All in all, the future citizens of Glory did a credible job of performing the rest of a half dozen songs.

When Charity turned and asked the congregation to stand and join in, Laura felt Brand step closer. Again her body reacted to him. A sudden rush of awareness flooded her when his arm pressed against hers.

She couldn't find her voice. Mute, she couldn't even mouth the words of the song. She glanced over to see if he noticed she wasn't singing. For far too long there had been no song in her heart.

His own voice was strong and melodic. When the song ended, she found him watching her intently. There was such warmth, such caring, in his eyes that she was forced to look away and take a deep breath.

"Are you all right?" he whispered.

She nodded. "I don't sing," she said lamely.

As they stood together, shoulder to shoulder, she felt herself shrinking inside. She was no longer afraid of what would happen to her if any of these good people ever discovered the truth—she was afraid for the man beside her, afraid of hurting him. If her past somehow came to light, no matter how innocent their friendship, she would drag him down with her.

The fact that she cared about what might happen to Brand scared her more than anything.

Charity dismissed the children's choir with a bow and a smile.

The program halted while they marched down the aisle to join their parents. Sam and Janie bounced down the steps and when they reached Brand, Sam quickly climbed over his father and then Laura. He plopped down in the empty space beside her.

"That's not fair!" Janie frantically whispered to Brand. "I get to sit beside Mrs. Foster. You said *I* would get to sit by her."

Janie's every word went up an octave. Laura instructed Sam to scoot to the next seat. She slid into his, opening a space between her and Brand and patted the now-empty seat beside her.

Janie sat and glared at Sam across Laura. Sam stuck out his tongue. Janie made a fist. Laura took hold of Janie's hand and Sam's and held them together in her lap.

"Watch your aunt," she whispered loud enough so that each could hear. "She's worked very hard and you really shouldn't ruin this night for her by misbehaving."

When Sam started to protest, Laura tightened her hand around his. He peered around her at his father, screwed his mouth into a pout, but didn't protest. Laura smiled and relaxed her hold.

"Now," she said, looking at each of them in turn, "isn't this nice?"

The adult choir needed work, but what they lacked in talent, they made up for in enthusiasm. Their new, bright-crimson robes were neatly pressed and their spirit rose with every song until finally the performance came to a close and the crowd applauded.

Brand walked her to the refreshment table. The children ran off to be with friends. As the rest of the crowd milled around, Laura looked for Amelia and Hank.

"Can I get you something?" Brand asked.

"I was looking for Amelia," she said.

"She and Hank said to tell you they've already headed home." Brand gave her a knowing smile. "They're still newlyweds, remember?"

She wondered about the wink he gave her until she realized that Brand thought of her as a widowed comrade who shared equally precious memories of her own honeymoon. Laura tried to smile, to give an appearance of understanding. Being with Brand, who was not just a gentleman but a minister, underscored not only all she had missed in her life, but all she would never have.

She tried to focus on the room, at the men, women, and children around them. People were talking, smiling, and congratulating Charity and the choir members.

I don't belong here. It wasn't a new revelation, but it hurt more than ever to realize a woman like her didn't belong anywhere—except in a brothel.

"Would you excuse me for a moment?" he asked.

The undisguised admiration and warmth in Brand's gaze threatened to be her undoing. "Of course."

She watched him walk toward a gathering of ranchers. He greeted them warmly, shook hands all around.

Alone in the middle of a crowd, she fidgeted with her gloves, adjusted the silk cords on her reticule, and promised herself never again.

"Mrs. Foster?"

She turned to find Charity there with Mary Margaret Cutter. Along with her husband, Timothy, Mary Margaret owned the First Bank of Glory, the town's only bank.

"You did a wonderful job with the choirs," Laura complemented Charity to keep the conversation on anything but herself. "Especially the children. You must have infinite patience."

Charity shrugged. "Not really. I just can't bring myself to correct them. I usually end up trying to hide a smile when they misbehave. I'll admit I had to use a touch of Amelia's nerve medicine before the performance—" She suddenly flushed with color.

Laura found herself wishing she'd remembered Amelia concocted nerve medicine and had bought some before tonight.

Mary Margaret leaned closer. "It's nice to see you here, Laura. I'm happy the reverend convinced you to join us."

"Yes, well ..." She'd never made small talk in this sort of a situation. "Thank you, Mary Margaret. It's nice to see you out from behind the teller window."

Mary Margaret was seventy if she was a day, yet she worked five days a week in the bank alongside her husband, Timothy, who was notoriously hard of hearing.

"We've been so busy lately. Not that I'm complaining, but with so many folks purchasing homesteads and ranches, most of them wanting some kind of loan, it's been hectic for us. It'll be interesting to see how many of these folks actually take. Not everyone adjusts to Texas. It takes a certain breed to fit in. The weather and the isolation out here will beat the stuffing right out of you, if you let it." She shook her head at Laura. "Never thought you'd last, but you did and we're mighty glad."

Laura was overcome by a sudden stinging in her eyes and wondered what on earth was wrong with her until she realized it was the threat of tears. Her carefully constructed facade was coming apart at the seams.

"I was thinking of starting a ladies sewing circle. Do you sew, Laura?" Charity asked.

"I've never even tried." She immediately realized they might wonder why not. "I ... have to admit, I'm spoiled when it comes to sewing. I ... my mother never taught me." She turned to Mary Margaret. "How about you?"

Mary Margaret shook her head. "Sew? When on earth would I have time to sew?"

"What about a Bible study group?" Charity was unwilling to let go of the notion of getting them all together. Laura feigned interest in the cuff of her gown.

"I don't have time for a lot of reading," Mary Margaret said. "By the time night falls, I'm tuckered out."

"Would you enjoy a Bible study group, Laura?" Charity asked.

"I'm afraid running the boardinghouse takes all of my time. I don't know how I could possibly attend a meeting," she admitted.

"I do love to read, though." Laura wondered what Charity would say if she told her she'd never even read the Bible.

"Maybe if you invited Brand, Charity, we could get Laura to join." Mary Margaret chuckled.

Laura nodded as her face grew warm. She glanced around the room. Coming tonight had made a statement to everyone. Their preacher was interested in her.

What now, she wondered.

She spotted Brand still in deep conversation with the men. As if he felt her gaze on him from across the room, he looked up, met her eyes, and smiled. It was such a simple, innocent gesture, and yet the unexpected thrill—that was becoming less unexpected by the moment—ran through her. It frightened as well as excited her.

"What *do* you read, Laura?" Libby wanted to know.

"Novels." Laura tried to focus on the conversation. Their little group had been joined by three other women who had moved closer, closing ranks around them. They were all listening intently.

"Nathaniel Hawthorne," she added. "And Dickens. I've read most of his work."

"How about Jane Austin?" Mary Margaret wanted to know. "I used to love reading her novels when I was young."

Laura could relate to Dickens' starving orphans, the underbelly of London's streets, and Fagan with his band of ragtag child thieves. She knew the polite constraint of the social world in which Jane Austin's characters moved merely masked what really went on beneath the varnish of polite society.

Standing there chatting with stout, hardworking Mary Margaret and Brand's sister, Laura was reminded that she didn't really know these women and had absolutely no real connection with them—and never would. She would never be able to fool them for long. She studied the faces of those who had joined them and wondered how they couldn't see right through her.

She took a deep breath and fanned herself with her hand. "This has been an enjoyable chat, but now if you'll excuse me, ladies, I'm going to get some air." She stepped away before anyone could protest and headed for the front door.

Hovering on the threshold, she stared out into the darkness that blanketed the town. Main Street spread out beyond the churchyard. Far in the distance, a light shone through the windows of the Silver Slipper Saloon. Closer, her own porch light still burned. It called to her like a beacon, drawing her to the safety of her gilded cage.

Bryce Botsworth and his family would be leaving after breakfast. If she snuck in the back door and up the servants' stairs to her room, she could lock herself away without ever having to see him again. She would have Anna deliver a note of apology; a headache would keep her from bidding them a personal good-bye.

A glance over her shoulder assured her that Brand had moved on to chat with yet another small group. She stepped outside and drew her shawl close. The breeze blew a cottonwood leaf down the street, the first of many that would fall in the coming days and weeks. Soon Glory's few trees would be as bare as the landscape surrounding the town — the open plains and prairies that rolled on forever would now and again be covered with frost and sometimes even a light dusting of snow.

Rain would come, then the cold, and thanks to the fertile range in Texas and growth in the region, guests would continue to walk through the door of the boardinghouse, insuring her future. The guests would never know what she had been before she became Laura Foster.

She had barely made it to the end of the path that led to the edge of the street when she heard footsteps quickly approaching from behind. She slipped the strings of her reticule open and reached inside. Her hand closed around the pearl handle of her derringer.

"I'm sorry, Laura." It was Brand. "Surely you aren't upset enough to walk home alone, are you?"

As she turned, she let go of the gun and slipped her hand out of her bag. She smiled.

"I'm not upset in the least——"

"I tried to get back to you and when that was impossible, I tried to catch your eye to call you over. I'm sorry I abandoned you like that."

A bitter laugh nearly escaped her. She knew what *true* abandonment was.

"Charity and Mary Margaret kept me company."

"You weren't even going to say good-bye?"

He had her there. He deserved better than to have her run out on him.

"You were busy chatting with everyone. I planned to send you a thank-you note."

He smiled. "I still have your note of regret in my pocket. Perhaps I'll start a collection. The congregation is going to wonder why I smell like lavender."

"You noticed." She was thankful for the darkness that hid her embarrassment. She kept a lavender sachet in her stationery box.

"I notice everything about you, Laura. I even noticed how uncomfortable you were inside."

She thought she'd been able to hide it.

"Why?" he asked.

"Why what?"

"You meet strangers every day. People from miles around rave about your hospitality."

She shrugged. "I'm simply more comfortable at home."

"Then let me take you there." He offered his arm.

"You should be inside the hall——"

"Right now, this is where I should be. Where I want to be."

No one had ever said anything as tender to her before. She didn't even know how to react. Silent, she slipped her hand into his elbow and let him lead her to his buggy.

The chatter and noise around Brand had receded the moment he realized Laura was no longer in the hall. Charity had explained that Laura needed some air. He headed for the door, expecting to find her just outside, but she was gone. His heart sank until he caught a glimpse of her headed down the shadowed walk toward Main Street.

Now, seated beside her in the buggy, the world felt right again. There was something about her that intrigued him and drew him to her. Something that made her stand out in a way no other woman had since he'd lost Jane. Granted, Laura was lovely, but there was something more, something haunting about her. He'd noticed the first Sunday she walked into the church. Since then he'd found there was so much more to her than her lovely countenance.

There was a wistful sadness about her despite her strength. Perhaps it was the way she gave the appearance of an observer of life, not someone who was part of it. Each time he'd seen her around town or on Sunday sitting in the back of the church, she had been alone. The more he thought about it, the more he realized she had few close friends aside from Hank and Amelia, the Cutters, the Hernandez family, and a few others.

People moved in and out of her life daily, but she was virtually alone.

He knew nothing about her past, where she came from, or who her people were. She'd never even mentioned her late husband by name. Her past was a mystery to him. One he hoped she would share when she came to trust him enough. Her isolation made him want to introduce her to another way of life — a life full of love, laughter, and family.

So far, he hadn't found a single flaw in her, except perhaps her stubborn determination. To her great credit, she was able to gently but firmly discipline his children, something neither he nor Charity had ever been able to accomplish. Laura managed to handle them without talking down to them, or bullying.

Her beauty hid a will of iron.

He was loath to say good-night, so he walked his horse down the street at a snail's pace. Even so, they reached the boardinghouse in what seemed like seconds. He set the brake and started around the buggy to help her, but this time she scrambled down before he reached the other side. A chuckle escaped him.

"Have I somehow amused you?" she asked as they made their way up the walk to her veranda.

"I was obviously too forward when I helped you down at the church." He remembered the feel of her waist beneath his hands. The shock on her face.

"It was . . . unexpected." Her words were so soft he barely heard them. He followed her up the steps to her door.

"Laura . . ." Unable to help himself, he stepped closer, which forced her to tip her head back to look up at him.

In the church hall, he'd imagined kissing her. He thought she'd protest this nearness now, but she didn't step back, didn't make an excuse to hurry inside. The lamp beside the door cast her face in flickering light and shadow, caught and played on the curls peeking from the edge of her bonnet. Her eyes were huge.

One kiss, he thought. *Just one.*

Brand found himself leaning closer. When they were mere inches apart, he heard her swift intake of breath just before their lips met.

That slight, whispered gasp before he covered her lips brought him to his senses. He would not risk any tomorrows by pressing her tonight. He ended the kiss so quickly that it was over almost before it started.

He stepped back, took a deep breath, and was tempted to tuck a stray lock of her hair inside her bonnet. Instead, he merely whispered, "Thank you, Laura, for accompanying me tonight. You have sweet dreams."

Without waiting for a reply, he turned and jogged down the steps. Fearing that one glance might make it impossible to leave, he didn't look back.

SIX

With her hands fisted at her sides, Laura watched Brand's carriage pull away. Her erratic heartbeat eventually slowed to keep time with the crickets under the front step. She lingered in the dry heat of summer's last sigh, picturing Brand's clear honest eyes, the intense tenderness in them. It was a look that would have brought her to tears, if she had been capable of tears. He was a man who would offer his heart. A man who would give and not take.

She had never kissed the men who bought her time unless they insisted. Most of them were too focused on other things. Surprisingly, kissing was almost too intimate for most of them. It was something they held sacred, meant for wives and lovers, not whores.

Brand's kiss had been short and sweet, but there was nothing tentative or awkward about it. It had been completely heartfelt and spontaneous. And seductive in its sheer innocence. Its brevity left her wanting more.

He is a preacher. A man of God.

She'd been powerless to stop him from making the biggest mistake of his life.

As she pressed her gloved fingertips to her lips, she knew he would be back. There was only one thing she could do when she saw him again.

She had to turn him away.

A bittersweet sadness swept through her as she smoothed down the front of her skirt. She reminded herself of all she had to lose, of all Brand stood to lose. She was being foolish, playing with fire. Falling in love was simply out of the question.

She had one hand on the front doorknob when she remembered Bryce Botsworth. She couldn't run the risk of running into him in the drawing room. She couldn't let him see the recognition on her face, couldn't give him any indication that they had met before.

She quickly tiptoed around the veranda to the back of the house.

The back door whined as she let herself in. Peaches slipped through before it closed and purred as she circled her ankles. When the cat started to meow, Laura scooped her up and held her close. She buried her nose in the soft fur on the cat's head.

"Shh. You want a bite to eat?" She set the cat down, slipped off the strings of her reticule, and laid it on the dry sink. Across the darkened room was the pie safe, where she found a piece of cheese. She was about to break some off for the cat when someone struck a match behind her.

Laura turned, expecting to see Anna.

Bryce Botsworth was lighting the candle in the middle of the kitchen worktable. Laura dropped the cheese.

She drew on every ounce of courage she had. "You frightened me, Representative Botsworth."

He moved closer. "No need to stand on formalities, is there, Lovie? I recognized you the minute you opened the door today. Do you think a man ever forgets a woman like you or the things you can do? Laura Foster, eh? Nice name. Certainly not as catchy as Lovie Lamonte."

"I have no idea what you're talking about."

"Oh, I believe you do, *Lovie*." He crossed the room and stopped not two feet away.

She tried to edge aside. He wasn't budging. He had her backed up against the dry sink with nowhere to go. Peaches was purring, circling, rubbing against her ankles. Laura's heart pounded.

"Cat got your tongue?" He laughed. "What was it? Fourteen, fifteen years ago? That was the last time I was in New Orleans before the war. I was younger then." He looked her over from head to toe. "You've filled out some."

The look in his eye told her he wasn't about to back down.

But he had as much, or more, to lose than she. Their brief acquaintance was a double-edged sword. She decided to have her turn.

"I seem to recall you had hair back then ... and a waist." She paused a second before she added, "Your youngest daughter must be what? Eighteen? She's older now than I was at the time. I'm sure your wife would be surprised to hear of our previous acquaintance."

"Are you threatening me?" His voice took on a hard edge. "Do you know who I am?"

She nodded. "You think you know me, but you have no idea who *I* really am or what I'm capable of, Mr. Botsworth."

He spread his meaty hands.

"Look, Lovie, why don't we let bygones be bygones?"

"Don't call me that."

"Laura, then. If you are running this establishment—"

"I own it."

"Fine. Whatever. I'm sure you have some policy in regard to seeing that all your guests have a pleasurable stay." He took another step and suddenly his hands were on her. His breath was hot and heavy in her ear. "Everyone else has gone to bed. We can do this here and now. A stolen moment. No one has to know. I'll make it worth your while. I'm a very wealthy man."

She braced herself, shoved him back at arm's length.

"Let go of me."

"Women like you don't change, Lovie."

"Pigs like you are the reason women like me can't wait to get out of the business." She gave him a harder shove and pushed him away.

His palm had connected with her cheek before she even realized he'd raised his hand. The sound of the slap echoed in the empty kitchen.

Laura refused to react. Ignoring the pain, she fumbled for her reticule, slid her hand inside, and closed it around the handle of her derringer. She pulled it out and pointed it directly at Botsworth's heart.

"Go back to your room and I'll forget this ever happened," she said.

Candlelight glinted off the derringer. He looked at it and laughed.

"What would your friends and neighbors say if you shot someone? I take it they have no idea who you really are."

"At this range I can't miss your heart. With you dead, they'd never find out. The sheriff is a personal friend—"

"Oh, I just bet he is."

She ignored the insult. "I'll say you surprised me. That I thought you were an intruder. This *is* my town; no one will doubt my word." Hank's face, Amelia's, the Cutters', Brand's all flashed through her mind. She could only hope it was true, that they would stand behind her.

"I don't think you're capable of killing, Lovie."

She wished he'd back up, walk out and leave her alone. If he pushed her past the breaking point, she'd show him exactly what she was capable of.

"I'm a very good shot. As I said, I can easily kill you at this distance. Why don't you just turn around and walk out of here, Mr. Botsworth? Go upstairs and crawl into bed with your charming wife. Live to see those lovely girls of yours married. I'm sure that idea is far more to your liking than your being hauled out of here feet first." She shrugged. "But that's up to you."

A moment of silence ticked by. Finally, his shoulders sagged.

Laura kept the gun trained on him. She wouldn't put it past him to lunge at her, to try and knock it out of her hand. She'd seen the same hungry look in men's eyes before. Lust was ugly.

Tension filled the air between them, but she was calm now. Her hand was cool and dry on the handle of the derringer. She meant what she'd said. She'd kill him if she had to.

Her resolve communicated itself to him. He dropped his hands, backed up a few feet before he stopped beside the table.

"We'll be departing tomorrow as planned," he told her.

"Good."

"I trust my wife won't be hearing about our little meeting?"

"This one, or the one in New Orleans?"

"Either."

"I think not. She might divorce you, Mr. Botsworth, and I'd run the risk of having you show up again, unencumbered by a wife and family. I wouldn't want that."

"Nor would I. Good-night, *Mrs. Foster.*" He gave her a curt bow and walked out of the room.

Her calm gave way to trembling. She was shaking so badly by the time he cleared the hall she feared she would collapse before she made it to the table. Pulling out a hard-bottomed chair, she sat, facing the door in case he returned. The derringer hung forgotten in her hand.

The candle guttered and went out. She sat alone in the dark.

As long as Botsworth was married and playing the faithful husband and public servant, her identity was safe.

When Peaches suddenly leapt into her lap, Laura gasped, then stifled the urge to laugh hysterically. As the cat began to purr and knead her skirt, she set the derringer on the table and scratched behind it's ears.

"You're lucky I didn't plug you." She held the cat on her lap until her trembling subsided. "Not many women have a night like this one. First a preacher kissed me and then I almost shot a man."

SEVEN

Even with her derringer within reach, Laura slept fitfully. By morning she'd decided that she wasn't going to let Bryce Botsworth keep her in hiding. She would send all her guests off with a proper farewell.

She dressed carefully, choosing a yellow-and-blue striped gown with a hint of a bustle. Draped ruffles adorned the skirt all the way around. Head high, she swept into the dining room and helped herself to the buffet. As she greeted all the Botsworths cordially, Bryce bid her good morning. When she refused to quail under his knowing stare, his face turned a ruddy crimson.

"Are you all right, dear?" His wife leaned over and felt his forehead.

"Of course. It's a bit warm in here, is all." He smoothed down his shirtfront and tried to smile reassuringly. When one of the other guests asked him how long he'd been in the state house of representatives, he quickly entered into conversation. He never engaged Laura directly again until the family was assembled on the veranda, ready to leave, at which time he somberly thanked her for her hospitality.

Laura bid Amber Botsworth and her daughters farewell and watched Richard load them into the buggy and drive them to the stage stop at the mercantile.

Most afternoons were hers to do with as she wished. Today she went up to her suite to pen a letter to Tom Abbott, the former Pinkerton agent.

A wooden bandbox decorated with floral decoupage held her stationery. When she lifted the lid, the heady scent of French lavender wafted out. She held the small sachet beneath her nose, closed her eyes, and inhaled.

"I still have your note of regret in my pocket. Perhaps I'll start a collection. The congregation is going to wonder why I smell like lavender."

"I notice everything about you, Laura."

She dreaded seeing Brand again, because somehow she had to muster the strength to turn his attentions when she did.

She sighed and drew a sheet of paper out of the box. Her stationery was a tasteful cream color with her initials engraved across the top.

L F M

She'd chosen the name *Laura* because she thought it pretty. For her middle initial, she used *M* for *Megan*. *Foster* she borrowed from the musical composer Stephen Collins Foster, who'd written "Beautiful Dreamer"—one of her favorite songs because of the melancholy melody.

She'd purchased a small volume on writing model letters and from it learned that the tone and skill a woman showed in her correspondence should mirror her position in the community. Proper communication showed one's culture, education, and genteel background. She kept her letters to Tom Abbott distantly polite and he always replied in like manner. Mr. Abbott knew her only as Laura Foster.

Taking pen in hand, she dipped the nib in the small bottle of india ink and began.

Glory, Texas, September 15, 1874

Dear Mr. Abbott,

Enclosed is your retainer for another three months of effort in the service of locating my sister. I have the utmost confidence in your ability and understand that you are facing near-insurmountable odds. Given the amount of time that she and I have been separated, the ensuing war years, and the widespread heartache that coincided with them, as well as the unthinkable notion that my sister may have died at a young age, I can only hope for the best.

Laura paused and stared unseeing out the window as she let her thoughts drift back to her own life after the war. The post-war years had given her the means to an end. She was free, though haunted by the memory of her sisters. She worried most about Megan, unable to forget their wrenching parting.

If, by some miraculous chance, her sister's life had become a fairy-tale, would Megan want to be found? Or was she living mired in degradation, beyond hope of rescue? And what of the others? Could she dare hope they'd been adopted by loving, caring families? She couldn't rest until she knew.

She picked up her pen again.

When and if you do find my sister, please take great care in approaching her. If she is living a secure life in a respectable household, I fear she may not wish to hear from me, as contact may raise too many unfortunate answers to any questions those around her may ask. I know that you will be discreet and I trust in your good judgment, just as I hold great hope that you will eventually succeed.

And so I close with my best wishes,

Yours truly,
Laura M. Foster

She enclosed a bank draft made payable to Tom Abbott and penned the man's New Orleans address. Then she lit a match and touched the flame to a stick of red sealing wax.

As she pressed her initialed stamp into the hot wax, she could almost hear her old partner Collier Holloway chiding her for pouring money down a rat hole. But Collier cared for no one in the world save himself. He'd told her so on more occasions than she could count.

She capped the bottle of ink, slipped her pen into a long carved box, and stood to shake the wrinkles out of her skirt. Downstairs, Rodrigo was putting together his own version of a peach cobbler. She set the letter in the empty market basket. He smiled and nodded in understanding. He would deliver it to Harrison Barker when he went to the mercantile tomorrow.

She heard the sound of someone splitting wood in back. "I'm going out for some fresh air. Call me when the new guests arrive."

She walked out the back door. From the shade of the veranda, she paused to watch Richard split some narrow logs into kindling. Unlike some homesteaders and ranchers who used cow paddies and buffalo chips in their fireplaces, she could thankfully afford to have wood gathered and split.

She gazed out over her garden. She loved it, with its struggling young fruit trees, her roses, and Anna's vegetable patch. It was nothing compared to Amelia Larson's profusion of herbs and flowers, of course. But Amelia's garden supported her livelihood. Dried, her friend's plants filled the apothecary jars in her store.

Laura often thought of the beautiful hidden gardens and courtyards of New Orleans, the sound of trickling water fountains and the soft green hues that tinted the ferns and Spanish moss. Central Texas was a hard, brittle land in comparison.

As she stood musing, Richard noticed her and waved. She waved back. When she had hired the Hernandez family, the boy had been twelve. Now he was almost sixteen, on the verge of becoming a man.

Across the yard, Peaches dashed out of the carriage house and raced around the horse and buggy still hitched up in the yard. As soon as she reached Laura, she started nagging with meows, rubbing against Laura's ankles.

"You, Miss Peaches, are a pest." Laura cradled the cat in her arms, ruffling the cat's fur, when Amelia appeared on the side veranda toting the heavy medical bag she'd inherited from her father.

"Anna sent me around," Amelia told her.

"You look like you're dragging. Is everything all right?"

Amelia sighed. "Not really." She waved to Richard. "Did you know he's not only delivering the *Gazette* for Hank, but he's learning to set type and run the handpress?"

Laura set Peaches down on the veranda, linked arms with Amelia's, and steered her toward the back door. "I heard. I'm glad Hank has someone to help him out too."

As they stepped inside Laura asked, "How about a nice cup of café au lait?"

"That sounds heavenly." Amelia took a deep breath as if she could already smell the brew. "I need some spoiling right about now."

Laura led Amelia to a tiny parlor off the larger drawing room. It was barely big enough to house two chairs and a table. Where the walls weren't painted a calm sea green, they were covered with the floor-to-ceiling cases that held Laura's vast collection of books. It was her own private sanctuary on the first floor, a retreat from the world.

She prepared the steaming cream-and-coffee mixture herself and poured it into a tall chocolate pot, which she set on a tray with a small dish of crescent-shaped cookies Rodrigo called wedding cakes.

Laura found Amelia seated in one of two comfortable armchairs upholstered in rose chintz. Head back and eyes closed, she appeared to be sound asleep.

Laura set the tray down on a butler's table without making a sound, but Amelia's eyes opened and she smiled.

"Mmm. I can smell that from here." She sat up straighter while Laura took the chair beside her and poured them each a generous cup.

"I love this room," Amelia let her gaze roam the bookcases. "Hank would too."

"No gentlemen allowed. This is my secret place."

"I feel honored that you invited me to share it."

Laura had first brought Amelia here when they were going over the Larsons' wedding plans. "You're the only guest who's ever been allowed in here—outside of Peaches, of course." Laura took a sip of coffee, then centered her cup on her saucer. "So, what's causing that troubled look?"

Amelia sighed and Laura leaned forward. "This has nothing to do with Hank, does it? Is he all right?" Laura hated to think some kind of infection lingered in his system from his gunshot wounds.

Amelia shook her head. "Oh, my goodness, no. He's healthy as a horse."

Laura glanced at the medical bag at Amelia's feet.

"Someone else, then."

She was surprised when Amelia said, "I was summoned to the Silver Slipper earlier. One of the young women there has fallen desperately ill. I did all I could, but unfortunately, I'm afraid I can't save her."

The Silver Slipper was Glory's only saloon and house of ill repute. It was a run-down, two-story building with a sagging balcony across the front and peeling paint on its clapboard exterior.

Laura found herself staring into her cup. She didn't have to imagine what the place was like inside. Above the saloon there would be a number of small rooms barely wide enough to hold a narrow bed, a washstand, and, if the occupant was lucky, a window to the outside world.

"You ... treat them? The women there?"

It was hard to believe someone like Amelia having any contact with the women of the Silver Slipper.

"Of course." Amelia drained her cup and rested her head on the back of the chair. "I'm surprised you would ask."

Laura flushed. "I didn't mean to offend. I just can't believe—"

Amelia studied her carefully. "Do you think less of me for treating them?"

Laura had forgotten Amelia knew her only as a wealthy, cultured widow. Naturally, if she truly was what she appeared to be, Laura would most likely be shocked at Amelia's actions.

"On the contrary. I admire you for it," Laura said truthfully. "Most people would turn their backs on those poor women."

"My father didn't. He would say that it's not up to us to judge them. Judgment is coming sooner than later for the poor girl I saw today."

Laura remembered the letter she'd just penned and thought of Megan and the countless lost souls like herself, of the untold abuse they suffered at the hands of men.

"Disease?" Laura asked softly.

Amelia shook her head no. Her eyes filled with tears. "She has ... self-inflicted wounds. There were complications. I really can't say more ..." Her words drifted away.

She didn't have to say more. Laura understood. She knew what lengths some women went to in order to keep from bearing unwanted children. She'd suspected as much before she even asked. Seeing how it affected Amelia, she was sorry she had.

"I'm sorry, Amelia."

Amelia wiped her eyes. "Sometimes it's very hard," she said. "Let's talk of something else. I didn't get to chat with you after the choir performance the other night. Hattie Ellenberg asked me to help with refreshments and then we left a bit early."

Laura watched Amelia blush. "Perfectly understandable."

"So, did you have a nice evening?" Amelia asked.

Nice evening? It had been a mistake from beginning to end.

Amelia might be her only close friend and ally, but Laura could never confide everything—not even after hearing about Amelia's mission of mercy to the Silver Slipper. She couldn't risk losing her only friend.

"It was a pleasant outing. More coffee?"

"Please." Amelia handed over her cup. "I hope we'll be seeing you out and about more often. Especially with Brand."

"Well—" Laura let her words drift away as she refilled the cup. "Here you go."

"He's very sweet on you, you know."

"That's what I was afraid of," Laura said, thinking out loud.

"You know, Laura, you can protest all you like, but I saw the way he looked at you—"

Laura cut her off. "We're not suited."

"Fiddlesticks." Amelia took a long sip and then asked, "Why not?"

For one thing, I'm no better than the women at the Silver Slipper.

"I'm not in the market for a husband," she said. She picked up the dish. "Cookie?"

"Maybe just one. You know, I wasn't looking for love when Hank came along either. In fact, I was fairly certain I was going to live my life alone. A spinster on the shelf. Then Hank and I discovered love finds us, Laura, whether we are looking for it or not."

Love.

Laura wondered what Amelia would say if she told her friend she didn't believe in love.

There came a soft knock on the door of Laura's study. It was Anna, whose concern showed in her dark eyes.

"So sorry, señora. A man asking for Mrs. Larson." She glanced at Amelia and then away. "He says it is an emergency."

"Thank you, Anna." By the time Laura turned around, Amelia had already set down her cup and had her medical bag in hand.

Laura asked Anna to collect the coffee tray and then followed Amelia to the entry hall. Beyond the front door, a grizzled older man, stooped and bearded, waited on the veranda. He held a stained and battered hat in hand, curling the brim as he passed it round and round through gnarled fingers. His faded eyes were deep set, sunken in an emaciated face, his clothing a collection no better than a rag bag. His trousers, stained and wrinkled, were barely recognizable as part of a Confederate uniform.

She'd seen men like him before, drunks that hung around bars and saloons begging for odd jobs, for a few coins and a place to sleep. She knew how to handle bums and beggars and was about to tell him to go around back to the kitchen. But Amelia stepped out onto the veranda to speak to him.

"Amelia—" she began.

Amelia smiled over her shoulder. "It's all right, Laura." She turned to the indigent. "What is it, Rob?"

"Mazie's taken a turn for the worst. Denton's afraid she ain't gonna make it this time. She's calling for you and a preacher. We're hopin' you got something for her pain, 'cause the liquor ain't working no more."

Laura watched the exchange, wished it wasn't unfolding here. She didn't have to imagine the scene at the Silver Slipper. She'd witnessed more than one death in just such a place before.

"I'll walk back with you." Amelia told Rob.

Laura knew better than to protest; she knew Amelia could most likely take care of herself. But Amelia didn't leave immediately. First she turned to Laura.

"Will you go get Brand for me? Bring him to the Silver Slipper? Tell him a young woman desperately needs him, and she hasn't much time. If he'll come, that is."

"Oh, he'll come," Laura said. It was the least the preacher could do for a dying woman begging for help. "I'll see to it."

At a trot, Amelia followed the man, who was already off the porch and limping down the walk. Laura hurried to the kitchen and told Rodrigo and Anna that she'd be back as soon as possible and to settle any guests when they arrived. She then ran upstairs and grabbed a bonnet and gloves and dashed outside, thankful the horse and buggy were still hitched up.

She hadn't driven in a long while, but the reins felt right in her hands as she headed out of the yard and down Main Street. Brand's home was next door to the church and not far from Amelia and Hank's. She found the place easily, though she'd never been there before. She pulled up in front, set the brake, and climbed down. It wasn't until she raised her hand to knock on the front door that she realized her gloves didn't even match.

Janie opened the door. Somewhere behind her, Sam was yelling, "I wanted to get it!"

When they saw who it was, they fell silent.

"Is your father home?" Laura asked.

"Why?" Janie demanded.

"It's an emergency."

"He's in his office. He said not to bother him."

Laura took a deep breath. "This is an emergency. Please bother him."

"But . . ."

Laura pictured the dying girl at the saloon. Her patience was ebbing.

"Please go tell him right now or I'll have to come in and find him myself. When I do, he's not going to be happy."

Sam bolted down the hall yelling "Papa! Emergency!" as if the house were on fire. Janie stood her ground.

"Do you love my papa?" the girl asked.

Laura closed her eyes and took a deep breath. "I like him. He's a very nice man. But I don't love anyone."

Janie crossed her arms and didn't invite her in.

Laura stood on the porch waiting for what seemed like hours. In reality it was mere minutes before Brand came down the hall. It was the first time she'd seen him without his coat. Collarless, with his shirtsleeves rolled up, he looked like any other man. Any other handsome man.

Her heart stuttered. She ignored it. This was no time for her emotions to betray her.

"Laura? Sam mentioned an emergency—" Concern was written all over Brand's face. "Are you all right?"

"It's not me." She glanced down at the children with their upturned faces, big eyes, and bigger ears. "Can we speak alone?"

He had to tell them twice to go find their Aunt Charity. They left, but not without exaggerated whining and foot dragging. Brand stepped outside and closed the door behind him. Laura thought he might take hold of her hand, so she locked them together.

"What is it?" he asked.

"A young woman is dying. She's asking for a preacher."

"Let me get my Bible," he said without hesitation.

Laura quickly added, "Amelia is with her. She's at the Silver Slipper."

"I'll be right back." Again, no hesitation whatsoever before he stepped back inside.

Laura walked to the edge of the modest front porch and tapped her toe while she waited. Seconds later, Brand was back. He'd collected his Bible and was donning his hat as he crossed the porch. He hadn't bothered with his coat or collar.

"Let's go," he said. He headed down the steps toward the buggy.

Once they were settled and she had taken the reins up again, he leaned back, watching her carefully.

"How is it you're here?"

"Amelia was at the house when they sent for her. She'd helped the girl earlier and now it appears the young woman is dying." Laura focused on the street, guiding her rig between other wagons and riders on Main.

She snuck a sidelong glance at the man beside her. When she found him studying her, she tried to concentrate on the road again. In no time she had pulled the rig up outside the saloon.

"Thank you, Laura." He jumped out of the buggy, lingered a moment. "Don't wait. I'll walk home."

"I'll wait," she said. "Amelia might need my help."

"This place isn't—"

"I'll wait," she insisted.

"But—"

"Go, Brand."

Bible in hand, he disappeared into the saloon.

She sat on the high-sprung front seat of the covered buggy staring into the saloon. Beyond the open front door, the interior was gloomy. It was afternoon, so there were fewer patrons inside. Of an evening when the air was still or a breeze blew in just the right direction, tinny piano music drifted as far as the boardinghouse. Just now, the piano was silenced.

Now and again as she waited and watched, a lone patron would walk inside the Silver Slipper. Thankfully, they were intent on their destination and paid her little mind. Laughter rang out. No one had any idea that a young woman lay dying upstairs. Laura doubted any of the men would even care.

When Brand stepped into the saloon, the barkeep, Denton Fairchild, immediately said, "Room two," and indicated the staircase in back with a nod. The air was stale and tainted with a sour smell. Brand took the steep stairs two at a time and paused at the second door from the top of the landing.

He knocked softly, heard Amelia say, "Come in."

A young woman with matted brown hair lay on a narrow iron bed. The only colors that distinguished her from the bedsheets were those of her hair and the purple shadows beneath her sunken eyes. A pile of soiled sheets and rags lay mounded in the corner of the room.

Brand focused on the woman in the bed. She appeared to be in her early twenties.

"How is she?" he whispered to Amelia.

"Feverish. Weak. There's nothing more I can do. She's lost too much blood."

"Is she conscious?"

"Barely. She's been begging for a preacher. I think she was just hanging on, waiting for you. Her name's Mazie."

There was barely enough room for him to slide past Amelia. He knelt on the floor beside the bed and set his Bible down.

"Mazie?" He took her limp hand in his. "I'm Reverend McCormick."

She didn't respond so he closed his eyes and began to pray. After a few moments, the hand inside his moved. He looked into her face and found her eyes open, glassy and feverish.

"I don't want to die a sinner."

"You won't, Mazie. Not if you believe."

"I do. I do and I'm sorry for everything I done. Will you pray for me?"

"I will. Close your eyes and pray with me. Ask for forgiveness. Put yourself in God's hands and He'll see you safely home."

"Preacher?"

"Yes, Mazie."

"My real name's Jenny."

Brand knelt and prayed for what seemed like hours while Jenny, barely breathing, clung steadily to his hand. Now and again she would moan in pain and Amelia would place drops of laudanum in water, lift the young woman's head, and help her swallow.

Finally, a slow, shuddering breath escaped the girl and her hand relaxed in Brand's. He raised his head and looked down upon her face. Her eyes were open, staring at the ceiling, but a blissful calm had come over her features. The corners of her mouth hinted at a smile.

Amelia reached over and closed her eyes. "What a tragic waste of life," she said. Then she whispered sadly, "Not one, but two."

Laura waited until the sun had slipped behind the western corner of the building. She knew that if she left, Brand and Amelia wouldn't blame her—they could walk home together—but she couldn't bring herself to leave.

It was late afternoon. The street traffic was gone. The saloon wasn't as crowded as it would be later. Laura stepped out of the buggy and walked up to the door. With every step she asked herself what she was doing, why she was walking into a situation that just might be her undoing, but she thought of both Brand and Amelia and their willingness to help.

Surely she could slip inside, tell the barkeep to let them know she had gone home, and then leave without incident.

Inside, the Silver Slipper was just as she imagined it would be, as down at the heels inside as it was out. There was nothing about the place to distinguish it from any other watering hole. The barkeep was wiping down the bar when he looked up and saw her framed in the doorway.

"Can I do something for you, lady, or are you just here to gawk?"

A few years ago she could have silenced him with one word, but she was Mrs. Laura Foster now. She drew herself up, took a step inside the door. One step. That was all. Only the veteran soldier, Rob, was inside, propped up at a table, staring into a glass of ale.

"Please tell Mrs. Larson and the reverend that I've gone home."

"I'll be sure to do that. Who should I say left 'em here?"

"They'll know."

He laughed and adjusted the garters on his shirtsleeves. "Anytime you're down on your luck, I could use a gal like you around. You wouldn't even have to do anything but stand in the doorway and lure 'em in."

Laura opened her mouth, about to tell him that he couldn't even afford her as window dressing. But remembering who she was, she closed her mouth and turned to leave. Unfortunately, four saddle tramps chose that moment to swagger in. Her heart stopped when she realized the man in the lead was the one who had slapped his daughter at the mercantile.

He took one look at Laura, snagged her in the crook of his arm, and without missing a step, pulled her across the room with him. When he reached the bar he ordered two whiskeys.

"'Pears to me things have changed, Miss High and Mighty. Where's your watchdog now?"

"Get your hands off of me." Laura was so furious she trembled with rage as she struggled to wrest herself from the man's grasp. His grip tightened. She instinctively reached for her reticule but realized that in her haste she'd left it at home. She had no derringer to protect herself with.

The man's companions bellied up to the bar alongside them.

"You got all the luck, Simon. That 'un's a looker."

Desperate to get away, Laura turned to the barkeep.

"Tell him to unhand me."

"Hey, lady, you walked in here on your own." He shrugged. "He's not breaking any laws."

Yet, she thought.

She caught a glimpse of herself in the mirror behind the bar. Her hat had been knocked askew, her hair was loose and cascading wantonly over one side of her face. The man beside her was leaning into her, trying to nuzzle her. She could feel his hot breath on her neck, his stubble against her cheek. She smelled liquor on his rancid breath and tried to shove herself back to gain some space between them.

She couldn't turn away from the image in front of her. It was only a reflection, but it was as if her new identity had been stripped away, as if her past was on display for all to see.

A reminder that one moment in time, one misstep, could change everything.

She stopped struggling and turned in the man's arms until she was facing him.

"Now that's more like it," he chuckled.

Laura smiled back at him as she brought up her knee and rammed it home. As he doubled over in pain, she raised her foot and stomped the heel of her shoe onto the toe of his boot. He gasped and reared back.

She turned toward the door but wasn't fast enough. The last thing she saw was his raised fist.

Brand was halfway down the stairs when he heard the commotion. He caught sight of Laura before she suddenly fell to the floor. The barkeep dashed out from behind the bar as Brand rushed toward the knot of men staring down at Laura. His heart stopped when he saw her lying on the filthy floor.

He tossed his hat and Bible onto the bar and shoved the men aside.

"What happened? Did she faint?" He wanted her out of the muck and mire. Wanted her safe. He knelt beside her.

The barkeep shook his head. "Sorry, Preacher. Everything happened too fast for me to do anything."

Someone made the mistake of volunteering, "Simon hit her."

Brand stood and scanned the men gathered around Laura. One was bent double, hands on his knees, gasping. He grimaced in pain even as he shot threatening glances at the circle of men crowding him. The minute his head came up, Brand recognized him.

"Abusing women and children appears to be a habit with you," Brand said.

The man tried to straighten. "Yeah. So?"

Without thought, Brand hit him on the jaw. Simon went down hard and was out.

Ignoring the man, Brand turned his attention to Laura again. Her hat had come off; her hair was a golden nimbus around her head. He hunkered down on one knee and scooped her up into his arms.

Amelia was at his side when he stood up.

"What happened? Let me see her."

"Not before I get her out of here."

Brand's footsteps were the only sounds in the room as he strode out with Laura draped over his arms. With Amelia hurrying to keep up, he headed for the buggy. He shifted Laura's weight and climbed aboard.

"Can you drive?" he asked as Amelia scrambled up and grabbed the reins.

"I drive my father's old rig all over the countryside when I call on patients."

He knew as much. He wasn't thinking straight. A cloud of fury had overtaken his senses. Not since the war had he felt such anger, such turmoil. Seeing Laura felled had been his undoing.

He looked down at the woman in his arms, brushed her hair back off her face. Her eyes were closed, her lips slightly parted. A welt was quickly rising on her cheek just below her eye. Upstairs he had just witnessed the damage a man could do to a woman. To see Laura this way only stoked his rage.

Fighting his anger, Brand tightened his arms around her, cradling her like a babe.

"Is she still unconscious?" Amelia slapped the reins and the horse picked up the pace. They were nearly back at the boarding-house but she didn't slow down until they reached the drive that circled around back. She stopped in front of the carriage house.

Amelia jumped down and turned to grab her medical bag.

Brand moved gingerly, afraid to jostle Laura. He was nearly across the yard when Anna came running out of the house.

"What happened to the señora?" She ran along beside him.

He kept walking. If Laura wanted her help to know what happened, she could tell them, but knowing what a private person she was, he kept silent.

By the time he crossed the veranda and reached the back door, Laura was beginning to stir. She turned her face into his shirtfront and mumbled something he couldn't make out.

Inside the kitchen, Amelia pulled a chair away from the table. Rodrigo was waiting with a wet towel.

"She's coming around," Brand told them. "Which way to her room?"

"Sit down, Brand," Amelia indicated the chair. "She wouldn't want to run into any of her guests. Let me tend to her here."

He sat but didn't relinquish his hold. Laura moaned and her eyelashes fluttered. Slowly she opened them and looked up at Brand in confusion. A second later, she began to struggle in earnest, trying to break his hold.

"Laura, it's me. It's Brand. You're all right." He expected her to melt into hysterics.

Instead she fought to climb off his lap.

"Let me go," she cried, pushing against him. "Let me up."

He put her on her feet but held on. She was noticeably unsteady as she touched her left hand to her cheek.

"Sit before you fall down." He guided her into the chair he'd vacated.

"Brand, move." Amelia nudged him aside.

When he backed away, he found his own legs less than steady. Leaning against the dry sink, he turned to Rodrigo. The cook was as shaken as the rest of them. He handed the wet towel to Amelia.

"May I have some water?" Brand asked.

Rodrigo took down a glass and poured water from a nearby pitcher. Brand drank it down without tasting it. His mouth was still dry, but he slowly recovered his senses as Amelia gingerly pressed the wet towel against Laura's cheek.

"Is she all right?" he asked the healer.

Amelia touched Laura's forehead and then her wrist. "She doesn't feel clammy. I don't think she has a concussion."

"I'm not deaf, you know," Laura said softly.

Amelia nodded. "It's a good thing you're hardheaded. I've got some smartweed steeped in vinegar that will help take down the swelling in your cheek. I'll bring it over after I see you settled. You're going to have quite a bruise."

Brand noticed Laura wouldn't meet his eyes.

"I'll tell Hank that man needs to be run out of town," Amelia said.

"No." Laura shook her head and winced. "Please. Just ... just leave it alone."

"But he struck you."

"I shouldn't have been there," she said softly. "I knew better."

Brand could imagine her terror, not to mention her outrage. To think of how she was manhandled only stoked his anger. He took a deep breath, asked God to ease his mind, to forgive him his transgression. He'd acted out of anger and fear.

"I should have made certain you left before I went in there," Brand said. "If it weren't for me, you would never have been there in the first place. For that to have happened to a woman like you—that place is so far beneath you. It's unthinkable."

A *woman like you.*

Brand's image wavered before Laura's eyes. She turned to Amelia, who was kneeling on the floor beside her, and tried to find her voice.

"I need to lie down. I have to pull myself together before dinner."

"Can you walk?"

"I'll carry her." Brand stepped forward.

"No!" Laura hadn't meant to sound so sharp, but she'd been shaken enough by simply waking up in his arms. "Please, Brand. Just go."

His expression immediately darkened with embarrassment. He stepped away.

"I'll help her get settled." Amelia said. "You should get home."

"If you're sure."

Both women nodded and then Amelia suggested, "Stop by Hank's office and let him know what happened—"

"No, please," Laura protested.

Brand gave her a look that spoke volumes. He wasn't about

to let the incident go unreported. He bid them good-bye, but not before promising to stop by tomorrow to see how Laura was feeling.

Amelia escorted Laura upstairs and insisted she recline on the bed and keep the compress on her cheek. Once she was settled, Amelia sat on the edge of the bed beside her.

"What happened in the saloon?" Keeping her shoes off the bed, Amelia crossed her ankles as they dangled above the floor.

Laura sighed. "It was a nightmare. I went to the door to tell the bartender to let you know I was leaving. All of a sudden, four men walked in — I think it was four — and one of them dragged me along with him. He ordered a whiskey. I tried to get away. He wouldn't let go so I rammed my knee — "

"Oh! You didn't!"

Laura nodded. "I did. It worked, but he was so furious he hit me. The next thing I know, I wake up in Brand's arms."

"Not such a bad place to be."

Laura refused to comment. She couldn't stop thinking about what Brand had said downstairs.

That place is so far beneath you. It's unthinkable.

That place, and others like it, was just where she belonged.

"You should have seen it," Amelia was saying. "Brand was on his way down the stairs and when he saw you go down — Why he was across the room like an avenging angel. Who knew the reverend could pack such a wallop?"

"What are you saying?"

"Brand hauled off and hit the man who mauled you. Knocked him out with one blow. Then he turned his back on the rest of them, swept you up in his arms, and carried you out of there."

"Oh, no." Laura moaned.

"Oh, yes." Amelia nodded. "It was something to see. I'll never forget it."

"But ... he's a preacher. And I — " Laura stopped abruptly.

"He's human, Laura. He may lose a bit of sleep and spend time praying over it, but no one, not even God, could blame him for defending your honor."

"But it happened because of me and my stupidity."

"Brand won't blame you."

God might forgive Brand, but she'd never forgive herself. If not for her, Brand would never have lost control.

"I shouldn't have been there," she said.

"What's done is done," Amelia said. "I'd like you to relax, at least until the dinner hour. Have you many guests?"

"Only two."

"Good. Perhaps you should excuse yourself tonight."

"How bad is the bruise?"

"Very colorful." Amelia stood up. "I'll have Hank deliver that tonic I mentioned while I'm making supper. Use it at least twice a day."

"I will."

Amelia headed for the door. "Send someone after me if you have a dizzy spell. Promise?"

"I will." Laura sighed again. "I'm sorry to have kept you so long. Thank you for everything."

Amelia paused with her hand on the door handle. "I'm your friend, Laura. That's what friends are for."

The minute Amelia was out the door, Laura got up and walked to the mirror on her dressing table. Her hair was a mess. There was a lump on her cheek the size of a ripe plum and of the same color. Amelia was right. She would excuse herself from playing hostess at dinner. No amount of powder would cover the bruise.

Any more than any amount of money or the guise of refinement could erase her past.

EIGHT

Early-evening shadows filled the corners of the empty church as Brand stepped inside. Only the sound of his own footsteps and his hushed breathing broke the silence as he sat down in the front pew. A peaceful calm enfolded him. Sitting in a room so often filled with prayer and communion of like minds was comforting in and of itself, as if blessings and petitions still whispered on the air.

He was stunned by what he'd done earlier. He hadn't planned to hit Laura's attacker. He hadn't plotted against the man with malice. He'd reacted instinctively, striking without thought to defend her honor. In the dark stillness, he asked God to forgive his loss of temper, his irrationality, his anger.

In his heart he knew God would forgive him. Forgiving himself would take a bit longer. For a split second in the Silver Slipper he'd turned into the man he'd left behind, the Brand McCormick of his youth — a headstrong, impulsive rebel fighting against the strict rules of an overbearing father. He'd been a carouser, a ladies' man with a devil-may-care attitude.

But one day on the battlefield, when men were falling around him and he was certain he would be next, he'd heard a voice in his head say over and over, *From this day on you will serve God and mankind. You have been given another chance. Take it. Use it for good.*

He was nearly blinded by regret for having wasted so much of his young life.

"Papa?"

He turned, found Sam standing beside the pew.

"Hello, son."

"What are you doing?"

"Thinking. Praying."

"What for?"

"I was asking God to forgive me."

"Did you do something bad?"

"I lost my temper." Until this moment, he hadn't thought about the story spreading. In Glory, if one person heard something, most likely everyone else would know about it within a few hours. Hopefully Sam wouldn't hear of his indiscretion.

"Maybe you should put your nose against the wall and think about it," Sam suggested.

Out of the mouths of babes. Brand tried not to laugh. "Sitting here alone in the dark is sort of the same thing."

"You think He'll do it?"

"Who'll do what?"

"You think God will forgive you?"

"I know He will."

"You promise not to do it again?"

"I promised to try not to."

"You're a man of your word, aren't you?"

"I hope so." Brand could see Laura's trust in Sam had made a lasting impression on his son.

"Then don't worry, Papa." Sam gave Brand a pat on the shoulder. "Everything will be fine."

Brand took the boy's hand and together they walked across the church grounds to the small frame house where Charity had the table set for dinner. Brand hoped, if his sister ever married, that her husband would have a strong constitution.

After dinner, he tucked the children in for the night, then

washed up, donned a fresh shirt, his collar, and a black jacket. He told Charity he had a call to make and left the house. He chose to walk to the Silver Slipper.

This time, when he strolled through the swinging doors looking like a man of the cloth, the room fell silent. The bartender glanced over and planted both hands on the bar, waiting for Brand to approach.

"You got some right hook for a preacher," he said.

"I came for my Bible and my hat."

The barkeep nodded and walked to the other end of the bar. When he came back he was carrying not only Brand's Bible, but two hats. One was the frilly navy-blue bonnet that Laura had been wearing.

"Sorry about your lady friend," the bartender said. "Hope she's all right."

Heat rose up in Brand.

"She's not my 'lady friend.'"

The image of Sam standing beside the church pew flashed into his mind and he remembered his promise. He was a man of his word. He wouldn't let his temper get the best of him again.

"Apology accepted," he said. He cleared his throat. The novelty of his appearance had worn off. Most of the men in the room had gone back to drinking. A poker game was underway in the back corner by the stairs. Brand glanced at the staircase.

"The undertaker came for Mazie just after you left." The barkeep anticipated his question.

"She deserved better. All the women who work here deserve better." Brand's hands tightened on the Bible.

"Hey—" The man shrugged as he reached for a glass. "I'm just the bartender. Some gent up in Austin owns the place. Pray for 'em all you want, just don't go trying to convert 'em. It's bad for business."

"If any of them come to me for counseling, I won't turn them away."

"I'll just bet you won't, Preacher."

Brand's jaw tightened.

"Are you a man of your word, Papa?"

He turned around and walked away.

It was a little after ten in the morning when Laura heard the doorbell ring. She left her library, closed the door behind her. There was a mirror in the hall tree near the front door, and she studied her reflection. Amelia had sent Hank over with smartweed vinegar tonic last night. So far, it had relieved the swelling, but no amount of face powder could hide the bruise. She practiced a smile, wincing at the pain, before she turned away from the mirror and opened the door.

Brand was standing there with her bonnet in his hand.

Her breath caught when she met his eyes and saw how deep was his concern. She could actually feel her heart contracting. She'd been an investment, a valuable commodity used and paid for, most of her life. No one had ever stood up for her. No one had ever protected her or made her feel precious in his eyes.

Until now.

"I had to see you," he said. "How are you?"

Laura glanced down the street. Thankfully, it was all but deserted. When she looked at Brand again, he was staring at the bruise. The muscle at the side of his jaw tensed. His eyes shadowed.

"Yesterday you sent me home without even looking at me," he said. "I lost my temper. I — "

"I was too embarrassed to look at you. I shouldn't have been there."

"No more embarrassed than I. I should never have struck that man. I was no better than he. My first concern should have been your safety."

"When Amelia told me what you did . . ." She couldn't finish.

"Let's not speak of it again." He handed her the hat and she saw the smudge on it where her head had hit the filthy floor. He reached for her free hand. "Come, sit with me."

He tugged her outside.

She should have stopped him but couldn't. His touch was like a lifeline to something good and true that she'd never known and never even dreamed she would find. Brand was the kind of man she'd only read about.

She reminded herself he might be a hero, but she was not a heroine by any means. Leading him on was wrong, but being with him felt so right that it was easy to deceive herself into stealing a few more moments alone with him. *Just a few more.*

He headed around the veranda to the far side where a wicker settee surrounded by potted plants and ferns faced a small side garden. It was her favorite view, a peaceful refuge that she rarely had time to enjoy. A bird bath was sheltered beneath a lacey oak.

He sat on the settee, gave her hand a tug.

"Brand—"

"Please. Just sit. We don't have to talk."

For once she didn't try to pull away. She sat. He didn't let go of her hand. Instead he tucked it between both of his.

They fell into silence, watched a sparrow splash in the bath that Anna filled each morning with fresh water. The sparse grass in the yard was turning gold. Thick white clouds scudded by overhead, destined for places she would never see.

As the minutes ticked by, Brand slowly relaxed.

"Mazie will be buried this afternoon," he said softly.

"Where?" She suspected it wouldn't be in the church graveyard.

"Outside of town a ways."

Laura imagined the burial. Few if any mourners would stand among the lonely paupers' gravesites on the open plain. She closed her eyes. The darkness behind her eyelids was terrifying in its bottomlessness, so she opened them and focused on the birdbath. Its water reflected the sky.

"Amelia and I will be there," Brand said, as if he'd read her thoughts. "She won't be alone."

Amelia and Brand had been there for the girl at the end. They would see her on her final journey. Laura hoped he didn't ask her to join them. She couldn't stand beside the grave of a soiled dove without thinking of Megan. It would break her heart.

But then she realized Brand would never ask that of her. He saw her as something she wasn't, something pure and good and wholesome. Someone like the other women in his church.

She looked down at their linked hands resting on his thigh and hated living a lie—he deserved so much more.

Tell him, she thought. *Tell him the truth, if that's what it takes to get him to walk away forever.*

They both spoke at the same time.

"Brand—"

"Lau—" He sighed. "I'm much better at preaching than I am courting."

"Courting?"

"See, you didn't even know that's what I'm attempting to do here." He laughed and then shrugged. "I'm rusty at it, I'll admit." He smiled off into the distance.

"I don't—"

"There's something good between us, Laura. I felt it when I kissed you. It's a feeling I'm not willing to ignore, even if you can. I'll wait as long as it takes. It's enough for me to enjoy hearing your voice and seeing you smile. When you're ready to admit that we're good for each other, I'll be here." His grip on her hand tightened. "I'm *not* going away."

You'll be here until the truth extinguishes the light in your eyes, she thought.

"Brand, there's so much you don't know—"

"Yesterday when I saw that man hit you, all I saw was red. I wanted vengeance. All I could think about was keeping you safe and taking care of you."

She wanted to get up and walk away.

"I'm not wealthy—" he began.

"Brand, please, *listen*—"

He touched his finger to her lips, silencing her.

"I don't have anything but my children and my faith, but if you let me into your life, I can promise you would always have the one thing I *can* give you, Laura—my heart."

Before he let go of her hand and stood up he said, "Please. Think about it." He straightened his collar, tugged on his cuffs and smiled. "Unfortunately, I promised to meet with the board from eleven to twelve. I should be going."

The ribbons of her hat trailed from her hand as she walked with him to the front steps. She may have been through the worst life had to offer, but she'd never been a coward. She drew herself up and refused to let Brand walk away thinking they had any kind of future together.

He paused at the top step and turned her way again, and she realized she ached to kiss him. It was another sign of just how far her control was slipping at the thought of this final farewell.

She glanced out at the street, saw Mary Margaret Cutter on her way to the bank. Mary Margaret waved. It was a blunt reminder of where they were and who he was. All notion of kissing Brand fled.

"I have a past," Laura blurted. "One I'm not proud of. I'm not what you think I am, Brand. I'm *not* the woman for you. If the truth ever came out—"

"We all have a past, Laura. There are things I've said and done that I would give anything to take back. No one is without sin, but people can change. They lead better lives. I don't even want to know what you did that you think was so wrong." He cupped her cheek with his palm. "I don't care. What matters is that you're not that woman anymore." He lowered his voice to a whisper. "Besides, looking into your eyes, I doubt it could have been all that bad." He let her go and stepped back.

"Think about what I said," he whispered.

She closed her eyes and fought to collect herself. Could he really forgive that easily? Without even knowing what she'd done?

"I'm simply not the woman for you, Brand. Not today, not ever. I'm sorry."

"I can't and won't believe it. You're not getting rid of me that easily. There are two things I have in abundance: faith and hope. I have enough for both of us. For now, that's enough."

His undaunted smile nearly broke her heart.

She heard him whistle a jaunty tune as he cleared the steps. Shoving his hands in his pockets, he headed down Main Street.

NINE

Laura was sipping a cup of tea the next morning when Anna brought the *Glory Gazette* to her in her study. She thanked the maid and, when the door closed again, opened the newspaper. When she scanned the headlines her blood ran cold.

"Prominent Widow Felled in Saloon."
"Preacher Defends Her Honor."
"Publisher's Wife Witnesses Fray."

Laura gripped the paper and read on:

Story by Hank Larson, Publisher and Editor in Chief.

Editor's Note: Touting the *Gazette* as nothing less than a fair and unbiased source of news, it is with dismay that we print this story, for not only was my own wife involved, but so was Reverend Brand McCormick, as well as Mrs. Laura Foster of Foster's Boardinghouse, both esteemed friends.

Two days ago, Mrs. Laura Foster was abducted outside of the Silver Slipper Saloon and dragged inside against her will. Mrs. Foster found herself in an untenable situation after volunteering to summon and drive Reverend McCormick to the site where he and Amelia Larson tended to an ailing young woman. When she stood up to her aggressor, Mrs. Foster was knocked unconscious. Reverend McCormick quickly came to her aid by subduing her attacker. The reverend was unhurt during the scuffle but the perpetrator was felled.

Mrs. Larson and Reverend McCormick rushed Mrs. Foster to her place of residence where she immediately came to her senses. The attacker was last seen riding out of town with his associates. Veteran Confederate Army Lt. Jenkins, known to most folks around Glory only as "Rob," declared he'd never seen anything like it.

"If push come to shove and I ever needed a man at my back, that preacher fella'd be the one I called," Rob told this reporter the day after the altercation.

Mrs. Foster is said to be recovering. Reverend McCormick had no comment.

The unnamed, ailing young woman formerly residing at the Silver Slipper passed away and was buried yesterday in Boots Up graveyard south of town.

Laura let the newspaper fall into her lap.
"Prominent Widow Felled."
So much for privacy and anonymity. She didn't have to rely on gossip. Hank had taken care of spreading the story.

She lifted the paper and reread the story twice. Hank made it sound as if she'd been dragged off the street into the saloon. She didn't know whether to thank him or give him a piece of her mind. What would Brand's congregation think of what he'd done? It was true, Hank's story made a hero of Brand, but he was still a minister. To think that he'd hit someone, lost his temper because of her —

She folded the paper and left it in her study. Her guests certainly didn't need to see it.

After asking Richard to hitch up the horse and buggy, she went upstairs for her hat and reticule. There was still a slight morning chill in the air, and she grabbed a shawl before she made her way back downstairs and headed over to Amelia's to ask for advice.

She found her friend in the apothecary shop that took up half of the front room of her home. Amelia was measuring a liquid into bottles and capping them with corks when Laura knocked and then let herself in.

"I'm so glad you're here," Amelia told her. "I was looking for a reason to stop working."

"Why don't I help?" Laura asked, eyeing all the empty bottles. "You'll be finished in half the time."

"That would be wonderful."

"What is this?" Laura set her reticule on the top of the display case and then took off her shawl.

"Rheumatism liniment. With cold weather coming on, people will be needing it for aches and pains." Amelia reached for Laura's chin, turned her face so that she could inspect her bruise. "Is the tonic I sent helping?"

"A bit. It's soothing, at least."

Amelia placed the funnel atop a small bottle. Laura carefully tipped the pan and poured the liniment. They spent a moment in silence, filling and corking bottles.

"I have a feeling I know why you're here," Amelia said finally. "I *told* Hank not to print that story."

"I guessed he wouldn't want folks thinking he was censoring the news and holding back the story because you were there."

"Exactly what he told me." Amelia set a full bottle aside and picked up the last one. The bottles were various sizes and colors; folks all over town saved their empties for her remedies.

"That's not why I'm here," Laura said. "I came to tell you that I've tried to discourage Brand's attention. He called on me yesterday to return my hat and see how I was faring. I told him I'm the wrong woman for him. I told him we didn't suit. That I wasn't who and what he thinks I am—"

"Don't you care for him at all?" Amelia held out the bottle.

Laura poured in the remaining tonic. "Of course I do. As a friend. He's a good man. The best. But trust me, I'm the wrong woman for him. I can only do him harm."

"You're one of the finest people I know, Laura. What you did for us when Hank was wounded, the way you spared no expense to host our wedding just so I'd have a wonderful memory ..."

"None of that makes me good enough for the Reverend Brand McCormick."

"Everyone in town thinks you two are well suited for each other."

"What do you mean *everyone?*" Laura paused, shocked.

"Ever since the choir performance, folks have been wondering when and where you'll show up on Brand's arm again. Even before the paper hit the street, word was out about how he defended your honor."

"My honor wouldn't fill a child's thimble," Laura whispered.

Just then Hank walked through the door and headed straight for Amelia.

"I'm the luckiest man in Glory," he said as he kissed her on the cheek and gave her a squeeze. "To have not one but two beautiful women in my house."

Amelia gave him a playful shove. "Don't make me spill this," she warned.

He kissed his wife again before he turned to Laura. The evidence of their love was more than apparent and left Laura filled with an aching emptiness.

"I hope you're not upset with me over the feature story," Hank said to Laura.

"What's done is done." It was impossible to be mad at him. She was more upset at herself for walking into the saloon. What happened was her own fault.

He went over to an armchair near the front door and sat down.

"The day after the incident, rumors were flying. I thought I'd put a stop to them by getting out the truth."

"Thank you for trying," Laura said.

"There's talk of Brand being honored after church on Sunday morning. I'm sure whatever the Auxiliary cooks up will involve lots of fried chicken and fixins. We'd be happy to pick you up, Laura. Around nine. That should get us there in time to get a good seat."

"Pick me up?"

"For Sunday service and the supper afterward."

"I'm much better at preaching than I am courting."

She glanced over at Amelia. Her friend was busy corking bottles. Hank expected an answer.

"I won't be going this week." The last thing she needed was to make more of a spectacle of herself. She picked up her reticule and threaded it over her wrist.

Hank didn't press her, but watched her closely. Laura looked up to Hank as a writer more than anything else. If she'd only been a man and her life circumstances different, she might have tried her hand at writing herself.

As it was, she could only live a fictionalized version of her own life.

"I hope you'll change your mind," Amelia said offhandedly. She bent down to line up the bottles of liniment inside the glass-fronted case. When she straightened, she looked directly at Laura. Her expression did little to hide her true feelings. "If you do and want to ride with us, just let me know. I can't imagine you'd miss an occasion where Brand is being honored for displaying courage on your behalf."

Laura bid them farewell, determined not to let on that Amelia's words had left her shaken. If she didn't go to the service, she'd be negating what Brand had done. If she did, she would not only bear the burden of being an imposter, but she'd run the risk of giving

Brand false hope. Not to mention stoking rumors that there was something more than friendship between them.

Who knew, she thought, that being respectable took so much time and effort? Such a toll on one's peace of mind?

Brand paced the wide veranda fronting Foster's Boardinghouse as he waited for Laura to return. He pulled his watch out of his pocket and pressed the knob that popped the lid. It was almost noon. Anna had said Laura would be back in time to preside over the midday meal.

He lifted his hat, shoved his hand through his hair, and took up pacing again. He was due home an hour ago. Charity was waiting for the bundle of things he'd picked up at Harrison's Mercantile. If Laura wasn't back soon —

Just then he saw her buggy coming up the street. She drove straight through to the back, toward the carriage house. He picked up his dry goods and headed around the veranda to meet her just as she was coming up the back steps.

"Brand." She couldn't hide her surprise. In fact, she looked downright startled to see him.

He took a deep breath. Tried to smile. "I've been waiting for you."

"So I see," she said. "I was at the Larsons'." Her brow knit into a frown. "What's wrong?"

"Are you in love with someone in New Orleans?"

Her hand went to her throat. "What are you talking about?"

"Harrison Barker told me that you have been corresponding with a man in New Orleans for some time now." He thought he'd feel better once it was out, but he didn't and wouldn't until he knew the truth. "Is that why you claim you're the wrong woman for me? Because there's someone else? If that's it, you could have just said so."

"I do correspond with someone in New Orleans. But that's none of Harrison's business, or yours, for that matter. His job is to collect the mail when it's dropped off, not go through it and spread gossip. I'll be having a word with him tomorrow."

"I've a right to know if you're in love with someone else."

Her chin went up and he knew immediately he'd made a huge mistake.

"What gives you that right?"

He set his bundle down on a nearby stool.

"I've spent more time confused and in prayer these past few days than I have since I found my calling."

He could see his honesty set her back. She took a minute to collect herself. Took a deep breath. His admission left her shaken.

"I told you I was the wrong woman for you. I don't know how else to say it."

"Then it is true. There is someone else."

"No. There is not. Now, if you'll excuse me, Reverend, I'm needed inside."

Brand watched her walk away no more content than when he'd first arrived.

TEN

The rest of the week crawled by at a snail's pace for Laura.
She kept to herself in the house, watched and hoped her bruise
would fade quickly. She thought of calling on Amelia, but she was
afraid her friend expected her to give in and attend Sunday service.

Days were growing shorter as fall shadows lengthened. She lit
the lamps, brewed pots of tea, and spent time closeted by herself
in her library. Yet of all the books in her collection, nothing held
her interest.

She found herself staring into space more often than not, picturing Brand's face as she'd seen him last. The day after their argument, she'd penned a note to Harrison Barker and given him a
piece of her mind. She told him her correspondence was none of
his business and she'd thank him to keep from reporting any gossip
that concerned her. The next day she'd received a note of apology
and a lovely tin of sassafras tea.

On Saturday night she had a houseful of guests, but she
couldn't summon her usual conversational wit and banter. All she
could think of was Brand and the Sunday supper to be held in his
honor after the service.

Would he care if she wasn't there? Would the congregation
think it rude if she snubbed the way he stood up for her? Not only

had she disappointed Amelia and Hank by turning down their invitation, but was she trampling on Brand's heart again?

She told herself that's what he got for wearing his heart on his sleeve. All that ever came of believing in love was heartache.

On Sunday morning, Rodrigo hitched up the buggy to take a young couple boarding with them to church. Laura stood in front of the bay window in her room and watched them leave.

The clock downstairs chimed the half hour. She walked to her dressing table and found she couldn't face herself in the mirror. Instead she went to the huge armoire that held her dresses—silks, satins, worsted, gabardines—and chose the most demure gown she owned. It was dove gray with black stripes and piping. She hadn't worn it since she first moved to town playing the grieving widow. She slipped it on and rang for Anna. The maid was there in minutes to help her button up the back of the dress.

"You look sad, señora." Anna stepped back, looked her over from head to toe. "Are you all right?"

"I'm going out for a walk. I'll be back in a little while."

"You want Ricardo to go with you?"

Since the incident at the Silver Slipper, the Hernandezes had been coddling her. Laura tried to smile reassuringly.

"I'll be fine after a little fresh air. Don't worry. I'm not sure how long I'll be gone." Laura pinned a small, boxy hat atop her upswept curls. "Thank you for your help."

Anna left her and Laura finished putting the final touches on her ensemble. The clock downstairs struck nine as she picked up her gloves and umbrella and headed downstairs.

The minute she left the house, she had known where she was headed, though she didn't fully admit it to herself until she was standing outside the church.

Glory's only church was nothing like the grand St. Louis Cathedral on Jackson Square in New Orleans. (Though she'd never been inside the cathedral, she had certainly traveled down the promenade on Rue de Chartres, beneath the triple spires towering over the square.) The simple white clapboard building in front of her might have been mistaken for a school if not for its high bell tower and steeple. Inside, the church was miniscule.

The doors were open in welcome. Choir music drifted out.

She paused to the right of the stairs until the singing stopped. A minute later, she heard Brand's voice, confident and strong as he spoke to his congregation, welcoming them. She took a deep breath, marched up the stairs, and peeked in.

The church was packed. As Brand read from the Bible, she stepped through the door and edged along the back wall until she reached the side aisle. Her heart began to pound when she realized there was nowhere to sit. She had no idea how long Brand would continue reading. Any minute now he might look up and see her.

As she hovered near the back, Laura noticed Mary Margaret Cutter sitting at the end of the second to the last pew. Mary Margaret glanced over her shoulder and smiled. She waved Laura over and nudged her husband, Timothy. The elder couple slid down the pew and Laura sat down and tried to make herself disappear.

She kept her eyes downcast, hoping Brand wouldn't spot her. He had finished his reading when she finally looked up, but he hadn't noticed her. Sunlight filtered in from the tall stained-glass window on the wall behind him. The rays reflected the many shards of color in an intricate mosaic of the Good Shepherd and his flock. As Laura stared up at the window, a gentle feeling of peace flowed through her.

The feeling was short lived. Brand spoke of his loss of temper that week in his sermon. She'd called upon all her courage just to walk in the door, yet Brand was able to stand before his friends, neighbors, and all those who turned to him for solace and advice and humble himself before them.

"Today you are congratulating me for standing up to a bully. A man who hit a defenseless woman. But the Bible tells us a wise man keeps himself under control."

He paused to scan the gathering. Laura knew the moment his

gaze found hers, for the slightest of smiles touched his lips. Mary Margaret noticed too. She nudged Laura with her elbow and when Laura turned, Mary Margaret winked. A few others noticed that Brand's focus had shifted. Heads began to swivel. Laura looked neither right nor left, but directly at Brand. In that moment, he was her lifeline. She could only hope she did not pull him down with her.

"Someone close to me was hurt and I lost control, which is no excuse. I'm a man of God and should always set an example, but in that instant, I wasn't thinking. Anger and fear took over and I struck out. At first I despaired of my actions. But what must we remember when we slip and fall? That everyone who believes in Him receives forgiveness in His name."

Brand made it sound so very simple: believe and your sins will be forgiven. Surely that wasn't all there was to it, especially when the will to believe in anything but survival had been taken away from her so long ago.

As she sat there listening, curious and attentive, the hollow sound of heavy footfalls rang out against the floorboards of the center aisle. Like everyone seated around her, Laura's gaze was drawn to a tall young man standing in back. Framed in the doorway, his face was shadowed by his wide-brimmed black hat. His shoulders were broad, his stance somewhat familiar. He wore dark pants, a dark-blue shirt beneath a leather vest. A holster rode his hips.

He didn't move as he stared at Brand.

"Welcome. We're happy to have you here," Brand said.

The man took a step farther into the room. When he failed to remove his hat or make any gesture, Laura's heartbeat spiked. Was this man somehow connected to the men in the bar? Was he here for retribution? She held her breath.

The stranger walked up the center aisle and stopped a third of the way down. Behind him, a couple seated near the side door got up and hurried out. There was some shuffling and hushed, nervous whispers. A few more people slipped out of the church.

Laura was too stunned to move, as were most of the others. The newcomer was far younger than Laura first thought. No more than eighteen or nineteen.

His dark eyes never left Brand's.

"I just heard you say that God forgives us our sins, Preacher." His voice carried across the room without shouting.

Brand watched him closely. If he was afraid, he showed no fear. "I did—"

"You think He'll forgive you for everything just as long as you believe? Is that right?"

"That's what the Bible says."

"Convenient." The word was barely audible but everyone heard it.

"If you'll have a seat, I'd be happy to talk with you later—"

"Happy? That's funny, seein' as how you don't even know who I am."

Brand moved away from the lectern and started toward the aisle. Before he took another step, the young man called out, "God might forgive you, but can you forgive yourself for what you did to my mother? Can you forgive yourself for walking out on her and leaving her in shame? Answer that, Preacher."

Brand's steps faltered. His eyes never left the young intruder. He whispered something only those in the front rows might have heard. Laura strained forward, grabbed the back of the pew in front of her.

The young stranger whipped off his hat. He was handsome in an exotic way.

"Look a bit harder and you'll see her in me. You might even see a little of yourself, Preacher. You don't know me, but I can see that you remember her—the woman you abandoned before I was born. The woman you deserted because she was Cherokee."

Brand's face drained of color.

A collective gasp filled the room. No one moved. Seconds ticked by.

Suddenly from the front pew, Janie's voice, high and thin, cut through the tense silence.

"Papa? What's wrong?"

Laura couldn't see Brand's children in the front row, but she could just imagine their fear and confusion. Charity was seated on the altar with the adult choir. Like everyone else, her gaze was riveted on the young man in the center aisle. Unlike the others, she looked as if she were seeing a ghost.

Before she realized she'd moved, Laura was on her feet, making her way to the front. Blind to everyone else in the church, she hurried to the end of the front pew where Janie and Sam were watching their father with wide, frightened eyes.

"Janie, Sam, come with me." Laura held out her hands and the little girl grabbed one and held on tight.

"What about Papa?" Sam wouldn't budge.

Thankfully, Amelia, steady and calm, suddenly appeared at Laura's side.

"Go with Laura, Sam," Amelia whispered as she scooted into the pew. She took hold of Sam's hand and drew him toward the aisle. "You, too, Janie. Stay with Laura."

"Tell Brand I've take them to my house," Laura whispered. Amelia nodded.

As Laura quickly whisked the children out the side door, she glanced back. Her breath caught. Brand was moving off the altar, walking toward the armed stranger.

"What was that man saying to Papa?" Janie wanted to know. "Why is he so mad?"

"He needs help," Laura told them, trying to smile. "Your papa will talk to him. Everything will be just fine."

Her mind raced, her thoughts focused on Brand as she walked down the street between his children, holding their hands.

"That man said Papa abamanned his mother. What's abamanned?" Janie wanted to know.

"*Abandoned*. That's when you leave someone behind," Laura explained.

She glanced over her shoulder. She picked up her pace. She could see the handful of people who had fled the church still milling around outside.

"Is he gonna abanmond us? Where are we going?" Janie planted her feet and refused to budge. "Where are you taking us, anyway? Why can't we stay with Papa?"

Laura sighed in frustration. "I'm taking you home with me. Remember Peaches? She'll be on the porch, most likely. You can pet her."

"Don't be such a baby. Papa won't leave us for long." Sam looked up at Laura. "You got anything good to eat?"

"Lots," Laura said.

"With sugar?"

"Plenty of sugar," she promised. Rodrigo always had an array of fresh baked goods on hand.

"See, Janie? It'll be okay." Sam let go of Laura's hand and skipped down the street.

"Don't get too far ahead," Laura called out.

Janie stuck out her bottom lip, but she started walking again.

Laura tried to ignore the feel of Janie's little hand in hers as well as the blind trust in Janie's eyes. She warned herself to guard her heart and tried to convince herself there were no feelings involved. She had merely acted on impulse to remove Janie and Sam from an untenable situation, that was all. Rushing to their aid certainly didn't mean she *cared* for them—or their father—anymore than she cared for anyone.

*L*ook a bit harder and you'll see her in me."

Brand did see *her* in the young man's eyes. Sarah Langley, the woman he had loved so long ago. She had been his first true love, though he'd been too young and foolish to see it then. He'd wooed and won many young women in the wild years of his youth—but unlike the others, he had fallen in love with Sarah.

As he stared at the young man standing in the aisle—Sarah's son, *his* son—Brand was aware of movement to his right. He'd heard Janie's voice, but was afraid to take his gaze off the young man with the gun.

A young man whose eyes resembled Sarah's, except they were cold and unforgiving.

A few minutes ago, Brand had noticed Laura sitting in the back of the church. His heart had soared. Now she and everyone else in the church was at risk.

Not only was there a slight commotion to his right, but Brand noticed that Hank Larson had silently slipped around to the back of the church. Hank was in the center aisle, gun drawn, inching his way toward the young man claiming to be Brand and Sarah Langley's son.

Brand raised his hand—just barely, but enough to halt Hank in his tracks. The sheriff hovered at the far end of the aisle, unseen by Langley.

Brand walked off the altar and started slowly toward the youth. He spoke calmly, and in truth, he wasn't afraid. Whatever happened, his faith was in the Lord.

"Why don't we step outside? I'd be happy to talk to you, son."

"Don't call me that."

The young man appeared at a loss, as if he hadn't thought past the initial confrontation. His gaze shot around the room, his face paled as if he were aware suddenly of where he was and how many people were watching.

When Brand reached his side he lowered his voice. "What's your name?"

"Jesse. Jesse Langley."

"Come with me, Jesse. Please."

Brand reached for Jesse's arm and began to walk him toward the side door. Once they were outside, Brand heard Hank addressing the crowd left in the church. Those who had already slipped out earlier had backed off to a safe distance to see what would happen. Brand ignored them and walked Jesse around the corner.

As if coming out of a trance, Jesse shrugged off his hold and stepped back.

"How is your mother?" Brand asked.

"Dead. She died over a year ago."

"I'm so sorry to hear that."

"Sorry? If you're so sorry, why weren't you there?"

Brand glanced back at the church. Under Hank's direction, folks were slowly, silently filing out, heading for the hall. A few stopped to gawk, hanging back to see what would happen. Brand turned away from the stares.

"Your mother left me. I looked for her, but there was no trace of the Langley family anywhere."

Jesse's stare was hard, unconvinced. "Why should I believe *you*?"

Brand spread his hands. "Because it's the truth. No one could tell me where they'd gone."

"That's hard to believe. It took me almost a year, but eventually I found you."

Almost a year.

Brand stared at the youth. Jesse was near the same age Brand had been when Sarah's family disappeared. He knew what determination and sheer stubbornness it must have taken the young man to find him. He was proud of Jesse's effort, not to mention stunned, to finally stand face-to-face with his and Sarah's child.

"Come home with me," Brand said. "We'll talk this out. You can meet the family."

The minute the word *family* was out, Brand knew he'd made a mistake.

Jesse's mouth became a hard line. His eyes narrowed.

"Your *family*?" Jesse sneered. "The perfect family, no doubt. The perfect wife. Children too?"

Brand nodded. "A boy and a girl. Nine and seven."

Jesse shook his head. "I've got nothing more to say to you, Preacher. Nothing at all. Coming here was a mistake."

"You don't know how many times I thought of your mother, how many times I've wondered about our child."

"Yeah. So you say. All I wanted was to hear you acknowledge that you knew my mother was carrying a child when you deserted her. I wanted to see the look on your face when I showed up here."

"I never *deserted* her."

Jesse Langley looked Brand over and shook his head, disgust marring his handsome features.

"The truth is I came to kill you, Preacher, but as it turns out, looking at you now, you're not worth the hanging." That said, Jesse Langley turned and walked away.

After settling the McCormick children in the kitchen where Anna dished them up a midday meal, Laura slipped upstairs to take off her hat. She washed her face and hands, tried to smooth down her hair.

The young McCormicks were perfectly happy, full of cookies and milk and surprisingly well behaved for a change. After they ate, Anna put them to work washing dishes. Janie complained that it was Sunday and they shouldn't be toiling, but Laura assured them that dishes had to be done no matter what day of the week it was. When Sam made himself a beard of soapsuds, she knew they were playing more than working.

In the drawing room, she paced in front of the window until Brand rode up alone. He tied his horse to the hitching post outside her low picket fence and came up the walk. She stepped outside to greet him, closing the front door softly behind her.

He looked exhausted. His step was slow, his usual smile was gone. She could tell by the slump of his shoulders that he was troubled by what had happened. She found herself hurrying across the veranda to greet him.

He paused when he saw her. As she closed the distance between them she found herself tempted to take his hand. The very notion shook her more than his presence.

"The children are fine," she assured him. "They're in the kitchen decorating a cake with Anna."

"Are they upset?"

"Curious. Happy because they've had plenty of sweets. How is Charity?"

"Upset. Lots of folks are. She said to thank you. She was afraid to move."

Laura led him up to the veranda where they both paused.

"I owe you an explanation," he began.

"Not at all," she said. From what she'd heard, she'd pieced a story together. The young man in church had claimed to be Brand's son, the son of a woman Brand had abandoned. She couldn't imagine Brand doing anything of the kind.

But from the suffering on Brand's face, it was clear he accepted the blame.

He walked to the white porch railing that surrounded the veranda and leaned against it. He took off his hat, set it on the rail. Looking into the distance, he said nothing. She stood behind him, staring at the back of his coat, at the cut of his sleeve, the wide shoulders beneath the black fabric.

Always before, he'd been the one to touch her, to take her arm, to gently guide her with his hand riding at the small of her waist, to lift her down from the buggy. He'd been the one to initiate a kiss.

Now it was she who wanted to reach for him. He was a man isolated in misery. She wanted so much to let him know that he wasn't alone, that she was there and willing to listen.

She stepped up beside him and rested her hand on his coat sleeve.

"Talk if you need to talk," she said softly.

Brand nodded. There was a tightness in him, as if he were an over-wound clock.

"The young man in the church—his name is Jesse Langley. He's eighteen. He is my son."

"You're sure?" It wasn't altogether impossible that the young man was lying.

"I'm sure," Brand said softly. "He's the image of his mother—"

"That doesn't prove anything."

"You saw him for yourself, Laura. There's some of me in him too."

The youth *had* walked like Brand, moved like Brand. He'd even sounded a bit like Brand from what she could recall. She'd been too stunned to take much note in church.

"Can we walk?" Brand asked.

She glanced down Main Street and hesitated.

"Not that way. Around back," he said.

She led him around the house, skirting the kitchen windows. If he'd been anxious to see his children he'd have said so. They walked through the rose garden and out beyond the edge of her property where the land opened up and rolled away from town and out onto the open plain. The horizon stretched on endlessly. A slight breeze blew, picked up grains of sand and whipped them into whirling cones that danced across the land and died away.

She had no hat, no umbrella, but she didn't care. The breeze teased the curls out of her hairpins. She feared it would become a tangled mess, but right now all that was important was hearing Brand out.

"He's been looking for me for months," Brand said.

"He's inherited your stubborn determination." She paused a moment, wishing he would smile. "Are you sorry he found you?"

She knew how she would feel if someone walked out of her former life and announced himself without warning. Botsworth had been a close call, but she hadn't been subjected to public censure.

Brand shook his head. "I'm not sorry. I always wondered if the child survived. If it was a boy or a girl. I searched all over for Sarah, his mother. After she told me she was carrying my child, her family up and left town."

"She left you?" Laura couldn't imagine anyone willingly walking away from Brand. "Why?"

"Her mother was Cherokee. Sarah and her family fought hard, trying to fit in. I was more shocked than happy when she told me she was carrying my child. I was only eighteen and never dreamed of settling down so soon. My father would have never given us his blessing. He thought she was beneath me.

"I wrestled with what to do. When I finally came to my senses and went to ask her to marry me, the Langleys were gone. Their place was deserted."

"You never saw her again?"

Laura read genuine regret in his eyes. "I looked everywhere. No one had seen them. No one knew where they went. It wounded me to the quick knowing that I had a child somewhere, a child I'd never know. All I could think of was how reckless I'd been. How I'd only been thinking of myself, not Sarah, and certainly not the baby. A few months later I enlisted in the Union Army."

He stared out over the open plain again. "After the war, I became a preacher and fell in love with Jane. But I never forgot Sarah. I never forgot that I might have a child somewhere."

"Until today." Laura thought of the defiant young man standing in the church denouncing his father before all. "Where is he now?"

Brand shrugged. "I don't know. The anger that drove him to confront me went out of him, but not before he admitted he came to kill me—"

Laura gasped. "Are you safe? Does Hank know?"

"Jesse changed his mind. He said I wasn't worth it."

"Oh, Brand." She ached for him, wished there was some way to ease his pain.

"Hank took over, got everyone out of the church. A lot of folks left right away. A few stayed for the supper. I couldn't face them."

Brand turned to Laura as if really seeing her for the first time since he arrived.

"I'm sorry I left the children here so long, but when Amelia told me you had them, I knew they were in good hands. I don't know what to do now," he admitted with a shrug. "I can't begin to guess what folks must be thinking."

"I'm sure they'll get over it," she said. "Aren't they supposed to believe in forgiveness?"

"God forgives. People have a harder time of it, especially when a man who stands before them week after week preaching moral fortitude turns out to be a sinner."

"You're human, Brand. Don't be so hard on yourself. Besides, that was eighteen years ago."

"This isn't something as simple as my lashing out in anger to defend the woman I love. This makes me a hypocrite."

She told herself to ignore what he'd just said about "the woman I love." He was upset. He had no idea what he was saying.

"Next Sunday, when the church is full, you'll see that they have forgiven you. They'll stand behind you." She tried to smile. "Where's that faith of yours?"

"Sorely battered." Finally, he smiled in return.

"Let's go get your children," she said, quickly turning away. "By now they may have Anna tied to a chair."

ELEVEN

It was noon on Monday when Laura walked into the mercantile followed by Rodrigo.

She told him she would be going along to help with the marketing, but in reality she was curious to hear what, if anything, folks were saying about the incident in church yesterday. She knew Harrison Barker would be dispensing gossip along with dry goods.

Sure enough, Harrison started asking questions as soon as she stepped into the mercantile.

"I heard you whisked the McCormick children out of harm's way yesterday. Is that so?" He paused, cocked his head like a hungry dog waiting for a bone.

"I took them home with me, if that's what you mean," she said. That was no secret. Everyone one in church had seen her leave with them.

"I'm surprised you weren't there, Mr. Barker."

"We would have been, but Mother wasn't feeling well. She's a member of the church board, you know."

"I believe I had heard. Do you have any rice?" Laura asked. "I need two pounds."

"Was it terrifying?"

"It was disconcerting." She sighed. "The rice, please."

He went behind the counter for a sack and then walked to the bin and started scooping rice onto a scale.

"Who'da thought it? A preacher having a child on the wrong side of the blanket. Folks are buzzing about it, believe me."

"They must have little else to do." She hadn't been there five minutes and already she'd had enough.

"Does this shed new light on your feelings? I mean, everyone knows you two have been keeping company."

"What are you saying?"

"Well, you know, he's been seen walking with you. Sitting on your veranda. They say a fine, respectable woman like you will surely show him the door now. He's got a lot of nerve, misrepresenting himself. He should have disclosed the truth straight out when he came here and applied for the job of pastor."

She looked around, lowered her voice. "How long does a man have to wear his past sins on his sleeve?"

"I guess until he gets to the pearly gates, that's how long." Harrison set the sack on the counter. "Besides, like I said, he wasn't forthcoming about it. Now he's got a mess on his hands. Earlier this morning I heard Bud Townsend wants to call a board meeting to discuss his dismissal."

"Brand's dismissal?" Laura almost dropped the rice Harrison handed her before she passed it to Rodrigo.

Brand had been right. It was worse than she thought.

A cold chill ran down her spine. If only there was something she could do to help.

She was the last person on earth Brand needed to fight his cause.

She couldn't wait to finish the marketing and get back home. There had been a few passing showers that morning so the street was not fit for walking. As she rode back in the buggy beside Rodrigo, she happened to glance down the alley between the Silver Slipper and the land office and see a man slumped over in the mud. He appeared to be out cold.

She'd only gotten a glimpse, but she thought she recognized his clothing. She was almost certain it was Jesse Langley.

"Turn right at the corner, Rodrigo, and go around behind the back of the buildings." She inched up to the edge of the seat, impatient to see if she was right.

"Stop between the saloon and the land office," she told him. "That's it, right here. Look." She pointed down the alley.

"A man, señora. Do you think he is dead?"

"I hope not." She looked around, then quickly climbed down out of the buggy. Thankfully, there weren't many people out and about in the weather. She heard Rodrigo call for her to stop.

She hitched up the hem of her skirt and hurried toward the fallen man with Rodrigo close behind. He complained all the while, grumbling how she should have at least waited in the buggy.

Sure enough, when she reached the man slumped over on the ground, it turned out to be Jesse Langley. His hat was lying upside down in the dirt. An empty whiskey bottle lay on the ground beside his outstretched hand.

"Can you lift him?"

"He is muddy." Rodrigo sounded less than enthusiastic.

"I'll buy you a new shirt."

"It is not that, señora—"

"Please, just carry him to the buggy."

"He smells like a *cantina*."

She paused, smiling to lessen the impact of her words. "Am I in charge here, or are you?"

Rodrigo shook his head. "I am trying to look out for you, señora."

"Another time, perhaps, Rodrigo. For now, tote this young man to the buggy. Let's get him out of here before someone sees us."

Rodrigo grabbed one of Jesse's lifeless arms and hefted him to his shoulder. Laura grabbed his hat and hurried after them. When they arrived at the buggy, Rodrigo dumped Jesse in back like a sack of grain as Laura climbed aboard.

Back at the boardinghouse, Laura instructed Rodrigo to drive inside the carriage house before he unhitched the horse. She didn't want anyone to see them unload their unconscious cargo.

"Where should I put him?" Rodrigo was still notably unhappy about the situation.

"Leave him in the buggy for now. I'm going inside to get a cot and some bedding, then we'll put him in the tack room."

She hurried inside and began to rummage through a storeroom for one of the folding cots she kept for families with extra children. Anna brought her a stack of fresh sheets and a blanket and Laura hurried back outside.

Rodrigo had the horse unhitched and was waiting by the buggy.

"He's going to get the sheets all muddy," the cook said.

"That's why you're going to undress him first. When I've got the bed ready, you can carry him in. Dump his dirty clothes in a pile and I'll put them in a wash tub to soak."

"All of them?"

"All." Before she turned to head into the tack room, she tossed Rodrigo the blanket. "Wrap him in that."

She made up the bed herself. Anna could sweep and dust the tack room later. Although ... that was a task Jesse Langley could attend to himself—if he decided to stay on.

Once Rodrigo deposited Jesse on the cot, Laura went to look in on him. It would be a few hours before he slept off the influence of the liquor. No telling how much he'd had. She doubted he'd stopped at one bottle after the scene he'd made at the church, the culmination of a life of anger toward Brand.

On close inspection, he was as handsome as she remembered given her brief look at him. He had black hair that curled softly, like Brand's, though he wore it long; it hung past his shirt collar. His skin was a shade darker than Brand's, his eyes slightly almond shaped. Any woman would envy his thick, dark lashes.

She smoothed his hair back off his forehead, wondering what would become of him. At least he was safely out of the alley. Whether or not he could pick up the pieces of his life and go on was anyone's guess.

The same could be said for all of them.

"He's awake," Anna told Laura four hours later. "I hear him making a noise like this." She proceeded to groan.

Laura laughed. "I can imagine he's not feeling very well right now." She gave instructions to ready a tray and told Anna that she would deliver it herself.

After seeing some new arrivals settled upstairs, Laura went back to the kitchen and found the tray ready.

"You want me to go with you?" Rodrigo started to untie his apron.

"I can manage. I doubt he could stand up to anyone at this point." She didn't mention she had tucked her derringer into the pocket of her apron.

Outside the door of the tack room, she heard Jesse Langley moan. Anna had done a fine imitation. She balanced the tray on one arm, knocked twice, and then let herself in.

He was lying on the cot with one arm thrown over his eyes. The blanket was pulled up, revealing only his bare shoulders.

"Whoever you are, go away," he mumbled.

"Sit up." She walked over to the cot and nudged it with her knee. "Now."

One bloodshot eye peered out from beneath his arm.

"Stop yelling," he whispered.

"I'm not yelling. Sit up."

"Where are my clothes?"

"Being laundered. We left some things for you." She nodded toward a pile that contained a pair of pants and a shirt donated by the Hernandez men. "Those will do until yours are ready."

"Who *are* you, lady?"

"My name is Laura Foster. I'm the one who dragged your sorry self out of the mud in the alley. Now sit up. This tray is heavy."

He wrestled around until he was sitting up with his back propped against the wall. He was careful to keep the blanket firmly in place. She wouldn't have guessed he was the modest type.

He squinted against the sunlight coming through a window set high on the wall.

"Headache?" she asked as she set the tray on his lap. He took one look at the plate of bacon and eggs along with a tall glass of tomato juice and paled.

"Are you trying to kill me?"

"Get this down and you'll feel better in no time. Guaranteed."

"You an expert on hangovers?" He looked skeptical.

"Just trust me."

"I can't stomach any of this."

"Start with the juice." She paced over to the workbench, unfolded a denim work shirt, and held it up. "This should fit." She draped it across the pile of pants and long johns before she turned around again. He'd drained the tomato juice.

"Now wait a minute or two and then eat the bacon and eggs. You need some grease on your stomach."

"What do you care anyway?"

"I know your father."

She thought it impossible for him to grow any paler, but he went gray and started to push the tray aside.

She walked over to the bed and put her hand on the top of his head and held him there. "Don't even think about getting up yet."

"Why not?"

"One, I don't want you heaving all over the place. Two, you're stark naked under that blanket."

"Please, get your hand offa my head," he groaned. "It's killing me."

"Stay put and hear me out. Please."

He pulled the tray up, picked up a piece of bacon and sniffed it. Took a bite, chewed, swallowed.

"You say you know McCormick." His eyes narrowed. "You his wife?"

"I'm just a friend. He's a widower."

Jesse snorted in satisfaction.

"I was there in church yesterday when you made your grand entrance." Laura said.

He didn't look up this time but concentrated on the tray.

"You caused quite a stir. Thanks to you, the reverend could lose his position here."

"You think I'm sorry?"

"You might feel justified, but he doesn't deserve to be ousted. He's a fine, upstanding man with two children and a sister who depend on him. He claims he tried to find your mother. He says he wanted to marry her, but she'd disappeared."

"Words are cheap."

"What are you planning to do now? Stay drunk until you run out of money?"

When he looked up, there was a bleakness in his eyes. "I'm already about out of money."

"I'll bet you never thought past that grand scene in the church. Not only have you embarrassed and possibly ruined Brand, but you have nowhere to go. What's left of your life now that you had your revenge?"

"He paying you to torture me? Is that it? As soon as I've eaten, I'll be on my way."

"Where to?"

"That's none of your business, is it?"

"What if I make it my business?"

"You got a smart mouth, lady."

"So I've been told. Do you have any money? Do you even have a horse?"

"I've got a little money left. I'm hoping my horse is still hitched outside the saloon. At least it was yesterday."

Her insomnia had given her hours to think about what had happened in the church, about this young man and his impact on Brand's life—and Brand's on his. It was a safe bet Jesse had spent his childhood dreaming of confronting his father. She'd spent hers seeking another kind of revenge, planning her future and that of her sisters. She'd been bound and determined to show the world that she didn't need help from anyone but herself. That she could succeed on her own.

But if Jesse Langley left Glory now, wallowing in self-pity, he'd most likely end up a wastrel or dead. He and Brand would never have a chance to reconcile either.

"If I offered you a job, you could stay on in Glory for a while."

"What makes you think I want to stay here?"

She took a deep breath. "Your father is here. You've spent a year looking for him. Why walk away now?"

"Because I hate him."

"You don't even know him."

"I don't *want* to know him."

She searched his face. "I don't believe you," she said softly. "I think you're here because you've wanted to know him all of your life."

"You're living in a dream world." He picked up the fork, ignoring her as he dug into the fried eggs.

"I've got to get back to the house," she said.

"Where am I, anyway?"

"In the carriage house of my boardinghouse. It's at the end of Main Street." She headed for the door, turned and paused. "How about you finish up, change into these clothes, and at least stick around until your laundry is finished tomorrow. By then you might have changed your mind about working for me."

"Doing what?"

"Odd jobs." She was certain she and Rodrigo could come up with something before tomorrow.

Langley didn't respond as he finished up the last of the eggs.

"Don't forget about your horse," she reminded him.

She left him without a good-bye. To her way of thinking, she'd already done much more than she intended for Brand's illegitimate son. He was just one more person she had to convince herself she cared nothing about.

TWELVE

It was no surprise to Laura when Jesse came to her the next morning and agreed to stay on. One day at a time was all he could promise. She said she understood but didn't explain how. She'd been living one day at a time for as long as she could remember.

He collected his horse and stabled it in the carriage house while Laura consulted with Anna and Rodrigo and came up with a list of chores that Jesse could tend to. She thought about the gazebo she'd always wanted and asked if he did any carpentry.

"I can do just about anything. Had to. Grew up making ends meet." His barb was obvious, but Laura ignored the attitude.

Laura hadn't seen nor heard from Brand again, which was a relief. She had no notion of how he would react to her taking Jesse in. She was writing out the menu that morning when someone tapped on the front door. By the time she reached the entry hall, the tapping had turned to pounding.

She brushed the lace curtain aside and found herself peering down at Sam and Janie.

"We thought you weren't home," Janie explained when Laura asked why they were beating her door to death.

She ushered them in, expecting Brand to come up the walk behind them, but Brand wasn't there. She looked up and down the street.

"Where's your father?"

Janie shrugged. "He told us to go outside and not to make any noise."

"Does he know you're here?"

"No," Janie said.

"Yes," Sam said at the same time.

"Sam?" Laura crossed her arms and stared down at him.

"Well, I kind of told him we were going to walk over and see you."

"Kind of?"

"Kind of softly," he admitted.

The children looked more disheveled than usual. Janie's hair had been braided but more strands were sticking out of the braids than in. Sam had a dirty smudge around his mouth. He had on short pants and one of his socks was sagging down his leg. One suspender was missing entirely. Janie's sash was untied and trailing behind her.

"Where is your aunt?" Laura led them to the kitchen table where she'd been working on her menu for next week.

"Mostly in her room bawlin'." Sam had wandered into the dining room and had his nose pressed to the glass in the breakfront cabinet where Laura kept her china.

She walked over to him, gently pulled him back, and used her sleeve to wipe off the spot left by his nose.

"You sure got lots of dishes," he said as she led him back into the kitchen.

"Is our brother here?" Janie had already made herself at home at the table.

Laura paused. "Your brother?"

"The man who came to the church on Sunday. Papa told us that he was our half brother and we wanna see him," Sam said.

"How do you know he's here?"

Sam wandered around the kitchen. "Yesterday at the mercantile we heard Mr. Barker tell Papa that Mr. Rodrigo said Jesse Langley was here."

Laura wondered why Hank bothered to print the *Gazette* when Harrison Barker was perfectly capable of spreading the news.

"Is he?" Janie had her elbows on the table and her chin propped on her fists.

"He is." Laura wasn't about to deny it to them and lose their trust.

"Can we see him?"

"He's busy right now."

"Doing what?"

"Cleaning the tack room. After that he's going to muck out the stalls in the carriage house."

Jesse had done every task she'd given him over the past two days without complaint. He kept to himself, ate his meals in the tack room, and didn't engage in conversation with anyone. Silent and sullen, but he was still there. She tried to imagine Jesse face-to-face with Brand's other children.

She looked down at Janie and Sam, wondering if it would do them more harm than good to meet Jesse.

Glancing out the window toward the carriage house, she thought of Jesse. He'd searched for Brand for a year. Fed on revenge and hate. Now he was left with nothing but anger and loneliness. She knew them both well, but she had replaced them with something tangible. She'd built a new life for herself. Yes, loneliness still had a way of creeping up on her, even with a house full of guests. Still and all, she believed anger was a waste of time. The sooner Jesse learned that the better.

She suspected that no matter how much he protested otherwise, he wanted to get to know Brand. Perhaps even be a part of his life.

These children were Jesse's kin. Maybe they would prove to be the bridge between Brand and Jesse.

There was only one way to find out.

"I'll introduce you to him on one condition." She walked to the dry sink where Rodrigo kept a dishpan full of soapy water.

"What is it?" Sam crossed the room and waited beside her.

"You let me clean you both up a bit first."

A few minutes later, the dirty smudges on Sam's face were gone. He was spit shined and polished, his hair still damp from where she'd wet it down so that she could part it. He'd been remarkably still the entire time.

"How old are you, Sam?" Laura asked as she held him at arm's length, inspecting her workmanship.

"Nine."

"Hmm." She made a great show of frowning.

"What are you thinking, Mrs. Foster?"

"Oh, just that you're old enough to make sure you look present-able before you leave the house. Anyone who's a man of his word should be manly about other things. Like washing his face and making certain his clothes are neatly worn."

"He doesn't wash behind his ears, either," Janie piped up. She took his place before Laura, ready for her turn.

Laura dipped a rag into the dishpan, wrung it out, and caught Janie's chin gently between her fingers. She tipped the child's face up. Her hand faltered as she stared down into Janie's innocent blue eyes. She had to take a deep breath, to steel herself and keep moving as if her heart wasn't aching with heavy memories of lining up her sisters and doing the same for them.

"You look funny," Janie said as Laura rubbed the rag around her hairline.

"I was just thinking," Laura said. "Or trying not to, actually."

"About what?" Sam asked.

"Something I don't like to remember."

"Why?"

Because it hurts. "No reason."

"Can I go outside?" Sam stood by the back door, looking out the window.

"Not yet. I'd rather we surprise Jesse together." There's safety in numbers, she thought. No telling how Jesse Langley would react.

She brushed out Janie's tangled locks and by the time she finished, the little girl's hair was parted in a straight line and two new braids trailed over her shoulders.

Laura stood Janie beside Sam and looked them over.

"How do we look?" Janie wanted to know.

"Passable. And a sight better than when you came in."

"Am I old enough to wash myself too?" Janie asked.

"You're old enough to try." Laura wondered if Brand had even noticed the state they were in before they left. Hadn't Charity recovered from her shock yet?

"Let's *go*," Sam prodded.

"All right. Let's." Laura took a deep breath and opened the back door.

The carriage house was cool and dim inside. The pungent scents of leather, horse, and dusty straw filled the air. Dust motes danced on a ray of sunlight that filtered in from the windows high on the side walls. The children were unusually solemn as Laura led the way across the open space between the buggy and the stalls toward the tack room in back.

The door was closed. As she raised her hand to knock, the door swung open and Jesse Langley filled the doorway. He looked at Laura and then down at the children. They stared up at him in silent awe. Laura knew that wouldn't last long.

"You need something?" He ignored both McCormicks.

"I do. You have guests. I brought them to meet you," she said.

Anyone who knew Brand well would immediately recognize Sam as his. Jesse stared at them both for a second before his expression imperceptibly tightened.

Before anyone could say anything, Sam stuck out his hand.

"I'm Sam. We're brothers."

Jesse stiffened. His gaze shot to Laura.

"What is this?"

"This is Sam and Janie McCormick. Your half brother and sister."

Janie smiled up at Jesse with a gap between her teeth and stars in her eyes. "Now I've got two big brothers. How old *are* you, anyway?"

Jesse stared at Laura. "Get them out of here," he mumbled.

"But —"

"You heard me, ma'am."

"I thought —"

He stepped back and shut the door.

"*That* was rude wasn't it?" Janie said. "Aunt Charity says there's no accounting for rudeness and that people should at least know their manners."

Laura curbed the urge to knock on the door and toss Jesse Langley out on his ear, but she reminded herself what he'd been through and how he'd ended up here in the first place and calmed herself down.

She reached for Sam and Janie's hands and marched them out of the carriage house and back into the kitchen.

"What now?" Sam asked, his footsteps dragging.

"Cookies," Laura told them.

"It's kind of early for cookies," Janie observed.

"It's never too early for cookies," Sam told her.

"My thought exactly," Laura agreed.

Rodrigo was in the kitchen when they walked back in. She settled them at the table with cookies and milk and then marched back out to the carriage house. The tack-room door was still closed. She didn't knock gently.

Jesse opened the door. "What now?"

He sounded surprisingly like Sam.

"I'm here to remind you that for the time being, I'm your employer. I suggest you rephrase that."

"You need something, *ma'am?*" He waited.

"I do. I need you to be civil to those children. They came over here on their own to meet their half brother and the least you could have done was say hello."

"They're nothing to me."

"They are children. All I'm asking is that you spend five minutes talking to them."

"Forget it."

Across town at the McCormick house, Brand had withdrawn to his office.

He knew that God never gave anymore than one could bear, but as he sat down behind his desk, he thought to himself, *This time He's pushing the load.*

Yesterday the church board had called an executive meeting and excluded him. He was convinced they were going to ask him to step down, as was their right. He wished they'd heard him out first. It may not have done any good to try and explain to those who had already made up their minds, but surely some were still undecided.

Afterward, Hank and Amelia had stopped by to tell him that they were behind him. She was on the board and assured him the majority wanted to wait and see how the congregation reacted before they took a vote of confidence.

He thanked them, assuring them everything would work out for the best, but when he closed the door and they were gone, doubt crept in.

He had a family to feed and shelter and no idea where he would go or what he'd do if he lost his position.

The Larsons had told him Laura found Jesse Langley passed out cold in the alley beside the Silver Slipper on Monday and had taken him in. Though the news surprised him, it only increased his admiration for her.

He turned to his Bible for solace. As he began reading, there came a soft knock at the door.

"Come in," he called, expecting one of the children. Or both. They'd been suspiciously quiet since he'd sent them outside to play.

But it was Charity. "I need to talk to you, Brand."

"Quite a shock we had, eh, Sis?" He stood up and came around the desk to join her.

"It wasn't just seeing that young man standing there claiming to be your son," she began.

"It's not an idle claim. He is my son."

"Do you mind if I sit down?" She indicated the chair in front of his desk.

"Of course not. I'm sorry this has been such a shock."

"No, it's me who's sorry," she said softly. "All of this might have turned out differently if I'd said something to you years ago. You might have found Sarah Langley and been there to raise your son."

A lone tear slid down her cheek and she quickly wiped it away. "But then you wouldn't have married Jane. You wouldn't have Janie and Sam and . . . I love them as if they were my own. I can't imagine a world without them."

"What makes you think you could have done anything? You were only a child when Sarah disappeared."

"I was seven." She took a deep breath before she went on. "Of course, I knew who the Langleys were. Everyone did. They were teased a lot about being half-breeds at school. One day I was outside Father's study and I heard him talking to Mr. Langley. Father told him to take his family, leave town, and not come back. He said he didn't want his son's life ruined. I thought Mr. Langley meant to hurt you in some way.

"I peeked around the door and saw Father take a roll of money out of the safe. When he handed it over, he told Mr. Langley to make certain no one ever found out where they went."

Brand's heart stuttered. He knew his father had been unhappy when Sarah caught his eye, but he would have never have believed the man capable of this—that he would stoop so low as to pay Mr. Langley to move his family out of town and to hide their tracks.

"It all seemed so secretive and strange. I didn't understand then, but the minute I heard what Jesse Langley said in the church,

I knew what it all meant. Father paid that man to take his daughter away, even though she was going to have your child, Brand."

Shaken, Brand sank into his own chair behind the desk. His gaze fell on the Bible he'd closed not five minutes before. His father had always been an authoritarian and unyielding. But he was gone now. There was nothing Brand could say, no way he could confront him.

It all comes down to forgiveness.

His father had done what he thought right for his son, but that didn't make it right. His father should never have played God.

"I'm so sorry, Brand," Charity said.

"Sis, there's nothing to forgive. How can I blame you for not telling me something you couldn't fully understand?" He got up and went around to her side of the desk again. "Don't forget, you were only as old as Janie is now." He couldn't help but smile a little. "In fact, she looks a lot like you did at that age."

"What about him? Jesse? What can we do to help him?"

"I thought he would walk back out of my life as suddenly as he walked in, but he's still in town."

"He is? Where?"

"Laura took him in. He's living at her place and working for her now."

"Maybe you can make him understand. Maybe there's still a chance he can be a part of our family."

"It won't be easy. Not to mention, I may have an uphill battle with the church board as well."

"Oh, Brand. Would it help if I spoke to them? Tell them what I know?" She was still shaking like a leaf.

"Hopefully they'll take my youth into consideration along with my years as a minister." He walked over to the window, watched the clouds trail across the open sky. "We have to trust in God, Charity, the way we always have."

He turned away from the window, smiled down at her, and offered his hand.

"Now, I think it's time we faced the world and find the children. They're suspiciously quiet."

"I'll see about getting the noon meal together," she told him.

Charity went to the kitchen. Brand called for Janie and Sam. When he couldn't find them in the house, he went outside and walked the grounds. They never went far and eventually came running when he called. He wasn't overly concerned until the image of Jesse Langley's face flashed through his mind.

If Jesse truly wanted to hurt him, it could be easily done through his children.

Brand started back to the house, his long strides eating up the distance. When he reached the front yard, he saw Richard Hernandez at the front door talking to Charity. She waved and called him over.

"Laura sent Richard over to tell you Sam and Janie are at her place."

Brand could finally breathe again. If the children were with Laura, they were in good hands.

THIRTEEN

Laura waited for Brand at the edge of her veranda. Beneath the wide brim of his hat, his face was shadowed. When he reached her, he doffed the hat but the shadows remained in his eyes.

She led him inside and paused in the entry hall as he closed the door behind them.

"I'm sorry about Sam and Janie pestering you."

"They haven't been any trouble."

"It's so good to see you, Laura," he said softly.

Without warning, he reached for her. She knew she should protest, but all she could do was go completely still inside. His hand rested on her shoulder for a heartbeat before he pulled her into his arms and held her close. Her first instinct was to push back, to break his hold, but the way he held her was so natural that her arms slipped around him without hesitation. Slowly she uncurled her hands, pressed her palms gently against the back of his coat. Her heart was beating frantically, like the wings of a caged bird.

She'd had countless encounters with men, but this gentle sharing was something she'd never, ever experienced. Standing within the warm circle of his embrace, she suddenly realized that she had been waiting for this moment for her entire life. She hadn't even realized what she'd longed for until this very second when she felt the beat of Brand's heart next to hers. She could no more let go now than stop breathing.

Because he needs someone to hold him, she thought.

That's all, she told herself. *That's all*.

They held each other until the sound of footfalls echoed in the kitchen, an abrupt reminder that they were not alone. Laura immediately let go. Brand opened his arms and stepped back. Another man might have acted as if nothing had happened. But something *had* happened and he had felt it as well. His gaze never left her face. His expression was filled with unspoken words.

A more innocent woman would not have understood their meaning.

A less honorable man would have voiced them aloud. Her face flamed. She dropped her gaze and fought to collect herself.

"The children are in the kitchen," she said softly.

They entered the kitchen, where Rodrigo was browning a pork shoulder.

"Where are the children?" she asked.

"They wanted to go outside. I told them to stay in the yard," the cook said.

"Jesse is here," she told Brand.

"I know."

They went out the back door. The children were nowhere to be seen, but Laura thought she heard Janie's voice coming from the carriage house.

"I'll go get them," she said, hoping to avoid a confrontation between Jesse and Brand.

"Is he in there?" Brand stared at the carriage house.

"He was. He's bunking in the tack room."

"I'll go with you," Brand said.

She saw the tension on his face. Tension tinged with worry.

"I'm sure the children are fine," she said, not really sure at all.

Together they walked toward the wide-open double doors of

the carriage house. As they approached, she heard Janie's chatter, her words loud and clear.

Laura stopped just inside the door. Brand hovered behind her. Across the open space, Janie and Sam were standing outside an open stall watching Jesse rake up straw and toss it into a wheelbarrow behind him. When Janie stepped close to the wheelbarrow, Jesse ignored her.

"How come you are so *old*?" Janie asked. "I wanted a *little* brother, not another big one. My papa said that we couldn't have another brother until he found a wife. So where did you come from?"

"You're in the way." Jesse's tone wasn't as sullen as Laura expected. He carefully sidestepped the little girl and dumped a pitchfork full of straw in the wheelbarrow.

"You got any muscles?" Sam wanted to know.

"More than you," Jesse said.

"Show me."

Jesse ignored the request and walked back into the stall. Sam rolled up his shirtsleeve, raised his arm, and made a fist. When Jesse walked out again, Sam pointed to his bicep.

"See? Muscle. My papa says I'm going to be strong as an ox."

"You believe him?" Jesse disappeared into the stall.

Sam nodded. "'Course I do. Why would he lie?" He shoved his fist up higher. "Feel for yourself."

Jesse stared at the boy for a second, then he reached down and fitted his thumb and forefinger around Sam's miniscule bicep. Jesse snorted. It was the only comment he made before he returned to his task.

Brand started across the room with Laura on his heels. She picked up her pace and reached the children first.

"Look who's here," she said.

"Papa!" Janie smiled and jumped up for a hug.

Sam, old enough to know they were in trouble, remained silent.

Jesse Langley turned his back and kept raking.

"Why don't you two go with Laura?" Brand said. "I'll be out in a minute."

"We're talking to Jesse," Janie said. "Can't we stay?"

Laura watched Brand study the young man in the stall. Jesse worked on, as if none of them were there. Brand looked to her for help.

"Come with me, you two," she urged, "Let's let Jesse and your father talk."

"Run along," Brand added. "I'll be out in a minute."

Laura held out both her hands and the children took them. As she led them into the sunlight, she glanced back. Brand was staring at Jesse with mingled confusion and something she'd had little enough of in her life. Hope.

Y ou're still here." Brand couldn't help but marvel at the strong young man mucking out the stall. He was tall and fit with thick black hair that reached his shoulders. He'd tied it back with a piece of black cord. His eyes were dark and clear, his mouth full, his jawline strong and determined. He was everything a man would want in a son—except that there was no love in his eyes. Only suspicion tinged with hate.

"Yeah. For now."

"I'm going to take that as a good sign."

"Take it as anything you want. I'm still here because I don't have the money to move on. I'll be heading out as soon as I do."

"I'd like you to give me a chance to get to know you."

Jesse leaned on his rake. "I know all I need to know about you."

"You don't know the whole story. I didn't either, not until my sister remembered something that happened before you were born. Seeing you sparked her memory."

Jesse turned around. "Sounds convenient, Preacher, but I don't want to hear it."

Brand looked through the open doors, out into the light of day where Laura strolled with his children through her garden. He turned around, spoke to Jesse's back, tried once more to reach this man who was his son.

"I'm not the kind of man who would abandon a child." He spread his hands, shrugged. "It's up to you to believe me or not. God knows the truth."

Jesse turned to stare at Brand in stone-cold silence before he said, "He's not talking, is He?"

Brand saw it was useless to argue. Badgering Jesse would get him nowhere.

Brand nodded in the young man's direction. "Thanks for putting up with the children. They've been curious and excited about you."

His gratitude was met with more silence. He knew when it was time to walk away.

Brand took a long look at Jesse Langley, knowing it might very well be his last.

As soon as Brand and the younger children were gone, Laura returned to the carriage house.

"What are you to him?" Jesse asked as soon as she drew near.

"What do you mean?" She felt herself flush. She knew very well what he meant.

"Are you lovers?"

"Absolutely not."

What am I to Brand? She didn't know how to answer and struggled.

"We're ... we're friends," she said.

"He'd like it to be more," Jesse said.

She remembered the way Brand had held her in the hallway. Remembered the warmth of his strong embrace, the way she'd felt in his arms—cherished, protected.

"He's an honorable man," she said softly. Far too honorable for her.

"Still. He'd like to be more than friends."

She drew herself up, reminded herself she was Jesse's employer.

"I'd like you to start painting the front steps when you're finished here."

"You sure you want me out there where everyone can see me?"

"What do you mean by that?"

"The black sheep? The minister's long-lost half-breed bastard?"

"Do not use that word here."

"It's the truth, even if it offends your innocent ears."

She folded her arms. Eyed him carefully. If he thought crudeness would have her on the run, he was sorely mistaken.

"You know, nothing you say could shock me. I prefer you keep your language clean. I have guests coming and going. If you're going to work for me, you're going to have to live by my rules."

"I'm not planning on sticking around long."

"So you say. I think you'll be around a long time because I know what you want. The only way you're going to get it is by not turning tail and running off."

He leaned on the top of the rake. "Oh, really? And what is it I want?"

"A father. The father you never had."

His gaze shifted. "You're crazy."

"I'm a lot of things, but crazy isn't one of them. I would have given anything to have my father in my life when I was a child, but he died young. You, on the other hand, have a chance to get to know yours. He wants you in his life. No matter what may or may not have happened between Brand and your mother, that's all in the past. This is the present. Your whole future is ahead of you. You can spend it with your father or without him. That much is up to you. Those children came to you with open arms this morning. You can be someone they look up to, a hero who can teach them right from wrong—but first you have to learn what that is for yourself." She thought of Brand, knew what he would say. "You're going to have to learn to forgive and to love."

She left before he could respond, before the anger he'd nurtured for so long had him tossing down the rake and walking out. She left him alone to think about what she'd just said.

As she crossed the yard toward the back of the house, her eye caught the pure white of the last rose of the season. She paused to touch its soft, layered petals, to inspect the perfect, fully opened bloom. It was a miracle unto itself.

"You're going to have to learn to forgive and to love."

She didn't know where the thought came from, but as she made her way into the house, she realized the words she'd said to Jesse she might just as well have told herself.

FOURTEEN

Time passed quickly, as time does when one is busy. It was Friday before Laura realized the week was nearly gone. She hadn't seen or heard from Brand again, but she'd heard of him from Hank when he stopped by to extend an invitation to Sunday supper after church.

When she politely declined, he asked if the scene on Sunday had soured her opinion of Brand.

"Of course not," she told him. "I took Jesse in, Hank, and I did it as much for Brand as for Jesse."

"Some folks might take it the wrong way if you don't show up on Sunday. People will be looking to see who is and isn't standing behind Brand. Your absence will be noted. Brand needs all the support he can get right now, and yours means a lot."

She thanked him and sent Hank on his way.

An hour later, the bell rang again. She was patting her hair into place when she entered the entry hall and looked through the window in the door. Seeing the tall, broad-shouldered silhouette behind the lace panel, she found herself smiling. She paused long enough to take a deep breath and calm her racing pulse before she reached for the door handle.

Brand's name was on her lips as she opened the door, but the man standing on the other side was not Brand.

She stared up in shock at Collier Holloway, her former business partner and paramour from New Orleans. He looked every bit the gambler, entrepreneur, and scoundrel that he was in a perfectly fitted black coat over a violet brocade vest, well-tailored trousers, and a black hat. She hadn't seen him since she left Louisiana, and their parting had been less than amicable. Collier had done everything he could to try and entice her to stay. Though he let her go, she could never convince him that her own dream, her future, meant more to her than the money they could continue to make together. When she'd told him she hoped it wasn't too late to salvage some scrap of decency in herself, he'd laughed in her face and called her a fool.

She looked up at Collier, too stunned to speak.

The day she'd dreaded for four years was here. It had begun like any other day. There had been no dark clouds on the horizon, no thunder or lightening, no warning of such an horrific turn of events.

Nothing but the ring of the doorbell. And now here was Collier, smiling down at her. She said the first thing that came to mind.

"What are you doing here?"

"That's a fine welcome for an old friend." He looked past her, over her shoulder, into the interior of her home. His gaze was a violation of her carefully constructed world. "No welcoming kiss?" he asked.

"Absolutely not." Thankfully, no guests were about. Rodrigo was within shouting distance in the kitchen. She was safe enough. The last thing she wanted was someone to see Collier standing on the veranda. She grabbed his sleeve, pulled him inside, and slammed the door.

"I figured you'd have missed me by now, but I didn't reckon on this," he said, doffing his hat and smiling down at her the way a snake might peruse a mouse.

But she was no mouse, no matter how respectable she appeared.

"What do you want?" She asked again. "Spit it out and leave."

"I want you. You were the best partner I ever had."

She'd been twenty-six the night she'd first laid eyes on him. She'd been seated on a velvet settee in the downstairs salon of the brothel on Rue de Lafayette, reading. Not only was she truly lost in the pages of a novel, but she'd found that putting on an air of complete disinterest was a challenge to many men. She always brought a book downstairs with her and was always the first chosen out of a dozen or so women in the room.

When Collier strolled in she had immediately recognized in him the qualities that would help take her from one world to another.

She could tell by his speech that he was a Yankee. The South was full of carpetbaggers, gamblers, and brash opportunists now that the war was over. Collier was definitely one of them. His appearance came at the perfect time—the upheaval and fighting had ended, the streets were somewhat safer, and she had made up her mind that she wanted out of this life for good.

But she was ruined. She was a soiled dove and no decent man would have her. She was no fool. She knew that for a woman like Lovie Lamonte, there was nowhere to go but onto the streets. Without capital, without a protector, she'd be turned away by decent folk, forced to live hand to mouth, and eventually continue to be what she'd already become.

She made certain Collier noticed her that first night by ignoring him. For a man who commanded a room with his very presence, being ignored was a new experience for him. She presented a challenge and she used her wiles as only she knew how to gain his admiration.

"What is it you want most, Lovie? Name it and I'll give it to you," he told her one night.

To live without shame, to find my sisters, to be free.

She couldn't tell him what she truly wanted and risk having him laugh in her face, so she said, "Money."

She ran her fingernail down his bare chest and added, "I want wealth beyond imagining and a place of my own."

He thought she'd meant a brothel of her own.

"That's easy enough," he laughed. "I can set you up tomorrow if that's all you want." He wrapped a lock of her hair around his finger and tugged on it until she leaned closer and kissed him. "I'd want exclusive rights to you, though."

She pretended to think about his demand for a moment. "I'd want everything in writing," she said. "We would be equal partners in the business and I would be able to walk away whenever I decided it was time."

He hesitated, but then nodded his assent. "Done."

"Once I've made my own money, I'd like you to help me invest it in other holdings."

Collier chuckled and shook his head. "There is a whole lot more to you than meets the eye, Lovie Lamonte — not that what meets the eye isn't enough."

"I've had fifteen years to listen and learn, Mr. Holloway. I've a knack for honing in on the most successful person in a room and finding out all I can from them — be it a businessman or a whore. It's time I put all my learning and 'experience' to work for myself."

He was true to his word and within a week she was running their new saloon and sporting house. The place was elegant; the women working there were the most refined and beautiful he could find in and out of New Orleans. Before long, patrons were lining up at the door.

There was plenty of money to be made off the misfortunes of others. Laura amassed collateral and soon had enough to invest in properties up for auction.

She and Collier made a fine team. He never once cheated her out of a penny and always gave her a hefty percentage of their profits.

As soon as she felt she was sufficiently wealthy, she had told him it was time for them to part ways. He wasn't happy about it, but he was a man of his word.

At least she thought so until now, four years later, as she watched him walk around her drawing room and pause to run his fingertips across the mahogany surface of a drum table. He picked up a framed photograph of a woman in a black dress with a prim white collar. Her hands were folded sedately in her lap; her hair was drawn severely back. He snorted, set the picture frame down.

"What about it, Lovie? Together we can't lose."

"I'm not interested in anymore partnerships. I'm not interested in anything you have to offer, Collier," she said. "I have what I wanted. I've moved on."

"I saw your 'Women and Families Only' sign. What does that mean?"

"Exactly what it says. I don't let rooms to single gentlemen. Ever."

"Why not?"

"People here think I'm a widow. I have a ..." She knew that to him it would sound ridiculous. "I have a reputation to uphold."

He threw back his head and laughed. "Oh, come on, Lovie."

"My name is Laura, now. Laura Foster." She turned away, walked to the fireplace, and stared down at the feather arrangement in a crystal vase she'd placed in front of the empty grate.

"So I heard," he said, wiping his eyes.

"Where?"

"From a certain Kansas state representative I ran into in San Antonio a few days ago." He was still chuckling.

"I'm glad you're amused. You can go now."

"Aren't you going to hear me out, at least?"

"No. I'm not interested."

"My proposal is for a place right here in Glory. Nice little town, but sorely in need of some life."

"What are you talking about?" She didn't want him in Glory. She didn't want him within a thousand miles of her.

Without invitation, he walked over to a wing chair, sat, and rested his hat on his knee.

"You can't sit there," she said, hurrying across the room.

"Sorry." He stood up and headed for the settee.

"You can't sit anywhere." She planted her hands on her hips. "You have to leave, Collier. I have guests arriving any minute now."

He wasn't fazed by her irritation at all. He sat down on the settee. "When Botsworth mentioned he'd seen you and told me where, I decided I'd stop by—for old-time's sake."

"Botsworth." She *knew* the scoundrel's stay would come back to haunt her.

"Exactly. The honorable Representative Botsworth. He told me you were running a boardinghouse and that you'd become somewhat of a bore." He glanced around the room again. "I can see you put all that money we made you to good use. No expense spared."

"I'm doing quite well, thank you."

He made a point of slowly looking around again. Then he shook his head. "But this isn't really you, is it, Lovie?"

She watched a smile curl his upper lip. She used to think him handsome, but seeing him here, surrounded by her lovely things, in her grand home, she couldn't help but notice the cool calculation in his eyes, the cynicism in his tone.

"I'll thank you to call me Laura. My name is Laura Foster and this *is* me now. This is my life. *My* dream."

"I find this little town very interesting. Definitely a new frontier for me. Or maybe the last gasp of the old frontier. Who's to say? At any rate, I stopped for a drink in that run-down establishment trying to pass for a saloon. The Silver Slipper."

Laura pictured the dingy, dimly lit watering hole with its sagging back stairs and dark secrets.

"I don't want to hear about it." She took hold of his elbow intent on dragging him toward the entry hall, but he refused to get up.

"Imagine my surprise when a gent came up to me, introduced

himself as the owner. He said that he's here from Austin for a couple of days looking for a buyer."

"What?"

"He's not looking any more. I bought it for a song."

"You *bought* the Silver Slipper?"

He nodded. "In the hopes that you'll run the place for me. In fact, I was thinking you could put me up here—until I saw that sign out front. Any chance that you'd make an exception for an old ... friend?"

"Absolutely not."

Collier Holloway in Glory was bad enough. Collier Holloway owning the Silver Slipper was horrible. She didn't know whether to rail at him or get her derringer and simply shoot him.

"Think about it, Lovie. The two of us together again. I'd run the saloon, you'd manage the women upstairs. The place needs someone like you to add a little class. You're already established in town—"

"Stop!" She held up her hand. "Listen to me very carefully, Collier. The answer is no. I'm established here as a widow. I run a respectable boardinghouse. I want no part of the Silver Slipper, or that life again. I want not part of—" She stopped abruptly.

"Go ahead. Say it." He got up off the settee, crossed the space between them, and looked down at her. "Finish."

"I want no part of you."

"That hurts, *Laura*."

"I'm sorry. But I've started a new life. I've moved on."

"Your old life wasn't all that bad. You amassed a small fortune. You had plenty of power. One word from you could bring down nearly every man of wealth and standing in New Orleans."

She thought of Bryce Botsworth, of how she'd blackmailed him into leaving her alone. She's had that same leverage over men in Louisiana, but that kind of power was nothing compared to the freedom, the independence she had now.

"What about the sordid, dark side, Collier? What about the

fact that my childhood was stolen from me? That I'm lucky to be alive?"

He indicated the room with a sweep of his hand. "You have everything money can buy, but this has to be boring for a woman like you. Sooner or later you'll grow tired of being alone."

"I'd rather sleep alone for the rest of my life than sell myself again."

He took a step closer. She stepped back.

"But you don't have to," he said softly.

"Get out, Collier. You've already overstayed your welcome."

"I don't recall you welcoming me in at all." He sighed. "So the answer is no?"

"The answer is no. Have you already paid for the saloon?"

"I signed a note."

"Too bad. Maybe you can take it back."

"Maybe I don't want to." He looked her over from head to toe.

"You'd never be happy here. This town is too small for you. Too boring. Besides," she said, thinking of all he owned in Louisiana, "what of your other holdings?"

He shrugged. "Still have them. New Orleans isn't that far away. That's why I was counting on you to go in with me. I could trust the management of the place to you when I'm not around."

She turned toward the entry hall. "I'll walk you out. Now."

Thankfully, he followed her. "If you change your mind, you can find me at the Silver Slipper."

"Don't hold your breath. I won't be changing my mind."

They reached the front door, where he put his hat on and stepped outside. He paused on the top step, turned to face her. "I'm a betting man and I'm willing to bet you will change your mind. When you do, you know where I'll be."

Anger flared. She tamped it down and suddenly found herself wishing Brand was there to hold her, to comfort her. She needed his steadfastness right now. His companionship. His goodness.

Instead, she was with Collier Holloway, who had the power to take away everything she had worked for, everything that had come to matter to her.

"You look peaked, Laura. Are you all right?"

"Of course not. One word from you and I'll be ruined in this town."

He put his thumb and forefinger beneath her chin. She turned her head, brushing him off.

"Don't worry. Your secret is safe with me." He put on his hat, gave a jaunty salute, and headed down the walk.

"Your secret is safe with me."

For how long? she wondered. *For how long?*

She caught a glimpse of movement out of the corner of her eye and turned to discover Jesse Langley standing off to one side of the porch, paint brush in hand.

"Does the good reverend know you're keeping secrets?" He set the paint brush down and pulled a rag out of the back of his waistband to wipe his hands.

"What do you mean?"

He shrugged. "Keeping secrets? It seems you and the preacher make a good pair."

"I've never lied to you."

Jesse walked around to the front of the veranda but didn't come up the stairs. He glanced down the street.

"You trust that man to keep a secret?"

"I don't have a choice," she said softly. Exhausted by it all, she was anxious to go inside, to shut herself up alone in her study. How much had Jesse heard?

What about you? she wondered. *Can I trust you?*

FIFTEEN

On Sunday morning, Brand stood behind the lectern. A quarter of his congregation was missing and those who were there looked uncertain.

The people he'd been closest to since coming to Glory had shown up—rancher Joe Ellenberg, his wife, Rebekah, and their brood; Joe's mother, Hattie; Hank and Amelia Larson; the Cutters; and more. They filled the front pews, lending him strength and reaffirmation of their faith in him.

Charity and the children were in the first pew. Sam and Janie were more somber than he'd ever seen them. They were aware that Jesse's appearance had set off this upheaval in their lives, but he was at a loss as to how to explain. Nor did Brand know how to spare them any concern.

He kept his sermon short and to the point, speaking as much to himself as the souls gathered to hear him. He told them what the Lord told Jacob—to forget the past. Only by turning their lives over to God would He lift them up.

Brand made no mention of Jesse's appearance. It was impossible not to feel responsible for the members who had chosen to stay away. Because of him they were not taking part in the morning's service.

As he spoke, his gaze continually went to the front door.

Though Laura wasn't among those who had come to support him, he hadn't lost hope of seeing her. He had avoided going to see her all week, stayed away because he didn't want the gossip surrounding him to taint her standing in town. He avoided her place because of Jesse too.

Everyone knew that his son was still working at the boarding-house. Brand feared another confrontation might cause Jesse to leave town, destroying any hope of ever healing their past.

By the time the service ended, Laura still had not appeared. As Brand stood on the church steps thanking all those who had attended, bidding them good-bye, he wished he could see her again.

Though the Larsons and the Ellenbergs invited his family to dinner, he had declined their invitations. Charity had put her all into making stew and it was simmering on the stove. As the four of them walked down the street together, Brand couldn't help but notice that instead of running ahead and taunting each other, Sam and Janie stayed somberly beside him and Charity.

"Papa, when are we going to go see Mrs. Foster and Jesse again?" Janie wanted to know.

"Maybe we should invite them to supper." Sam scuffed his feet as he walked along the dusty street. "Do we have enough stew, Aunt Charity?"

"There's always enough, but today might not be the best day. I'm sure by now they have other plans," she said.

"That's a very charitable notion, though," Brand said.

"If he's our brother, how come Jesse lives at Mrs. Foster's and not our house?"

Brand looked up at the cloudless sky. He had resorted to silencing Sam by telling him that he would understand when he was older.

Janie practiced skipping. "Mrs. Foster has the prettiest house. And the best cookies. You should see, Aunt Charity. I just love the way she wears her hair, don't you?"

"She's a fine lady," Charity agreed.

Too fine for the likes of me. Brand tried not to let his spirits sink.

"Don't you think she's just about the most beautiful person in the whole world, Papa?" Janie bobbed along beside him, looking just like her mother.

What would Jane think of me now? he wondered.

Jane had loved him. He was certain she would have understood that Jesse had been conceived when Brand was a different man. A lifetime ago.

But what of Laura? The last time he saw her, he had held her close and she had eased his burdened heart with her sweet embrace. Not seeing her was taking a toll on him. There was no way of knowing what Jesse had told her. No way of knowing if her opinion of him had changed.

SIXTEEN

Laura took in the view of the rolling Texas plain as she rode alongside Amelia in an old covered buggy that once belonged to Amelia's father. Dr. Ezra Hawthorne had made a habit of visiting ranches and homesteads around Glory, and Amelia, though she wasn't a certified doctor, kept up the practice.

In the past she had turned down Amelia's invitations to accompany her, but today Laura welcomed the chance to escape, especially since they would be paying a call on the Ellenberg family at the Rocking e Ranch.

She hoped the outing might take her mind off of the fact that she hadn't seen Brand for over two weeks. Nor did she want to think about when Collier Holloway would show up again.

So far he'd kept his word and not told anyone about their former association. She'd run into him one day on her way past the livery stable. He had made a great show of introducing himself to her, as if she'd never seen him before in her life.

The Ellenbergs proved to be as concerned about Brand's future as Amelia. Their conversation centered on the closed-mindedness Brand might be up against.

On the way back to town, she and Amelia rode in silence. Laura stared out across the wide-open plain, marveling at the stark landscape. The robin's-egg-blue sky seemed to go on forever.

After awhile, Amelia said, "I can't believe it's been over two weeks since Jesse Langley showed up." She shook her head. "It's too bad we can't turn back the clock."

Lost in thought, Laura failed to comment. Amelia flicked the reins over the horse's rump and it picked up the pace.

"I'm surprised he's still around," Amelia said.

Laura nodded in agreement. "No more than I. He keeps to himself and does his job. I'd hoped Jesse would open up. That he'd at least try to know Brand a bit better by now, but he's made no attempt to see him at all."

Laura reached for the side of the buggy and held on as they approached a pockmarked portion of the dirt road. She admired the way Amelia handled the rig.

"Have you seen Brand lately?" Amelia asked.

Laura studied the leather traces as they slapped against the horse's backside.

"No, not lately."

Not for eighteen days, to be exact. Eighteen days during which he'd never been far from her mind.

"He needs to see you, Laura."

"I don't—" Laura tried to imagine the shock on Amelia's face if her friend knew exactly how much she wanted to see Brand and how much she missed him.

"He needs you now more than ever." Amelia sounded as if she was losing patience. "He needs your support. He's hurting, Laura. If you care for him at all, let him know it. Tell him that you're behind him."

Laura wondered if Brand truly thought she had turned her back on him.

"He's a good man. You know it, I know it. The whole town should know it. He doesn't need me to remind him," she said.

"All it takes is a few strong-minded people to believe that he's not fit to lead. Bud Townsend is a rancher with both money and influence. He's on the board and he's speaking out against Brand."

Laura was worried enough about Brand without Amelia pressing her and now that Collier was in town, she was on tenterhooks, terrified that he would expose her. She took a deep breath. Somehow she had to convince Amelia that she was the last person Brand needed to stand up for him.

"Surely you and Hank have just as much influence as Townsend," she said. "And what about the Ellenbergs? Aren't there others doing all they can to show their support? Why doesn't Hank write an editorial?" Laura let go of the buggy and braided her fingers together in her lap.

"He's planning to. We're doing all we can." Amelia's patience was definitely slipping. Laura heard it in her tone. "You're well respected in the community. We could definitely use your help."

Amelia paused, looking thoughtful. "Has Jesse turned you against Brand?"

"No, he doesn't talk about his father. He doesn't talk much at all."

Laura's insides were churning. She wanted nothing more than to stand by Brand, to support him in every way, but the only way she could really help was to keep her distance.

"Are you afraid if you side with Brand, it might hurt your business?"

"Of course not! Amelia, please, stop. I'd certainly back him if I thought it would help, but trust me when I say I'm the last person on earth Brand needs on his side right now."

Amelia wasn't about to back down.

"I don't understand why you're so convinced you two aren't suited. It seems—"

"There *is* no two of us. There never will be." Suddenly, without warning, Laura blurted, "Amelia, before I moved to Glory, I was a prostitute."

She watched as a myriad expressions played across Amelia's face. *What have I done?* A feeling of dread held Laura in its grip. She had a sudden memory, long buried, of a worn kite made of string and scraps of paper. Her papa had made it for her and Megan. The kite was flying high in the Irish sky over the green hill where their whitewashed cottage sat with its view of the sea.

Suddenly, the string broke and the kite sailed higher and higher until it spun and twisted and fell to the ground, where it crashed and was broken beyond repair.

She had the same feeling of loss now that she had then. Surely her bond with Amelia was as shattered as that flimsy paper kite.

The words had left a poisonous taste in Laura's mouth. She turned to Amelia and saw her staring straight ahead, her face as pale as chalk. Without warning, Amelia pulled on the reins and stopped the buggy.

When she turned to Laura, her eyes were clouded with shock and disbelief.

Laura had had no intention of ever exposing her secret. But the wall she'd built around her heart had simply crumbled.

This, she told herself, *was what comes of letting yourself care.*

She had no idea what to do or say. There was no way to call back the truth.

"Surely you can't be serious," Amelia whispered. "I don't believe it."

Laura looked away. "Unfortunately, I am dead serious."

"But ... you're a widow."

"No. I'm not. I have never been married. Nor will I ever be." Laura clenched her hands together in her lap. "What you see, the woman you think I am, is a façade. There's nothing respectable about me. I was a prostitute for most of my life, and until Brand took it into his head to court me, I've been able to keep my feelings locked inside where they belong."

"So you do care for him."

"And now you know why that's impossible. You know why I shouldn't be anywhere near Brand and why I won't be showing up at the church to stand up for him. It's not because of what he's done, it's because eventually I will end up doing him far more harm than good when and if the truth comes out."

She watched her friend struggle with the truth, trying to come to terms with it.

"Please, take me home, will you?" Laura was afraid she was about to break into a million pieces and when she did she wanted to be in the privacy of her suite. She fully expected never to see Amelia again and the thought was almost too much to bear.

"How did you—" Amelia took a breath and started over. "When did you become a ... a—"

Laura spared her. "My uncle sold me to a brothel when I was eleven years old."

"Oh, Laura," Amelia's voice broke. When she covered Laura's hands with her own, it was Laura's undoing.

"I could never be the right kind of wife for Brand and his children," she whispered.

"What if no one ever finds out?" Amelia's brow furrowed as she tried to reason it all out. "How could they?"

"I've always feared I would run into someone who knew me before. That happened very recently, but I managed to threaten him and he left without anyone being the wiser—or so I thought. But now he's led a man named Collier Holloway to town. He was my business partner after the war. He advised and made investments for me. When I cashed out, I moved to Glory because it was such a remote town buried in the heart of Central Texas."

She sighed. "But now Collier is not only in Glory, he bought the Silver Slipper and wants me to go into a partnership with him again."

"No!"

"I'm afraid it's just a matter of time before he exposes me for what I am."

"Then *you* must bring the truth out into the open. That way you'll no longer have to fear exposure. You can explain to everyone first—tell your story in your own words."

"Oh, yes. And just look at what happened to Brand. He made a mistake nearly twenty years ago and is *still* being judged by it."

"Not by everyone."

"I wouldn't stand a chance. I'd be run out of town."

"Those who know you and have come to care about you would stand by you. Most of all, if you tell the truth, you would be free of the threat of exposure."

Laura couldn't imagine what freedom would feel like.

"Do they tar and feather people in Texas?" she wondered aloud.

Amelia tried to smile. "We haven't had a good tar and feathering for years."

"I can't do it," Laura admitted. "I'm not brave enough," she whispered.

"You aren't alone," Amelia said.

"I won't bring you and Hank down."

"Hank and I can take care of ourselves. And you're a strong woman, Laura. I always thought so and now I know so. You have the strength to tell Brand the truth and stand up to everyone in Glory."

Amelia reached for her medical bag on the floor of the buggy and pulled out a lace-edged handkerchief. "Here," she said, handing it to Laura.

It wasn't until that moment that Laura realized tears were streaming down her cheeks. The bodice of her gown was dappled with tear stains.

"I never cry," she said, dabbing at her eyes. "Never."

She hadn't cried since she was a child. Since . . . before.

She knew how to fight, scratch, argue, tease, tempt, and flirt. But she never let herself show weakness. Never let herself cry. Now she couldn't seem to stop.

When will it be enough? she wondered. *When will I have paid enough for my sins? How far do I have to run? How many times will I have to start over?*

Was it really so much to ask, to be free of the past? To be happy? Were her dreams too far out of reach to ever be realized?

She mopped at her tears, took a deep shuddering breath. And then, angry at herself for such a blatant show of weakness, she turned to Amelia again.

"I'm sorry. I'm sorry I've embarrassed you and myself."

Amelia lifted the reins, threaded them through her fingers. "There's no need to apologize. You just sit back and let me drive you home. We're almost there."

Laura wiped at her eyes, but the tears kept coming.

"Just remember one thing," Amelia said before she signaled the horses to start again. "You are *not* that woman anymore. You're Laura Foster." Then Amelia looked Laura in the eyes and smiled. "But most of all, you're my dearest friend."

SEVENTEEN

Though they'd only been gone a few hours, Laura was more than relieved to be home. She had heard confession was good for the soul. As far as she was concerned, it was exhausting.

Amelia guided the buggy up to the fence in front of the house. Bidding her good-bye, Laura climbed down and started up the drive, intending to go in the back way. She wanted to change, brush the trail dust out of her hair and wash up, before she met a gathering of guests in the drawing room for late-afternoon tea.

She wasn't halfway up the drive when Jesse came out of the carriage house trailed by Sam and Janie. Each of the children had shouldered a long stick with a small bundle attached to it.

What now, Laura wondered.

Jesse studied her face. "What's wrong? You been crying?"

"Of course not. I'm perfectly fine." She reached up, brushed back a lock of hair.

"Coulda fooled me."

She looked past him at Sam and Janie. "What are you two doing here?"

Sam scuffed the toe of his shoe in the dirt. Janie's face crumpled. She started to cry. "We ran away from home but Jesse won't let us stay. He's mean. He hates us."

Laura turned to Jesse. He shrugged. "They want to live in the carriage house with me. I told them to skedaddle."

181

Laura lowered her voice. "Did you actually tell those children you hate them?"

"'Course not."

Laura knelt down and gently took hold of Janie's arms. "Jesse doesn't hate you. It's just that you *can't* stay here. Your father is probably worried sick about you. He'll most likely be here in a minute—" She didn't know whether to be thankful or irritated. She was shaken and definitely not in the mood to face him.

"No, he won't," Sam interjected. "All he does is worry about folks not coming to church anymore and where we're gonna go if we have to move away. We don't *wanna* move away. We wanna stay here. You got a big place, Mrs. Foster. Why can't we live with you? Jesse is our brother—"

"Half brother," Janie amended.

Sam went on. "We wanna live with him. I want him to teach me how to ride and shoot. Papa doesn't even carry a gun."

"Papa says we might have to leave town!" Janie wailed.

"What makes you say that?" Laura asked.

"We were listening at the keyhole when he was talking to Aunt Charity in his office," Sam volunteered.

Laura looked at the thin sticks bending under the weight of their small clothing bundles. The arm of a rag doll was sticking out of the top of Janie's pack. She had the urge to pull them into her arms, to cuddle them as she had her sisters when they were small. She wanted to assure that all would be well and that they wouldn't have to move away.

But she'd failed her sisters and she knew better than to make these children a promise that was out of her power to keep—especially when she wasn't even certain of her own fate.

Her carefully constructed life might be unraveling but right now these children needed her help. She looked at Jesse and thought, *All of them.*

Laura took a deep breath and got to her feet.

"So are you taking them home? Or do you want me to have Richard go tell the preacher they're here?" Jesse asked.

Laura stared at him for a moment, thinking. The children were watching the exchange with interest. Suddenly she had an idea.

"No," she said. "I'm not taking them back. You are."

"Me? But—"

"They're here because of you. You take them back."

"We don't wanna go back," Sam said.

Laura planted her hands on her hips. Her own world might be teetering on the brink of disaster, but she was still capable of trying to help Brand's family survive.

"You two don't have a choice. Your father loves you. He needs you at home right now." She glanced toward the carriage house where Jesse's horse was saddled and tied up outside.

"Go get Jesse's horse and bring it over here," she told the young McCormicks.

They hurried away, arguing over who would get to hold the reins.

"Hey," Jesse started after them. "Wait just a minute here."

Laura reached for his shirtsleeve and pulled him back.

"I have my own problems, Jesse," she said. "This one is of your own making. Because you chose to confront Brand in public, he's being forced to resign."

"Listen, I—"

"Because of your resentment and anger, those children's lives are being turned upside down. It's time you and Brand talked things out. You're still around because in your heart you want to get to know him."

"You're crazy, lady."

"I'm a lot of things, but crazy isn't one of them." She glanced up the drive and saw the children leading the horse behind them. "You are taking those children home and while you're at it, use the opportunity to talk to Brand. Listen to him when he tells you what happened to him and your mother. Think of someone besides yourself. You've hurt him deeply and if that's what you wanted, you've won. Now maybe it's time you try and make something good happen."

When he sighed and rubbed his jaw, she could see that he was weighing her words.

The McCormick children were back. Janie was trying to balance both bundles as Sam held the reins.

"Give me those," Laura said, taking the bundles and sticks from Janie. "Now Jesse is going to let you ride on his horse while he walks you home."

"We're gonna be in trouble," Sam mumbled.

"You shoulda thought of that before you ran away," Jesse told him just before he grabbed Sam around the waist and hoisted him up into the saddle. The grumbling stopped immediately.

"Me too! I wanna ride too!" Janie started jumping up and down, holding her arms up to Jesse.

He looked at Laura. "Thanks a lot."

"Anytime."

Once Janie was securely settled, Laura handed Jesse both bundles.

"Have a nice walk," she said.

As Jesse grudgingly led his horse down the driveway, Laura listened to their exchange.

"What's his name, Jesse?" Janie reached down to stroke the horse's mane.

"Horse."

"Will you teach me to shoot?" Sam wanted to know.

"No."

If she hadn't been so bone tired and drained, Laura would have smiled.

Brand was ushering Timothy and Mary Margaret Cutter out of the house when he saw Jesse leading his horse up the street. Both Sam and Janie were mounted in the saddle.

"Why, that looks like *him*," Mary Margaret stood aghast at the top of the porch stairs. "What's he doing with your children?"

"Jim who?" Timothy squinted down the street.

Mary Margaret shouted in his ear, "Not Jim. *Him*. The one that started all the fuss."

The fuss Mary Margaret referred to was the reason why the two of them had come to call. They assured Brand they were on his side come what may, but as members of the board, they were very concerned about the future of the church.

"Thank you so much for stopping by," he told them. Distracted by the sight of Jesse with the children, Brand added, "Things will work out for the best."

One way or another, he thought. *One way or another.*

Mary Margaret and Timothy negotiated the steps, supporting each other as they moved along the uneven walk. Brand escorted them out to the street, where they bid him good-bye, though Mary Margaret stalled a bit as she watched Jesse approach with the children. She gave Jesse a cool nod and hooked her arm into her husband's elbow.

As they walked away, Timothy shouted to his wife, "Are you sure his name is Jim? I thought it was something else."

It was a second or two before Brand realized Jesse was holding two small bundles. He handed them over to Brand.

"What's this?" Brand recognized Janie's doll named Sadie. It was stuffed into the top of one of the packs.

"Their things. They ran away."

Brand cradled the bundles in the crook of his arm. Everything his children valued fit inside two flour sacks.

"Look, Papa! I'm riding Jesse's horse named Horse," Janie cried.

Sam beamed. "Janie wiggled all over. Jesse told me since I'm older I had to hang on to her so she didn't fall off and break her neck."

Jesse reached for Janie first. She giggled as he swung her down. It was obvious from his expression that bringing them back wasn't his idea. But when he set Sam on his feet, Jesse said, "Nice work, sport."

Sam seemed to grow an inch.

Brand saw Laura's hand in this fragile camaraderie between his children. Somehow she'd managed to bridge the gap. He was filled with an intense longing to see her.

"I'm sorry they've pestered you again," Brand apologized. "They talk about you all the time."

"Somebody ought to keep a better eye on them," Jesse advised.

"Things have been in a bit of upheaval around here."

The children, he noticed, were staring up at Jesse as if he'd hung the moon.

Just then, the front door opened and Charity appeared on the porch.

"Look, Aunt Charity, this is Jesse," Sam said proudly.

"So I see," Charity came down the steps to join them in front of the house.

"He's our half-a-brother," Janie told her. "Yours, too, I 'spose."

"Actually, he's my nephew." She smiled up at Jesse. "I'm your Aunt Charity. Welcome."

Jesse nodded and tugged his hat brim. "Ma'am."

Charity turned to the children. "Why don't you two run inside and set another place at the table?"

"A place for Jesse?" Sam's eyes went wide.

Charity nodded. Without her having to tell them twice, they ran off to do her bidding.

Once they were gone she said, "I was just a little girl when … when your mother's family left town. If I'd have understood what was going on back then, I could have given Brand the information that might have helped him find your mother. Our father paid your grandfather to take Sarah away and ensure none of you were ever found. He did his job well. It was as if your family never existed."

She made an attempt to reach for Jesse's hand and then stopped

and dropped her gaze. "I'm so very sorry," she whispered. "If I'd
only known—"

Brand waited for Jesse to comment, but his son merely shifted
and appeared uncomfortable.

Charity eventually found her voice and a smile. "I've fixed an
early supper," she said. "We'd be pleased if you'd stay."

"I don't think—" Jesse started to refuse.

"The children would love to have you here," Brand said.

Jesse hesitated, tapping the horse's reins against his thigh.
Brand gently placed his hand on Jesse's shoulder. He felt the young
man stiffen and fully expected to have his touch shrugged off. A
silent second passed and then another before Jesse slowly relaxed.

"I'd like you to stay too, son," Brand said.

When Jesse turned to Brand, his jaw was tight, his eyes suspiciously bright. He cleared his throat before he turned to Charity.

"I 'spect it would be all right. Mrs. Foster won't be needing me
any time soon."

"Wonderful. I'll go in and have the children wash up." Charity hurried inside and left the men alone. "Don't dawdle out here,
you two."

Brand showed Jesse where to tether his horse. Silence hung
heavy between them as Brand struggled to find common ground.
He thought immediately of Laura, as he did most every hour of
every day.

"How is Mrs. Foster?" He asked.

Jesse paused, appearing uncertain. "She went for a drive this
morning with Mrs. Larson. When she came back she looked upset.
Like she'd been bawling about something—"

"Laura? Crying?"

"Not in front of me." Jesse took off his black hat, wiped his
brow with his forearm. "She pretended to be fine, but her eyes were
all red and puffy. She was in some kind of a mood, that's for sure.
I'm hoping it was none of your doing." He eyed Brand suspiciously.

"I haven't seen her for days," Brand admitted.

"You think that might be part of the problem?"

Brand's first impulse was to rush to Laura's. He very nearly excused himself and told Jesse to tell Charity to start dinner without him, but Jesse looked uncomfortable enough as it was. Brand figured Jesse might take off at the least provocation.

"Do you have any idea what might be wrong?" he asked.

Jesse checked the reins he'd looped around the hitching post, made certain they were tight. Then he rubbed his hand across his jaw for a second before he met Brand's gaze head on.

"No idea." He shrugged. "If you care so much, maybe you ought to go see for yourself."

EIGHTEEN

After Jesse left with the children, Laura went upstairs to wash her face and hands, then brushed out her hair and pinned it up into a simple chignon. She changed into a fresh gown, a simple, demure day dress of dark blue with a round collar, long sleeves, and cuffs trimmed in dove-gray piping.

The entire time she was freshening up, she thought about Amelia's suggestion that she tell Brand the truth. It might only be a matter of time before he heard it from someone else anyway.

She rested her elbow on the dressing table, covered her eyes with her hand. If she were a praying woman, this would be the time, but she knew nothing of God. She'd never even opened a Bible and didn't even own one. There had been no curiosity about God on her part. She was certain that He did not exist. Not for her, anyway. She went to church on Sunday to keep up appearances. Nothing more.

She raised her head, turned away from her reflection in her dressing table mirror, and hurried downstairs.

"Is Jesse back?" she asked Rodrigo.

When he told her that as far as he knew, the hired hand hadn't returned, Laura hurried outside. There was no sign of Jesse in the carriage house. She wondered what was keeping him. Brand's house was across town, but easily within walking distance.

She hoped it hadn't been a mistake to send him off with Brand's children.

She stared down the empty drive at Main Street. She pictured the children, their short, skinny legs sticking out over the sides of Jesse's horse. They'd left with him so trustingly.

It suddenly occurred to her that if Jesse wanted to get back at Brand for abandoning him and his mother, what better way than through his younger children?

Practically at a run, she started down the drive. When she reached the street, she slowed but didn't stop. Late-afternoon shadows appeared to grow longer as she passed the livery and reached the boardwalk. Trying not to panic, she searched for Jesse's horse among those tied up along Main. All she could recall was that his horse was brown and little else. Before she knew it, she realized she was about to pass by the Silver Slipper.

She lifted the hem of her skirt, about to cross to the other side of the street, when Collier came strolling casually through the open doors of the saloon.

"Well, well, well." He slowly looked her over. "Look who's here."

"I'm *not* here. I'm just passing by."

"That hurts, Lovie. Just passing by? I can't believe you wouldn't stop in to say hello."

Too late, she realized she'd run out without a hat or her reticule. She reached up, tucked a loose curl behind her ear. She felt her face flame as he slowly perused her modest dove-gray gown and then smiled.

"My, my. That schoolmarm costume certainly does something for you—Mrs. Foster. Very intriguing. Sparks my imagination."

"It's not a schoolmarm *costume*, thank you." She made a move to walk away but he stepped in front of her.

"Hold on a minute. What's the rush? I honored your request. I've steered clear of you, but now here you are in front of my saloon. I'd say that's more than a consequence."

"I told you I have my own business to attend to. Now let me pass."

"I've given you plenty of time. Am I going to have to resort to blackmail to make you realize this is where you belong? Keep the damn boardinghouse if it means so much to you. You can run both places."

"I'm not going to change my mind, Collier. That's final."

"Then don't blame me if word gets out about who and what you are. One way or another, I want you here and I mean to have you."

She felt her insides turn to ice water. She was aware of movement on the street, but wasn't about to take her eyes off of Collier.

"Aren't you even a *bit* curious to see what I've done to the place?" He nodded toward the front door.

"No. I'm in a hurry—"

"Laura?"

She recognized Brand's voice and looked up in time to see him swing out of his saddle. Dressed completely in black, wearing his white collar, he looked every inch a handsome gentleman preacher as he closed the gap between them.

Please, please, no. Not now.

She tried to wish Brand away.

"Are you all right?" He stared down into her eyes in a way that made her want to melt into him and let him carry her away from Collier's knowing leer. "You look a bit pale."

Instead of bringing relief, his appearance only compounded her anxiety. Not to mention Collier's threat.

"Did the children get home?" she asked.

He nodded. "They did. Thank you for sending them home with Jesse."

"I was worried about them, thinking perhaps I'd made the wrong decision, sending them back alone with him—"

"Not at all. In fact, he stayed for dinner. He should be returning soon. I was just on my way over to thank you."

He studied Collier, obviously waiting for an introduction. Laura couldn't bring herself to say anything.

Collier offered his hand. "I'm the new owner of the Silver Slipper. Collier Holloway."

Weak in the knees, Laura held her breath.

The men shook hands. Brand introduced himself.

"Nice to meet you, Preacher." Collier's manners were smooth as silk.

Unfortunately, Laura knew when he appeared to be behaving that he was at his most dangerous.

She found Brand studying her far too closely.

"Will you walk me home?" Anxious to get home and to get him away from Collier, she took hold of Brand's arm.

"Of course." He didn't smile as he tipped the brim of his hat in Collier's direction and then walked her to the edge of the boardwalk to collect his horse.

She knew Collier would take note of her familiarity. Sure enough, when she looked back at the gambler, Collier smiled and gave a slight nod. If he wanted to hurt her, all he had to do was use Brand.

"Have a nice evening, *Mrs. Foster*," Collier said. "Stop by again anytime. You, too, Preacher."

Brand led his horse as they walked along in silence, each of them lost in thought for a few strides. When they finally spoke, it was at the same instant.

"I did *not* stop by that place—"

"You seem upset—"

She tightened her fingers on his sleeve, knew she should let go, but didn't.

"I was worried about the children. I hope you aren't mad about Jesse."

"On the contrary. I'm very thankful you sent them home with him. When Charity first invited him to supper, he refused, but then he changed his mind. When I saw him sitting there at the table with us, I knew the problems he brought into our lives paled in comparison with what I've gained, and I have you to thank for it. You could have turned your back on him, left him lying in the street, but you took him in and now you've brought us together. Thank you doesn't seem nearly enough."

If only she could put her own life back together that easily.

"I think deep down, he's a good-hearted young man." For the moment, Laura tried not to dwell on Collier and what havoc he might cause in all their lives. "All Jesse's ever wanted is to know you, to have you acknowledge him."

They were nearing the boardinghouse and she slowed her steps. She didn't want Brand to walk away and leave her there alone. She couldn't bear to tell him good-bye.

"Thank you for walking me back," she said, making no move to turn toward the house.

"I've missed you, Laura."

She looked into his eyes and the undisguised desire was there again. She could no more deny it than she could the air she needed to exist.

"Oh, Brand." She wished she could tell him how much she'd missed him. That she thought of him with every passing hour.

"Tell him the truth."

Amelia's words came to her.

Brand started walking again. She fell in beside him as they crossed the street.

"I heard that you went out with Amelia this afternoon and returned upset," Brand said.

Had Amelia spoken to him already? What exactly did he know?

She knew that he must have heard it from Jesse when he asked, "Did that have anything to do with that man, Holloway?"

She nearly lost her footing but then caught herself. "Of course not."

"He seemed to be playing loose with your feelings, Laura. As if he had the right."

"He has absolutely *no* rights where I'm concerned," she said a bit too harshly. "Not anymore."

Brand stopped walking. He wanted to say more, she could tell, but he didn't. They had nearly reached her drive. The sun was hurrying toward the horizon. She'd missed tea. It would soon be time to dine with her guests.

"So you do know him."

Afraid of saying too much, she said absolutely nothing.

"What is it, Laura? Please, let me help you."

She shook her head.

Tell him.

She let go of his arm, prepared to walk away. He had enough worries of his own. "Everything is fine," she said.

He reached for her hand, kept her there with the merest touch.

"I'd do anything for you. I hope you know that."

She tried to don a carefree smile. An image of the Ellenberg family gathered together in their humble sitting room earlier came to her—a vignette of a life that was but a distant, faded memory for her. Thinking about the scene she'd witnessed, their shared laughter and joy, caused her smile to waver. It was the kind of life that was as out of reach for her as the moon.

Unable to deny herself, she reached up, patted the lapel of his coat, and smoothed her hand along the black fabric.

"Go home to your children and hold them close, Brand. And don't worry about me. I can take care of myself."

B rand waited until she disappeared into the house before he mounted up and headed back down Main Street. He slowed his horse to a walk as he rode by the Silver Slipper, but he didn't see any sign of Collier Holloway. Until he had more information, he wasn't about to make another scene. That was the last thing his battered reputation needed right now.

There was something Laura wasn't telling him; he was sure

of it. She'd tried to reassure him that everything was fine, but she couldn't disguise the haunted look in her eyes.

She was anything but fine.

He was tempted to go back and demand she tell him what was wrong, but with a woman as headstrong as Laura, he figured that would be the worst thing he could do. He hated leaving her, hated not being there to help.

He rode past the *Gazette* building. It was dark inside and there was no sign of Hank. Amelia had been with Laura earlier. If anyone could tell him what was wrong, it was her.

He nudged his horse into a trot and headed toward the Larson house. When he arrived, Hank and Amelia were just finishing up their evening meal. He sat down at the table and unable to resist sweets, opted for a piece of apple cobbler.

"So what brings you here, Brand?" Hank hooked his arm around the back of his chair. "Some good news for a change, I hope."

"Jesse ended up having supper with us today." He went on to explain how Jesse came to be at the house—how Janie and Sam had "run away" to Laura's and how she'd sent them all home together.

"Good for her," Hank said. "She's not one to shy away from anything."

"How is Charity?" Amelia asked. Brand noticed she seemed quieter than usual and often lost in thought.

"She invited Jesse to stay to supper. She let him know he was welcome any time."

They chatted awhile longer as he finished off his apple cobbler and complemented Amelia.

"Would you like more coffee?" she offered.

"No, thanks. I've got to be going." He stood up, collected his hat. "Before I leave, I'd like to speak to you about Laura. If I may?"

Amelia seemed so hesitant that Brand became certain something had, indeed, happened on their outing. Something Laura wasn't willing to tell him. His gut twisted. Amelia glanced over at Hank and smiled.

"Excuse us, would you, dear? I'll walk Brand out alone."

"Should I be jealous?" Hank teased.

"Only if I'm not back within the hour." She walked Brand to the door and they stepped out onto the porch.

Brand thought he'd have to initiate the conversation, but Amelia surprised him.

"Have you spoken to Laura this afternoon?" she asked.

"I just left her," he admitted.

"And?"

"Jesse mentioned he thought she was upset earlier, so I was intent on seeing her. I was on my way to her place when I ran into her on the street talking to a man named Collier Holloway outside the Silver Slipper. It was such an unlikely place to find her—"

Amelia couldn't hide her alarm. "Did she say why she was there?"

"She said she'd been out looking for Jesse, that she wanted to make certain he'd brought the children home."

"That's all?"

"Yes."

"Well, then," Amelia didn't look at all relieved.

"If she's in danger, I need to know, Amelia."

"You need to talk to Laura, Brand, not me."

"So she *is* in danger."

"I don't think so. At least, she's not worried about anyone harming her."

"But she's worried about something."

"I really can't say."

"Harrison Barker said she has been corresponding with a man in New Orleans—"

Amelia stopped him. "I know how much you care about her, but there's really nothing I am at liberty to tell you. You need to talk to Laura."

"I've been hesitant to lay my troubles at her doorstep."

"You've both been trying to protect each other when what you need is to lean on each other."

"What are you saying?"

"Love is the strongest thing there is, Brand. You know that. I've heard you preach that over and over. Love and forgiveness." She took his hands, gave them a squeeze, and then let go. "Go see Laura tomorrow. Take her somewhere where you can talk in private. Tell her how you feel—"

"But with everything that's happening—"

"None of that matters. She needs to know how much you care about her."

"Of course, but what are you hiding, Amelia? What has you so upset?"

"Laura is my friend, Brand. I can't say any more. The rest is up to the two of you."

NINETEEN

Laura awoke long before dawn the next day feeling completely out of sorts. By the time breakfast was cleared, she had the urge to hit something.

She bid the Hernandez men carry the dining room carpet out back and hang it wrong side out on the clotheslines behind the carriage house, out of view of the guestroom windows. There, she felt free to take out her pent-up anxiety on the Peshawar rug without anyone watching.

A good ten minutes went by as she whacked and pounded, wielding the carpet beater against the hand-knotted threads, taking great satisfaction in each muffled thump.

She finally rested for a second, rolled her head to stretch her neck and shoulders, and then drew her arm back to start again.

"Is it dead yet?"

With all her weight behind her swing, she nearly toppled head first into the carpet when Jesse appeared without warning. He chuckled when she spun around and pushed her hair back out of her eyes.

"That's not funny," she grumbled. "You frightened me."

"You look all right to me."

Though his coloring was darker than his father's, his wide, confident smile reminded her so much of Brand's she had to look away.

"I'm fine."

"Good, because you've got company." He jerked his head toward the carriage house. "The preacher is coming up the drive."

She didn't want to see Brand. Not now. Not after yesterday afternoon and certainly not while she was looking like a fishwife in a simple cotton gown fit only for dirty work. There was dust in her hair and no doubt all over her face.

"Tell him I'm not here."

"You want me to lie to him for you?"

"Tell him I'm not seeing anyone right now. Tell him I'm too busy. Tell him it's impossible. Tell him—"

"Tell me yourself."

Brand came around the corner of the carriage house, leading not only his horse but also a brown mare with a star on her forehead. As he paused to give her a lingering look, Laura blew a stray curl out of her right eye. She lifted the carpet beater and shrugged.

"As you can see, I'm busy."

Beside her, Jesse said, "Busy beating a carpet to death."

When he walked away whistling, Laura wished she could escape as easily.

Undaunted by her excuses, Brand came toward her. His eyes never left her face.

"It's far too beautiful a day to be working so hard. I came to see if you'd spend an hour or so with me. Charity packed us a picnic. I thought we could take a ride south of town. There's something I'd like to show you."

He was tempting. She'd give him that. Too tempting now that he'd shed his usual black coat and was wearing a butternut-colored jacket and a light-blue shirt. Without his clerical collar, it was easy to forget what he was, forget who they were. She reminded herself to hold fast to her resolve.

She glanced at the horses behind him.

"I don't ride."

"You're a Texas woman now. It's high time you learned. We'll take it slow. It's not far."

"Really, Brand, I can't."

She expected him to say something witty. To try and cajole her with a smile. Instead, without warning, he reached for her hand. The shock of his touch still disturbed her more than anything he could say.

"Please, Laura. Come with me."

"Please. Come with me." Such a simple request.

She remembered Amelia saying, *"He needs you more now than ever."*

Brand McCormick needed more than she could ever give. He needed someone he could love who loved him in return without reservation. A woman whose past was as spotless as new fallen snow.

Once they were alone, away from the house and any interruptions, she'd have no excuse not to tell him the truth.

"All right," she said, suddenly nervous. "I'll go. But I can only spare an hour or so."

He gave her hand a squeeze.

"Just let me run inside and get a hat." She turned and he walked beside her toward the house.

"A pair of old gloves, too, if you have them," he suggested.

"I'm not certain I can do this." She caught herself thinking aloud and quickly glanced up to see if he had heard.

"Don't worry. I won't let you fall." Obviously he thought she was talking about riding.

I already have, Brand. I've already fallen.

She expected riding to be more difficult, but the hardest part was mounting the horse. Brand had rented a mare from the livery and asked for a side saddle. He told her that Big Mick Robinson, the smithy, had rolled his eyes at the request.

"Any female worth her salt doesn't ride sidesaddle. At least that's what Big Mick claims." Brand made certain the horse didn't

move as Laura tried to mount from the chopping block near the
woodpile.

Getting her left foot up into the stirrup while keeping her skirt
hem and petticoats down was more of a challenge than actually settling into the saddle. Once she was there, she grabbed the pommel
with both hands and held tight.

"From up here, the ground looks very far away. And hard." She
was afraid to move.

Brand walked around the horse. Before he slipped her right
foot into the stirrup, he adjusted a series of straps and buckles while
Laura concentrated on keeping her balance. Brand then walked
Laura's horse around the yard so that she could get the feel of the
saddle and the sway of the animal beneath her. He gave her cursory
instruction and then turned the reins over.

Finally they were off, walking the horses across the open plain.
When she felt more comfortable, Brand tried a slow trot and Laura
bobbed up and down until her hat almost flew off. She was afraid
to let go of the reins to hold it down.

Without thinking, she yelled, "Help!"

When she saw Brand's face, she laughed.

"Very funny, Mrs. Foster," he said. "You just took a year off
my life."

She hadn't realized how completely vulnerable they were out in
the open until she saw him recover from his concern. Suddenly the
grove of trees ahead wasn't as inviting.

"Are we in any danger of running into Indians?" she asked.

"The Comanche haven't raided this area for a couple of sum-
mers now. This time of year, the renegades start heading back to
the reservation to let the government feed them for the winter."

"You don't wear a gun."

"No."

"Do you carry one in your saddle bag?"

"No."

She wondered if he thought he could look a renegade Comanche in the eye and pray him to death. She'd brought along a hat but not her reticule. Now she found herself wishing she'd brought it and her derringer along.

"I wouldn't have brought you out here if I thought it would put you in harm's way."

"I know, but—" She quickly realized she was only looking for an excuse to turn back and put off the inevitable.

"Laura, don't worry."

"I won't." She figured it would be easier to face a whole tribe of Comanche than to do what had to be done.

The land seemed to roll on forever, unbroken except where trees crowded around water sources. She spent most of the ride staring straight ahead, holding tight to the reins, but now and again Laura braved a look at Brand. He seemed to have relaxed once they left Glory behind. Now and again, his eyes met hers and he smiled.

"Where exactly are we going?" In many ways, she hoped they never reached the mysterious destination. If she hadn't been so uncomfortable and in need of a stretch, she'd have been content to ride beside him forever.

"We're almost there." Brand pointed to a spot where cottonwoods and mesquite lined a meandering stream.

He dismounted and helped her down. For a moment she didn't think she could take a step on her own. He gently held her arm and started to lead her to a rock so she could sit in the shade.

"Oh, no," she shook her head. "From that saddle to a rock? I prefer to walk around a bit first."

"Stretch your legs while I unpack the picnic."

As he began to pull a surprising amount of carefully wrapped food items out of his saddle bags, Laura strolled along the stream. The water level was low, more than a trickle, less than a rushing waterway. She marveled at the crystal clarity of the water. It shimmered with glints of sunlight as it rippled over multicolored stones.

She walked down into the bare rocky section of the streambed, then moved closer to the center where the water ran two feet wide

204 JILL MARIE LANDIS

and six inches deep at the most. Careful to keep the hem of her skirt out of the water, she knelt on the rocks and dipped her fingers into the stream.

The water was cooler than she expected. She thought it would have been warmed by the rocks. She lifted her fingers to her lips, smelled, and then tasted the moisture there.

Footsteps crunched on the rocks behind her. Brand's shadow merged with hers. She looked up, saw him silhouetted against the sun.

He handed her a tin cup. "Thirsty?"

"Thank you."

There had been streams, rivers, dense forests of green near her cottage in the Irish countryside, but her life in New Orleans had been that of a city dweller. The act of dipping a tin cup into a trickling stream had become a novelty.

"What are you thinking about?" Brand had hunkered down beside her, watched as she took long swallows of water until the cup was empty.

"About how long it's been since I've had fresh water directly from a stream."

"How long?" He reached out and tucked a curl behind her ear.

It was a spontaneous gesture. She could tell he was as surprised by it as she and so she didn't step away.

"A very, very long time." She tried to keep the sadness from her tone. Soon enough, she told herself. There will be enough time for regret and sorrow after he learned of her past. For now, she would enjoy their picnic and the stunning fall day.

"Everything's ready." He rose and offered his hand, ever the perfect gentleman.

She let him help her up, stifled a groan, and tried not to think of the ride back to town.

He had spread a plaid-wool blanket on the ground in the shade. Assorted packages were stacked in the center. There was another cup and a bottle of sarsaparilla. Laura stood at the edge of the blanket taking in every detail, tucking the memory deep in her heart so that whenever loneliness crept up on her she could take it out and remember this moment.

"Is something wrong?" he wanted to know.

"I've never been on a picnic before," she said softly.

"Never?"

"Not that I can recall."

"Then I'm happy that you're sharing your first with me. Charity will be pleased too. She wanted to make certain everything was perfect. If it was up to her, she'd have packed the good china."

He knelt on the edge of the blanket and began unwrapping the bundles tied in butcher paper. "She sent along some cold beef, bread, cheese, and some apples."

"I'll be sure to thank her." Laura lowered herself to the opposite side of the blanket, untied her hat, and set it down beside her. As the sun bathed her face, she leaned back on her hands. Suddenly she was starving. "It looks wonderful. Being outdoors has whetted my appetite."

"No doubt attacking that rug the way you did helped too," he laughed.

"No doubt."

She ate slowly, aware of his nearness, as well as the fact that they were completely alone. There was no need to remind herself that she was safe in his company. She had nothing to fear from this man. Each time he passed her a hunk of bread, a piece of cheese or beef, she waited in anticipation for the touch of his hand.

There was no sound except for the hush of breeze across the land, the whisper of leaves in the cottonwood trees, the lilting sound of water bubbling around stone. Her heart cherished the peaceful moment, a respite both precious and stolen from their busy days and hectic lives.

Laura paused often to glance over at Brand. Each time she found him gazing at her.

"How did you find this spot?" She flushed and broke the silence.

"Joe Ellenberg brought my family out here one day. You haven't seen the best part yet."

"Which is?"

"Not far away."

The sun's warmth seeped through her cotton gown. If she were alone, she would be tempted to lie back, feel the sunshine on her face, and forget her worries. But she was not alone and she had worries that couldn't be forgotten, so she sat primly on her side of the blanket and finished her portion of the midday meal.

Brand wrapped the leftover bread. When everything but the blanket had disappeared back into his saddlebags, he held out his hand. Laura gazed up into his eyes, slipped her hand into his, and let him draw her to her feet.

She stood before him, unmoving, unable to think of anything but his nearness. For a moment she thought he was going to kiss her. Her breath caught.

But Brand didn't move. He held tight to her hand, cleared his throat, and then stepped back.

"Bring your hat," he advised softly. She reached for the wide-brimmed straw bonnet she'd borrowed from Anna. When she fumbled with the ties, he brushed her hands aside and tied a bow beneath her chin.

"Perfect," he said with a smile. "Now, for the surprise. Actually, it's not all that much. I may have been overly enthusiastic."

"What do you mean?"

He shrugged. "For a woman who's probably seen the world, it's not very spectacular —"

"I haven't seen much of the world, actually."

"Someone like you? I can't believe that." He held out his hand with familiarity, and she could not resist giving him her own as she walked beside him. He was careful to measure his stride to match hers.

"We're walking up the stream just a ways."

She was thankful for the shade of her hat brim. The walk was a bit farther than she had expected. They stopped when they neared a gathering of stones on their side of the stream.

"We're here." He indicated the collection of large rocks and boulders along the stream bed.

"Is this it?" She wondered what she was missing.

He pulled her up to the rocks and pointed to the surface of the nearest. "Look closely."

She bent closer, noticed the rock was covered with indentations—spirals, swirls, outlines of sea shells, imprints of ferns and plants. She traced the patterns with her fingertips, braced her hand on the top of the rock as she bent down to get a better look.

"Fossils?" She had read about such things, but never hoped to see one. She straightened and noticed all the rocks in the immediate area were covered with them.

"Joe thinks a flood or a storm unearthed them long ago. He and his father came upon them one day and marveled at this evidence of the sea having once been here in the middle of Texas. Hattie claims they are proof of the Great Flood."

"Ah," she said as if she knew what Great Flood he was talking about.

They walked from rock to rock. She stopped to wonder and admire stones older than she could imagine. Now and again traced the impressions with her fingertips.

He was standing beside her, near enough to feel his warmth, to hear him breathe. She was aware of everything—the clear, warm fall air, the sound of the brittle dry grass moving as the wind skimmed through it. The song of the stream.

Most of all, she was aware of Brand.

She looked over her shoulder, met his eyes.

"They are a wonderful surprise, the fossils," she told him. "I'll always remember this day."

And you. No matter what happened, she promised herself, she would never forget this day.

B rand was lost in the depths of her eyes, thrilled that seeing the fossils and sharing the simple picnic had pleased her. He saw it in the way her eyes shone up at him, the way her smile played around her lips, teasing her dimples into view.

He was tempted to kiss her, but before he could, she turned and walked on to inspect another boulder covered with impressions. This time when she paused, she clasped her hands together and kept her back to him. He watched her shoulders rise and fall on a heavy sigh.

"Something happened yesterday," he said, gently touching her shoulder. She turned to him again. "I wish you trusted me enough to tell me what upset you."

He stared out over the rolling landscape, picturing the man he'd met in front of the Silver Slipper. Collier Holloway was tall and dark, and women probably considered him handsome in a rakish way.

Brand took a deep breath. "If there's someone else —"

Her answer was swift and certain. "No. No one else."

"Marry me, Laura."

"What?" Her color faded. She looked as shocked as he was.

The proposal had slipped out without warning, but there was no way he was going to take it back. He knew the obstacles, but the offer had come from his heart, from his very soul.

"I've no right to ask or to expect you to say yes when my future is so uncertain, but I believe God brought us together, Laura. I love you —"

"Don't," she said, touching her fingers to his lips. "Please, don't. I can't marry you, Brand."

She reached up and tenderly cupped his cheek. Her eyes glistened with unshed tears.

"Are you still mourning your husband?"

"No, definitely not. I simply can't marry anyone," she whispered.

She hesitated, pale as ash, then closed her eyes and raised a hand to her temple.

"Are you all right?" He took hold of her elbow and led her to a rock, guided her to a sitting position.

"What is it? Are you ill?"

She was shaking so hard that she held her hands together in her lap to stop their trembling. He sat beside her, covered her hands with his own. Despite the warmth of the sun, her fingers were as cold as ice.

"I'll get the horses and we'll start back." He wanted to get her back safely. She was definitely not well.

"No, please, Brand. I have something I want to tell you. Something I should have told you weeks ago. I can't let the beauty of this day or your kindness dissuade me any longer."

He asked no questions. He simply waited for her to go on.

"It's about me. About who I was before I came to Texas." She pulled her hands out from beneath his, unlaced her fingers, and then wound them together again. Her gaze never left his eyes. She spoke slowly, haltingly, as if each and every word was painful to utter.

"I was born in Ireland. When the famine came, my family immigrated to New Orleans. I was ten years old. My parents and my three younger sisters and I moved in with my uncle and aunt in a section called the Irish Channel."

She must have seen he was unfamiliar with the area, for she went on to explain.

"That was a section of the city near the docks where the poor Irish lived. My father found work digging the canals that protect the place from storms and flooding. He caught yellow fever and died. We lost our mother shortly after him. My aunt and uncle couldn't afford to feed four extra mouths, so they sent my two youngest sisters to an orphanage."

"Oh, Laura." He started to slip his arm around her shoulders but she edged away. She was no longer looking at him. "You never saw them again?"

"No."

"It must have been terrible—"

"I wish that was all there was to it."

He could see that she was gathering the courage to go on. There was the briefest of pauses while they both looked up to watch a pair of red-tailed hawks circle overhead before the birds flew off together.

Her voice was barely above a whisper when she began again.

"My uncle sold me and my nine-year-old sister to what they call a sporting house—a place where men go to amuse themselves with women. I lived there most of my life."

He knew perfectly well what she meant. He was too stunned to speak as he tried to comprehend. His mind could not wrap itself around the idea of someone as genteel, as perfectly mannered and caring, as Laura in a brothel. Not now and most certainly not as a child.

Shock, anger, and disbelief warred inside him at the injustice of it. He stared at Laura, her finely etched profile, her delicate coloring and mannerisms.

She's a whore.

Reeling, he closed his eyes. He struggled to stop the images that assailed him; Laura in the arms of other men, countless, nameless, faceless other men. He shook his head.

No. It was all he could think. *Not Laura.*

When he opened his eyes again, he found her staring at him. Her face was drained of color. He could tell by her expression that his reaction had deeply wounded her. His silence had reinforced his shock louder than words.

She started to stand. He reached for her.

"Laura, stop."

When she tried to step away, he said, "Wait. I'm sorry. I'm so sorry."

She gave a slight shake of her head. "No. You don't need to apologize. Anyone would be reviled."

"Shocked, not reviled."

She looked down to where his hand was still gripping her upper arm.

"Please, sit back down," he encouraged. "Go on."

At first he thought she would refuse to stay, refuse to continue, but she sank back onto the rock as if she no longer had the strength to stand.

Brand fought to conceal his confusion. He didn't want her hurt any more than he'd already hurt her. Any more than she'd already been hurt by life. He'd been so proud of the way he'd counseled his flock. So certain of his role as not only their minister, but as a town leader and a man they all looked to for guidance.

First Jesse's appearance had shaken the foundation of his reputation, and now he had lost his heart to a woman who had just confessed to being a whore since childhood. Would loving Laura cost him his position and whatever standing he had left in Glory?

Above all, he wondered if his love could weather such horrific truth.

He struggled for words of consolation and found none.

Stunned, all he managed was, "It must have been horrible."

"Horrible doesn't come close to describing that first night. An innocent child is a prize the most vile of men will pay anything to use . . .

"My uncle told me I'd have fine clothes and everything a girl could want. But my sister and I were separated and when they dressed me up in satin and lace and tied my hair up in ribbons, I didn't enjoy my new treasures. I was taken downstairs into a grand salon where everything glittered, gold and crystal. Rich brocade covered the furnishings. I was forced to stand on a stool and sing a song. My voice shook as I sang a lullaby my mother used to lull us to sleep with. It's the only song I could remember right then.

"I was sold to the highest bidder. A man who ..." She rested her head on her hand and refused to meet his eyes. "A man who hurt me.

"I was a valuable commodity, so afterward I was given the best of care. An old woman, a slave, was there to care for the women of the house. She nursed me through the worst of it. I mistook her gentle care for friendship and begged her to help me escape — until I realized she would never give in. She was only doing as she was told, saving me so that I could be used again.

"I'm not sure what happened to my sister. I saw a man take her away and never laid eyes on her again. To this day I cling to the hope that she's still alive. There's no difference between the guilt I carry for what I became and the guilt of not being able to save her. I was the oldest, the one who was suppose to protect my sisters and I — " Her voice finally broke. "I couldn't save Megan. I couldn't save any of us."

"You were just a child yourself. What could you have done?"

"Something. I should have done *something*, but I didn't. I couldn't even pray for them.

"At first I hated the other women. I was determined not to become like them. I watched and waited, hoping to escape. Eventually I realized there was no escape. I discovered money was power. I thought that in order to leave that world behind and find my sisters, I would need as much money as I could make. As I grew older, I singled out the most sought-after women, the ones who had the most power over the patrons, and I learned from them. I made certain I became a favorite. I discovered what men desired most and gave it to them.

"I hardened my heart. I stopped feeling and escaped into a fantasy world where I dreamed of building a fine home and of finding my sisters. I dreamed we'd all be together again.

"I was torn, knowing I should escape that life at any cost, but I was a captive of the promise of a dream. I stayed until I had enough money to start my life over as someone else, someone new. But now I know that inside I'll always be that ruined child, that desperate young woman willing to sell herself. A young woman who became the very thing she so despised.

"When I left New Orleans, I changed my name to Laura Foster and didn't look back. But I'm still that woman, Brand. I'm still Lovie Lamonte. I'll never be free of my past or my sins. I know that now."

She wouldn't look up at him. Her shoulders were bent under the weight of her confession.

He fought the images her words conjured, but the horror was nearly overwhelming. The memories were something she would live with for the rest of her life. He found himself asking, *Now that I know, can I ever forget?*

He reached down, placed his hand beneath her chin, and raised her face so he could gently thumb aside her tears. When he looked into her eyes, he knew the answer.

"That's not who you are now," he whispered.

"But—"

"That isn't who you are, Laura. Not anymore."

"That's who I *was*, don't you see? And then I wouldn't quit until I had enough money to become completely independent, to surround myself with lovely things that would give the illusion I was wealthy, respectable, and beyond reproach. I was still a whore when I didn't have to be." She shook her head, her tone filled with long-pent anger. "What does that say about me? Amassing money meant more to me than walking away. More than freeing myself of the degradation and shame."

"You were a child when you were forced into that life. You grew up in a world not many women can even imagine, let alone survive. It colored your thinking, Laura. That poor, abused child grew up doing what she thought she had to do for her own survival. You've left that woman behind."

"I saw the look on your face when I began, Brand. I may have left the brothel behind, but I'll have to live with my past forever."

"God forgives, Laura. Never forget that."

She turned away and whispered, "Can you forgive me for not telling you before?"

Brand ached with the pain she was feeling. Seeing her there, so vulnerable and broken, he wanted nothing more than to take her in his arms and comfort her, to convince her that his heart was still hers alone.

"Of course. I can forgive you anything."

He watched her as she studied his face, searching his eyes for the truth. He could see that she didn't believe him. She shook her head, tried to deny his words of assurance.

"The past will always be dogging me, threatening my world and the people in it. I didn't set out to make friends like the Larsons or the Cutters or the Ellenbergs. Most of all, you. I can't have you or any of them hurt because of me. I can't ignore my past anymore now that Collier—" She stopped abruptly and dashed the tears from her cheeks.

"Holloway? Who is he to you, Laura? What hold does he have over you?"

"He threatened to tell you the truth."

"Is that why you're telling me now?"

"I couldn't let you hear it from him."

"Is Collier the man you were writing to in New Orleans?"

She shook her head. "No. I told you I was sold with my sister, Megan. She disappeared our first night in the brothel. One of the women later told me that Megan was purchased outright by a man from New Orleans."

Laura refused to look away from the undulating landscape. Her words were carried by the constant breeze blowing across the plains.

"Before I moved to Glory, I hired a detective to search for her, but I don't have much to go on. I doubt the man who bought her used his real name."

She paused, finally turning to face him. Brand was shaken by the fathomless pain in her eyes.

Before he could try to draw her close again she said, "The man I've been corresponding with in New Orleans is a Pinkerton detective I hired to search for Megan. Eventually I hope he'll find my two other sisters as well."

He remembered what Jesse had said about Laura appearing upset after her drive with Amelia.

"Amelia knows, doesn't she?"

"I told her yesterday." She refused to face him and continued to stare out over the open plain.

"What did she say?" He silently credited Amelia for keeping Laura's secret.

"The same thing you did. That I'm not that person anymore."

"But you don't believe us."

"People see us as the accumulation of all the things that we've been and done."

"That's no reason to give up trying to convince them otherwise," he told her.

"But look at you," she shook her head, her mouth a taut line. "You are a minister. Your life has completely changed since you were a young man. And yet what of your good Christian flock? You preach to them of forgiveness and they still condemn you."

She laughed. It was a brittle, hopeless sound. "Imagine their reactions when the truth comes out about me? If they can't forgive you, do you honestly believe those hypocrites will forgive me? When does it end, Brand? When have we paid enough?"

She touched her heart. "Even if by some miracle I was forgiven, no matter what I do, it's all still in here, Brand. All that shame. All those memories are in here no matter where I go or what I do. No matter who forgives me, I'll still carry them all with me."

So fragile, he thought. It was clear that the *other* Laura, the confident wealthy widow, masked a damaged, frightened child within. He tipped her face up again, forced her to look at him. He prayed she saw acceptance in his eyes, that she saw all the love he still felt for her. Then he slowly lowered his lips to her trembling mouth and kissed her.

She kissed him back at first. Then, with a small cry, she pushed him away and scrambled to her feet.

"How can you stand to touch me now?"

He rose, reached for her before she could walk away. Drew her into the circle of his arms and held her close.

"Because I love you, Laura, and I believe that you *will* find the strength it takes to truly turn your life around. Your life in Glory has been beyond reproach. You have already proven yourself to everyone who knows you. Ask for God's forgiveness."

He smoothed a curl back off her face, grazing her cheek with his fingertips. Her skin was smooth as satin, as flawless as rich cream.

"But—"

"Ask Him to forgive you."

"You make it sound so simple."

"Because it is."

He saw a glimmer of hope in her eyes, but it quickly flickered and died.

"There are still the town folk, not to mention your congregation, to consider. Some of them won't even forgive *you*, Brand. What I've done is so much worse."

"I want you to marry me, Laura. I know now why God led you to me. Even if we have to leave Glory and I have to give up my ministry, that's what I will do to have you with me."

"You can't mean that. Your children—"

"Will understand."

"I can't do that to you, Brand. To yourself or your family. After you've had time to think this through, you'll see that I'm right."

"I can't live without you."

"If there's one thing I'm certain of, it's that we have the strength to do whatever we have to in this life."

She turned her back to him and walked a few steps away. When she stopped, she stared out across the open plain. The breeze lifted her hair away from her face, exposing cheeks stained with tears. Her gaze was intent on the horizon.

He let her be until he saw her shoulders fall on a heavy sigh. The burden of keeping her secrets was a heavy one. Sharing them with him had taken a toll.

"Laura." He started toward her, determined to convince her that his love was steadfast.

She turned before he reached her. She tried to smile and failed.

"Please," she whispered, "take me home."

TWENTY

Somehow Laura endured dinner in the dining room that evening. Presiding over the table full of guests, she was able to smile and keep the cordial conversation moving, but throughout the meal she felt as if she were outside herself—watching the woman she had become pretend to be something she was not.

After dinner, she took a few moments to go over the breakfast menu with Rodrigo and then gave Anna instructions for the morrow. Alone in her room, she slipped into her long, white nightgown and tried to read, but when she found herself going over and over the same paragraph, she gave up. Even the antics of the women in the novel *Cranford* couldn't distract her tonight.

She carefully set aside the book and walked to the window, drew the drape back far enough to stare out into the darkness. The nights were growing colder, crisper. Soon it would be time to light fires in the fireplaces throughout the house. The harvest moon looked exceptionally close tonight, huge and golden. She sighed and let the drape fall back into place.

"Ask God to forgive you."

Lost, she looked around the room and for the first time found the opulence stifling. The heavy draperies at the window, the figurines scattered here and there on the tabletops, the gilt-framed oil paintings of still lifes and landscapes. For the first time she thought its overblown garishness all too reminiscent of a brothel.

She took a deep breath.

How? she wondered. *How do I pray?*

Could God enter a heart of stone?

She stopped pacing when she found herself at her bedside. Before she could change her mind, she knelt down, folded her hands, and rested them against the bed.

"God," she whispered, "if You are up there, I need Your help. I ... want to say I'm sorry."

She closed her eyes and pictured Brand and found it easier to pray for him than herself. She asked that he be able to stay in Glory. Sam and Janie deserved to grow up in this place they'd come to call home. She prayed that Brand and Jesse would one day get to know each other.

Finally she asked God for forgiveness and for the first time in her life, she didn't let herself question why she'd been given the life she'd led. She didn't curse the fact that she and Megan had been sold into darkness, or why her parents had to die. She concentrated on now.

When she got to her feet, however, she felt no different. She certainly felt no lighter than when she'd knelt down. There had been no lightening bolt of revelation, no voice from above, no sound of a heavenly choir filling the air.

There was only silence and the muffled tick of the grandfather clock downstairs.

The next morning Brand woke with a spring in his step and renewed determination. No longer was he fighting to save his own reputation and his position as minister of Glory's only church, to make certain his children's lives weren't uprooted. He was braced to stand behind Laura and make her his wife.

The thought of losing her was far worse than having to go before his church community and ask for their forgiveness and understanding. He knew the challenge ahead. He knew he had the faith to survive it.

It was up to him to convince not only his congregation but the entire town that both of them had proven themselves and deserved a second chance.

Losing Laura was something he couldn't fathom. He'd awakened this morning picturing Laura's face as she'd told him goodbye yesterday. Looking back, he realized that her smile had never really reached her eyes. Now he was anxious to see her, to make certain she was all right.

He whistled as he dressed, choosing his best coat, his new white shirt.

"You look good, Papa," Janie said, smiling up from her bowl of oatmeal as he walked into the kitchen.

He reached for a piece of dry toast and pulled out a chair. As he started spreading butter on the toast, he paused to smile at each of them in turn, Sam, Janie, and then Charity.

"I've asked Laura to marry me."

"Oh, Brand, that's ... that's wonderful." Charity didn't look quite as certain as she sounded.

"Three cheers for Papa!" Sam shouted. "Does that mean we get to live in her house? We'd see Jesse everyday."

Janie's eyes were wide as silver dollars. "Will we, Papa?"

Brand took a bite of toast as Charity set a cup of coffee beside him.

"I'm not sure where we will live." He realized he wasn't sure about anything, really. "I'm not even certain she'll say yes."

"But we're hopin', right Papa?"

"If we have 'ta move away, will she come with us?" Sam wondered.

He hadn't had time to think past proposing. He didn't know what they would do if he lost his position here. Would Laura want to leave the place she'd worked so hard for, suffered so much for to build? After hearing her story, he wasn't certain she would be able to walk away from her dream.

His sister was at his side with a bowl of oatmeal in hand. "Brand?"

"None for me, thank you," he said offhandedly.

"Are you all right?"

"I'm fine. I'm just anxious to see Laura." Brand noticed the children had finished eating. "Why don't you two collect your books? I'll walk you to school."

When they both jumped up and headed for their rooms, Brand walked over to where his sister was still fussing at the stove, stirring oatmeal that didn't need to be stirred.

"What's wrong, Charity?"

She shook her head but didn't answer. He put his hand on her shoulder, nudged her into turning around.

"I don't want to be a burden to you and Laura," she said.

"You're as much a part of this family as any of us." He gave her shoulder a squeeze and made sure she was listening. "You gave up your own life to help me when Jane died. Do you think I'd ever turn you out?"

"No, but Laura might not want to take in an old spinster aunt."

"Laura hasn't even agreed to marry me yet, but can you really see her *not* accepting you too?"

"I don't know her all *that* well."

"You'll get to know her and you'll see how wonderful she is." He held her at arms length and smiled. "Besides, you're hardly an old spinster. We both know you've turned down at least three proposals, Charity. You're still alone by choice."

"If I wasn't so afraid of ending up married to someone like Father I'd have accepted."

"I don't think there's any worry about that, do you?"

"What if I can't see past my own infatuation and end up with a controlling, overbearing, authoritative—"

He held up his hand. "I get the picture, Sis."

"You left for the Army," she reminded him. "I grew up under his thumb. I won't give up my freedom that easily just to be married, but I do long for children and a home of my own."

"How about I make you a promise," he said. "When you fall in love, I'll let you know if I think your man will turn out to be anything like our father."

"Promise?"

"I promise."

"Thanks, Brand."

"You're welcome."

He walked back to the table wondering what his sister would think when she found out about Laura's past. Would Charity question his own judgment? She might not be the best disciplinarian in the world, but she had raised and protected the children like a mother hen. Would she protest for their sakes?

Brand reached for his coffee, drank half of it before he set the cup down again. He called out to Sam and Janie, asked them to hurry.

"Be sure they take sweaters," Charity said. "There's still a bit of chill in the air."

He paused in the doorway, smiled. "I'll tell them. Don't worry. Everything is going to be fine."

"I'll pray that it is."

"Thank you, Sis. That's all we can do."

After walking the children to school, he headed through town. As he passed by the *Gazette* building, Hank waved him inside. He had a message from Amelia. There was to be a church board meeting that afternoon and Hank indicated Amelia was going to call for a vote of confidence so that the matter of Brand holding on to his position would be put to rest.

"She believes wholeheartedly that you will gain the board's vote of confidence and this whole issue about Jesse's mother will be behind you."

Brand wondered what Amelia, and Hank for that matter, would think of his proposal.

When he finally reached the boardinghouse, he expected Laura to answer her front door. Or if not her, then Anna Hernandez. When Rodrigo greeted him with his dark brows drawn tight, his expression one of confusion and worry, Brand's gut knotted.

"*Señor* Preacher," Rodrigo said. "Please. Come inside."

Once Brand stepped into the entry hall, the cook obviously didn't know how to proceed.

"Where's Mrs. Foster?" Brand glanced into the parlor first, then the dining room across the hall.

The portly Mexican's shoulders drooped. "She's not here, señor." He called for his wife and Anna came running. Her hand shook as she reached into her apron and pulled out a folded letter.

"My son, he read it to us earlier," Anna said softly. Her nut-brown eyes were huge and brimming with worry.

She handed the letter over. The familiar lavender scent wafted over Brand as he scanned the words.

> *To Whom It May Concern:*
>
> *Until further notice, Foster's Boardinghouse is to remain closed to business. I am sorry for any inconvenience this may cause travelers with reservations. I hereby appoint Rodrigo and Anna Hernandez as caretakers of the boardinghouse until further notice. They may continue to reside in their home on the property for as long as they wish.*
>
> *Sincerely,*
> *Laura Foster*

Brand stared at the letter, not knowing what to make of it. When he looked up at the Hernandezes, he saw they were equally baffled.

"She didn't say anything? Didn't tell you where she was going?" Rodrigo shook his head. "No, señor. *Nada*. She gave me a letter to deliver to the bank and other instructions, things I am to do for her."

Brand carefully folded the letter and handed it back to Anna. There was still no explanation of where Laura may have gone or when.

"Did she give you the letters personally?"

Anna nodded. "Yes, this morning. When we first stepped into the kitchen. She had one bag packed with her things. We were to feed the guests breakfast and then tell them the place was closing. That they had to leave." She rolled her eyes. "Some of them were not happy."

"Did you drive her to the stage?" Brand calculated how long Laura might have been gone if she'd caught an early ride. It would be easy enough to find out where she was headed. Harrison Barker's store was the stage stop.

Rodrigo shook his head. "She would not let me. She said it was not necessary."

"Don't tell me she simply walked away?"

If so, surely someone must have seen her on the street. How far could a woman get on foot?

Anna glanced at Rodrigo before she added, "She told us to stay here. To wait three hours before we went out or spoke to anyone. She did not want to be followed."

"Where is Jesse?" Brand glanced toward the back of the house. "Does he know where she is? Did he take her somewhere?"

Rodrigo shook his head. "He went to hunt wild turkey yesterday afternoon. He was not sure when he would return."

"She may have run into him, hired him to escort her out of town," Brand said. "Did she ..." He was forced to clear his throat before he could go on. "Did she leave a letter for me?"

Rodrigo slowly shook his head. "Nada, señor. Nada."

Nothing. No word. No letter.

"What should we do, señor?" Rodrigo asked.

Brand thought for a moment. "Do as she asked. Take care of

the place and stay in your house out back. Deliver the letter to the Cutters and make sure Hank Larson sees the letter she left you. That way no one will question your being here. He'll know how to advise you. Maybe the Cutters should keep your letter in the bank vault until Laura returns."

He figured if she had left instruction for the Cutters, she had provided funds for the Hernandezes as well to keep the boarding-house in order.

But where was she? How had she disappeared so quickly?

And when, if ever, would she be back?

Shaken, Brand thanked the couple, left them as worried and bewildered as he. Once he'd stepped outside onto the veranda, he stared down Main Street, weighing his options.

He hesitated going straight to the mercantile to ask Harrison if she'd purchased a stagecoach ticket. He might just as well stand in the middle of the street and announce that Laura had suddenly left town.

He would go to Amelia first. Laura had chosen to tell her friend the truth about her past. Perhaps she had also confided in Amelia about where she was going and when she'd return.

Within minutes he was at the Larson's front door. He rapped on the wood frame, praying Amelia would answer. When she opened the door, he was so relieved he could barely string a sentence together.

"Have you ... Did Laura ... She's gone." He pulled off his hat.

"Come in, Brand. Why don't you give me your hat before you completely ruin the brim twisting it like that?" She held out her hand. He gave her his hat and she began to smooth the brim back into place. "Now, what do you mean, she's gone?"

"Have you seen her?" He stepped into the apothecary shop, which was also the Larson's drawing room. "She's left town."

Amelia sobered immediately. "Where did she go?"

"I have no idea. She's not at the boardinghouse. She left this morning after handing the Hernandezes a letter appointing them caretakers." He began pacing the long, narrow room. "She walked away with one bag. She told them she didn't need a ride to the mercantile to catch the stage so I don't know if she's taken a coach or if she's on foot." He shoved his fingers through his hair. "Supposedly, Jesse went hunting."

He took a deep breath and started over. "I don't know much of anything at this point. Yesterday she confessed her past to me, told me all about her former life in New Orleans. She said that you knew too."

"And?" Amelia was watching him closely. "How did you react? Were you shocked?"

"Of course I was shocked, but once I recovered, I told her that I didn't care. That I loved her. I even asked her to marry me."

"Oh, Brand. I know you love her, but — "

"Now she's gone." He walked over to the window that faced the street.

"Maybe she just needs time. You both need time. Was it wise, proposing to her on the heels of her revelation? You know how much I care for Laura, Brand. She's a wonderful woman who has done a remarkable job of turning her life around, but you are a minister and she is a woman with a checkered past."

"I have no doubt that God has brought her into my life for that very reason. Who better to love her unconditionally? Who better to find forgiveness in his heart?" He shook his head. "When I think about the look on her face when she told me good-bye yesterday, it scares me to death. There was such ... finality to it."

Amelia came to his side. "Let's stay calm," she said too quickly.

"You don't look calm," he noted.

"She has no one to turn to. Nowhere to go." Amelia's eyes were suddenly bright with tears. "All those photographs and daguerreotypes in her drawing room? She bought them, Brand. She's completely on her own."

"She has us," he said.

"She doesn't feel worthy of us."

As he stared down the street, a swift, dark thought came to him.

"Collier Holloway," he said. "Maybe she went to him."

"Oh, I surely hope not. I think that's the last thing she would want to do."

"Is it?" His heart was hammering. "She believes herself unredeemable. That the life she led is unforgivable. All my talk of forgiveness fell on deaf ears. She was more concerned about me and worried about how I was going to maintain the trust of the congregation and the church board when they learned the truth about her. Maybe she thought going back to Collier was the only way to discourage me—"

Amelia shoved his hat into his hands. "Go. Go to the Silver Slipper. Don't waste another breath. If she's there, drag her out by her hair."

He shoved his hat on as he stepped outside and headed for the porch steps.

"I'll walk down to the *Gazette* office and tell Hank she's missing," Amelia called out.

Brand stopped in his tracks and turned around.

"Before you do, wait to hear from me. If she is in the Silver Slipper, I don't want anyone to know."

"If she *is* in that saloon, do whatever it takes to get her out."

The saloon doors were already open even though it wasn't yet ten o'clock. Brand reined in, dismounted, and tied his horse to the hitching post in front of the Silver Slipper.

He walked inside without hesitation. The barkeep, Denton Fairchild—the same man who'd been there the day the unfortunate Jenny died—recognized him.

"Hey, Preacher. What can I do for you?"

Brand glanced toward the office door in the back wall. "I want to see Holloway. Is he here?"

The barkeep hesitated a second too long before he said, "He's out."

If the man hadn't glanced up toward the last door on the

second-floor balcony, Brand might have believed him. He started across the room and took the stairs two at a time.

"You can't go up there! He's busy." Fairchild started around the end of the bar after him.

Brand hurried along the balcony, passing the various doors until he reached the room at the end of the line. At the end of the hall were double doors, larger, grander in scale, with brass hardware.

He reached for the knob. It was locked. He rattled it, tried to twist it open.

"Holloway! Open up." He had visions of Laura on the other side of the door. "Open up!" He pounded on the doors.

The barkeep was behind him now, trying to pull him away. He shrugged the man off just as the door whipped open. Collier Holloway stood on the other side of the threshold in a half open, quilted satin robe. His hair was a tousled mess, his eyes red from excess.

Brand steadied himself, ready to save Laura from a fate worse than death.

"Well," Holloway slowly smiled. "If it isn't the preacher. How are you doing this morning, Reverend?"

Brand looked past him. There was a woman in the bed on the other side of the room, a wide-eyed brunette clutching the covers beneath her chin.

Not Laura.

Relief coursed through him.

"I take it there's a reason for your unexpected appearance?" Collier leaned against the doorjamb and crossed his arms over his chest. "Or were you just dying to see me?"

"I'm looking for Laura. Is she here?"

"Lovie?"

"Who's Lovie?" Brand was sick of the man's stalling.

Something flickered in Holloway's eyes. A conceit and a familiarity Brand despised.

Holloway watched him intently. "So, she didn't even tell you her real name?"

"She did, but she's Laura Foster to me. Where is she?"

Collier Holloway stepped out into the hall and closed the door behind him. He nodded to the barkeep.

"You can go, Denton," he said. "I can handle him." Holloway focused on Brand. He kept his voice low, his gaze steady. "What makes you think she's here?"

"Yesterday she told me everything. This morning I went by the boardinghouse and it appears she's gone. She didn't tell her help or her friend, Amelia, where she was going."

"And I guess she didn't even tell you, eh, Preacher?"

"No." Brand shook his head, fighting a sinking feeling around his heart. "She didn't."

"Then it appears the *lady* doesn't want to be found." Holloway rubbed the night's growth of stubble on his chin. "What did you do, Reverend? Start ranting and raving when she told you? Did you send her packing?"

"I proposed."

Collier shoved away from the wall, his expression a study in contempt and barely restrained anger.

"You happy now, Preacher? You asked her to be a preacher's wife? Who are you kidding? She's a smart gal. She knows she can *never* be what you want her to be, so she ran. Good luck finding her. It took me four years to track her down after she left me."

Brand kept his hands fisted at his sides. He took one long deep breath after another. It would be so easy to let himself go, to fall into the yawning pool of anger that beckoned. So easy to lash out and knock Holloway senseless.

It was a struggle, but Brand finally reined in his temper and held himself in check.

"I can see you're worried, Preacher," Holloway said. "Don't be. That woman's like a cat. She always lands on her feet."

Holloway laid his hand on the doorknob behind him. Before he stepped back into his room he said, "If and when you find her, be sure to tell Lovie I said that if she ever comes to her senses, my door's still open."

Brand was headed back to the Larsons when he heard the loud, hollow sounds of footsteps beating against the wooden walkway along Main Street.

"Reverend!"

He turned around just as Richard Hernandez reached him. The young man was out of breath. Bracing his hands on his knees, he bent over and drank in long draughts of air.

"Is she back?" Brand asked.

Richard shook his head and looked up. "My ... my father sent me. He said to tell you he looked in the carriage house and the horse is gone. The horse that pulls Mrs. Foster's carriage. Maybe she left on the horse."

"Alone?"

Laura had no experience riding save yesterday's. Brand hoped she hadn't gotten it into her head to take off on her own. If so, she could be lying somewhere on the open prairie with her pretty neck broken.

"Is Jesse back yet?" At this point, Brand could only hope she might have talked Jesse into helping her.

"No, sir. He's still gone." Richard hesitated.

"What is it?"

"If you are thinking he went with Mrs. Foster, you are wrong. I saw him leave yesterday. He had a bedroll with him. He never came back yet."

"But you didn't actually see Laura leave?"

"No, sir. I was at the *Gazette* office early helping Sheriff Larson with this week's newspaper."

Within twenty minutes Brand was back at the Larsons'. Amelia had been waiting for him, watching through the window. She sat him down at the kitchen table and poured him a cup of strong coffee.

"No word at all, you say?" She filled his cup almost to the brim and then passed him the sugar bowl and creamer.

"She's not with Holloway—"

"Thank heaven," she whispered.

"The Hernandez boy told me that her carriage horse is missing. Harrison Barker said she didn't board the stage this morning."

"Do you think she rode off on her own?"

"If she did, I don't think she'll get very far very fast." He sighed, took a sip, and set the cup down again. "Maybe she paid Jesse to take her somewhere."

"Good. With Jesse she'll be safe. When he gets back, he can tell us where she's gone."

"Why would he come back to Glory?"

"Because you're here," she said.

"Richard said Jesse left to go hunting yesterday."

"Laura may have sent him off early to avoid suspicion. Maybe they met up outside of town," she mused.

"That would mean she was planning to leave *before* I proposed."

Brand stared at the worn tabletop. A pottery vase filled with dried flowers served as a centerpiece. Hank and Amelia's home was neat but sparsely furnished. The couple had been tested, but their love had survived. Brand knew his love was true. His belief in his and Laura's future just as solid.

Amelia made him finish the coffee before he took his leave and even managed to tempt him with a bowl of the chili bubbling on the stove.

"I'm going to head back to the boardinghouse," he told her. "See if Jesse's back yet. See if he knows anything."

She walked him to the front door for the second time that morning. "Let me know."

"I will," he promised.

She reached out and touched his sleeve. "Don't worry, Brand. You'll find her."

"I hope you're right," he said. He refused to accept the notion that he would never see Laura, never hear her voice or kiss her sweet lips again. "I sincerely hope you're right."

TWENTY -ONE

That afternoon, Brand sat in uncomfortable silence during the emergency board meeting. It was the last place he wanted to be with Laura moving farther out of his life with each passing moment. He was tempted to get up and walk out, but he couldn't leave with his fate still among the topics yet to be discussed.

The board members had appeared uncomfortable from the minute he joined them. There were seven in total counting Brand, and all were present except Timothy Cutter, who was at the bank. Mary Margaret Cutter was there along with Barbara Barker, Harrison's mother; Amelia, whose father had been instrumental in building the church; Bud Townsend, a wealthy rancher; and Raymond Pettigrew, a retired lawyer who was new to town. He and Townsend were friends and Pettigrew had a habit of siding with the rancher whenever it came time to vote.

The underlying, unspoken question was still whether or not Brand should be retained. At the moment, though, the topic was whether or not to reroof the church. He wondered how long they would put off the inevitable vote regarding his tenure. He hadn't the stomach to fight his own case today, not with Laura missing. All he could think about was where she might be, whether or not she was safe, and how to go about finding her—especially if she didn't want to be found.

Across the table, Townsend had a tentative hold on his temper. His weather-worn face was two shades redder than usual. Two years ago, the rancher had donated funds for a new roof for the hall. This year the church itself was in sore need of reroofing, but Bud had balked when Mary Margaret asked if he could again be generous. If not, she suggested, perhaps he could donate half the amount needed.

Studiously avoiding meeting Brand's gaze, he told the rest of the board, "There's no way I'm handing over any more of my family's hard-earned cash for anything as long as McCormick is still minister."

The rancher had a demeanor as tough and abrasive as his leathery, weather-weary hide. Townsend wasn't about to mince words even in front of Brand. Everyone else shifted uncomfortably in their chairs when he turned to Brand directly.

"It's bad enough you got yourself a half-breed son, Reverend. The fact that you never married the buck's mother compounds the problem. What are people gonna think of us when they hear? Those aren't exactly the qualifications we were looking for in a preacher when we hired you on. We're trying to attract upstanding, God-fearing folks to this town."

"I, for one, don't care what anyone else thinks," Barbara Barker said. "Brand has done a wonderful job of—"

"Right up until his 'son' showed up and spilled the truth about him," Townsend interrupted. He drummed his fingers on the tabletop. "And now I hear he's been spending a lot of time courting that highfalutin widow."

"I call for a vote of confidence." Mary Margaret Cutter quickly cut off all discussion. "Otherwise we're not going to get anywhere."

Amelia shook her head. "This isn't the time to—"

"When is the time?" Townsend had a full head of steam and was running with it.

Brand pushed back his chair and got to his feet.

"There's no need for a vote of confidence." He looked at each of them in turn—friends, supporters, and his outspoken opposition. "Before this meeting, I wrote to an old friend and asked if he could stand in for me as acting minister until you can find someone of your own choosing. He's recently retired. I'm sure he'll agree to come and arrive within a couple of weeks. In the meantime, please consider this my resignation. I quit."

"Brand!" Amelia was on her feet. "You can't—"

"I just did."

He was free now. Free to go after Laura. Free to find her and make her his wife without repercussions from his flock. He was beholden to no one but God and he knew without a doubt that was one vote of confidence he could always rely on. The only one that really mattered.

"Now, if you'll please excuse me." He hated to walk out on Amelia and Mary Margaret like this, but the time to act was long overdue. Bud Townsend was right. He *had* been focused on Laura of late. Right now, she was his entire concern. If he didn't go looking for her, who would? Even if she refused to marry him, there was no way he could let her walk down the dark and twisted road she'd once traveled. No way he could live with himself if he did.

He left the hall and went directly to the church, opened the side door, and went in. It was chilly inside, cavernous and empty. Slipping into the closest pew, he closed his eyes and began to pray for guidance. He'd barely started when the door opened behind him. He suspected it was Amelia, until he heard spurs chink against the floor.

He opened one eye, expecting to see Bud Townsend or Raymond Pettigrew standing there.

But it was Jesse. Hat still on, hands riding his hips just above his holster.

Brand stared at the hat. Jesse shrugged then took it off. "Sorry. I need to talk to you."

Brand slid over. Jesse appeared uncomfortable, but sat down beside him. He gazed up at the high-peaked ceiling.

"Where's Miz Foster?"

"I wish I knew. I hoped you might. Thought maybe you'd helped her leave town."

"I went hunting yesterday and just got back. Rodrigo told me she left. Permanent-like. Rode over and saw you walk in here." Jesse scratched his ear. "You know why she might have packed up and took off?"

"Maybe." *Because I asked her to marry me.*

"How long are you going to sit here doing nothing while the trail gets cold?" Jesse looked Brand over. His son didn't say a word, but Brand could tell he was thinking, *Is this how you went about trying to find my ma?*

"I had a board meeting. I'm finished here and just about to pack up and go looking for her."

"I hope you're better at preaching than you are tracking somebody down."

"I am, but I just quit."

Jesse looked at his hands. "Because of me showin' up, no doubt."

"I need to find Laura and I wasn't getting anywhere listening to small-minded folks arguing over old news."

Brand spun out his theory about Laura taking the carriage horse. Told Jesse that he'd checked with Harrison Barker and found out Laura hadn't bought a ticket for the morning stage.

"I don't even know which direction to go."

"She didn't take the horse. Rodrigo found it wandering around in the pasture behind the house."

"Then how did she leave town?"

Jesse shook his head. "A headstrong woman with money can do just about anything she wants."

"Do you have any idea where we should start looking?"

His son stared at him as if he were crazy. "You asking me to help you?"

"I am."

Laura wanted him to get to know Jesse, or rather, Jesse to get to know him. Now her disappearance might be the catalyst for bringing them together.

"Why should I?"

"For one thing, she took you in, gave you a place to live and an honest day's work. I'm not asking you to do it for me, I'm asking you to do it for her. The consequences, if we don't get her back, are unthinkable."

"Pretty strong words."

"You don't know the half of it."

"If it's got anything to do with that scallywag who owns the saloon, I can't imagine it amounts to anything good."

"He doesn't know where she is either."

"Then I reckon that's good news." Jesse sat there a minute or two. Dusted the brim of his hat.

Brand tried to clear the lump in his throat before he said, "I can't give you back the past or the years we lost, but I can give you the future. I'm not convinced I can do this alone. I don't know the first thing about tracking anyone."

Jesse sat for so long Brand thought he ought to take the silence for a no.

Then Jesse turned to him again. "I don't have much else to do. I'm in."

"We'll find her. I know we will." Brand said. The alternative was unthinkable but he had no guarantees they would succeed. And if he found her, then what? Not only was his own reputation in question, but there were those who would never, ever come to accept the woman who had won his love.

"I'll go pack some things," Jesse said. "We could be gone awhile." He stood up and stepped out of the pew. "If I were you, I'd say a few extra prayers."

"Don't worry, I plan to." Brand was already giving thanks for Jesse's help. "Meet me over at my place when you're ready."

Jesse walked out. Alone again, Brand clasped his hands, lowered his head, and prayed for strength and guidance.

Turning to his faith and following his heart had always gone hand in hand. Laura had seen his initial shock, his doubt and hesitancy as he had tried to absorb what she was saying. What she couldn't see was that his love was stronger than his doubt. That he was willing to stand by her. If he was blessed enough to find her, it would be up to him to convince her that if God was willing to forgive the worst sinner, then man could surely do no less.

When he left the church, he found Amelia waiting for him outside.

"We took the vote and we want you to stay. It was four to one. Pettigrew went against Bud Townsend. If Timothy would have been present it would have been five to one." The hem of her skirt flared out around her ankles as she jogged to keep up with him. "Please say you'll reconsider your resignation."

He shook his head. "Sorry, Amelia, but this is for the best. Now I'm free to go after Laura and I don't intend to stop until I find her and bring her home. The board may have confidence in me now, but what will they think of my decision to marry her when they find out about her past? What then?"

His words gave her pause. After a few more hurried steps in the direction of his home, she grabbed onto his sleeve. "Please, stop a minute. I can't keep up with you."

"I've got to hurry. Every minute we lose puts her that much farther away."

"You can't go off alone. Looking all over Texas is like looking for a needle in a haystack."

"Jesse has agreed to go with me."

"That's good, I guess." She nodded. Her expression brightened some. "That's real good. I hate to think of you riding around unarmed. Hank has a gun he can loan you."

"No, thanks. Please don't worry about me. I'll be fine. It's Laura we should be worried about."

"I hope you're not too late."

"I pray I'm not."

She took his hands in hers. Held them tight. "You listen to me, Brand McCormick. You find Laura and then you bring her home. I wish I could speak for the whole board, but I can't. You won the vote of confidence, but I have no idea how long we can hold your position for you."

"I understand. Just watch out for Charity and the children. I've got enough in savings to see her through for a while—"

"Hank and I would never let them go hungry. You know that. You have plenty of friends here. Friends who want you to stay on."

"Friends who will still back me when Laura and I marry?"

She didn't answer. Even he didn't know if those friends might find his commitment to Laura untenable once they learned the truth.

"Everything will be fine. You'll see," Amelia said. "Just start by finding Laura and bringing her home."

Charity followed him around the house as he grabbed a couple of clean shirts and long johns.

"Are you sure you should leave in the middle of all this trouble?"

"Laura is gone because of my initial response to what she told me. I'll admit I was stunned, but who wouldn't be? I love her, Charity. I'm the one who sent her running. Because of me she's walked away from her home, her dream."

He couldn't voice his true concern aloud. Now wasn't the time to add any more to his sister's pile of worry.

"I'm entrusting the children to you, as always. Amelia and Hank will help you out with anything you need. See Mary Margaret at the bank if you need any money. I've left some cash in the water pitcher in the pie safe."

"But what if you don't find her?"

"I'm not going to stop until I do."

She planted her fists on her hips. "You can't be serious."

"You're more than capable of handling things until I get back."

"Will you stop by the school and tell the children good-bye?"

He walked into his room. Opened a tall wardrobe and pulled out a coat he hadn't worn in a long time—a jacket of suede lined with lamb's wool. He shrugged out of his collar, took off his black coat, and changed into the heavy jacket.

"I don't want a scene. I'll leave them a note. That way they'll have something to reread until I get back." He scanned the room before he picked up his extra clothing. "Tell them Jesse is going with me and I promise to bring him home with me when we get back. That ought to make them happy."

"Brand, what if something happens to you? What if you don't come back? How will I know you're all right?"

He slipped his arm around her shoulders.

"Where's your faith, Sis? I'll try to write once a week to let you know where we are." He let her go and shrugged. "Who knows? We might be back in a couple of days."

"Maybe so." She smiled. "You're right. Maybe you'll be back by supper."

"How about you pack us some vittles? Something to eat so we don't have to stop along the way." He didn't need her to remind him he had no idea where they were going or how long they might be gone. With any luck, they just might be back for supper after all.

TWENTY -TWO

Laura was thankful she knew what to expect when she boarded the old Concord stagecoach at Brady City. After her long journey from New Orleans to Glory, she had promised herself that she would never undertake such a miserable experience again. Yet here she was, dusting off the cracked leather seat with the handkerchief she'd brought to cover her nose and mouth when the choking road dust became unbearable—which it surely would.

For now, it appeared she would be the only occupant of the stage until the next stop.

Escape had been far easier than she expected. The old veteran Rob Jenkins had been more than willing to swear allegiance when she slipped out of the house before dawn, found him curled up on a wooden bench outside the Silver Slipper, and shook him awake. She offered him twenty dollars and a gently worn gentleman's coat—one a guest had left behind three years ago along with a pair of nearly new boots—if in exchange he would rent two horses at the livery and escort her out of town.

She wouldn't let herself think of Brand, didn't question what she was about to do. She simply went back to collect her things and bid the Hernandezes farewell. Leaving them in stunned disbelief, she quickly stepped outside and circled around the house. Thankfully, Jesse had gone hunting, so she'd asked Rob to meet her behind the carriage house on horseback. True to his word, he'd brought along a gentle mare for her and strapped her carpet bag to the back of his own mount. Shielded from a view of Main Street — not that anyone was out and about in the violet light of the breaking dawn to see them — they slipped away unnoticed. The fact that morning turned into afternoon and no one had come tracking them was both reassuring and bittersweet.

Now, refusing to allow herself the luxury of emotion, she settled into the coach, prepared for the initial jolt as it pulled away from the depot. The driver, thankfully, had appeared to be sober. She couldn't say as much for Rob, but he'd been lucid enough to escort her all the way to the Brady City depot and do exactly as she'd instructed.

While she remained bundled up in her hooded cape, her hair, and face hidden from view, he purchased her a ticket that would take her as far as the New Mexico border.

"My wife's been ill," Rob told the stationmaster in his slow southern drawl. "I'm sending her to her folks in Albuquerque."

When he handed her the ticket, his concern was evident.

"You sure about this, ma'am? I kin have you back to Glory 'fore nightfall."

She wasn't sure of anything anymore, but that wasn't something Rob Jenkins needed to know. She looked back the way they had come, searched the horizon.

Was she doing the right thing?

Surely if she wasn't meant to leave, she'd know it in her heart. There would be a sign.

She felt nothing but the resolve to go on. There was no one in sight. No one coming after her.

"I'm sure, Rob." She reached for his palsied hand and gave it a hard squeeze before quickly letting go. "I've paid you well for your silence. I'm counting on you to keep it. When you get back to

Glory, if you hear of anyone asking about me, do *not* play the hero and tell them where I've gone."

"No, ma'am." He tugged on his hat brim. "If there's one thing you don't have to worry about, it's me bein' a hero." He studied the ground for a second then said, "Fine lady like you shouldn't be out here on her own like this, no matter what she's runnin' from."

"It's none of your concern what I'm running from," she told him gently.

"No. I 'spect it's not. But we're all runnin' from something," he said, "even if we're not going anywhere."

"Promise me, Rob," she urged.

"I may be an old broken-down sot, but I know how to hold my tongue. 'Sides, in a day or two, I'll probably forget all about this."

She hoped he was right. She watched Rob ride off leading the mare behind him, trying to convince herself she wasn't searching the horizon for Brand, when a nice-looking gentleman appeared outside the coach. He opened the door, gazed around the cramped interior, and tipped his bowler hat to her before stepping inside.

Instinctively she lay her hand over the reticule on her lap. The hard metal of her derringer was reassuring to the touch. The man didn't appear to be threatening in the least, but appearances could be deceiving.

The driver yelled, "Hold on," gave a whistle to the team, and the coach was off with a lurch, swinging and swaying with the pitch and roll of an oceangoing vessel — but one that bumped and jarred when the wheels slipped into ruts and holes. Laura held on to the strap dangling from the roof above her and let herself roll with the motion of the coach rather than fight it. Once she had grown somewhat accustomed to the jolting, she could spare a look at her fellow passenger.

He appeared to be in his late thirties with kind, soft-brown eyes and a well-trimmed beard. His wool suit coat and pants matched the vest he wore beneath them. There was a parcel wrapped in brown paper and tied with twine on the seat beside him. He kept his hand on the package to keep it from tumbling to the floor.

If the constant sway and bounce of the coach bothered him, he didn't let it show.

He smiled and Laura returned it with a slight smile of her own, then turned her attention to the passing landscape. They rode in silence for miles. She had no idea where they would stop next and didn't care as long as they were headed away from Glory. Away from Brand and the madness of accepting his proposal.

After nearly an hour, the stranger shifted on the seat and set the parcel on his lap. "I'm Michael Noble," he said with a nod. "A book drummer."

Laura fanned the dust off her face with her handkerchief and adjusted the folds of her cape. The day had progressed from a chilly morning to a pleasantly warm fall afternoon.

"I'm Mrs. Foster." She told him her name without thinking and hoped she would not regret it. She sized the man up for a moment or two more. "You sell books?"

"I do. Books of all kinds." He patted the package on his lap. "Do you read, Mrs. Foster?"

She took him to be asking if she enjoyed reading as a hobby, not if she was literate. "I do. I have ..." She paused, remembering her extensive collection. In her haste she'd forgotten to bring along the copy of *Cranford* she hadn't finished reading. "I have quite a few books."

"What are your favorites?"

She began to list some of her favorite novels and he commented as to whether or not he'd ever read them. Soon the journey became somewhat more enjoyable and the miles and hours flew by.

"We should nearly be there," he finally said, opening the gold watch he'd slipped from his vest pocket.

"Where?"

"Why, San Angelo," he told her, amazed that she had no idea where they were headed. "Speaking of books," he added, "since it seems your taste runs more to stories of heroes and adventure, passion and history, have you read the greatest book of them all?"

"Which book would that be, in your opinion, Mr. Noble?"

"The Bible."

His answer momentarily silenced her. A thousand thoughts ran through her mind.

"I can see my question has taken you aback. Why is that?"

"My life has taken a few twists and turns of late. I have friends who recently suggested I might find answers there—"

"But you doubt it." He nodded. "I see."

No, you don't see, she thought. *You have no idea.*

When they reached their first stop, which was little more than a way station, the driver helped her out and she assumed Mr. Noble would follow her inside. It felt good to stretch her legs, but when she saw the interior of the depot, she hoped this was not their overnight stop. There was little inside save a dirt floor, some hard benches, and a filthy table. Besides, she had hoped to be farther away from Glory before nightfall.

She ordered coffee and a plate of something that resembled hash. Though it tasted like the inside of an old boot, she ate as much as she could stomach. It was the only thing she'd had to eat all day.

After twenty minutes the driver appeared. "Time to get a move on," he told her.

She left her plate half full of food, finished off her coffee, and walked back to the stage. After she took a look inside the empty coach she turned to the driver.

"Where is Mr. Noble?" When he hadn't shown up inside the depot, she assumed he must have taken a stroll around the grounds to stretch his legs and was probably napping in the coach.

"This was his final stop," the driver said. "He unloaded his books, bought a horse, and headed off."

She thought it odd the man didn't say good-bye but dismissed it when the driver offered to help her into the coach.

"The next stop isn't all that far. It'll be dusk in a couple of hours."

The coach swayed as the driver climbed aboard. He cracked the whip and they were off again. Laura heard something thump against the carriage floor.

She looked down, and there, in the corner in the narrow space between the seats, lay Mr. Noble's parcel. Carefully bracing one hand on the seat across from her, she quickly leaned down and grabbed it up before the jostling threw her off balance. It was heavier than she expected and, from the feel of it, a book.

She stared down at the twine tied in a thin bow and the words written across the heavy brown paper.

To Mrs. Foster. May your journey lead you home.

With a shiver, she slowly pulled the ends of the bow. The paper rustled as she opened it. She ran her fingertips over the tooled leather cover, fingered the gold-embossed title, and her vision wavered. She closed her eyes as a tear slipped out from beneath her lashes.

She'd asked for a sign. A fingerboard pointing the way couldn't have been any clearer.

Brand and Jesse headed north and east, toward Stephenville and Dallas, thinking Laura would try to lose herself in a larger town. They traversed a high tableland broken by a jumble of hills and fertile valleys. Eventually, the road slid down into the Bosque River valley, where post oaks, elms, and sumacs thrived in the uplands.

There was no sign of Laura in Stephenville.

Brand would always remember the town, not because it was their first stop, but because it was where he told Jesse the truth about Laura. There was no way he could walk into a brothel and ask for her without telling his son why she, of all people, could possibly be there.

Jesse remained thoughtful for a long while afterward. "It makes no difference to you?" he finally asked. "You don't mind what she is? Knowing what she's done?"

Brand answered without hesitation. "I love her. She's not that woman anymore."

"Yet you're looking for her in those places."

Brand hesitated before he took a deep breath and admitted, "I'm praying I won't find her there."

There was no sign of Laura at any of the stage stops along the way to Dallas. No one admitted to seeing anyone answering to her description.

It was at the small towns and depots that Brand noticed the looks Jesse got whenever he walked into a room. Texas wasn't a land that forgot or forgave easily. After years of wars with the Comanche and Kiowa—after raids and abductions of hundreds, if not thousands of settlers—a man with his son's looks and heritage would never be easily accepted.

He found Jesse to be tireless, stubborn, and wise. Surprisingly, his son knew when to smile and try to charm anyone who might have an objection to his presence, and he knew when to stand up and fight for himself.

Thankfully, the fights were few and far between.

They rode through the Brazos Valley, level in places, gently rolling in others. Spring-fed creeks were full of fish—perch, bass, catfish. Cedars and small oaks covered low, rolling hills. Bois d'arc hedges surrounded fields.

When the Houston and Texas Central brought the first train to Dallas, the population had doubled overnight. The Texas and Pacific Line arrived a year later and the town boomed. The streets were packed with wagons and folks vying for space. One hotel proprietor laughed and told Brand that the town was growing faster than warts on a toad.

Jesse and Brand were there nearly a week before they gave up. No one, not at any hotel, boardinghouse, sporting club, or saloon had seen anyone fitting Laura's description.

Brand refused to give up. They headed south, where the land opened up again and towns were few and far between. There was still no sign of her.

Before they headed west, they took a circuitous route to return to Glory to see Charity and the children. When they arrived at the house at suppertime, the children were nearly as excited to see Jesse as they were Brand. To Brand, it seemed as each of them had grown a good six inches in the last two weeks.

The children were allowed to monopolize the dinner conversation and hung on Brand and Jesse's descriptions of all they'd seen. Once they'd been hustled off to bed and Jesse left to head to his room at Laura's, Charity started clearing the table and doing up the dishes.

She was scraping chips of soap into the dishpan of hot water when she said, "John Lockwood arrived a few days ago. He's boarding with the Cutters."

The Reverend Lockwood, a friend from Brand's divinity school days, was not only a minister but a teacher.

"Hopefully he'll meet with the board's approval." Brand realized he hadn't even asked about his replacement, a reminder of where his mind was now.

She set the soap and a paring knife down and turned to face him.

"The board made it clear to him that he's only here temporarily. Just until you return. Amelia and the Cutters have fought hard for you. Folks want you back, Brand."

He rose slowly. Days in and out of the saddle, miles spent riding in unpredictable weather that could fall forty degrees between dusk and dawn, were wearing on him. Jesse, on the other hand, seemed fueled by the hunt. He met each new town, each new day, with dogged determination.

"I'm in their debt, Sis, and yours." Brand smiled at her from beside the kitchen table.

"You know I think of Sam and Janie as my own."

"Believe me, I know, and I'm thankful for everything you're doing."

"Just come back safe. We'll be all right."

It was late afternoon when Laura woke up, startled when she didn't immediately recall where she was. If the small window with its faded gingham curtain hadn't been enough of a hint, then the narrow bed with its worn, lumpy mattress was enough to remind her of her present situation.

Sleep had never been her friend and still wasn't. She'd been here going on three weeks and more than ever before, she'd managed very few hours of uninterrupted sleep. Whenever she finally did manage to doze off for a nap as she'd just done, she awoke within minutes, aching all over. She'd made up her mind to ask for a newer mattress as soon as she'd been here a month — which wasn't far off at all.

She missed Peaches and sometimes imagined she saw the cat curled up at the foot of the bed. The room was barely big enough to swing a cat in. Along with the bed, there was a chair and a small bedside table just wide enough to hold a lamp and her one book. Gone were all the gilded trappings of wealth she'd possessed. Gone was the library collection she'd held dear. Gone were the friends she had made in Glory. And the love of her life.

She slipped out from beneath the covers. The minute her feet hit the cold floorboards, her toes curled away from the late November chill. She doubted she'd ever grow used to the cold or the dryness. She doubted she'd ever feel warm again.

The clink of glasses and dishes in a wash tin filtered up through the floor. She heard the muted sound of masculine voices. After slipping into her underclothes she donned one of the two simple gowns she'd brought with her, hoping not to call attention to herself. She parted her hair down the middle and wove it into two thick braids, which she wound around and anchored to the crown of her head.

She was forever trying to poke escaped curls back into place.

She picked up the book the illusive drummer had given her, intent upon stealing a few minutes of reading before she went downstairs. Pulling the straight-back chair over to the window where the weak fall light filtered in, she set the book on her lap and tried to forget about the lovely, cozy study she'd left behind. Specifically, she remembered the steaming pots of flavorful tea and chocolate Anna had brewed for her the day she shared her private retreat with Amelia. She'd never forget Amelia's heartfelt words the day Laura had revealed her secret.

"Most of all, you're my dearest friend."

Thinking of Amelia and how strong her friend was, Laura refused to give into tears. Turning to the window, she looked down the empty street. Soon the lamp outside the building would be lit, throwing a haloed glow out into the night. Customers would begin filing in. Word of her addition to the staff had quickly spread by word of mouth. Men came from miles around. Some nights there was standing room only downstairs.

Before she left the room she stopped to study her reflection in the small, clouded mirror in a frame on the wall. Her gown hung loose around her waist. Since she left Glory, with none of Rodrigo's wonderful cooking to tempt her, she had lost weight. Not only that, but shadows filled the hollows beneath her eyes. She attempted a smile but failed miserably.

The next day, after meeting with Reverend Lockwood, Brand and Jesse were soon on the trail again.

They stopped at every stagecoach depot along the route south and west. It wasn't until San Angelo that they were rewarded with a glimmer of hope.

Morning rain had forced them to wrap up in slickers. By afternoon, the rain had turned to sleet. Jesse said little, but set on forging through an area of cattle ranches where *vaqueros* worked the herds. Most of the white ranchers they questioned didn't hide the fact they wanted Jesse off their land.

Brand finally called a halt for the night at the stage depot near San Angelo, a trading post across the river from Fort Concho. The stage stop was a sparsely furnished one-room outpost managed by a wiry-bearded man in his sixties. He was stoop shouldered and intent upon "rustling up some grub" for them.

Brand warmed himself a few paces back from the low fireplace on the wall opposite the small cast-iron stove. He described Laura to the station manager. The man paused in the act of stirring a batch of refried pinto beans and nodded.

"Didn't catch her name. Not sure she even said it, but she's a hard 'un to forget."

The cold immediately seeped out of Brand. Jesse sat up straighter on the bench across the room.

"Where was she headed?" Brand asked the depot master.

"South, toward Presidio." The man tossed a stack of tortillas atop the stove. "It's the last stop, on the border. 'Course, she coulda stopped somewhere along the way. Not many places to light, though."

Jessie looked at Brand. "We going to follow her into Mexico?"

"You think I'm not up to it?"

Brand pictured Laura the way she'd looked in the sunshine that day by the creek. She was so lovely, so fragile, despite the stubborn strength that helped her win her independence.

Would he follow her into a foreign country with his children and his sister to think of? Was love coloring his common sense? He was a preacher. She was a fallen woman. The odds were against them. And yet, it that quiet place in his heart, he knew that they belonged together, and with God's help, they *would* be together. He would follow her to the ends of the earth if he had to. He walked over to a grimy table marred by rings from the bottom of a hot kettle. He sat down across from Jesse on a hard wooden bench.

Jesse studied him carefully. "Nobody would blame you for turning back."

"I loved your mother, Jesse, but I gave up too soon. I regret the years I lost knowing you. I'll never get them back." Brand looked down at his hands. They were still reddened by the cold. "I love Laura. I couldn't forgive myself if I didn't try to find her." Brand met Jesse's eyes again. "If you're ready to stop, I'll go it alone."

Jesse shrugged. "I figure I can keep going as long as you can."

TWENTY -THREE

Laura found herself wishing she'd brought her fur coat instead of her wool cape. Then she smiled, trying to imagine the reaction if she walked into the crowded room downstairs in ermine.

Today her room was cold as Collier Holloway's smile. She'd hung an extra blanket over the window hoping to keep out the wind that seeped in through the missing chinks in the plaster around the frame. She draped the quilt off the bed over her shoulders whenever she was chilled. It wouldn't do for her to fall ill and miss a day of work.

Not that she needed the money. She'd tucked the pile of emergency cash she always kept in the house into her corset the morning she left Glory. Though she'd deposited most of her savings in an account at Cutter's bank, she never fully trusted all of her funds to any one source. She had brought along enough to cover her needs for the next few months.

Thankfully, those needs were few. She'd lived on nothing for most of her life. The money she earned here didn't compare to what she made in New Orleans, but her pay was piling up as fast as the wind-driven snow that had just started to fall.

The sound of men's voices drifted up through the floor, a low, deep murmur that blended with the shuffle of heavy boots and the scrape of chairs across the floorboards. She glanced at the small silver watch she'd pinned to her bodice, a trinket she'd bought years ago.

With fifteen minutes to spare before she went downstairs, she picked up the book on her bedside table and turned up the flame in the hurricane lamp.

The bed sagged as she sat on the edge of the mattress and opened her Bible. It was still the only book she had and for now it was more than enough. Michael Noble had been right. The pages were full of all the drama, history, and pageantry that she ever wished for in a novel—and so much more.

She glanced down at the page she had marked with a dried desert marigold.

"The publicans and the harlots go into the kingdom of God before you."

Maybe the publicans, she thought, *whatever they are.*

Although she'd prayed over it, though she tried so hard to believe, she still wasn't entirely convinced there was such hope for prostitutes. She imagined Brand saying, "That's where faith comes in, Laura. In belief."

"I'm trying," she whispered into the silent room. "I'm trying."

Brand and Jesse left San Angelo, traversed high, rolling prairies, and crossed rugged hills to the valley of the Pecos. The trail twisted down canyons and over high passes with towering ranges that slashed across each other. They saw signs of mountain lion, deer, coyotes, and bobcats.

There was a new stationmaster and his wife at the first stop they came to. It was a lonely outpost and the woman was more than willing to chat. If Laura had passed through after the couple arrived, the woman would have definitely remembered her. She didn't.

Heading southwest, they moved on toward Fort Stockton and

nearby St. Gall. The hills were covered in cedar, oak, mesquite, and agrita. The sky darkened and the air felt cold enough for snow as they followed Spring Creek. Thinly wooded rocky hills offered no protection from the elements with the daylight hours at their shortest and the weather fierce.

By the time they reached Fort Stockton and St. Gall at Comanche Springs, Brand was never so glad to see signs of civilization in his life. The Army supply center had been established near Comanche Springs, the crossroads for wagon trains, mail stages, and travelers.

They boarded their horses at the town livery. A hot meal was in order before they searched for lodging, so they took the stable proprietor's suggestion. Jesse pulled his coat collar up against the biting wind, shielding the lower half of his face as they headed for the only café in town, a few doors down.

The buildings were mostly made of adobe — mud and straw bricks covered with a coat of whitewashed stucco. Second stories fronted by narrow balconies had been added to a few places. They reached the Old Coyote Café, which was full of Army personnel. Jesse shot a doubtful glance at Brand, but there was one table left in the corner of the room, so Brand walked in and sat down.

A middle-aged, harried-looking waitress said she'd be right with them. Jesse chose a chair that put his back to the room. Brand eased himself into a chair in the corner and tried to stifle a groan. Jesse noticed.

"Riding all day too much for you?" he chided.

"In this weather?" Brand laughed. "I expect it's too much for you too. You're just too stubborn to show it."

Jesse chuckled and slid a glance around the room before he took off his hat and brushed a dusting of frost off the brim. The soldiers seated around them eyed Jesse closely.

"I can't picture Laura here," Brand said, lowering his voice as he leaned across the table. "There might be more soldiers than civilians, but even so, this place makes Glory look like a metropolis."

"Whatever that is," Jesse said.

Brand was about to explain when the waitress walked over. Whip thin and lanky, she appeared to be in her mid-forties. Her hair was the color of watered-down cocoa. She gave them a once over and stared hard at Jesse for a second too long.

"We don't serve Indians," she said.

The room went dead silent. Jesse didn't move.

Brand introduced himself with a non-threatening smile.

"I'm Reverend Brand McCormick and this is my son, Jesse." He knew there was no ignoring Jesse's heritage. He added, "He's not Comanche."

Every eye in the place was on them by now.

"I understand you have the right not to, but I'd appreciate it if you'd serve us both. We've had a long, hard day's ride," Brand said. "We're just passing through."

He watched Jesse casually lean back in his chair and fold his hands on the table in front of him. "I'd hate for you to toss my pa out in the cold because of me," he said.

My pa. Though the situation was tense, Brand found himself smiling.

The woman glanced around the room and then back at Jesse. She raised her voice just enough so that every man in the room heard her.

"I suppose, seein' how this is my place, I have a right to decide who I serve and who I don't." She frowned and worried her bottom lip for a second before she said, "I'll bring you two coffees while y'all decide whether you'll be having meatloaf or venison stew."

It was a moment or two before conversation took up around the room again. Jesse said nothing, but Brand saw his shoulders rise and fall on a sigh of relief.

They had a cup of coffee and decided on the stew when the waitress confided she preferred it to the meatloaf. She disappeared into the kitchen and then was back in no time with two huge bowls of stew. She set them down and walked away.

They'd barely had two bites when she was back. "Here's some sourdough to sop that stew gravy up with, Reverend." She folded her arms at her waist. "Where you two headed?"

"Actually, we're not sure. We're looking for someone," Brand told her. He knew better than to expect more than a word or two out of Jesse, what with a room filled with Fort Stockton's enlisted men.

Brand went on to describe Laura. When he saw a hint of something akin to recognition behind the woman's eyes, he feared his heart might stop beating. She recovered so quickly, he almost doubted what he'd seen — until he noticed that Jesse was suddenly sitting a bit straighter, listening intently.

"Have you seen anyone fitting her description?" Brand asked.

"Doesn't sound like the type we usually see around these parts." The woman hesitated a second before she added, "Why are you looking for her?"

Brand tried to choose his words carefully, afraid he'd put the woman off and not get another word out of her. The truth was always the way. "I asked her to marry me and she took off." He quickly added, "If she's still not willing, so be it. I just want to see that she gets back home safely." He stared down at his stew, certain he couldn't eat another bite.

"*Maybe* she came through here. Maybe she didn't. How about I go back in the kitchen and talk to the cook?"

"Thank you kindly," Brand said, watching her go, trying to keep his hope from walking away with her.

When he looked over at Jesse, Brand found him staring after the waitress.

"She's seen her," he said softly. "She might not be willing to tell you anything with me here. How about I go back to the livery stable? See if there's a place I can bed down in for the night?"

It wouldn't be the first time they'd slept in a barn. Brand wouldn't stay in a hotel or boardinghouse that refused Jesse.

"Sit tight and finish your stew. One of us ought to have a good meal under his belt."

He stared at the men in the room. Wondered if the cook might have seen or heard of someone who looked like Laura. He tried to imagine her living in St. Gall. Not only was it a far cry from New Orleans, but it was the exact opposite of a well-settled, family-oriented community like Glory.

Holloway's words came back to haunt him. *That woman's like a cat. She always lands on her feet.*

Maybe she'd landed here because the town was full of men.

He looked up and found Jesse chewing a mouthful of stew. He swallowed and washed the bite down with some coffee. "You really ready for what we might find?"

Brand nodded, but he was thinking, *Not really.*

As Jesse concentrated on the stew again, Brand found himself praying he'd be ready for whatever they found.

L aurel? We're getting pretty busy downstairs. I could use a hand."

Although the sound of Betty Jean's voice came through the door just fine, the woman knocked again just to make sure. "Come on, honey. We got a passel of men down there and they're running out of patience."

"Coming, Betty," Laura called back. She tossed the quilt off her shoulders and pulled the edges of her thick sweater together and buttoned it up tight. Heading out, she paused long enough to lift an apron off the hook behind the door and slip the strings around her neck. She tied the apron around her waist and smoothed the front down.

When she opened the door to step out into the hall, she nearly ran smack into Betty Jean Frank.

"What are you doing out here if things are so hectic downstairs?"

Now that she was outside her room, Laura didn't think the place sounded any busier than usual for this time of day.

"It's a madhouse. I just came to hurry you up, is all." Betty Jean was watching her closely as they hurried down the hall together.

"What's the matter?" she asked.

Betty Jean shrugged. "Nothing. It's just … I hope you know how much we appreciate all the help you've been, even though we can't pay much."

"It's not about money," Laura shook her head. "I told you that in the beginning. I'm just grateful to you and Ansel for taking a chance on me." She'd told them she hadn't any experience, but that she needed the work and promised she'd try to please. It had been hard at first, the long hours excruciating, but waiting tables was second nature to her now. Though St. Gall wasn't the kind of place she'd want to stay in forever, it was fine for the time being.

She followed Betty Jean along the upstairs hall and then down the stairs. The heat rising from the kitchen was a welcome relief. In no time at all she'd have to shed her sweater.

Betty Jean pointed toward a group of men at a table near the stairs. "See what you can do for them, honey," she said before she left Laura's side and headed across the room.

Even the heady aroma of venison stew couldn't tempt Brand into taking another bite. Jesse, on the other hand, was having no trouble shoveling it in. When he finished with his own bowl, he nodded toward Brand's.

"Go ahead. Have at it," Brand said, sliding the bowl across the table. Jesse broke off another hunk of sourdough and dipped it into the thick gravy.

Brand looked up and found the waitress back at his elbow. "I'm going back to the kitchen. Laurel will be helping you folks." She had a curious expression on her face as she nodded across the dining room.

As she walked away, Brand had a clear view of the interior of the café. He noted the appreciative stares of the enlisted and other men around the room, followed their gazes, and found himself staring at Laura.

All breath left him.

"Hey, Miss Laurel. Evenin'," one of the soldiers said. "It's about time you showed up. You know we're all here just for the pleasure of seeing you." There was nothing impolite about the way the solider addressed her, only the deepest admiration and respect.

Laura's smile lit up the room. She was thinner, but her dimpled grin was her own. More than that, there was a new, radiant peacefulness about her.

"Thank you kindly, Private Tipton," she said. "Now what'll you gentlemen have tonight? Stew or meatloaf?"

Laurel.

Laura.

He'd found her.

She knew each man at the table by name. She smiled politely, but demurely. Her hair—he'd never seen it so severely styled—was braided and pinned atop her head. He missed her curls and found himself wishing he had the right to walk across the room, take her hair down, and separate the braided strands into a fine, shimmering nimbus.

Content to watch her, he remained as still as the frozen sleet caught in the nooks and crannies outside the adobe. Rather than risk a scene, he chose to wait until she noticed him.

Everything he'd practiced saying for when he found her left him. All he could do was drink in the sight of her and say a silent prayer of thanks.

"You wanna pick your jaw up off the table?" Jesse paused with a spoonful of stew halfway to his mouth to stare at Brand. "What's wrong?"

When Brand didn't answer, Jesse looked back over his shoulder to see what had caught Brand's eye.

Laura had learned to become aware of every nuance of movement at the tables. When customers turned to look for her, it was because they needed something—more coffee, some water, another helping of food.

She scanned the tables, immediately arrested when her gaze stopped on the familiar face of a young man. His dark hair was long enough to skim his shoulders. His eyes were black. She watched them widen in disbelief.

Jesse Langley.

When she realized it really was Jesse, her breath caught and her heart began to pound. Everything around her—all movement, all sound—faded. Slowly, slowly, she raised her eyes and looked past Jesse to the man across the table from him.

Broad shouldered, the same full mouth and strong jaw, but with eyes of blue.

Brand.

Without warning, the room started to spin. Laura reached out to steady herself. She ended up planting both hands on the nearest table. She closed her eyes and hung her head, hoping the dizzy spell would fade.

The soldier seated beside her was on his feet in an instant, helping her into his vacated chair.

"You all right, Miss Laurel?" he asked.

She tried to nod while keeping her head down. Maybe it was her imagination. Maybe her mind was playing tricks on her, showing her what she wanted more than anything else in the world.

She was afraid to look up. Afraid Brand wasn't really there at all.

Beside her, the soldier stepped away and someone else took his place.

"Laura? Are you all right?"

There was no denying the sound of Brand's voice. The warm, solid touch of his hand on her shoulder. She felt it though her sweater and the fabric of her gown. She would know his touch above all others.

She took a deep breath and found the courage to lift her head, to look into the depths of his eyes and search his face. She reached out. Her hand shook as she touched the cuff of his sleeve, not daring to let her fingers graze the skin on the back of his wrist.

"Is it really you?" she whispered.

He nodded. Slowly smiled.

"How did you find me?" In her heart she knew how he had found her and she knew why.

"It wasn't easy," he said.

The soldiers at the table were hanging on every word. The man who had given up his seat leaned over Brand.

"Are you all right, Miss Laurel? Is this man bothering you?"

"No," she said, not daring to take her eyes off Brand lest he disappear. "He's not bothering me."

Now Betty Jean was there, too, hovering behind Brand. The lines on her forehead were drawn into the deep creases of a frown. She instructed Brand, "Take her into the sitting room behind the stairs. I'll be in as soon as I can manage." She looked Laura over. "If that's all right with you, Laurel?"

"Of course. It's fine, but—" Her gaze scanned the crowded room. The men waiting to be served were all watching. She smiled, hoping to reassure everyone she was fine.

Brand slipped his arm beneath her elbow and helped her to her feet. She didn't take a step until she was certain her legs weren't going to give out. She tried to walk and was forced to grab hold of Brand's jacket. Before she could protest, he picked her up in front of everyone and carried her over to the room just beneath the stairs.

There was a small fireplace built into the far wall, which was crowded with heavy furniture fashioned of knobby wooden branches. Burning mesquite gave off a piquant scent. The thick adobe walls retained the heat. The warmth in the room would have been a welcome relief if not for the fact that Laura felt so flushed.

Brand carried her to an overstuffed chair covered with a striped serape and set her down.

"Jesse is here too" she marveled, not knowing what else to say.

"Wolfing down the last of my stew like a starving man." Brand glanced at the door. He'd left it partially open.

Always thinking of me, she thought. *Of my reputation.*

She tried to stop smiling but couldn't. She had missed this man terribly, but hadn't realized how very much until now.

"Please, sit down," she urged. He chose the chair beside hers.

Before either could speak, Betty Jean appeared bearing a tray with two mugs of hot tea. Laura tried to rise.

"You shouldn't be waiting on me with that crowd out there."

Betty Jean waved her back down. "They'll wait."

She turned to Brand. "Mind if I send your boy in, Reverend? He's paid the bill and I'm afraid if he stays out there alone much longer, things might go bad. None of the men have taken too kindly to Laurel looking so undone."

"Of course. Send him in." Brand accepted the tea tray and Betty Jean walked out again. "Things aren't all that comfortable for Jesse in a town like this—with the fort so close by and all the soldiers around."

"I imagine not." Laura had overheard enough snatches of the enlisted men's conversations to know why. "These men are paid to fight the Comanche. To keep the peace in these parts. It's not easy."

She drank in the sight of him, still finding it nigh impossible that he was here.

When Jesse walked through the door, Brand fell silent. Laura tried to smile up at the young man who looked so much like his father and yet so different.

"You both should leave as soon as possible," she said softly.

"I'm not leaving without you," Brand told her.

With his back to them, Jesse hovered near the fireplace and rubbed his hands together. Brand noticed his son's discomfort.

"Do you know of a place where we can spend the night?" Brand asked.

She contemplated his question. The soldiers would have to be back at the fort within a few hours. There was no hotel, no boardinghouse. The stage depot, like most, was nothing more than a one-room adobe. She doubted Jesse would be welcome there.

"There's a house not far from the south edge of town. Surrounded by a low adobe wall. The Garcias will take you in for the night. Señor Garcia is a hunter who sells game to the Franks — the owners of this place. Tell him that ..." She hesitated. "Tell him you're friends of Laurel's."

"Laurel," he said.

She shrugged. "It was close enough to Laura."

Across the room, Jesse said, "I'll go ahead and find the Garcia place and wait for you there." He gave Brand a nod and headed out a side door.

Laura's gaze followed him.

"He'll be all right," Brand assured her. "Despite how he chose to announce his arrival in Glory, he's got a level head on his shoulders."

"I know that. I'm just surprised to see you two together." She didn't admit that she was shocked to see them at all, let alone together.

"You wanted us to get to know each other."

"I'm glad you're on good terms."

She thought of Jesse in a town full of enlisted men stationed at nearby Fort Stockton. Men who had battled the Comanche as recently as August. Men who had seen their comrades fall in skirmishes all over southwest Texas. "You should probably leave here as soon as you can," she urged again.

"That's up to you now. I'm not going anywhere until you agree to come back with me." He leaned forward in his chair, reached for her hand, and covered it with his.

"What happened with your congregation?"

She watched him wrestle with the answer.

"I resigned," he said.

"Oh, Brand. No."

"They asked me to stay. Finding you was more important."

"I won't come between you and your church."

"Say you'll marry me, Laura."

"I won't let you trade the life you've built for me. Please, Brand, don't do this."

"Then don't give up *your* dream to spare me, Laura." He sounded angry, frustrated by her refusal to give in. "Don't walk away from everything you've built. Your home, your business—"

She looked at his hand, so tan against her own. "You still want to marry me, knowing the truth?"

"Yes."

"You would still marry me knowing I didn't hold to your beliefs? That I was sitting in your church on Sundays just to keep up appearances, but I wasn't a believer?"

"I know in my heart that we've been brought together for a reason. I'm the one man who can not only love you but help you find forgiveness."

"I saw the revulsion in your eyes, Brand. I saw the horror mirrored there the day I told you the truth—"

"Shock, not revulsion. Not aimed at you. Not ever."

She closed her eyes and took a deep breath. Above all, he deserved the truth.

"The night before I left, I tried to pray, Brand. I asked for a sign, something, anything to show me the way, but nothing happened and I left you. But being here alone, not as Laura or Lovie, without the trappings of wealth, I found honest work for an honest wage. I don't know if I'll ever be the woman you think I am. This person you call Laura Foster. I'm trying to find the courage and faith I need to believe in forgiveness, and the strength to fight for the right to be with you, as your wife."

She reached out to cup his cheek. "I'm slowly finding my way, Brand. If you'll still have me, I'll marry you," she whispered.

Reaching for her, he cupped the back of her head in his palm and kissed her. This time he held nothing back. In his kiss she felt not only respect and reverence, but desire.

"Thank you," he whispered afterward. "Thank you for making me the happiest man on earth. We can do this, Laura. Together and with God's help, we can do anything."

"I won't hide behind a lie any longer, though." she said. "The truth has to come out."

"Just promise you'll let me be the one to tell your story."

"I promise," she whispered, pressing her palm against his cheek.

There was nothing she wouldn't promise this man who had given her everything simply by loving her.

A branch crackled and popped in the fireplace. Sparks shot out, fell harmlessly upon the hard-packed earthen floor of the adobe. Outside, darkness shadowed the land. Through a narrow window in the thick wall, Brand saw that the sky had cleared. Stars glimmered exceptionally bright in the cold winter air and a brilliant half moon was on the rise. Milk-white light splashed across the hills.

Laura watched him expectantly, waiting for him to make the next move. He wanted to do more than kiss her. He wanted to hold her in his arms, to take down her hair and run his hands through it. That was what he wanted. What he could *have* was a different matter. He called upon all the patience he could muster.

"I'll buy your ticket tomorrow. You'll be on the next stage headed back," he told her.

She shook her head no. "I have money. I can buy my own ticket—"

He laughed. "Promise you'll always be stubborn and independent?"

"I'd like to continue running the boardinghouse," she said.

He tried to picture Sam and Janie tearing through her house full of expensive things.

"The children—"

"Will make the place a real home. If you don't mind moving your family in, that is."

"My sister—"

She didn't even let him finish. "Charity will live with us too—" She paused before adding, "Though she may not want to move in once she hears the truth."

"She may surprise you. She's not one to let anyone tell her what to do."

"There are those who will always be disgusted by me," Laura said.

Shadows filled her eyes again. He knew what the truth would cost them, just as he knew that even when it was out in the open, Laura would never forget the dark years of her past.

He had no notion how the town would react. There was nothing to do but leave the future in God's hands.

He pulled her into his arms and pressed his cheek against hers.

"You've made me the happiest man in the world," he assured her. "Now let's get you on the first stage out of St. Gall tomorrow before another storm hits."

By two o'clock the next afternoon, Laura was safely tucked inside the stagecoach outside of the depot. She was wrapped in not only her cape, but the quilt Betty Jean had gifted her with to use as a lap robe. Just as before, she was the only passenger, but she no longer had to search the horizon for Brand. He had found her. And no matter what, she knew now that even if he hadn't, she was never truly alone.

The Franks had driven her to the depot in their buckboard. Brand and Jesse rode alongside.

"I hate to up and leave you without help." Laura apologized over and over to Betty Jean while Ansel waited nearby.

"I knew a gal like you wouldn't be here long," the café owner said. "The pretty ones always got a man chasing after them. Yours seems nicer than most. Then again, he *is* a preacher."

"Thank you for the job and the room." She didn't tell Betty Jean she'd left behind all the money they'd paid her; the hardworking couple needed it far worse than she did. The accommodations above the café may have been Spartan, but the neat little room had been the perfect retreat.

"We'll always have a place for you, if you ever want to come back." Betty Jean laughed and shook her head. "We won't have near as many men lined up for dinner without you here to take their orders."

Betty Jean shed a tear or two when she said good-bye and left Laura in Brand's care.

"You sure you'll be all right on your own?" He wasn't pleased that she was heading back on the stage alone.

She smiled. "I got this far alone, didn't I? Besides, the children need you at home."

"Then I'll have Jesse accompany you."

"Brand, no. Please. Give me this time alone."

"But—"

"Please. We have the future ahead of us." She wanted time to reflect, to prepare herself for the challenges ahead without having to think about Brand spending any more time away from his family, without Jesse trailing along as escort.

"You're sure?" he asked.

"I'm positive." She paused, thinking a moment. "Does everyone know that you left town to look for me?"

He nodded. "They do by now."

The stagecoach driver was asking Brand to step aside so he could close the door. The driver made certain it was shut tight and climbed aboard.

Brand rested his forearms on the window frame. He wanted to

kiss her good-bye—she could see it in his eyes plain as day—but he held himself in check.

Laura leaned toward the window until she was close enough to kiss him. She closed her eyes and touched her lips to his. When the kiss ended, she smiled into his eyes, refusing to say good-bye.

"Soon," she whispered instead. Soon they would be married, their union blessed.

Then it would be her right, her wifely duty, to give him so much more than a kiss.

TWENTY
-FOUR

Bad weather dogged Brand and Jesse as they arrived in Glory late Saturday afternoon. Brand insisted Jesse have dinner with the family before he went to the boardinghouse to ask the Hernandezes if he could move back into the carriage house and tell them Laura was on her way home.

The minute the men started up the front porch steps, shouts of welcome greeted them.

"Papa and Jesse are back!" Sam called from the front room.

Before Brand could open the door, the children raced out to greet him. He knelt down to wrap his arms around both of them at once in a crushing bear hug. He savored the feel of their strong little bodies in his arms, their boundless enthusiasm and energy.

"You're just in time for dinner, Papa," Janie announced. "Jesse too." She ran to Jesse and grabbed his hand. "Are you hungry, Jesse?" She swung his hand back and forth between them. Brand could see he was uncomfortable, but he didn't try to pull away.

"'Course he's hungry," Sam decided. "They been out on the road. A man gets hungry on the trail, don't he, Papa?"

"A man surely does," Brand laughed. "I could eat a bear."

When Charity came to the door her face was flushed from the

heat of the oven. She was wearing her best gown, the pink one she usually saved for Sundays and special occasions. Brand gave her a hug too. She met his gaze and her blush faded. Worry shadowed her eyes.

"What's wrong?" Brand asked.

She glanced down at the children, pursed her lips, and shook her head as if to say "Not now." "I'm just so glad you're back safe and sound. You, too, Jesse. Come on in and wash up. We're having company for dinner," she told them.

Amelia, Hank, and Reverend John Lockwood were all waiting to greet them in the front room.

"Charity invited us for dinner," Amelia said. "We were just about to sit down."

Brand took one look at Amelia and knew something was wrong. Amelia was uncharacteristically quiet. Even more telling, she didn't ask about Laura.

If Hank knew what was wrong, he didn't show it. He pounded Brand on the back and then welcomed Jesse home as well.

"I'll get two more plates and some silverware," Charity said as she headed for the kitchen. As she passed Reverend Lockwood, she smiled. "Would you mind bringing two more chairs up to the dining table, John?"

"I'm glad to see you, Brand. I've had a wonderful stay here in Glory these past few weeks, but I'll be happy to hand you the reins tomorrow." The reverend grabbed a side chair and carried it into the small dining room. Sam tried to drag another over by himself. Jesse took one look and helped him out.

"John's been a wonderful replacement." Amelia smiled, though she appeared distracted. "The board *was* hoping that you had changed your mind—" She fell silent and Brand had the feeling there was much more she wanted to say.

It didn't escape him that no one had yet asked about Laura. Taking his cue from Amelia and Charity, he didn't volunteer anything. Charity urged them all to sit down again. Amelia helped carry dishes out from the kitchen. They brought in a platter of fried chicken and a bowl heaped full of mashed potatoes, plus gravy, corn, beans, and biscuits. Hank kept the conversation flowing, but the expression on Charity's face assured Brand something was definitely wrong—something that no one would address with the children in the room.

Lockwood was still on his feet. He pulled out Charity's chair when she made her final trip in from the kitchen. Hank assisted Amelia, and everyone finally settled into silence.

"Reverend Lockwood, would you say the blessing?" Charity asked.

After the blessing, everyone began passing serving dishes and filling their plates.

Sam was the first to speak up between bites of a drumstick. "So are you gonna preach again, Papa?"

"I am, son."

"You changed your mind," Hank said. He didn't sound particularly relieved.

Brand took a deep breath. "Laura changed it for me, actually."

"You found her?" Charity laid her fork on her plate.

"We found her and I convinced her to come home." He glanced around the table and found the adults studiously considering their next bites.

"Are you gonna get married?" Janie wanted to know. "Can I have a purple dress with lots of ruffles to wear to the wedding?"

"Not now, Janie. I'm sure your papa is far too tired to discuss it." Charity handed the gravy to John.

Brand studied his sister for a moment. The look she gave him was a silent warning not to ask what was wrong.

"We'd better see about getting you that dress," he told his daughter. "Mrs. Foster has agreed to marry me."

He waited for congratulations and good wishes.

Charity reached for her water goblet.

Silence fell. Brand noticed that except for Jesse and the children, no one was even looking at him.

Amelia spoke up. "Would anyone care for some mashed potatoes?"

When Brand looked across the table at Hank, he wasn't sure he liked what he saw in the publisher's eyes.

"When you getting married, Papa?" Sam wanted to know.

"Sooner rather than later."

An awkward silence descended once more. Everyone concentrated on eating until the meal was over. Charity was in a hurry to serve up apple cobbler with fresh cream. As soon as most everyone was finished, she turned to Sam.

"Why don't you and Janie bundle up and show Jesse that new litter of kittens. You wouldn't mind going out to the barn with them, would you, Jesse?"

Jesse glanced at Brand and tossed his napkin on the table. "Not at all, ma'am."

Sam and Janie raced down the hall to collect their coats. As soon as the three of them were outside, Brand leaned back in his chair. He looked at Amelia, Hank, Charity, and Lockwood in turn.

"Now, who would like to tell me exactly what is going on?"

His sister's face turned the color of a ripe raspberry. She opened her mouth, closed it, and shook her head.

Brand turned to Amelia. "What is it? Did the board retract their votes and accept my resignation? Is that it?"

Before Amelia could comment, Charity found her voice. "Not yet, but people are saying terrible things about Laura, Brand. Things I can't even repeat."

So it's happened, he thought. Laura would arrive and be ambushed by gossip. He had wanted to be the one to bring the truth out into the open. Coming from him, he'd hoped to make a difference as to how the news was received.

"Collier Holloway let it out," Amelia said. "I was afraid this would happen."

Brand was furious.

Charity stared at him. "You knew about this? It's all true?"

Brand slowly nodded. Charity turned to Amelia. "You knew too? Why didn't anyone tell me?"

"Laura took us into her confidence just before she left," Brand explained. "If I could have told you, I would have."

"That's why she left town, isn't it?" Charity glanced back and forth between them. "She told you and she was too ashamed to face you afterward."

"Actually, she left to spare me embarrassment when and if the truth came out," Brand said.

"And yet you went after her." Charity shook her head in disbelief. "What were you thinking, Brand?"

"I love her."

John Lockwood folded his napkin and slid it alongside his plate.

"Maybe I should excuse myself," he said softly.

Charity turned to him. "Please, don't leave." She took a deep breath before she turned to Brand.

"First Jesse shows up and now this. I like Laura well enough, Brand, but I don't see how you can expect folks to accept her, let alone as your wife."

Amelia and Hank had yet to voice their opinions, but Brand thought their silence telling enough. He looked around the table again. He'd overcome doubt because of his love for Laura, but if those closest to him couldn't accept it, he didn't know how he was going to convince anyone else that Laura was worthy of becoming his wife.

"Forgiveness is the foundation of my belief," he said softly. "Love and forgiveness go hand in hand."

Amelia nodded. "We only want what's best for you."

"Laura is what's best for me," he said, daring anyone to object.

"Both Amelia and I think so too," Hank said. "But we also think you'll have a long, hard row to hoe." He turned to Amelia, slipped his arm around her shoulder. "Maybe we should be heading home," he suggested.

Brand walked the Larsons to the door and told them good-night while Charity collected Reverend Lockwood's overcoat and brought it to him.

"Thanks again for agreeing to preach tomorrow," Brand told John after the Larsons left. "I'm going to need some time to prepare for more than stepping up to the pulpit again. From the reaction tonight — and I'm in a friendly camp — it looks like I've got an uphill battle to fight."

"I'll stay on as long as you need me," John volunteered. "Things will work out for you, one way or another."

Lockwood went into the kitchen and took an overly long time thanking Charity for dinner and bidding her goodnight. When he came back in he asked, "Would you mind stepping outside with me, Brand?"

Lockwood appeared to be concentrating on buttoning up his coat.

"I could use some fresh air," Brand assured him.

Together they crossed the front porch and stopped at the end of the walk. He was certain the reverend would try to council him about his feelings for Laura.

"I meant what I said. I've truly enjoyed my time here," John told him. "Everyone has made me feel quite at home."

"You have my undying gratitude," Brand said. "It wasn't easy leaving Charity and the children here. You might have noticed they're a handful, but my sister does a fine job with them."

"She's not only competent but beautiful. If I were younger, I'd ask your permission to court your sister. She's just the kind of woman I've always wanted to marry. She's dedicated and hardwork-ing and would do a man proud. She should have children of her own to love." John's face was a shade darker. He shook his head and tried to make light of his comments. "She probably wouldn't want anything to do with an old goat like me."

Brand studied him. "How old are you, John?"

"The very late side of forty-five." He shoved his hands in his coat pockets and glanced down the street. "Tell me about this woman you're in love with."

"She's a good woman with a dark past." He gave John an abbreviated account of Laura's life and situation.

"People around here are in shock," Lockwood told him. "They knew you were courting her and that you went off searching for her when she up and left. Some have asked for my opinion."

"What *do* you think? What do you tell them?"

"I trust your judgment. I know what's in your heart, what you believe. If you think she's the right woman for you, then I don't doubt it."

"I made no secret that I was courting her. There is nothing to hide. I didn't know about her past until she told me a few weeks ago. Then she left—to keep from hurting me."

"Still, you might want to think this through, Brand."

"I have. Believe me, I have."

"Then I'll pray for you both," John promised.

"Thank you, John. That's all I can ask."

Brand found Charity finishing up the dishes.

"Did Jesse and the children come back in yet?" he asked.

"They went into their rooms to change into their nightclothes."

"Did Jesse leave?"

"I suppose. He didn't stop in to say good-bye."

He was surprised Jesse hadn't come in to thank her for dinner. No doubt Jesse was as bone tired as he and longing for a good night's sleep in his own bed—if he still had one.

Brand wanted to tell Jesse that Laura's story had come to light before he heard disparaging talk from someone on the street and wound up in a brawl.

Suddenly he felt like the walls were closing in. He ached for a few minutes alone. Instead he watched his sister dry her hands, slip off her apron, smooth her hair. Her forehead was creased with worry lines.

"We've a new organ at church." She avoided his gaze. It was more than evident she didn't want to speak of Laura right now.

"Purchased by the board? That's surprising. At the last meeting, the treasury had been sorely lacking."

"It was donated by someone and delivered right to the church door. It's very grand. Amelia has been accompanying the choir on it and we had the old upright piano moved into the church hall."

Though she was trying to keep the conversation light, worry lines creased her brow. He figured she could use a compliment right about now.

"You know, John is quite taken with you."

"He is?" Her face turned as pink as her gown, but she didn't sound surprised.

"In fact, he said if he were younger and staying on for a while, he would ask my permission to court you. I don't know what he's thinking. He's far too old for you." Brand shrugged. "Still, it's always nice to know when someone admires—"

"He's not that old."

"He's forty-five."

"I wouldn't care if he was fifty. He's educated and still very handsome. He loves my cooking, which is passable at the most. He thinks I've got a way with children, and he thinks I'm beautiful."

"*I* think you're lovely."

"That doesn't count. You're my brother!"

"Then I'll tell him he's welcome to court you, but he'll have to work fast if he's set on leaving town—" Brand stopped. "Would you go with him, Sis? Would you leave if he asked you to marry him?"

Tears glistened in her eyes. Irritated, she quickly wiped them away.

"I want what you have, Brand. I want a family. I want someone to love me."

"We all love you."

"I know that, but it's not the same."

He put his arm around her. "I know, Sis. And I do want you to be happy, if this is what you want."

"What do you really think of him, Brand? You promised you'd tell me if you thought the man I fell in love with was anything like our father."

"John is nothing like Father. He admires and respects you. I think you'd be very well suited and happy together."

"Then please tell John I'd be happy to have him court me." She moved away, hung the wet dishtowels on a rack near the pie safe. "And I'd like you to think about what you would be doing by marrying Laura. I can take care of myself and I'll stand beside you no matter what, but you've got Sam and Janie to think of. What will this do to them?"

"The woman I've come to know will make a kind and loving mother to them, but you're right. There is more than just myself and Laura to think of." He paused. "If you don't mind, I need some fresh air."

"Of course." The steaming dishwater had dampened her hair. She smoothed it back away from her face.

He grabbed his coat off the rack in the hallway and headed out the back door. Outside, wind from the southwest was picking up. There were stars in the eastern sky, but storm clouds were fast approaching. He pictured Laura tucked into the coach and hoped she was warm enough. He thought of the crude depot stops along the route and chided himself for not following his instincts and escorting her home.

Now he was more determined than ever to be waiting at the mercantile when her stage pulled in. He had to be there to soften the blow and warn her about Collier's revelation.

He took another deep breath of frigid night air, lingered to watch the stars blinking in the indigo heavens before he turned around to see if the barn was locked up tight. He noticed the glow of a lantern seeping out from the cracks around a shuttered window in the side wall. He'd have to have a talk with the children. They could have burned the barn down if the unattended lantern fell and started a fire.

When he got to the barn door, he noticed the heavy bar had been dropped in place on the outside. He was about to lift it when he heard a loud thump from within and then Jesse shouted, "Hey! Lemme out!"

Brand raised the bar and the door swung open. Jesse was standing inside.

"What are you doing in there?" Brand asked.

Jesse shrugged. "Ask your children. They locked me in."

"What?"

Jesse nodded. "Had me look at the kittens and then they told me one was missing. I fell for it. Got on my hands and knees and while I was digging through the straw, they slipped out and barred the door. I tried yelling but nobody heard me. I figured I'd bed down and try to stay warm."

"Why would they do that?" Brand muttered.

"I can't figure out why those two do anything. You mind if I head home now? See if I've still got one, that is?"

Brand held out his hand. Jesse took it and they shook.

"Thank you for your help. I couldn't have made it through that country on my own," Brand admitted. He told Jesse that Laura's past had been revealed. "Just remember you'll always have a home with us if you want it. Come on back tonight if you need to."

"Yeah. Those tadpoles can lock me in again."

Brand returned to the house and knocked on Janie's door. She opened it so quickly he was convinced she'd been standing on the other side, waiting for him.

"Yes, Papa?" She smiled up sweetly.

"Come into Sam's room with me," he said.

She hung her head as she walked with him to the room beside hers.

Sam was in bed with the covers pulled up over his head. His imitation snores didn't fool Brand for a second.

"Sit up, Sam. Don't make me ask you twice."

Sam sat up and peered at them over the edge of his blankets.

Brand looked at both of them in turn. "Who wants to tell me why you locked Jesse in the barn?"

"Jesse was locked in the barn?" Sam's eyes grew round as wagon wheels.

"You know Jesse was in the barn. Don't make things worse."

"We wanted to keep him." Janie shrugged.

"Keep him?" Brand anchored his hands on his hips. "You wanted to keep Jesse so you locked him in the barn?"

"We thought that if he spent the night in there with the cat and her kittens, he might like it as much as he does sleeping in Mrs. Foster's barn." Sam folded down the blankets and tucked them under his arms.

Brand found himself biting the inside of his cheek. "He has a *room* in Mrs. Foster's carriage house. He doesn't sleep in a stall."

"Can't we make a room for him in our barn?" Janie asked.

"I'll help you build it," Sam volunteered.

Brand pinched the bridge of his nose, fighting a headache. Any other time he would see the humor in the situation. Tonight, he just wanted to get to bed and try to get some sleep.

"I *have* invited Jesse to stay here," he told them. "If things don't work out for him at Mrs. Foster's, he just might do that, but the choice will be up to him. Locking him in and trying to force him to stay isn't going to work. You owe him an apology."

"Yes, Papa," they chimed together.

By the time Brand left them tucked in again, he was dead on his feet. But that night, sleep was a long time coming.

TWENTY -FIVE

It was late afternoon on the day Laura's stage finally pulled up in front of the mercantile. A light dusting of snow covered the frozen ground and Main Street was nearly deserted. Laura roused herself and straightened her hat, then folded the quilt Betty Jean had given her. It had come in mighty handy inside the freezing coach.

The driver opened the door and helped her down the step before he retrieved her heavy carpetbag. It had been lighter when she left home, much lighter without the Bible. She thought it better that her soul had grown lighter and her bag heavier than the other way around.

She'd been the only passenger on this leg of the trip. There was no one there at all to greet the stage, no sign of Brand. Because of the weather, her arrival was not only hours, but days behind schedule. She hoped he didn't think she had broken her promise to return.

She headed into the mercantile to warm up and say hello to Harrison. If she was lucky, someone shopping inside might offer her a ride down the street.

She glimpsed Harrison through the front window. He was behind the counter as usual. She waved but figured he hadn't seen her when he didn't wave back. The small silver bell above the door tinkled as she walked in, but he took his time looking her way. The polished smile he beamed on customers faded faster than a snowflake in July when he saw her. Gone was his solicitous greeting. He didn't offer to take her bag.

She carefully closed the door against the cold and tried to strike up a conversation.

"How are you, Mr. Barker?" She set the heavy carpetbag down at her feet and folded her gloved hands at her waist.

"Something I can do for you?"

No kind word of greeting. No response to her question. He didn't even ask where she had been or how her trip was. He said absolutely nothing.

"Is everything all right?" she asked. "I hope your mother is doing well."

There was a pause and then, "She's fine. Thank you." Still no smile.

A prickle of concern nagged her. She gave up the notion of trying to cheer him. "Is there any mail for me?"

Without comment, he walked to the row of small wooden mail slots at the end of the counter. Her box was empty.

"None in quite awhile." He turned around and began adjusting perfectly straight canned goods on the shelf behind him.

His cut was direct and obvious. Suddenly she was even more anxious to get home.

There was no one around to hitch a ride with, but she could definitely walk. She picked up her bag and was set to leave when a woman Laura had never met hurried in. Frigid air swirled in around her. Dressed for the cold, she carried a large, empty basket. When she saw Laura, she came to an abrupt halt and simply stared.

Suddenly Harrison's ingratiating smile was back.

"Let me help you, Mrs. Simmons." He took the woman's market basket from her and set it on the counter. Then he came around the counter and ushered her away from Laura. As they moved on,

Harrison said over his shoulder, "You'd best be moving on, Mrs. Foster. We don't cater to your kind here."

It couldn't have hurt any more if he'd slapped her. Laura blinked and watched him guide the woman across the room, moving quickly away, as if she had the plague. Harrison and the woman had their heads together, whispering.

So that's how it is.

The inevitable had happened. Armed with her newfound faith, she thought she'd been prepared to face this battle, but she wasn't ready for the pain inflicted by Harrison's insult.

If the shopkeep knew, the truth was out. Had Brand told everyone after he had promised to wait until she returned? Maybe he'd wanted to hurry and try to turn the tide in her favor. If Harrison was any indication, things weren't going very smoothly.

She kept her head high. She'd suffered disparaging looks and remarks before. She'd seen the condemnation in the eyes of folks who thought themselves above her kind on the streets of New Orleans. But here in Glory she was used to living a lovely charade as Laura Foster. Harrison's cool dismissal hurt her more than she expected.

She clutched her bag close and opened the door. The bell chimed above her, the tinkling sound mocked her as the freezing cold outside slapped her in the face. Unthinking, she moved too quickly and nearly slipped on a patch of ice on the boardwalk. She caught herself and slowed down, picking her way along, thankful that there was hardly anyone out today.

There was no sign of Hank in the *Glory Gazette* building. A CLOSED sign sat in the lower right corner of the window. No doubt he'd stayed at home to sit by the fire with Amelia. She pictured the two of them warm and cozy inside their little house and tried not to envy them.

Her toes were freezing inside her black leather shoes as she trudged down the street. When a buckboard driven by a rancher passed, the driver didn't even look her way. For that she was grateful. Far better to be ignored than openly scorned.

Brand wouldn't have told anyone before warning me. Nor would Amelia.

As she walked alone, shoulders back, spine erect, she knew that there was only one explanation.

Collier.

She reached the Silver Slipper and stopped outside. In milder weather, the door was always open. Today it was closed. She tried to peer through the stained-glass design of a woman's slipper surrounded by garish ruby and garnet glass. The bartender was behind the bar. Rob Jenkins was mopping the floor in back. There was, oddly enough, no one else inside.

She took a deep breath, opened the door, and stuck her head inside.

"Could you call Mr. Holloway for me, please?" she asked the bartender.

Rob stopped mopping and nodded a silent greeting before he went back to his task. No matter how thoroughly he cleaned — which didn't appear to be that thoroughly — it would never be enough to eradicate the odor of spilled liquor permeating the floorboards or the smell of tobacco that had seeped into the walls.

"Come on in from the cold," Denton Fairchild suggested. "No need to freeze while you wait."

"I prefer to stay outside," she told him.

"That's up to you, but close the door and keep the cold out." The bartender rudely eyed her before he went to do her bidding.

Laura closed the door and waited outside on the boardwalk. Her hands were freezing inside her gloves. She could barely feel her toes.

Collier appeared in surprisingly good time.

"Come on in, Lovie."

"No, thank you."

"If you think I'm going to stand out there and freeze, forget it." He started to close the door.

She stuck her bag in the opening. "All right."

She glanced around. There was no one on the street to see her enter the saloon anyway.

"I'm glad to see you," Collier smiled down at her before he turned to Denton and signaled for the man to bring him a drink. He took her by the elbow and tried to lead her farther into the room.

She shook off his hold. "You told someone."

"I won't lie to you. After you left town, everyone was talking about how *noble* it was for the minister to go off looking for you, how *wonderful* it was that he was so in love that he was willing to run after you and bring you back. Ridiculous, given that I knew why you were running and what you were running from."

"You have no idea—"

"That he proposed? Not at first, but when he told me, the reason you left became crystal clear to me. You wanted to save him from ruination." He picked up the whiskey Denton had set down in front of him, threw back his head, and finished it in one swallow.

She couldn't deny it so she didn't even try.

"Are you ready to give up this charade now?"

"Actually, I should thank you. I'm glad the truth is finally out."

"When you finally realize your business is ruined, I won't mind taking the place off your hands. That fancy house of yours would make a mighty fine brothel." Collier ran his finger around the lip of his empty tumbler.

Without another word, she grabbed her bag, stood, and headed for the door.

"You think things will just go on as they have before? You think the truth won't make a difference in this town? You've got another thing coming, Lovie. You're ruined."

When Collier didn't bother getting up to open the door for her,

Rob moved with surprising agility for a man who'd been looking at the world through a liquor-induced haze for years.

"There you go, Miz Foster." He opened the door with a flourish, ignoring Collier's dark glance. Unfortunately he didn't close it fast enough.

Collier's parting words rang in her ears as Laura headed home. "When you're out on the street again, remember I told you so."

By the time Laura reached her front door, her spirit had sunk as low as the heels of her sodden shoes. She thought the sight of her house would cheer her, but as she walked past the side of the porch on her way to the front door, she noticed the cement birdbath had been knocked over, the bowl was cracked, and the pedestal broken in half. She stared at it for a moment, tightened her grip on her valise, and hurried up the walk to the front door.

She tried the knob and found the door locked. It wasn't until she reached for the bell that she realized the oak finish on the front door had recently been re-varnished. There were telltale remnants of paint slashed beneath the surface. She took a step back to study the marks and realized they were not random. The word *whore* had been scrawled across the front door in bold, black letters.

Someone, most likely Rodgrigo or Jesse, had tried to remove the damage, but beneath the shiny finish, the word was faint but still visible.

Like me, she thought. *Polished on the outside but forever ruined no matter how hard I try to change, no matter who I become.*

Doubt assailed her as she rang the bell.

Have I done the right thing by coming back?

Anna answered, opened the door, and stared until she quickly recovered and reached for Laura's bag. She stepped back to let her pass.

"*Entra*, señora. Entra." Anna started to usher Laura into the drawing room. The shades were closed and there was no fire burning in the grate. The shadowed room seemed cold and lifeless. Laura's teeth were chattering.

"Come. It's warmer back here," Anna said.

It was indeed warm as toast in the kitchen. Laura wasn't surprised to find not only Rodrigo there, but Richard and Jesse seated at the table. Jesse was sporting a black eye.

All three men shot to their feet, but she waved them back down.

There was a moment of shocked silence before Rodrigo said, "Welcome home, señora. Everything is just the way you left it." He smiled, but it quickly faded. "Almost."

"What happened to your eye?" She had a feeling she knew what Jesse was going to say.

"Nothing."

She looked around the table. Four pairs of dark eyes looked back.

"Tell me," she insisted.

Jesse spoke up. "Let's just say nobody will be trespassing around here again anytime soon."

Anna brought Laura a cup of tea. She thanked the woman, doubting even the steaming brew could warm her. She was chilled to the bone and not merely by the inclement weather.

"We will fix the birdbath, señora," Rodrigo promised.

"The door isn't perfect yet, but we're working on it," Jesse told her. He leaned back in his chair and hooked his arm around the top rung of the ladder back. If his shiner bothered him, he didn't show it. From the way he was smiling a cocky half smile, he seemed to be wearing it like a badge of honor.

"I wasn't sure you'd actually show up," he added.

"I promised your father."

"He's been trying to second-guess the weather. Figured the storm would hold you up. I know he wanted to be there to meet you so you wouldn't step off alone."

He was watching her closely. She knew why.

"I received a chilly reception from Harrison Barker as soon as I stepped off the stage."

"Amelia figures it was that Holloway fella who —"

"It was." She nodded. "It was bound to happen sooner or later."

"You sure it was him?"

"I stopped and asked. I knew it wouldn't have been Amelia, and Brand promised he would wait until I returned."

"You *wanted* Brand to tell folks?"

"I did."

When Anna set the tea down, Laura wrapped her hands around the cup to warm them.

"May I take your coat, señora?" Anna offered.

Laura shook her head no. "I'm still too cold." She wondered if she'd ever be truly warm again. "How is Brand?"

Jesse's gaze strayed to the window and back before he said, "Handling this better than most men would be about now."

She could tell by the Hernandezes' expressions they knew what was going on. She could only imagine how Harrison was treating Rodrigo whenever he shopped at the mercantile.

"Would you excuse us for a moment?" she asked the family.

"Of course, señora. We will dust upstairs now." Rodrigo left his chair and walked toward the front of the house with his wife. Richard put on his coat and went out the back way.

Jesse leaned forward and explained, "When we got back from St. Gall, everyone already knew."

"How is Brand?"

"Stubborn as all get out."

"Meaning?"

"He's bound and determined to state his case to his congregation. He intends to marry you no matter what."

"He could lose everything," she said softly.

She thought of Collier's offer to buy her house. The last thing this town needed was a brothel. She sighed, planted her elbow on the table, and rested her chin on her fist.

It had been a long, exhausting trip across the southwest corner of Texas. She was cold and tired, and all she wanted to do was to drag herself upstairs and sleep for a week.

"Brand's not the only one in town who is speaking up for you." Jesse reached behind his head, laced his fingers together, and stretched. "You've got more friends than you thought."

"Not that it will do any good." Not if Harrison's reaction was any indication.

Jesse pushed his chair away from the table and stood up. He rapped his knuckles on the wood surface a couple of times.

"I rode into this town full of hate. I was just as likely to kill Brand McCormick as not—"

"You don't have it in you," she said.

"Maybe not, but I *thought* I did. I came looking for revenge." He spread his arms wide. "Look at me now. I'm still here. I'm getting to know my pa, and I've got a couple young'uns who hang on my every word and believe I can do just about anything."

"I don't see what that has to do with my situation."

"I guess what I'm trying to say is that life is kinda like riding a buckin' horse. You just have to relax and hang on." He smiled one of his rare smiles. "I do know one thing: Brand is still dead set on marrying you. If you were to call it off, you'd break his heart."

The deep cold had abated but the night was still brisk as Brand rode through town headed for Laura's. The boardinghouse, always cheerfully alive with light when it was open, was shrouded in darkness except for a single lamp burning in the corner window on the second floor.

He dismounted and walked his horse up the drive and around to the back door. There was no lamp burning in the kitchen. A light in the carriage house indicated Jesse was home.

After knotting the reins over the hitching post near the back door, Brand crossed the veranda and pulled the bell, hoping Laura could hear it. He knocked again and was about to walk around to the front door when he saw candlelight moving down the hallway toward the kitchen. He watched through the window as Laura set the candle down on the dry sink beside her.

"Who is it?" she called.

"It's me. Brand."

She opened the door. Her hand clutched the lapels of her robe together, just below a band of lace that teased her chin. Her hair was down, flowing around her shoulders.

She smiled up at him, warming him from head to toe.

"What are you doing here so late?"

"I had to see you." He shuffled from foot to foot and blew on his gloved hands in an attempt to keep warm. She glanced behind him, surveyed the darkness beyond. Her reputation couldn't get any worse, but there was his to consider.

She hesitated a moment longer before she said, "Come in before we both freeze to death."

He stepped through the door. "I was called out to a ranch twenty miles outside of town. One of the hands fell off his horse and was trampled. I went to console the family and when I returned, I heard you'd arrived this afternoon."

"I'm sure that's all over town by now. It appears I'm quite the topic of conversation these days."

"Are you all right?"

She nodded. "The thing I feared for so long has finally come to pass and aside from worrying about you, I find there are far worse things that could happen to a person than being the object of gossip." She took his hand. "Losing you would be one of them."

"I didn't want you to hear like this. I went to the mercantile every day, waiting for word, hoping to be there when your stage arrived. I'm so sorry I missed meeting you. The one day I wasn't there—"

"Please, I'm fine." She stepped farther back into the room and picked up the candle. "Let's go into the drawing room. There's no fire, but there is wood in the grate."

He followed her down the hall, drawn to her the way a moth was drawn to a flame as she led the way through the darkness. He opened the sliding double doors into the drawing room. Kindling was stacked beneath the logs on the grate. Brand knelt down and had a low fire burning in no time. When he got to his feet, he looked around the room.

Reflected firelight shimmered off of the gilt frames bordering her paintings and the silver candelabra on a library table near the window. Laura touched the flame of her taper to its brace of candles and stepped back.

"It seems there is something missing." He looked around. The room seemed bigger somehow.

"Guests," she said, "for one thing."

"Your photographs are gone." Those images of unknown faces from other times and places she'd collected.

She nodded. "Other peoples' people. I put them away this evening."

She moved to join him in front of the mantel. He took both her hands in his.

"You will have family again, Laura, as soon as we marry. More than you ever dreamed of."

"If so, I'll be the happiest woman alive."

"No ifs," he said. "It's a certainty. Sam, Janie, Charity. And we'll find your sisters one day too."

"And Jesse," she reminded him. She prayed it wasn't all just a lovely fantasy.

He nodded. "And Jesse." He looked around the room. "Are you still sure, Laura?"

"More sure than I've ever been about anything in my life. Are you?"

"Yes, but if I were to lose my position—"

"If the boardinghouse fails, we'll all move on and start over."

"You would do that? Leave this house behind?"

"When I walked in today, I realized that's all it is. It's just a house. The joy and hope that I felt while I planned and built this place aren't the same as the love and peace in my heart now. I know

now that I can live anywhere, Brand, and be happy. I can still look for my sisters. They'll be welcome wherever I am."

"Wherever *we* are," he amended.

She indicated the room with a wave of her hand. "*Things* don't bring us happiness. Happiness is something we carry in our hearts. Like love."

They stood in front of the mantle hand in hand, facing one another as firelight gilded them with its golden glow. Having her back, seeing her here where she belonged, solidified his resolve. She was kind and loving, passionate in her selflessness. She would be a perfect wife and companion.

"Sunday will be my first time preaching since I returned," he told her. "I plan to announce our engagement."

"We don't know what God wants for certain, Brand."

"We'll know soon enough. Either the congregation will accept you or they won't. If they don't, then they lose me."

"Maybe you should wait a while. Let the talk die down a bit. I can certainly weather the storm."

"I want you to be my wife, Laura. The sooner everyone knows I'm not going to change my mind about it, the better."

"Jesse said Charity seemed upset."

"She's worried about the children."

"As well she should be." She shook her head.

"I can't think of a better mother for them than you. People can talk all they want about having faith, but when they have to prove it, when they have to open their hearts and live the truths they claim to believe, that's when they are truly tested. We'll come through this and so will this town."

"Sunday," she whispered, "is the day after tomorrow."

"Sunday it is."

"Must I be there?"

He watched her courage waver and understood. It was one thing to pray for forgiveness alone in her room; it was another to seek it from a church full of people.

"No. Not at all."

She clung to his hands.

"I should go," he said.

But instead of moving toward the door, he ran his hand up her sleeve, threaded his fingers through her curls. Before he knew what he was doing, she was in his embrace. He kissed her long and thoroughly, kissed her with the passion of a man long starved for what he most desired.

He felt her hands on his shoulders, her fingers curled around the fabric of his coat. She kissed him back until a soft cry of protest escaped her. Her fingers uncurled. She let go and stepped back.

"This is insane," she said softly. "You have to go. If anyone sees you—"

"I know. Forgive me, Laura."

"I'll walk you to the door."

He placed the screen before the glowing embers of the fire. She snuffed out the candelabra and carried the lone taper again as they moved back down the hall toward the kitchen.

When he opened the back door, cold air whirled in and extinguished the flame, casting them in darkness. He wrapped his arm about her shoulder, drew her against his warmth. Still, she shivered against the cold.

"Our love belongs out in the open," he told her. "In the light of day."

She reached up and slipped her hand around his neck. He lowered his head and kissed her again.

"Go, Brand," she whispered as she pulled back. "Be safe."

"I'll be back on Sunday, right after the service."

"Until Sunday," she said.

"I love you, Laura. Never doubt it."

"I ... I love you too."

TWENTY -SIX

On Sunday morning, Brand watched the sun come up on what promised to be a warm, beautiful day. He relished the time alone while the house was still quiet, before Charity was up preparing breakfast and getting the children spit shined and dressed in their Sunday best. He walked into his office, carefully avoiding the squeaky board in the hallway, and sat at his desk, where he prayed and gathered his thoughts for his sermon.

He thought he would be nervous this morning, given the gravity of the situation, but he was filled with a contentment and peace the likes of which he'd never known.

When it was time, he escorted Charity and the children to the church. After they went inside to put on their choir robes, he waited on the steps to greet the congregation just as he'd always done. The change in the weather brought more folks out than he'd expected. As far as he could tell, most everyone was happy to see him back. Whether or not they assumed he had ended his courtship of Laura remained to be seen. Everyone was too polite to mention her or his month-long absence.

Since she had returned a good week after he did, most likely they assumed he was no longer interested in her.

Bud Townsend and his family climbed the steps. Mrs. Townsend nodded in greeting but didn't smile as she trailed her sizeable brood inside.

Bud paused long enough to lean close to Brand and mumble, "Close call, eh, Reverend? Good thing word got out about your fancy lady friend before you tied the knot. You dodged one bullet over that half breed. The second scandal would have brought you down."

Though he couldn't go so far as to tell Townsend it was good to see him, Brand was able to say, "I hope you enjoy the sermon, Bud."

He took a deep breath and turned to the family behind Townsend, relieved to see the Ellenbergs. Knowing Joe, Rebekah, and Hattie Ellenberg were there lightened his mood instantly.

A dramatic hat with a spray of long pheasant feathers adorned Hattie's head. It was like nothing she'd ever worn before.

"That's some hat," he told her. "I like it."

Hattie nodded and the feathers bobbed. "Ain't it though? It was a gift." She walked inside with a smile wide as the Brazos on her face.

When the last of the worshippers had entered, Brand followed them in and found there was standing room only inside. The service opened with the adult and children's choirs. The addition of the new organ made both choirs sound better than ever. Charity beamed with pride as the children filed off the altar.

Brand had noticed John Lockwood standing in the back of the church. The minister was smiling to beat the band as Charity took her seat in the front pew.

Brand walked to the lectern, took a deep breath, and scanned the crowd. An expectant hush fell over the gathering. The adults were intent, waiting for him to start his sermon. Even his children were not squirming as usual. In that moment he knew he had made the right decision. It was best he cleared the air.

He looked down at the open Bible on the lectern and took his strength from the words on the page. He didn't have a single note to refer to. He hadn't written a sermon for this most important day.

He began with a quote from the gospel of John. "He that is without sin among you, let him first cast a stone at her."

Folks shifted nervously, looking around, making not so subtle eye contact with each other before they focused on him again.

Later, whenever anyone asked Brand what he said that day, he wasn't able to tell them word for word. He only knew he was inspired as he spoke of forgiveness and new beginnings, of how they were called to leave their lives of sin and begin anew. He spoke of the story outlined in the Bible, told the tale of the woman who had been an adulterer and how, after Christ asked those of her accusers without sin to stone her, those accusers walked away.

When he finished speaking, he looked at his congregation. He saw Hattie beaming up at him from where she was seated beside her son. Amelia was wiping tears from her cheeks. Beside her Hank Larson nodded as if to say, "Well done."

Others he didn't know as well sat expectantly when, after a pause, he instructed Charity and some of the older girls and boys present to help her escort the younger children to the hall.

"I have an announcement to make to those adults who are willing to stay a bit longer."

No one else chose to leave.

Brand slowly looked around the crowded church again before he began.

"You may have heard that before Laura Foster recently left town I was courting her. When she suddenly disappeared, I went searching for her."

He couldn't help but notice the exchange of glances around the room, the whispers, the awkward shifting around in the pews. Undeterred, he went on.

"After hearing things that have come to light about her past, you may be of the opinion that I am no longer interested in pursuing our relationship. I have asked you all to stay so that I could tell you myself that neither my intent nor my feelings have changed."

A swell of conversation filled the church as a shock waved rippled through the crowd. Brand raised his voice and everyone fell silent again, hanging on every word.

"Laura Foster is the woman I intend to marry. She has accepted my proposal and—"

Bud Townsend was on his feet, effectively cutting Brand off.

He indicated the crowd with a wave of his hand.

"Just how far are you willing to push these fine folks, Reverend? You may have convinced the board to pass a vote of confidence after your son called you out, but this is going too far. It shows you're not worthy to stand up there and preach God's holy word."

"What difference is there in asking you all to forgive the sins of *my* past and asking you to forgive those of Laura Foster?" Brand looked around, "Or of anyone else here?"

"Something you did twenty years ago isn't the same thing. No telling what she's been doing in that 'boardinghouse' of hers. Even if she has repented, what kind of preacher's wife is she gonna make?"

Hank Larson shot to his feet. "Before things get out of hand, I'd like to say what she *does* in her home is rent rooms to 'women and families,' just like the sign on her front porch says."

Bud Townsend wouldn't be silenced. "You're trying to railroad everybody again, McCormick," he said. "Your friends on the board might have saved you once when that son of yours showed up, but they're not gonna abide by this. I can guarantee it."

"I'm not relying on just the board, Bud. I'm here to ask the entire congregation—the good people of Glory and those from ranches around the area, the hardworking, honest folk who are the backbone of this community—to hear the truth about Laura's past. Then they can tell me whether or not they will accept her as my wife. If not, then I'll step down."

Laura pulled dress after dress out of her closet and tossed them on the bed until she settled on one of her best. No matter what happened today, she was determined to make Brand proud. She walked over to her dressing table and chose a strand of pearls, put them on, studied herself, and pinned up a few stray locks of hair.

She was who she was — all the struggles, the misery, the determination, the joy.

She donned a coat, picked up her reticule, made certain her derringer was inside. She might be headed to church, but there were just some things a woman shouldn't have to do without. Protection was one of them.

Judging herself ready, she went downstairs, outside, and crossed the drive to the carriage house.

Jesse answered her knock immediately. The bruise around his eye had faded some.

"You look mighty fine. Where are you headed?"

"Will you drive me to the church?"

He hesitated. "You sure?"

"The least I can do is meet Brand after the service." She wondered if Jesse could hear her knees knocking. She was afraid, certainly, but she wasn't ashamed. Not anymore.

"Let me hitch up the buggy," he said. "With any luck, you'll get there by the time it's all over."

They pulled up in front of the church. Jesse set the break on the buggy. There wasn't a soul in sight. The church doors were closed.

"They must still be inside," she said.

"I'm not going in." He stared over at the church from beneath the brim of his black hat.

"That's up to you."

He turned his gaze her way. "Someday. Maybe."

"Someday. When you're ready." She was the last person to try to persuade him to change his mind.

He climbed down, walked around to her side of the buggy, and held out his hand like a gentleman. Stepping down, she thanked him and started up the walk alone.

When she reached the church doors she tried the handle but it didn't turn. She was staring at the wooden doors, wondering whether to go around to the side, when the door opened a crack. A man she didn't recognize stood on the other side. He was dressed in black with a white clerical collar banding his shirt.

"Come in," he whispered.

She nodded her thanks and slipped in. The entire church was full. There wasn't a seat left. People were standing along the wall in back. She ended up with her back pressed against the door, standing slightly behind and between the tall, salt-and-pepper-haired minister and a gangly cowboy with his hair neatly parted and slicked down.

A heated discussion was going on. When Laura realized it centered on her, she reached for the door handle again. Then she glanced up at the visiting preacher beside her. His smile steadied her.

He leaned down and whispered in her ear. "Mrs. Foster, I presume?

She nodded yes.

"Reverend John Lockwood." He introduced himself in a hushed whisper. "I stood in for Brand while he was away. If you would like to leave, I'll escort you out, but I believe you owe it to Brand to stay."

She tightened her hands on the folds of her skirt and held her head high. "I'll stay."

As Laura watched, an angry, barrel-chested man in a gray suit sat down. A second later, Amelia rose. All eyes were on her friend when she started speaking.

"If it hadn't been for Laura's help, I wouldn't have been able to pull Hank through when he was severely wounded. She showed up unasked and stood beside me while I operated. She never batted an eye. She was right there for us. She's been there for us ever since."

On the other side of the church Mary Margaret Cutter got to

her feet as soon as Amelia sat down. Laura closed her eyes against a
rush of tears. When she opened them, she found it better to focus
only on Brand as he stood tall and confident behind the lectern. If
he was nervous or worried in the least, it didn't show.

He is doing this for me. For us.

She could be just as strong. She would do him proud.

Mary Margaret gazed slowly around the church. "I know most
all of you. You've given your trust over to Timothy and me for
years. We've trusted you in return whenever you come in to the
First Bank of Glory asking for loans, or for help with paying your
taxes. We've loaned you money to see you through until the next
roundup and the next harvest, so I hope you'll believe me when I
say that there is nothing Laura Foster has done to be ashamed of
since she moved to Glory four years ago.

"You want to know where the money came from for those fancy
new choir robes some of you and your children are wearing? Well,
half of it came from the pie auction and the masquerade ball. The
balance was donated anonymously. Laura Foster was the one who
made up the difference—but I wasn't supposed to tell."

As she took her seat, Timothy shouted, "Did you just say you
were having a spell?"

Richard Hernandez was seated alone, close to the back door.
When he stood up, hat in hand, folks swiveled around in their
seats to have a look at him. Laura was thankful she stood in John
Lockwood's shadow.

In a clear, strong voice Richard said, "If not for Señora Foster,
my family would have nothing. She took us in. She gave us a home
and work. And that organ there—" He pointed to the altar. "She
had my father deliver it to the church after she left town. It came
out of her drawing room."

He had no sooner taken his seat than Mick Robinson, the
smithy, stood up.

"Old Rob's been wearing a new winter coat and boots. He told me Mrs. Foster gave them to him 'fore she left town." Mick sat down.

When Barbara Barker suddenly stood up, Laura held her breath. Surely Harrison's mother had nothing good to say.

"A couple of years ago when the school was built, that woman put in an order at the mercantile for enough McGuffy readers for all the students," Barbara announced. She looked over at Mary Margaret. "Anonymously."

Blinded by tears, Laura covered her lips with her gloved hand.

Hattie Ellenberg stood up the minute Mrs. Barker sat down. Her face was hidden behind the brim of her bonnet. She waited for the buzz of conversation to die down and then her voice rang out loud and clear. "About three weeks ago, Rodrigo Hernandez showed up at my place with a pile of hat boxes. Mrs. Foster sent out five fancy hats with a note saying they were for me to wear when I came into town. I'd told her how I liked to cover the scalpin' scar on my forehead so as not to alarm other folks, and she remembered."

Hattie reached up to touch the brim of her bonnet and the pheasant feathers danced. "You all just heard the reverend tell you exactly how she wound up living in such a sinful state. She had no choice in the matter. She was robbed of her innocence and her childhood. She had no family to stand by her.

"You've all heard stories of captives, like my son's wife, Rebekah. She survived. But there are many who take their own lives rather than live in degradation. Or women like me who have suffered physical indignities. But I believe only God has the right to claim our lives in His own time. It isn't up to us to decide. Because of those beliefs I survived what the Comanche did to me. Every day since is a day I've devoted my life to the Lord.

"Laura Foster lived through unspeakable trials and now she's trying to live a good life and make amends. What right have any of us to judge her, or anyone else for that matter?"

As soon as Hattie sat down there was a general buzz of

conversation around the room until Brand demanded everyone's attention again.

"What Hattie said so well is true. There's no shame in surviving. We learn from our trials. It's not how you start out in life, it's how you finish that counts. Laura Foster has learned more than most of you will ever know about hardship and struggle. I thought so before and now, after all I've heard today, I know she's the better for it. You've put your trust in me as your minister for nearly four years now. I've fallen in love with a woman who has proven again and again that she's good and kind and true. If I thought loving her was wrong, if I thought for a moment that she wouldn't be the kind of mother my children deserve or the kind of wife I need beside me as I strive to lead a congregation, then I wouldn't have asked her to marry me.

"It's up to the Lord to forgive Laura Foster, just as it's up to Him to forgive all of us our past sins. It's up to you to believe in His infinite wisdom and forgive Laura and me our past sins, just as He does. That's all I can ask of you."

Before anyone else could respond, the rancher who had been so upset earlier was on his feet again.

"I know what's right," he said. "I'm resigning from the board and taking my family and my contributions elsewhere. Anyone who agrees with me is welcome to come with me."

The woman beside him stood up and together they worked their way out of their pew and went out the side door.

Except for a few whispers here and there, the room was silent. Everyone was watchful, expectant, as they held a collective breath and waited to see who would leave next.

Brand braced both hands on the lectern.

"I would like to thank all of you who spoke up on Laura's behalf. I'm moved and grateful for your show of support."

His gaze swept the room again and suddenly stopped on Laura. She knew the moment he had seen her; his smile lit up his face.

"For those of you who have never met Laura Foster," Brand said, "I'd like to introduce my fiancée."

When he motioned her to come forward and all heads turned her way, she found she couldn't take a step.

Reverend Lockwood came to her rescue. "At your service, Mrs. Foster." He gallantly offered his arm.

"Thank you," she whispered.

"Ready?"

Laura turned toward the front of the church where Brand was waiting for her. Her heart slowed to an even, steady beat as she smiled back at him.

"I'm ready." She slipped her hand into Reverend Lockwood's arm and he escorted her up the aisle toward the promise of forever.

TWENTY
-SEVEN

"Janie, please. Stand still." Laura sighed with frustration as she tried to anchor one more hairpin and put the final touches on Janie's hair. "If you insist on wiggling around that way, this entire right side of curls is going to tumble down, and we haven't time to start over. We're already running late."

Laura glanced around her suite, which was in complete upheaval. She shook her head, wondering if she would ever get used to such confusion.

Janie was seated on the low, padded stool in front of the dressing table, pulling out the stoppers on one after another of Laura's collection of crystal perfume bottles.

"May I wear some, Laura? Please?"

"Only if you sit still for one more minute, and then only a dab."

"I'll sit still," Janie promised. A second later, she said, "Uh-oh."

By now, Laura knew nothing good happened whenever one of the children said uh-oh. She took her eyes off of Janie long enough to survey the room. On the opposite side of her lovely, hand-carved bed — now littered with petticoats, socks, hats, and Brand's best black coat — Sam stood near the bedside table stuffing a chocolate bonbon into his mouth.

"Sam McCormick, please put the lid back on that candy dish and come over here."

He mumbled something unintelligible around a mouthful of chocolate.

"If you drip one bit of that on your clean shirtfront, you will not be allowed to carry the ring," Laura warned.

"Bu—"

"Close your mouth, please. Your father will be so disappointed if you ruin your new clothes."

Janie tried to turn around to see what he was doing. Laura held her still.

It didn't keep the little girl from talking.

"This is the most important day of our lives, Sam. If you don't behave, Laura might change her mind and tell Papa she won't marry him."

When she saw that Janie was about to cry, Laura quickly chose a light, floral-scented perfume and dabbed just a hint behind Janie's ears.

"There you go," she said. "You look pretty as a picture, Janie. Now sit on the edge of the bed and don't move. You, too, Sam. Sit beside your sister."

Janie skipped over to the bed. "Are you going to have the vapors, Laura? Amelia says sometimes brides have the vapors. She sells a lot of her nerve tonic to women who are getting married."

"I don't have time for vapors," Laura assured her.

It was her wedding day and she hadn't even had time for more than a cursory glance in the mirror since breakfast, and yet she felt blessed. She dabbed a bit of perfume on herself and decided that was the best she could do.

Sam had finally swallowed the chocolate. He was eyeing the candy dish from the edge of the bed.

Janie ran her hand over her ruffled purple skirt. "I heard Aunt Charity say it was a shame you and Papa can't go on a honeymoon, Laura."

"What's a honeymoon?" Sam flopped onto his back.

"Everyone knows that, silly." Janie spit on her fingers and shined the toe of her shoe.

Laura paused in the middle of brushing lint and cat fur off of Brand's black coat and stared at Janie. "And exactly what do you think a honeymoon is, young lady?"

"It's when two people get married and go outside to look at the moon and call each other 'honey.'"

Laura bit her lips together and concentrated on the coat brush.

Just then, Charity came rushing into the room.

"John is downstairs waiting to start the ceremony," she told Laura. "And Brand is afraid you're going to call off the wedding."

"She might be having the vapors," Sam informed him.

"She said she doesn't have time for vapors." Janie reminded him.

"Why don't you two go downstairs and keep Reverend Lockwood company?" Charity suggested. As they went running out of the room, she turned to Laura. "Brand sent me up here for his coat."

"Tell him I'm almost ready."

"You're still in your dressing gown."

"It'll just take a minute to change." Laura handed the coat to Charity and had to laugh. "I hope your wedding day is calmer than mine."

"I can't believe that in a month I'll be married too." Charity's cheeks took on a rosy glow. "Who would have guessed?"

"Reverend Lockwood is a lucky man."

"I'm so happy he wants to stay in Texas. We'll still be near all of you."

"I hope so. Is Jesse ready?" Laura walked over to the closet where the gown she'd chosen hung waiting for her to slip into.

"He's with Brand. He refused to wear the suit you bought him."

"It was worth a try. Perhaps it will fit Richard."

With the rest of the McCormicks moving into her home, Laura had assured Jesse he was welcome too. He'd only had to take one look at Sam and Janie as they thundered up the stairs armed with their toys and books, bickering about who would get which room.

"Thanks for the offer, but I'm just fine out in the carriage house. There's a lock on the door."

As she slipped into her dress, Laura reflected on the turn her life had taken. In the two weeks since their engagement became official, her precious routine had been turned upside down. Her days were hectic and unpredictable, and yet she loved every minute of them. There were still people who avoided speaking to her on the street, but most of the citizens of Glory had closed rank around her, including Harrison Barker, whose mother had threatened to "box his ears" if he didn't apologize.

She still worried what the children would think when they found out about her past, as they were bound to someday. She prayed that she'd be given the words to explain and she knew Brand would be at her side when she did.

Charity picked up Brand's coat and headed for the door. "I'll get this to Brand. Unless there's anything else you need?"

Just then Brand himself called out from the hallway, "Are you ready, Laura?"

Charity handed him the coat on her way out while Laura scrambled to cover her dress with her robe. A second later, she found Brand smiling down into her eyes.

"Everyone's ready, but I can't guarantee how long they'll be able to wait. Sam's eyeing the frosting on the cake. Are you getting cold feet?"

"I'll be ready in five minutes."

He took out his watch and checked the time. "You said that five minutes ago."

She held out her hand for his coat, then held it for him while he slipped it on. When he turned around, she was reaching for a stray piece of lint on his lapel. Instead he drew her into his arms for a kiss.

"I think you're supposed to save that for after the wedding," she whispered.

"One little kiss won't hurt."

"It's not going to help. Is everyone here?"

He nodded. "I think so. Harrison and his mother just arrived, which is actually why I came up here."

"They aren't making trouble are they?"

"Not at all." He reached into the back of his waistband and pulled out a letter.

"Harrison brought this for you. I hesitated giving it to you, in case it's bad news, but there's a fifty-fifty chance it's the news you've been waiting for." He handed it over.

She immediately recognized Tom Abbot's clear, bold handwriting.

"Take your time," he said, kissing her again. "You've got four minutes."

"Send Anna up to fasten up my gown, would you, please?"

"Of course." He was almost out the door when he paused and turned around. "Remind her that will be my job from now on, would you?"

"Go." She tried not to blush as she pointed toward the door.

Once he left the room, she went to the bed and sat down. She held the letter on her lap unopened and took a deep breath.

Today was a new beginning. No matter what the Pinkerton had found, this was still the best day of her life.

She closed her eyes, thanked God for everything she had, for everything He had blessed her with already.

Then she picked up the letter and carefully broke the sealing wax.

The Pinkerton had written but two lines:

I believe I have found your sister, Megan. I will write again when I am certain.

A tear splashed on the page. She quickly wiped it away before it smeared the ink. She refolded the letter and carried it to her dressing table where she slipped it into her decoupage stationery box.

Anna arrived as if on cue to fasten the row of buttons up the back of the dress.

"Congratulations, señora," she said when she was finished. "We will see you downstairs." She gave Laura a spontaneous hug before she hurried out of the room.

Laura took one last look in the mirror. She'd had Charity help her with an upswept hairstyle that morning. By now there were wayward curls popping out all over. She ignored them and concentrated on choosing a pair of simple earrings and a matching pearl necklace from her jewelry box. Staring back at her own reflection, she nodded. Good enough.

She started to leave the room, but stopped, clasped her hands together and closed her eyes.

"Thank You," she whispered. "Thank You for everything."

READ AN EXCERPT FROM BOOK TWO OF
THE IRISH ANGELS SERIES: *HEART OF LIES*.
COMING SOON!

LOUISIANA 1875

Beneath a crescent moon, a crudely built cabin rested on crooked cypress stilts planted in the chocolate brown water of the bayou. A dock lined the front. The back of the cabin touched the edge of marshland that was illusive at best. At its worst, it became a muddy bog.

A thousand eyes watched from the slowly moving water, tall reeds and rises; alligators, muskrats, mink, rats, deer, an occasional bear—silent denizens of the swamp. Like the human inhabitants, they existed here at the whim of the water and the storms that blew in without warning.

Fall had arrived. The muggy heat of summer was gone, tamed by cool air that drifted down from the north. Soon, hundreds of thousands of birds would flock south to the marsh to escape winter's cold.

The bayou was a place of refuge for more than winged fowl. Humans, too, easily hid where back roads curled through dense overgrowth and gave way to miles of shallow, narrow waterways that crisscrossed the swamp.

Inside, the walls of the cabin were made of rough-hewn cypress planks lined with old newspapers. The silence of the night was broken only by tormented sounds as Maddie Grande whimpered her way through a recurring nightmare.

It was always the same, always terrifying. Maddie was a child again, running in mid-stride when the nightmare began. Her bare feet slapped the cobblestoned streets of New Orleans as she fought to keep up with the tall, lanky man in the lead. A blonde girl, not much taller than Maddie, tugged Maddie by the wrist.

All Maddie could see of the man was his back. His greasy dark hair hung beneath his wide brimmed black hat and his hunched shoulders. His coat was well worn, threadbare around cuffs that didn't reach his wrists. It swayed loose from his shoulders, flapping as the three of them ran.

313

The other child, an inch taller, tightened her grip on Maddie's wrist and whispered a warning, "Keep up. You can do it."

Somehow Maddie knew that if she fell behind, a beating would be her swift reward. Like Mercury, fear fashioned wings on her feet.

The nightmare unfolded through a fog of time and forgotten memories that swirled around the man and the child leading Maddie along. The edges of the vision were blurred and tattered, like the stained pages of a book left too long in the rain. The streets they traversed were cool and damp, the air close and warm. The sounds and smells around them familiar.

New Orleans in early morning; street lamps were being extinguished as vendors at the French Market set up their wares and shouted to customers and each other in a patois of languages. Indians sold furs and herbs, farmers hawked fruits, vegetables, and spices. Hunters and butchers offered meats of every kind. Fishmongers promised a fresh catch and a bounty of seafood. There was always snow-white rice for sale, a staple in every home, along with Indian corn.

People of every hue crowded the stalls. Behind the scene, slaves hauled hogsheads loaded with tobacco, cotton, indigo, and cane to nearby ware-houses. No one noticed the ragtag trio fleeing past. Refreshment stands lined the blocks near the market. The smell of gumbo and fresh brewed coffee tainted the heavy, humid air.

Maddie, urged on by the blonde, kept running. Eventually, they reached an area where homes stood alongside businesses. Now and again she glimpsed cool, shaded courtyards through gateway grilles. She longed to stop and dip her hand into one of the trickling fountains, to take a sip of water. But she was not allowed to tarry. Air burned her lungs as she fought to keep up the breakneck pace. She had no doubt that the blonde girl would drag her body down the street if she stumbled and fell.

When the man suddenly halted, surprising Maddie, she clasped her free hand to her side where a stitch ached like fire. Thankfully, it quickly passed and she was able to straighten. She stared up at the wooden planks in a huge door before them. It was anchored to a thick stucco wall.

The older girl turned, but the face of the blonde child who so protec-tively clung to her hand never fully materialized. In its place was nothing but a pale oval, a wavering, shadowy void where a face should be.

That faded, faceless image filled Maggie — not with fear — but with feelings of intense sorrow and loss.

The faceless girl slicked down Maddie's hair and whispered, "I'll watch out for you. No matter what."

Maddie suffered through the same nightmare countless times.

Who was this child she mourned for? Why did the nightmare haunt her, even in the best of times?

There were those she mourned, those with faces she would never forget, whose memories were engraved upon her heart. She counted this unknown, faceless girl among them, though she didn't know why.

The skeletal man, just as unidentifiable, gave a phlegmy cough before he raised his hand and lifted the wrought iron ring on the door knocker and let it fall. It hit the wooden door with the hollow, ominous ring of a final heartbeat.

As the door swung open, the man faded from the nightmare. Maddie's hand tightened; she clung to the older girl's, and together they stepped over the threshold and through the doorway. They walked slowly forward and the space around them narrowed to become a blood red hallway. Flames licked the amber glass globes of flickering gas lamps evenly spaced along the hall. The girls' shadows wavered and danced over a decadently expensive textured wall covering.

Maddie's heart began to pound frantically. Heavily scented perfume weighed on the close air in the hall. She heard the sound of a door open and close. Now and again there came a throaty laugh, a moan, a cry.

Another man, different from the first but just as indistinguishable, suddenly appeared and came slowly toward the girls. Maddie's blood ran cold. He was as tall as the first but not lanky. His crooked top hat reminded her of a sooty stovepipe. The tails of his black coat flapped behind him as he strode forward.

Maddie was ever aware of the child beside her. She felt the other girl's panic, felt her stiffen, heard her cry out. Suddenly, the older girl's hand was torn away, their hold broken.

The faceless child shouted, "No!" and tried to grab Maddie. Her cries were abruptly ended by the sound of a slap that cracked on the air between them.

Without warning, the man in the black coat hoisted Maddie to his shoulder. Handled with no more reverence than a bag of rice, she dangled from his shoulder, staring down at the whirling patterns of the red and gold carpeted floor. Her head began to swim. As the stranger scuttled along the crimson lined hallway carrying her away, the other girl started screaming again and so did Maddie.

She kept on screaming as darkness closed around her. She screamed until suffocating shadows that seemed to go on forever choked out the light and everything faded away but the sound of her own voice.

Now, her muffled cries broke the stillness on the bayou and filled the small cabin. Startled awake, no longer a child, Maddie Grande sat up drenched in perspiration and stared into the dark void around her. With the screams echoing in her head, she swung her legs over the edge of the mattress stuffed with moss and set her bare feet on the rough floorboards. She rose and stood for a moment beside her narrow cot listening to the creaks and groans of the cabin as the water lapped around the pilings. It was a comforting, familiar sound.

She padded across the room to where a tall pottery crock stood on a crooked shelf nailed to the side wall. Staring out of a window above the shelf, she reached for a ladle, dipped fresh water from the crock, and brought the ladle to her lips.

Outside the window, a scant spoonful of moonlight filtered down through the tall cypress trees making a wall of deep green that appeared jet black in the darkness. Draped with gray Spanish moss, the ghost forest towered over the swamp.

Maddie stared past her reflection in the wavering glass and out into the darkness, acutely aware that she was alone in the cabin, alone in the swamp. Yet she had no fear. She'd survived on the streets of New Orleans for as long as she could recall. Out here on the bayou, most of what she feared was of nature, not of men.

Besides, she was not frightened of death anymore. She had already lost those she held most dear. She had nothing left to lose.

She sighed, listened to the barely audible sound of slow moving water. She reached out, pressed her palm against the cool glass. Her own image stared back at her, illusive in the muted light. Thick brown hair with barely a hint of a wave tumbled past her shoulders. Eyes of nearly the same color as her hair stared back. There was just enough moonlight to reveal the small scar that parted the end of her right brow. How it came to be there, she had no memory.

As she turned, intent on returning to her cot, she heard the scrape of a wooden pirogue against one of the piers. Relieved, she let go another sigh. The twins were back.

She gave up going back to bed and fumbled with the oil lamp on the table in the middle of the room. It was one of the few pieces of furniture other than four mismatched wooden chairs and three cots. The golden glow from the lamp illuminated the interior, revealing the small, neatly kept side where Maddie slept. It was in stark contrast to the twins' cots and the littered floor around them. Their side was a jumbled lair where the two of them had nests of clothing, old pieces of traps, and things they were "due to fix" or things they had "found."

She heard footfalls against the dock outside and turned as the door opened. Lawrence walked in first. His blond hair caught the light. The freckles that spattered his face were golden red in the lamplight. His eyes were blue, shadowed by heavy lids that gave him the appearance of a young man who was constantly drowsy. Lawrence had always been thought of as slow witted, most likely because he was so accustomed to letting his twin brother, Terrance, think for him. He was so adept at sleepwalking through life, Lawrence rarely needed to think at all.

He nodded to Maddie and headed straight for a brown and white jug full of white lightning on the shelf of foodstuff. He hooked his forefinger through the ring on the neck, lifted the cork, and took a swig. Smacking his lips after a long swallow, he finally turned and smiled at her.

But when he glanced back toward the open doorway, he wore a look of concern.

"What are you doing up, Maddie?" As if it were an afterthought, he took another swig from the jug and then set it in the middle of the table where Terrance would find it waiting.

She shrugged. She never talked about her nightmare. Her father never let her show any sign of weakness. Cowardice had always been ridiculed. Fears were not to be mentioned aloud, as if silence could wither them in their tracks.

She'd known the twins as brothers for as long as she could remember. Together, they worked the streets of New Orleans, growing up as street urchins in the back alleys. They knew how to pick pockets, work a crowd begging, how to steal anything that wasn't nailed down. They ate from market stalls, slipping fruits and meats and baked goods into their grimy little hands without anyone being the wiser.

They'd been taught how to bite and scratch and escape the law and they embraced their lives of thievery even as they matured.

When Terrance decided they should move to the bayou she had welcomed the change. There was nothing left to keep her in the city. Nowhere she called home.

No one cared what she did or where she lived.

Where she lived? She almost laughed aloud at the idea. No one cared where she existed was more like it.

Lawrence shifted and turned away as he headed for his cot. He brushed the shirts and pants off, ignoring them as they fell to the floor. The cot sagged as he sat down.

"Where's Terrance?" She glanced toward the open door. If it was left gaping long enough, a rat as big as a housecat could slip inside.

He shrugged. "Tying up his pirogue, I guess. He'll be along any minute."

She knew better than to ask where they'd been or what they'd been doing for the past three days. Even if they would tell her, the less she knew the better.

"Are you hungry?" She asked.

"I can hold 'til mornin'." He looked as if he were about to bed down for the night when they heard Terrance's footsteps. Maddie turned and watched the second twin walk in.

Shock hit her in a mighty wave when she noticed the bundle cradled in his arms. She gave a gasp when she saw two small feet shod in ankle-high black leather shoes dangling from beneath the frayed hem of a gray Confederate Army issue blanket. The war had been over for nigh on to eight years and the blanket had definitely seen better days.

"What have you done?" She whispered, tearing her gaze away from the bundled child to meet Terrance's eyes.

His eyes, identical to his brother's except that they were cool and emotionless, narrowed in defiance as he dared her to criticize him. Terrance was the schemer, the planner.

"I'm lookin' out for our future, that's what." He shot a glance at his brother seated on the edge of his sagging cot. "That's more than I can say for some around here."

He carried the bundle over to Maddie's cot and gently laid his burden down near the wall. He gave the blanket a slight tug downward and Maddie found herself staring at a beautiful little girl with a head full of coiled brown ringlets. She was sound asleep and wearing a fur-lined red cape worth more than everything in the ramshackle cabin put together.

A twinge squeezed Maddie's heart. Unable to speak, she ached to reach out and touch the child's porcelain cheek so badly that she had to fist her hands in the folds of her skirt.

"Why?" She turned on Terrance, afraid there was only one explanation for the child's presence. "You're not thinking of starting a new tribe—"

Lawrence laughed from across the room. Maddie and Terrance, locked in a battle of wills, ignored him.

"Those days are over, Terrance. They died with Dexter," she whispered.

Dexter Grande was their leader, their father, keeper, guide, and judge.

He was the visionary, the glue who had held their tribe together, the one who "recruited" his band of children, the one who taught them to steal and how to survive on the streets.

"Some would look down on us," Dexter would say, "but this is our way. We take from those who have. We are the have-nots of New Orleans and this is our due."

But no one lives forever, especially in a city plagued by war and yellow fever. As Dexter Grande grew older, the young men of the tribe became harder to control and were told to leave. Apoplexy brought Dexter down at the ripe old age of sixty-five, and without him, what was left of their tribe quickly scattered.

"It worked for Dexter, why not me?" Terrance speculated. "Just 'cause Dexter died doesn't mean we can't start a new tribe and run the same games."

Maddie turned on him. "Look around. We don't live in New Orleans anymore."

She didn't want to think about moving back to the city. For the most part the twins were never around and she was alone, which suited her just fine. There were no reminders of her own losses here, only the gentle, healing sound of the water lapping against the dock and the hush of the wind through the lacy cypress.

He was at the table now, lifting the jug to his lips. He took a couple of deep draughts, set the jug down, and swiped the back of his hand across his lips.

"Just because I haven't started a new tribe yet, that don't mean it might not happen sooner or later. Right now though, I'm thinking bigger than that."

He nodded at the sleeping child on the cot. "Why should we waste time havin' her dance for a dollar or two on the street when there's real money to be had?"

"You tell me," Lawrence said. It was one of his favorite sayings. Terrance always obliged.

Terrance's eyes glittered, lit by greed. "One word. Reward. Easy money and lots of it from the look of her."

Maddie's heart still hadn't settled. She didn't know which would be worse, hiding the child until they could collect a reward or contemplating the start of a new tribe.

One thing she knew for certain, this was no orphaned street urchin needing shelter. This child belonged to someone wealthy. This child would be missed.

Share Your Thoughts

With the Author: Your comments will be forwarded to the author when you send them to *zauthor@zondervan.com*.

With Zondervan: Submit your review of this book by writing to *zreview@zondervan.com*.

Free Online Resources at
www.zondervan.com

Zondervan AuthorTracker: Be notified whenever your favorite authors publish new books, go on tour, or post an update about what's happening in their lives at www.zondervan.com/authortracker.

Daily Bible Verses and Devotions: Enrich your life with daily Bible verses or devotions that help you start every morning focused on God. Visit www.zondervan.com/newsletters.

Free Email Publications: Sign up for newsletters on Christian living, academic resources, church ministry, fiction, children's resources, and more. Visit www.zondervan.com/newsletters.

Zondervan Bible Search: Find and compare Bible passages in a variety of translations at www.zondervanbiblesearch.com.

Other Benefits: Register yourself to receive online benefits like coupons and special offers, or to participate in research.

ZONDERVAN.com/
AUTHORTRACKER
follow your favorite authors